RIVER ROAD

RIVER

ROAD

C. F. Borgman

NAL BOOKS

NEW AMERICAN LIBRARY

NEW YORK AND SCARBOROUGH, ONTARIO

Copyright © 1988 by C. F. Borgman

All rights reserved. For information address New American Library.

Published simultaneously in Canada by
The New American Library of Canada Limited.

 NAL TRADEMARK REG. U.S. PAT. OFF. AND FOREIGN COUNTRIES
REGISTERED TRADEMARK—MARCA REGISTRADA
HECHO EN CHICAGO, U.S.A.

SIGNET, SIGNET CLASSIC, MENTOR, ONYX, PLUME, MERIDIAN
and NAL BOOKS are published *in the United States* by NAL PENGUIN INC.,
1633 Broadway, New York, New York 10019,
in Canada by The New American Library of Canada Limited,
81 Mack Avenue, Scarborough, Ontario M1L 1M8

Designed by Julian Hamer

Library of Congress Cataloging-in-Publication Data

Borgman, C. F.
  River road.

  I. Title.
PS3552.07527R58 1988   813'.54   88-1796
ISBN 0-453-00612-4

First Printing, September, 1988

1 2 3 4 5 6 7 8 9

PRINTED IN THE UNITED STATES OF AMERICA

for
M. Borgman
D. Freelander
J. Negron
R. Umans
G. Person
M. Smith
A. Warhol
C. Trungpa
A. Feldman
F. Cantelope
D. Copeche
D. O'Neil

"That the river is everywhere at the same time, at the source and at the mouth, at the waterfall, at the ferry, at the current, in the ocean and in the moutains, everywhere, and that the present only exists for it, not the shadow of the past, nor the shadow of the future?"

"That is it," said Siddhartha, "and when I learned that, I reviewed my life and it was also a river, and Siddhartha the boy, Siddhartha the mature man and Siddhartha the old man, were only separated by shadows, not through reality. Siddhartha's previous lives were also not in the past, and his death and his return to Brahma are not in the future. Nothing was, nothing will be, everything has reality and presence."

Hermann Hesse, *Siddhartha*,
translated by Hilda Rosner

2012, Panacea, Florida

On shore, Eugene Goessler licked his index finger and dipped it into the envelope marked "Clara." It contained his third of his mother's ashes. Some of the ash stuck to the wet fingertip. He sucked it, tasting the grit and powder. His tongue pushed against the roof of his mouth. He flooded the dry of it with saliva. For a splash of a wave, he saw his mother in a kind light. A holy communion. He swallowed. His eyes watered up. He followed the ash as it slid down his throat. He took a long slow salty-aired breath, then exhaled just as slowly and said, "Now, that's what I call barbecued!" He shook the rest of the third of her into the palm of his right hand and pitched the ashes into the Gulf of Mexico.

At sixty-one, Eugene Goessler was a tall and lean sunburnt man, wearing white shorts that hung baggy on his hips as he stood with his back to his bungalow #4. Since 2006, each winter he rented #4 at the secluded El Caribe Bungalows outside of Panacea. Panacea was located south of Tallahassee where the pan and handle attached in Florida.

"If Florida is America's dick," Eugene once said to his friend Lola Hampton on the phone, "if Florida is America's dick, then my bungalow is where the root rises, where the shaft begins, the top of the sack, the crossroads. You can travel the veins down shaft, or go west into the chickenskin hilly ball country toward New Orleans."

"It isn't America's dick, Eugene," Lola replied, studying her globe. "Florida is a big overworked clit. Get out a map, Goessler. Now, New England has possibilities if we're talking only the United States."

"We're talking geographallus, Lola, geographallus."

"Then let's face it," Lola said decisively loud, "Africa is the great cock of the earth, Goessler!"

He stood barefoot in the white sand in the sun in the push of a warm wind that dispersed the ashes like pollen. His face was red from the sun and worn from weather and lined from life. His face revealed a history of emotions, handsomely elder, from the deep furrows that ran down his jaw to a pronounced dimple in his chin, so that the furrows and dimple formed the letter W. From the creased ledges that puffed below each of his green eyes, to the fans of crow's feet that formed river deltas at the lips of his eyes. Green eyes, not hazel or yellowish, but green on the edge of a sea-blue. His eyebrows were still reddish blond, holding out from the transformation to white that his other hairs had accepted, and there was a splinter of a scar running through his left brow. His lips were thick, even as they stretched into a smile, flattening wide against his front teeth, as he moved them open and shut trying to wring a taste of his mother from the residue of grit that he still felt in his mouth. The edges of his mouth curved sharply up when he smiled or spoke because the lips could go no further out as they collided with the rounded creases that curved from his ruddy cheeks to his nose. His nose was long, but not pointed like a beak. It was more like a hound dog's snout, somewhat rounded at the tip. When he was breathing deeply or talking, his nostrils' movement would cause the tip to sharpen.

He squatted down to the white sand and set fire to the "Clara" envelope, shielding the weak flame from the wind with his large worn hands. He was no longer smiling as he studied the quick flicker, almost invisible in the sunlight. The envelope seemed to be turning black and disintegrating over nothing. His forehead wrinkled into a tan grid of lines that could be read like a a street map. His back curved as it arched over the burning envelope, emphasizing the frets of his spine, the steps climbed by friends and lovers and even his mother over the years. He saw the inked word "Clara" burn away.

"Clah-rah, clah-rah, clah-rah, clah-rah," he said over and over.

The famous "performance-poet" Eugene Goessler had long blond-white, almost fiber-optic translucent hair that he wore tied back in a ponytail that fell below his freckled shoulders. The hair had thinned at the top of his head, and his hairline was dotted with age spots. Sweat surfaced on his brow as the fire faded. He rose erect and kicked sand around the ashes with his feet. His chest was covered with white hair. His skin seemed loose, despite his lack of fat or flab. It tightened when he reached with his arms high toward the sky as if he were his mother hanging wash on the line.

"Clah-rah, clah-rah," he stretched, seeing the blue above, "clah-rah, ah-qua, ah-qua, ah-qua," and then he dropped his arms down to the sand, down to the laundry basket, down to the sea. His tall bony body seemed strong and lithe for a man of his age, and the keen glint in his eyes as he repeated the word "ah-qua" vented in chant the emotions that were surfacing with his ash ritual. The emotions that were rings in his trunk, steam from his heart, the fuel to the furnace of his poet. Like a gurgling contented baby, delighting in its own noise, Eugene alternated between "Ah-qua" and "Clah-rah," performing bows to the sea and holy glory to the blue sky up. He felt the sand on his soles and curled his toes into the warmth of it, and for another flash of wave, he saw himself at Ipanema in Brazil.

Inside bungalow #4, Eugene saw his reflection in the window glass, and through him, he saw the beach and the Gulf acting up a storm.

"Mr. Goessler," his phone announced, "Octavio calling. Mr. Goessler, Octavio calling. Mr. Goessl . . ."

Eugene hit the button with his big toe, "Octavio?"

Octavio spoke from the speakers in the wall on either side of the bed, "Hello sweetie," he said with his Brazilian accentuation and lilt, "I am only calling to verify the plan. How is everything for you?"

"Bueno," Eugene said, grinning as wide as possible at the sound of the Brazilian, "just bueno. It is all perfect and I will look for the lights tomorrow night."

"We are in the Keys," Octavio explained, "and Tonio is refitting one of the hydro belts, sweetie, so I think we must plan on two nights."

Eugene wanted the hydro to be fit, and agreed, "Another night it is then, and let me know if there is any change."

Octavio laughed and disconnected.

The marblelite desktop in the bungalow was covered with shells and rocks and scraps of paper, photographs, envelopes and other jewels of Eugene Goessler's memory. There was the cedar box from his son, Jason, and the old green canvas knapsack Eugene had carried all over the earth. This was the baggage he'd brought down to Panacea for his final winter there.

He climbed up onto the desktop, pushing the relics of his life aside so that he could sit cross-legged, lotuslike, and watch the storm come in across Apalachee Bay.

"Earth," the old man said, past his slight reflection, through the glass, and out. "Earth. Gravity. Earth."

1958, Ohio

"What is the earth?" Eugene asked his mother.

Clara was hanging wash on the line in the side yard of their house high up the hill from River Road and spoke with a clothespin in her mouth. "Now what kind of question is that?" She was a heavyset woman, claiming that after having baby Debbie four month's ago in May, she couldn't lose the pregnancy weight. She wore a checkered housedress that had a row of wooden clothespins snapped down the front of it for easy reach. Her brown hair was pin-curled tight to her skull. Her face was red from the sun and from the exertion of washday and her resentment that she had so much work to do. Her face was puffy and porous and her eyebrows were penciled in dark over eyes that looked around the diaper she was hanging. Her eyes were green, like Eugene's, and as they fastened on the gangly boy on the kitchen doorstep she said, "I'll be darned if I know, honey. Lord," she grunted, stooping for a sock and, in a single motion, grabbing a clothespin from her dress and snapping it to the line, "Lord, what is the earth? Well, let me think now."

Eugene watched the flab of her arms shake as they reached down to the wicker laundry basket, and then up to the line that crossed and crisscrossed the little yard, the only level spot around the old house. He was not allowed to play with his trucks in the dirt pile because it made too much dust and would get all over the clean wash.

"Earth," Clara repeated slowly drawing it out. "Well, I reckon it is the globe like you have at your school, Eugene. It's where we're living, though Lord knows some got it better than others.

It ain't all even. Some have got, like the rich do, and some have not got, like us."

Eugene's question was not being answered. He ran his hand over his head, patting its fresh-mowed stubble. He sat on the wooden step that led into the kitchen. His long legs were bent up so that his chin rested on his knees.

"But what is all of this?" he asked his mother, rewording the question. "What is the earth doing?"

Clara tisk-tisked with two clothespins in her mouth like fangs, and she thought that Art Linkletter on television was right when he said that "kids say the darndest things." She hung a heavy pair of Melvin's work pants on the line, and the weight caused the line to dip. "Hand me one of the clothes poles. Eugene. The old wringer doesn't wring good at all."

Eugene took a thin wooden post that was leaning against the clapboard of the house and ran it over to her. It was whittled in a V at one end to catch the washline, and she shoved it under and raised the wash across the yard to new heights. The diapers now waved white and high like sails on the river, Eugene thought. He went back to the step.

"This ain't a school question is it?" Clara asked. "You ain't trying to trick me into doing your homework are you, mister smarty pants? What kind of question is that for a Catholic school anyways?"

"No," Eugene laughed, "I was just wondering. Sister Joseph said that Jesus said there is heaven and earth and hell and . . ."

"So you are trying to trick me!" Clara aha'd, looking over to the boy. "Now you should just keep that kind of highfalutin thinking in school where it belongs, Eugene. Lord know, it costs extra to be Catholic."

"But Jesus said . . ."

"I only turned Catholic for your daddy's sake, Eugene. I don't know much about them deep goings on. Just obey your parents and be good and you'll get to heaven."

Clara had never really thought much about the Catholic religion. Her biggest gripe was the sacrament of Confession. She felt that Melvin could get drunk for days, then go confess his sin, and walk away with a clean jug ready to be filled at Stogie's tap.

That evening, on the porch, Eugene asked his father what the earth was.

"Dirt, boy," the man replied, picking his teeth with a toothpick. "Dirt."

1968, Ohio/New York

In the yellow taxi from La Guardia Airport, Eugene strained to take in all of what he was passing. New York! He had the window open. He passed where the World's Fair had been. Then, above a massive graveyard baking in the August heat, he saw the towers and spires and monoliths of Manhattan stretching forever like thousands of Carew Towers, the forty-eight-story Cincinnati skyscraper.

"First time in New York?" the cabdriver asked.

"No," Eugene lied, remembering his friend Leslie's warning to not let anyone know how green he was.

The cabdriver stopped at the address he'd been given on West Twenty-second Street. The building was decrepit, sooty, and foreboding. Eugene wondered if anyone could really live there. He saw laundry hanging from the fire escape. He paid the driver, tipping him only after the man had explained, "Tipping is something new, that's why you don't remember it if you haven't been to New York in a while."

Eugene carried his bags into a dark brown stinking vestibule and found Sue Neiman's name listed among many under the apartment numbered 2-B. He pressed the buzzer, and re-pressed over and over, till he realized he was staring at a paper taped to the wall that said, "Door Open, Bell Out of Order." He climbed the stairs and knocked on the purple-painted door.

"Yeah?" he heard from behind it.

"I'm looking for Sue Neiman," he said. "I'm a friend of her cousin Katherine."

The door opened wide. A large young woman with long fine

8

black hair and flushed pink face leaned on one of her broad hips, puffed a cigarette, and skeptically said, "Yeah?" The tips of her ears protruded through the black.

Eugene Goessler, freshly turned eighteen, stood tall and lanky in his boots full of feet and extended his long arm out to shake the woman's hand, wide grin and green-eyed friendly.

The day before, stretched out in the long white claw-footed tub on River Road, Eugene examined his plan on how to tell his mother. He would tell her that night, when she returned from bingo. He hoped she would have won, even just a door price. It wasn't as if his departure was falling out of the clear blue, he'd been saying for months that as soon as he turned eighteen he was leaving for New York, to study at the School of Arts, which was only a bit true. The school idea was to soften the blow. A lot of kids left home to go away to college, but he told himself that he would have to enroll somewhere at some point in order to avoid being drafted into the Vietnam War. Each time Eugene had said anything about leaving, Clara had either screamed at him that he would be deserting "your poor widowed mother who has already known more grief than all the Kennedys combined! You are the man of the house!" or she would snicker meanly, insisting that he simply was "not allowed to go till I say you can go, buddy." He remembered how June had stood up to her. June. He took a breath and sank under water, blowing air to bubbles through his nose, descending into a wordless world of ringing sounds and gurgling.

Eugene had what looked like a reddish rash on the side of his neck, below his jawline. It was not a rash, it was scarred skin from the fire. His eyebrows were blond and red and brown, but mostly blond from his summer of outside full-time construction work. He had saved over twelve hundred dollars. He had a strapping torso, tanned to his waist, proportionately drawn down to the hairs at his growing outpost. He was a continent floating in the tub. His chest hairs were the jungle, his bent legs were the Alps, and his cock and balls were bobbing like Hawaii, becoming sweet on him, a choice spot for a holiday. He could, even with his years of sin, guilt, and accusations, at his most relaxed, as in a tub of warm water, enjoy touching himself. He had learned, almost forced himself to learn, what anyone could want from him. They'd said he was handsome, and saw the reactions in faces, yet he had been taught to hate vanity. Hate love, especially conceited self-love. "You think wonders who you are, mister," Clara would berate him if she ever saw him at a mirror or dressing. Eugene was always surprised that people liked him. "Like you? Are you crazy, Goessler?! You're a beauty!" Leslie had said to him one Sunday afternoon when he had confided in her just how insecure he felt. She was trying to talk him into posing for some pictures that a friend of hers was doing, "for a book on the male physique. I'll give you his number, he lives in Greenwich Village, and when you get to New York, maybe you'll look him up." What he felt inside, and what he looked like outside, he learned, were almost opposites. Letting go of his restrictions in the lukewarm water, in his head accepting a brief descent toward the Hell of sexual touching, he allowed his insides out. A touch, a grab, a shakedown, lickdown, eatup, chew tongue gobble wet and slobbering, not just him, others too, kissing all over, kneading the musculature, and then stopping himself, leaning forward, the excitement subsiding, and picking clean his toenails.

Out of the tub, in the humid air, he looked in the mirror over the sink. "Who the hell do you think you are?" he said, drawling as his mother would have. He cleaned the tub with cleanser and thought, "Tomorrow at this time I'll be in New York City." He had his ticket and his money, withdrawn from his bank account, hidden in the boys' room. He was flying there. His first plane ride, and it was cheap, half-fared because he was under twenty-one and willing to, as he assumed, "stand." His friends, Kevin and Leslie, were going to pick him up and take him to the airport in Kentucky. Everything was set except for telling his mother. He had already decided to leave notes for his little sister, Debbie, and his brother, Frank.

"Dear Deb, Put this money in your piggy bank, and don't tell mother about it. You use it to call me if you have to, when I get a phone somewhere, and if you have to, you can come to me if it gets too weird here. I love you, Eugene."

"Dear Frankie, Well, as you know by the time you are reading this, I've gone and done it. I feel sorry for leaving you and Deb. Watch out for her, brother. Here's $100. I left $100 for Deb too. If you have to leave because mother starts flying off the handle, please bring Debbie with you and come to New York and join me. I will try to send money when I can. Don't let her beat on you. Peace, brother. Eugene."

At the purple doorway, Eugene asked, "Are you Sue?" He suspected she was because Katherine had mentioned in her letter that "Sue is real dumpy looking."

Sue moved her cigarette to her other hand and shook Eugene's, nodding with a small-toothed smile, that she was "the one and only Sue Neiman, Arthurian expert and chocolate sugar loving freak." She sized up the tall Ohio cub.

Eugene's smile broadened his long clean-shaven face. His lush-lipped grin curled up into his cheeks and his eyes clearly said, "I am a good guy, you can trust me." He was wearing a yellow boat-necked shirt that stretched across his broad shoulders. His light hair was in a curled mess from the wind out the taxi window, and he ran his hand in and through some of it, revealing the white-blond beaches at the sides of his forehead that introduced his hairline. His ears were nearly hidden by the tangles of curls, some almost as red as his earlobes. He stood straight, a foot higher than Sue Neiman in her bare feet, toenails painted green "like Sally Bowles," tipping two very meaty legs that squeezed at the thigh into paisley shorts. June had once said to Eugene on the porch as they watched Melvin climbing the steps, "You have the best posture, Eugene. Look how bent over Daddy moves, and to think how he looked in the pictures from way back when he was a ballplayer."

"Did your cousin Katherine write you about me coming to New York?" he asked, sounding very accented, even to himself.

"Uhhhh . . ." Sue wondered, not sure if she remembered a letter. Of course, the mail was always a big mess with eight people living there off and on, and even more using it as their address. Katherine? Hadn't she been sent out to her dad's in California? Katherine? The beauty who never seemed to have acknowledged her for more than a brief card at the holidays?

"She said you might know of a place for me to stay," Eugene explained. "I was her boyfriend when she lived in Cincinnati."

"Uh, sure," Sue said, charmed by his healthy looks and slow drawled accent, then sizing herself, her potential with him as a possible fuck, shaking her thin long hair dyed black-black, remembering the pimple on her forehead, getting self-conscious over that, and then her weight, and then her bitten fingernails, and then thought to herself, "Ah, fuck it, fuck the whole come-on trip. Why bother? It's all such a plastic game," and she said out loud to Eugene, "I don't remember a letter from her, but I lead such a crazy life, who knows what happened yesterday, you know? Now, I'll let you in, but you must tell me exactly who you are."

"Eugene Goessler," he said, following her big paisley butt. Her hair ran down to it, "I'm glad you were home. I guess I would have just waited down on the street."

He would have paced in defined strides, listening to his heels hit the pavement, just as he had on the tile at the airport, waiting for the bus he'd been told about, finally gathering the courage to mimic the other people whom he had watched hailing cabs. Physically, Eugene was fit, from running track and swimming in high school, from the heavy construction work he'd done for months after school and then all of June and July. There was a conscious reliability on his muscles, and an unconscious tender underside that was aching in the emotional maze he'd assembled. It was just as strong as his stride. His adrenaline was flowing, and he was striking. He crouched and looked directly at the cabdriver, shaking the man's hand.

"Up, up, and away," he'd sung to the stewardess, looking directly at her, distracting her actually, with his green-to-blue eyes, framed in long lashes of summer, carrying the sun onto the plane. He wanted to act nonchalant. Kevin and Leslie could not believe, as they drove to the airport, that he'd never flown before.

"Ticket, please," the woman at the boarding gate had asked.

He reached for his ticket, he had no pockets in his shirt, and he patted his jeans, looking to her for help. "I know it's here somewhere," he half-chuckled, lightening his sweat, having learned what flying standby really meant, not knowing till the last minute if he really was going to be breaking all ties or not. He was lugging more than sun and bags. He was carrying the emotional weight of his mother's desperate cries, the love for his sister and brother and his friends, everything familiar and sure, all of that, as if he'd been dared. "Go ahead and jump." He had tied the tourniquet tight, so as not to bleed all over the strangers.

Since he was fourteen, and saw how June left, he'd been dreaming of his own getaway. New York. For a while it had been

California. He was thinking of being a surfer. But New York was the stronger draw. The big city where he'd heard, especially from Leslie, everybody was free to do whatever they wanted, shamelessly. "If God is dead," Leslie had said, "he's buried in New York." New York, where everything was open all night. Where nobody cared if you had hair down to your ass. Where drugs were openly sold right on the street. Where nudity was right on stage. Where people applauded anarchy. Eugene thought that he might try to get a part on Broadway, in *Hair*. He wondered how difficult that would be. Kevin had told him, "First thing, Eugene, is get a good agent, and then get a vocal coach, and a drama coach, and you'll need a portfolio," which was when Leslie told him about her friend who was the photographer in the Village. The Crowd, as his friends called themselves, were all either artists or musicians or actors. His friend William, from Bishop Miller High School, had introduced him to this self-acknowledged clique. They all encouraged him, coaxed him, and applauded him. Eugene would do anything they dared him to do.

"See that man in the suit," Kevin had said once. "Walk up to him and tell him that he is a fucking hawk and that one day a psychedelic dove is gonna take a long runny crap on his bald head." Eugene did, adding a little rub on the man's head, prompting the man to raise his fists, calling Eugene a "drugged-out hippie!" To which Eugene replied profoundly, "Your only reaction is violence. Violence! Murderer!" And he retreated to the laughing clutches of the Crowd, who repeatedly bolstered Eugene's bravado with, "You are just too far-fucking out, Goessler!"

He was far cockier with an audience than without. On the plane, he felt almost timid, watching intensely the instructions for oxygen, hoping he had gotten the procedures correctly and that he would survive the inevitable crash. His fear of death almost loosened his grip, but everyone else seemed oblivious to the stewardesses' forewarnings. He told himself that once he was alone, on his own, without anyone to answer to or get prodded by, he would finally be able to feel completely integrated, the extrovert and the introvert, united and happy. But first, he had to survive the flight and be on guard for the dark underside of New York. He was prepared for the muggers who would be waiting for him at La Guardia as he stepped from the plane. "Don't trust anybody" was the last thing Kevin had said to him, kissing each cheek at the boarding gate, right in front of all the hicks. He still heard Clara's guttural screams as he descended the steps with his two bags. "You can't leave! You're killing me! Eugene! You'll have to live with this the rest of your life! Shame on you!" He was tight. The river across the road shimmered a severe golden good-bye to one of her sincerest lovers. Kevin and Leslie held the door to the Volkswagen open. Clara screamed from the fortieth step, holding her heart. Eugene could not turn around. He felt June beside him, almost helping with the bags. He stood for a second, looked out to the river and said, "River, you're coming with me."

"This place is a pigsty," Sue Neiman said, accepting her slovenly ways, and everyone else's. She was not about to apologize for the garbage and piles of clothes and the full-up ashtrays all around her corner of the room. She thought, "I am simply not into the whole facade trip. AmeriKa has sold out on cleansers to support militaristic, imperialistic capitalism." She pushed a big pillow toward Eugene, indicating he should set his bags down, and himself on it. "Now," she said, flopping down onto her mattress, her teats showing through her tie-dyed tee shirt, "how do I know you're not some kind of weirdo, Yew Jean?" She said his name, mimicking his accent.

He laughed, knowing his meekness, knowing his intentions were definitely not toward raping her, if that was what she was implying, which, if it was, she seemed to have spread her thighs for him already, smiling batty, butting out her cigarette in the incense burner on the floor. She was definitely weirder than him. "Hey, I really went with Katherine. She lived at 2227 Backbone Road till her mom sent her out to Oakland. She went to Mother of Perpetual Faith and I went to Bishop Miller, both of them right on top of the hill in Delhi Hills . . ."

Sue jumped in, mimicking the way he said "Delhi," "Dell High!" Her family on Long Island all made fun of the midwestern accents of their Ohio relatives. She thought Eugene was incredibly cute, and thought, "Of course Katherine would have someone like him." She had never liked Katherine. She had always been compared to her, always unfavorably. "I believe you, I believe you!" she laughed. "Yew Jean. How's them thar crops doin?" She felt she could say what she wanted to him. He was at her mercy. He was the one in need of a place to stay, and deserved to be taken down a peg or two, considering how he had lucked out in the looks department. She felt that she had lucked out in the brains department.

"It is kind of a weird name, isn't it?" Eugene said, very aware of how he was sounding. A vocal coach would change all that.

"Smoke?" Sue asked, offering a Marlboro. They both lit on the same match. "Now, Yew Jean, as you can see, it is a little crowded here, but let me first explain the rules."

"Sure," he smiled, sensing he would not have to call his next prospective help, Leslie's friend in Greenwich Village, whom Kevin had said was a definite homosexual.

"I know it sounds fucked up, but rules have to be made after all the shit that has gone down here. Now, Linda and I found this place, she's really cool, you'll like her, and so we are the ones who have to pay the rent to Matilde, the landlady. Now she is really crazy and acts like she hates everyone, carrying on out in the hall, sometimes all night."

"Sounds familiar," Eugene said, "like my mother."

Sue did not like him acting as if he could possibly understand the drama. She practically spit smoke at him, "You don't know, farmboy, just wait! Anyway, so it'll be twenty-five bucks a month, whether you use the place or not, and it has to be paid before the first."

"Sure," he agreed, wondering just how much the place could possibly cost.

"And food is a real trip. You have to be real careful about food, Yew Jean. We have had all kinds of fucking bummers over fucking food. Whose this is, whose stuff is on somebody else's shelf, and all this petty shit that really gets in the way of what we're all really into, peace and love and all that shit, you know what I mean? So most of the time you just buy what you're going to eat that day, and, oh yeah, this is like the really most heavy rule, if you are balling somebody, you can't expect privacy."

Eugene had never heard of the term "balling" before, but he liked the way it sounded, rolling and round, but male. Maybe it was his affection for his balls. "Fucking" seemed less exciting, that is, if "balling" was what "fucking" was. He was assuming it was, although he realized he'd have to listen further, because he was not about to ask Sue, who would think he was even more of a hick. Maybe balling was two guys banging their balls together, he thought, and maybe what Sue was saying was that she thought he was queer. He was confused, but remained facially attentive, as if he was taking down notes on her rules, nodding in overall agreement.

"And, Yeeeeew Jean, this is really really the law, if you use the tub in the hall, you have to fucking clean it out. We made Tony the Bone split because he never fucking cleaned up after himself. He thought he was god's gift to women, and figured they'd get off licking his scum rings. You know, I just thought, do I shock you? Do you think I'm vulgar and crude?"

Eugene shook his head, and was going to say that his friend Leslie had a really foul mouth, but he felt that Sue was proud of her vulgarity. He was kind of shocked, although everything seemed shocking to him.

"And, if you do, that's tough shit," she said, laughing and reaching over to touch his knee. "Just kidding, Yew Jean, you know, I can be a real mindfuck sometimes. It's like I was born in the wrong century, you know? But anyway, I'll tell you all about my other lives later. God, where was I? I swore that I would lay down the law the next time somebody new came to crash here . . ."

"Clean the tub," Eugene said, stubbing out the cigarette on the sole of his boot, foolishly catching the ashes in his hand as if they would mess the floor any more than it already was.

"Yeah," Sue said, "and there's two other guys paying right now, but I haven't seen Dave the Douche in days, so it's really just Nelson who's been around, and he's always with Linda lately, so if she's cleaning up after him, that's her fucking trip. All I can say is, you really have to clean the tub."

"It's in the hall?"

"Yeah," she said, surprised at the question, staring, caught by his eyes, his voice, the way he leaned toward her, a bit of sweat above his sculpted lips. She hated herself for a moment, knowing she would consider cleaning out his tub and sharing her food if she was his old lady, and then she let out her stomach noticeably big, thinking, "Fuck it, it isn't worth it." She said out loud, "Yeah, it's in the hall, you silly. There's one door that opens to the loo, and the next one down opens to the tub. The sink is in here," she pointed over the stacks of books to the kitchenette.

Eugene did not know what a "loo" was either, but it sounded enough like "poo" to obviously be the toilet.

"And we keep the toilet paper on that nail," she pointed toward the purple door, "and just cause you guys don't use as much as us girls, don't be shy about buying some once in a while." She offered Eugene a suck on the straw that stuck in her can of chocolate cola soda.

He took a suck. He'd never heard of such a drink. There was so much to discover.

"Finish it," Sue said, "there's more in the fridge. I love straws, don't you? I think we all have something to work out about nursing and our mothers. Some guys have really been into my breasts."

Eugene kept the straw in his mouth so he wouldn't have to respond to her possible offer, not wanting to jeopardize his acceptance into the crash pad.

"Well?" Sue said, looking up through strands of her black hair as she lit a stick of sandlewood incense.

Eugene sucked bottom, loudly, swallowed, and asked for clarification, "Huh?" He had decided that if he had to, he could get into sucking on her teats, if he would then have a place to live.

"Well, are you going to join us?" Sue said, as if that was the obvious question.

"Yeah! Sure!" Eugene said loudly, relieved. "I'll pay you right now."

He took his wallet from his boot where he'd put it for safe-keeping, and he gave Sue thirty dollars, "Five toward toilet paper and stuff." He saw the picture of June that he carried behind the plastic inset. He closed the wallet thinking, "Hey, June, look at me, here in New York City!"

She put the money in her striped rope purse and said, "I'm fresh out of weed, or I'd offer you some, Yew Jean. Do you have any on you?"

Eugene shook his head and explained that he didn't bring any because he thought they might check for it at the airport. He failed to mention that he never had actually purchased grass, although he had smoked it. Clara was always accusing him of being "high on something," especially if she read accounts in the paper about "long-hairs and protests." She forbade him to ever be near Calhoun Street, near the university, where the paper claimed drugs were sold openly on the street. Eugene's friend Leslie lived on Calhoun Street, and in all the times he'd walked it, he had never been confronted about purchasing any-thing more intoxicating than incense.

"I heard that in New York you could go out on any street and buy grass," he said.

Sue laughed and shook her head as she continued to rummage through her bag. "Maybe I've got a roach."

"I heard that everyone has roaches in New York," Eugene said, and then realized she was not looking for bugs in her purse, and clarified himself, hoping to cover his greenhorns, "I mean cockroaches, you know."

Sue looked up, frustrated from her messy search. "Yeah, they're all over the place. Nothing kills'm, and that idiot, Dave the Douche, got all bent out of shape when Nelson sprayed poison here one day. He claimed that the little fuckers should be left alone and we should share our space, at which point I told him that he would be responsible for paying their share of the rent."

"Maybe we could go buy some grass," Eugene suggested, as Sue was cursing and throwing the contents of her bag out across her mattress.

"Dynamite notion, Yew Jean," she said gruffly sarcastic, "but who the fuck has bread to cop weed? What you gave me goes to Matilde."

"I'd pay for it," he said, stopping himself from telling her how much money he had in his boot. It made him feel comfortable to see her disposition relax at his offer. He looked around the room, his new home, feeling not only accepted, but necessary. There were three windows at the far end of the room, each hung with Indian print cloths. One was pulled to the side with a ribbon, revealing the black iron fire escape and a slit of sunlight. There were two mattresses leaning against the wall, obviously not used on a daily basis. The wall was covered with posters. An-other mattress was spread out neatly and had a coverlet and a round peace symbol pillow on it.

"That's Linda's bed," Sue explained. "As you can see, she's really hung up on cleanliness," and then Sue described what she thought Eugene was looking at, "and that's Vicki's stained glass stuff in the box. She's seeing this dude in the East Village so she's not around much. She made that butterfly in the window, but you can't see it through the curtain."

Eugene crossed the room and pulled back the cloth. He saw

the glass butterfly hanging on a string. He saw a group of Puerto Rican boys sitting on a stoop of a vacant cinderblock-sealed building. He wondered if they were muggers.

"She's a good artist, don't you think?" Sue said from her mattress.

Eugene thought it was ugly. He did not think of himself as any judge of art but the butterfly looked like something his mother would like. He leaned his head out the window and looked up and down Twenty-second Street. One of the boys yelled something up to him and he pulled his head in, resetting the Indian curtain. "Where would be a good place for my stuff?" he asked Sue.

She directed him to Tony the Bone's old spot, explaining that he had left the mattress, and Eugene was welcome to it, but he would have to get his own linens. The word "linen" provoked images of white clean fresh sheets on the line in the side yard at River Road. It seemed like linens would not be caught dead anywhere in the crash pad, except possibly undercover on Linda's bed, and even that seemed abused and gloomy. His spot was obviously the worst spot, the farthest from the windows, the closest to the in-and-out traffic at the door, and the nearest to Sue's pile of corner. He looked around and realized that there was no real "best" spot, and said, "Fine," moving in, carrying his bags three feet.

Sue was now sorting her purse contents and in a sweet coo of a voice that took Eugene by surprise she purred, "Do you really want to go buy grass?"

"Sure. I should celebrate, right?" Eugene did not sound very enthusiastic as he studied the stains on his mattress and wondered if they were blood or urine or shit or cream stains, or maybe all of that.

Sue pushed herself up so that for a moment, through her tee shirt, Eugene saw her large breasts shake free. "Yew Jean, we could get a good pad to cover all those stains," she said, seeing his lip turned, and then, imagining a shopping spree, Sue spoke excitedly, imagining walking arm in arm with him, smoking a joint, buying things, and maybe falling in love, or at least "like." "There's this great Salvation Army down by the Elgin and you could buy a pillow and a blanket, though it's so hot, you really don't need it, and on Eighth we can cop the grass and maybe a couple hits of acid, and we can get a key made."

In October, Eugene flipped out on acid at a Halloween party on Eldridge Street, below Houston, on the Lower East Side of Manhattan. Nelson had met the tranvestite superstar, Charity Ball, "Lucy's funnier, younger, redder sister," at a happening and she'd invited him to her party on Halloween. Eugene had met some people who had invited him to The Electric Circus, but Nelson convinced Eugene that "that scene is dead, man. This party will be a fucking blowout." In two months, Eugene had become close friends with fast-talking, street-wise, Nelson. Nelson had talked him into attending one of the acting classes he took at the New York School of Drama. He got Eugene a job at the head shop he worked in on St. Mark's Place. He knew something about everybody, it seemed, and Eugene's friends back in Ohio seemed like bumpkins compared to Nelson. Nelson was wiry thin and jumpy and looked like a New York actor, dark brown hair and eyes, rough at the edges and quick with a line. He was twenty-two, four years older then Eugene. He had "split Bensonhurst for the big time" and had convinced himself and everyone he met, if only slightly, that one day, he would make it.

Nelson and Linda, they were still sharing the same mattress, came as vampires. Sue made Eugene up to look like a cowboy, and she made herself up to be a witch. She would never admit it, but she always wore black to social events because years before she had heard that black slimmed you down. Eugene sat next to Linda on the train as a way of telling Sue that he was not her date. It seemed that the four of them were always together, and Sue acted as though Eugene was her old man, especially in public.

The party was in a large six-room tenement apartment above a bodega. The rooms were dark and full of pulsating lights and costumed people crowded where the music was loudest, not quite dancing to Vanilla Fudge, and then The Doors, and then The Velvet Underground. Eugene had three cups of punch before Nelson warned him that he had overheard someone saying that the punch was laced with acid. Nelson seemed to think that three cups was enough for him, and told him to have a nice trip.

The air was thick and sweet-smelling from incense. Someone stuck a joint in his mouth, and as he inhaled, he felt a hand on his cock, and then whoever it was disappeared into the smoke. Everyone was in costume. He looked for Sue. He looked for her pointed hat. He moved from room to room, feeling as if he was peeping through a keyhole rather than the black Lone Ranger mask. Ideas fell like running water over his forehead.

"I had no idea," he repeated over and over, as his consciousness disintegrated and the strychnine caused a tightening in his jaw and at the back of his neck. "I had no idea." He found his witch, Sue, a familiar stranger, and he said, "I had no idea." She was also starting to trip, but she knew what to expect.

"Just relax, cowboy Yew Jean," she cackled wickedly. "I'm here, so just relax and have fun."

Eugene wanted to say he was scared. He was. He had been scared since he descended the stairs from River Road. Who were all of these people? Were they laughing at him? The man who called himself Rasputin passed him and called him "Buckoe," or "Buckeye," or "Bucky" and he wanted to fight him for that. He was bigger, and could beat the shit out of him, he thought. What if he was losing his mind? Nobody would help him. Nobody would know or care. Nelson would, if he could find Nelson. He was scared of New York. He was scared at the pleasures he'd felt walking through the dirty side of the city. Old men made propositions to him and he would hurry away from them. He learned that if he looked directly at someone, they would think he was available for sex, or looking for a fight, or about to mug them. One striking man with black curly hair came into Patchouly, the head shop where he worked, and asked him if he wanted a blow job. Eugene had laughed, and had he been free to run away he would have, but he was the only one behind the counter. He'd felt himself getting hard and wanted to blurt out, "Aren't you embarrassed to just come out and ask such a thing?" But he shook his head "No," and looked away flustered, and then condemned himself when he saw the guy leave. "Do it! Why not? You've thought enough about it. Jerked off enough over all these guys in posing straps. That guy was neat!" Back at the party, he felt that everyone passing him in costumes, as he stood cornered, could read his thoughts like lighted signs running around that building in Times Square. He believed that if he stood perfectly still, he would be invisible, and he was. He saw himself. Why had he let Sue put black eyeliner around his eyes? Why did he leave three buttons open on his shirt showing off his chest? Why were his pants worn so low on his hips and tight in the crotch? Was he so innocent? Hiding in the corner? He began to laugh, realizing that he was attracted to himself, that he wanted to be wanted, and his fears were founded in all the shame and judgments from his past. "I had no idea," he mumbled, not knowing if he had spoken out loud or not. "Wow," he grinned, feeling the tension in his jaw crack. He understood the word 'wow" that Nelson always said. It was for when words were meaningless. He felt wise. Everything made sense, there just were no words for it. Everyone was beautiful. The music was beautiful. He felt his fingers, and then the muscles in his arms and legs. He moved them and laughed. He had a body! He flew to be nearer the music. To dance as he had with June. She had always used him to practice new dances before she went out on a date. Katherine had said he was a good dancer. Katherine would be shocked at the wild scene he was in. Some people were completely naked and painting themselves with music stripes. The blacklight posters were no longer posters. Jimi Hendrix was right there in the room, singing "This is the End!" as if he was Jim Morrison. He could see the music streaming like wet colors from the speakers. Someone dressed like a queen twirled around and around, stirring up the sea of colors. He thought that this was why men danced. They had to. To jump and sidestep all the streamers of colors.

Nelson came over to him and asked how he was doing. Eugene wanted to say something, but couldn't find his mouth. Then Nelson reached up and removed Eugene's mask, and said, lost in his own trip, "Come on, mister farmboy, there are no masks in the free age of Aquarius."

"Wow," Eugene smiled, feeling like a veil had been lifted. Nelson spoke the truth, he thought, and he pushed out his arm, seeing it tear through the confessional screen that separates the confessor from the priest.

"Stop in the name of love, darling," a beautiful blond said to Eugene. She smoked a cigarette from a sparkling holder, and mimicked his arm outstretched. "Baby, baby, I'm aware of where you go," she rubbed against him. "Are you a star?"

Nelson sang out, "Andrea! Hey!" to the young woman who said she was "Julie Christie in *Darling*, darling."

Nelson became Eugene's boyhood friend Bobby Schneider, dressed like a vampire, biting the neck of the blonde woman. He took a step back, and fell onto a couch. He sank deep into the soft cushion of it. He became the couch. Linda came in and led Bobby away and Eugene was surprised that she would know his old friend. He thought it was a small world. Another truth blazed before him. And then, the hostess of the party, the transvestite star of the underground, Charity Ball, dressed in a red sequined gown, and her hair teased out in a magenta Afro laced with sparkles, sat down swiveling onto Eugene's lap, pushing a joint to his mouth. He had found his mouth!

"Here, honey," Charity said in her low range, "I saw you come in. Now suck this in deep. That's it. They don't call me Charity for nothing."

Eugene felt the smoke open his throat. He laughed at the thought that he was the couch and she was only burning a hole in it. The sequins pressed into his chest.

"What's you name, cowboy?" Charity pursed her overdone lips. "I stopped the formalities hours ago. I'm too wasted."

Eugene coughed. Charity felt his stomach muscles, sliding her hand through his open shirt.

"Ooooo!" she squealed in her high range. "You're gorgeous! Did you bring your six-shooter?"

Eugene felt like a god. He traveled through his body flexing and thrusting like a vibrating recliner chair.

Sue, the witch, was hovering nearby, and saw Charity fondling Eugene's crotch. She came over to the couch and sat on the arm, next to Eugene. Charity smooched the air to her and explained, "I'm sizing up my guests." Seeing Sue made Eugene feel guilty. He felt she had caught him bragging. He felt his cock soften and disappear. Sue asked him if he was okay. He couldn't speak. It seemed that everything was echoing in his head, layers and layers of noise.

"Cowboy," Charity said, running her hands all over him, "I got a feeling this here body of yours could use some affection."

Eugene's green eyes watered.

Sue reached over and pushed Charity back a bit, "Hey, I think maybe he wants you to keep your hands off him. You're fucking with his head. He doesn't need your trip, man, or woman, or whatever you are. He's my old man."

Charity screeched, "Your old man! Now who is the mindfuck here? Look at him, he's beautiful, and hey, honey, let's face it," the hostess moved close to Sue's tight lips, "let's face it, honey, you're a witch."

Sue looked to Eugene. His eyes were closed and tears were streaming down his cheeks. She ran into the other room.

Charity unbuckled his jeans and managed to pull his pants down, along with his underwear. She oooed and ahhhed enough to attract a few voyeurs as she proceeded to suck his floppy cock.

Eugene opened his eyes at the warm wet feeling. He wanted to tell her to stop. He saw everyone watching. He felt his cock harden. Janis Joplin was singing. The magenta Afro seemed to be bouncing between his legs.

"Suck the cowboy, Charity," someone said.

Eugene brazenly looked in the bystanders' eyes, and that excited him more. He felt like he was fucking the entire room and everyone in it. He felt great. He felt like an animal, growling for the crowd, displaying himself, feeling like he had broken through to a higher plateau, reborn to be wild. He felt wet heat shooting through his flexed legs, and then a stab of burning up his spine to his neck, as if his head was encircled by a collar of fire. He jumped. His cock popped out of Charity's face. She frantically grabbed for it. He jumped again, this time standing straight up, gagging Charity, his cock turning her head like a turnstile, and he fell forward onto the wood floor, shooting come and screaming "Fire! Fiiiiiiirrrrreeee!" Charity put her red heel on his white ass, as if he were a captured prize, and everyone applauded. She crawled over to him and turned him face up. She kissed him. Her face was covered in smeared red lipstick, as was Eugene's dripping cock. He was breathing heavily, eyes squeezed shut.

"He's gone," Charity said, wiping her face with his kerchief, standing up, leaving him splayed on the floor, amidst the stoned-out wandering dancers.

Crazy-haired, Rasputin knelt down and took a few licks at Eugene's cock and balls.

Eugene was back in Ohio, helpless. Watching the flames. Hearing the screams. And then he started singing "Sugar Shack" as

Rasputin tried to pull his boots off. Again Eugene cried out, "Fire!" and a few people said. "Oh, wow!" because "Light My Fire" had just started playing.

At the back of the apartment, Nelson was trying to talk Linda into turning off the water in the sink. She had washed her face and hands so much that her skin was raw and bleeding. Sue tried to help, explaining how Linda's need to be neat and tidy had gone to her head. Then someone came in talking about the naked cowboy Charity had supplied for anyone to eat, and Sue pushed her way through to the front room.

Andrea Superstar, the blonde "Darling," was straddling Eugene and burning his chest hairs and the trail leading down to his pubic hair with her cigarette. Sue shoved her off.

"Hey!" Andrea said indignantly. "Who the hell are you, darling? He wants fire, I'm giving him what he wants!"

Sue screamed for Nelson, and she buttoned Eugene's shirt. His jeans and underwear were nowhere on the floor.

"Boo!" a few people hooted, watching from the sidelines.

A gypsy said, "Bummer. Let's burn the witch."

Sue started crying, and again called out for Nelson. Andrea was flicking lit matches at Sue's black dress.

"Fire!" bellowed Eugene. "Throw me your life!"

Nelson, the vampire, came in whining, "Wow, what did I miss?"

Sue screamed, "We've got to get out of here! They're all crazy!"

Charity came in and dove into the scene like a Hollywood star, slapping sense into Sue's abundant cheeks, "Listen up, honey! You go run along. I'll take care of this doll. What's his name?"

"None of your beeswax!" Sue cried, catching herself, mouth open at such a stupid childish remark.

Nelson pulled Eugene by his shoulders from the middle of the floor and propped him, bare ass, against the wall. He went back to get Linda out of the sink.

Sue called after him, "I'll wait here with Eugene, Nelson! Get Linda and let's get out of this madhouse!"

"Madhouse!" Charity flared, turning southern, "I'll have you know that cowboy almost killed me with his big kindness, and I want him to stay. It's my party!"

"Then go cry," Sue said, at a loss, sitting down next to Eugene, taking refuge at the side of the mute shaking young man. She made sure his shirt covered his cock, and rested her head on his arm.

People danced.

"Fire!" Eugene cried.

1969, New York City

Sue and Nelson celebrated Eugene's nineteenth birthday in their new apartment on St. Mark's Place. In his year in New York, Eugene had taken speech and acting lessons where Nelson studied. He had taken every drug. He had come up a high number in the military draft lottery. He had had an affair with Andrea Superstar and met Andy Warhol and Paul Morrissey and Viva and Ultra Violet. He learned to strip for the camera, and made fifty dollars for one day's work at the photographer's studio. He started writing a rock musical about Jesus, "the first hippie," and he was including parts for himself, Nelson, Charity, Andrea, Joe, and Viva. Then he heard that there was a hippie Christ play scheduled for Broadway, so he stopped working on it. He visited Ohio in June for two weeks and spent most of his time away from home and up in Mount Adams with Kevin and Leslie, his Crowd, till it was time to leave. Clara threatened to have him committed for the way he acted, "So drug-crazed and dirty, laughing at nothing at all like you was a lunatic."

In that year, Eugene clung to his three fucks of Andrea because interspersed with her, he was hanging out with men for money. One of the directors of the drama school asked him to his apartment, where they got stoned. The man told him, "Eugene, I am intrigued by your potential and would like to offer you private coaching. I have been watching you, and I think you've got what it takes." He asked to see him naked. He told him to stand and strip, slowly, and to act like he was alone. Eugene did as he was told, trying not to laugh, and trying not to get hard. He let the man fondle him and suck him off. It was all

27

he could do to not let on that he was enjoying it and that he was tempted to reciprocate. Over the weeks, the man coached Eugene privately in his bedroom.

One day Nelson confronted Eugene, "I heard you've been dicking Mr. Taylor."

Eugene laughed, coolly, as Nelson would have, "If you call that sex. I let him blow me and he's going to help me get into Equity, and he said I could take his classes for free."

Nelson shifted his weight from untied sneaker to tied sneaker. "So it's true. Man, everybody was talking about it behind your back after your scene today, you know, the way he tore Loretta apart and said you had 'found Williams' inner mote.' Fuckin 'A,' Eugene, I think you better dig what kind of rep you're getting."

Nelson had the habit of shortening words, chopping them off, similar to the way he moved, in quick jerks. He talked as if he was too cool to waste time with all the syllables. At Odessa's Ukrainian Diner on Avenue A, where Nelson, Eugene, and Sue ate three or four times a week, Nelson called pirogis "pees," kielbasa "bas," and sauerkraut "rot." His critiques in scene study classes were always abbreviated in one or two words. When asked his opinion of a scene, he would throw his head back as if he'd been hit by a thought of real weight, adjust himself, loosen his hands from his wrists as if they were wet, and then say something terse, like "shall." Then, asked to explain himself, he would twitch and squirm and add an adjective, like "trans." Eugene learned to understand him, and if he was in the class, he would yell out, "Nelson means transparent and shallow!" Eugene was infatuated with him.

Nelson said, "I'd say, 'Mr. Taylor can I have it in scratch?' Will you do that, Eugene? Get his word in ink." Then he put his hand on Eugene's shoulder and said, "Check it out. Linda split. My dick's got the time if he's giving grants. Wonder why he's not made a move my way?"

Eugene had wondered that too. He wondered why he had been singled out to be propositioned. He wondered if he acted available in some way that he was unaware of. Was it in his eyes? Did he look too closely at Mr. Taylor, or was it the way he would look away if Mr. Taylor caught his stare? Why was it him and not Nelson who received the school director's attentions?

He chose to accept Nelson's shrugged explanation, "He must

know not to mess with me. You, man, no way do you have your shit together, you act like a dude. You smile too fast." Nelson mimicked Eugene, acting goofy with a big toothy grin and walking in circles in wide strides around the room with his thumbs hitched in his jean pockets. Eugene laughed but punched Nelson in the arm and denied he acted, as Nelson put it, "Rube, man, easy touch, rube," but he was willing to allow his innocence the accountability for Mr. Taylor's focus on him and not someone else.

Linda, Nelson's girlfriend, moved to Tennessee with Dave the Douche in July, "to get away from the paranoia, pollution, and egomania," to live on a commune the Douche had heard about. The crash pad on Twenty-second Street had become "just too crazy and sick," according to her. Nelson was hurt. He, as well as Eugene and Sue, agreed that too many freaks had keys to the place and the only solution was for the four of them to find a new apartment. Linda argued that "it's not just this dump, it's the whole civilization!" Eugene and Sue sat on one side of the bookcase listening as they argued. Finally Linda agreed to drop acid with Nelson one more time. He hoped to convince her that their love was stronger than Tennessee, and she hoped to convince him to give up his "jivy New York scene and find out who you really are."

Hours later, Nelson and Linda made very loud love while Eugene peripherally watched from his pillow on his mattress. The sight of Nelson's white ass humping in the hot July moonlight, and the sound of his grunts and gasps, sent pangs of strange hunger through Eugene. The room was full of a sexual headiness. Eugene breathed in the rhythm that Nelson was thrusting. Sue snored in unison. Eugene felt a contact high. He came when Nelson came.

It seemed Nelson impressed Eugene more than Linda with his prowess, because she packed and left the next day. Eugene and Sue comforted Nelson by pooling their money to buy cocaine and the three of them went to Central Park and decided that they would move to a "real apartment." The place they found was a five-room railroad over the head shop Patchouly where Nelson and Eugene worked sometimes. They moved in on Eugene's nineteenth birthday.

Sue arranged chocolate Ding-Dongs to spell Eugene's name,

and they sang "Happy Birthday" and went down to the Fillmore on acid. Eugene was aching to talk to Nelson about the feelings he'd been having, and the LSD dissolved his doubts and fears. It was obvious. He had to stop pussyfooting around and admit it, Eugene realized, he was bisexual, and at that point in time and space, he was in love with Nelson. All the lyrics from the band playing on stage seemed to verify his vision, "Love." He realized that if he was honest, he had to admit that he had been attracted to males since high school, and it wasn't just sexual. He was in love with Nelson! Each time he admitted that to himself, he whooped and hooted and the entire theater agreed, joining him in chanting, "Love! Love! Love! Love!" Only Nelson seemed oblivious to the obvious. He was trying to roll a joint and kept spilling grass onto the floor. Eugene cried in joy at the truth, sometimes consciously wondering who had organized such a birthday for him. Only Nelson could have pulled off such a feat. That was why he was being so sheepish. Eugene grabbed him and kissed him on the lips and declared, "I love you! What a surprise party!"

"Fuck, man!" Nelson pushed him to the seat. "Look what you fucking did! I dropped the fucking lid!" Nelson felt around on the floor, cursing and calling Eugene a crazy fucking rube.

Eugene pushed his way to the aisle. Sue shouted for him to hurry back. He had to get out of there, he knew. It was all some fucked-up hallucination. Out on Second Avenue, he wept and decided that he had to see Charity. He ran down the street, knocking into people and cars, his ears ringing with a hideous chant of "Love!" and then maniacal jeers of "Queer!" He finally reached Charity's building on Eldridge Street and knocked hard, yelling for her.

Charity's male voice yelled, "Who the fuck is it?" and she opened the door wrapped in a towel. Her red hair was dripping wet. Her voice rose to a shrill, "Cowboy!"

Eugene was covered in sweat. He fell toward her, crying, "I was afraid you weren't home."

She held his head down to her shoulder and patted him, "There, there, you're safe here, cowboy. Just tell me what drug it is this time."

Eugene melted and felt like a dead baby in her arms. She rocked him.

"Drug?" he thought. "That's right! I'm tripping!" His cries turned to laughter. He said, "Acid."

Charity led him to her bedroom. She said she had a surprise for him. "A waterbed!" she announced proudly. "I just finished filling it up. That's why I'm all wet. The hose kept pulling out and spraying all over," she sighed, batting her plain un-made-up eyes. "The story of my life, right, cowboy?"

The room was soaked. The walls were wet, the mirrors were wet, and the floor was wet. She said the witch who ran the bodega below her had probably gotten the first shower of her life. She told Eugene to lie down and initiate it while she finished drying off. He sat down apprehensively. The room swayed. He giggled like a boy, feeling free to, and the chant in his head faded like the end of a song. From the other room, Charity sang out, "It's all so perfect, cowboy!" The phone rang and Charity shrieked and talked. He told himself, "Anything goes." He felt like he was on an air mattress floating on the river.

Charity said into the phone, "I know, I know, honey, he said she had shaved her pussy but they had to shoot fast before her Lebanese cracks .... mmm-hmm, I told *you* that!" She appeared in the doorway holding the phone and making faces to Eugene referring to the long-winded gabber on the other end. She mouthed "Jackie," to him. "Mmm-hmm, honey, I was shocked too but he's afraid of his own shadow since the shooting." She said to Eugene, "Take your shoes off, cowboy, or your heels will puncture it." She said to Jackie, "Yes, *the* cowboy. You know Paolo is after him. He called me yesterday and today. I don't know what he's shooting."

Eugene took off his shoes.

"Cowboy's from Texas or Ohio or somewhere out there where they don't chop'm down till they're full grown." She kissed the air in Eugene's direction.

Eugene liked hearing himself talked about. He became aware of how he must have looked to Charity. He consciously flexed his arms and spread himself out on the waterbed. Looking down his tee shirt, he saw his crotch packed and rising in his cutoffs. If Charity wanted, he decided, he would let her blow him again. They never went beyond that in the few times she'd gone down on him since her Halloween party. He was a stud, he thought, just the way she wanted it.

She hung up the phone and said to him, about the waterbed, "Fabulous, n'est pas?"

He nodded and adjusted himself for her.

"Oooo, honey, you look so much more yourself than when you got here. I think I can safely say, cowboy, that you cannot hold your liquor. Now, before I get my face on you, let me call Paolo. I didn't give him your number because I knew you were moving."

Eugene thought of Nelson and Sue at the Fillmore. He thought of their new home, and of the Ding-Dong cakes.

"Paolo? Miss Ball here. I've got Cowboy in my new waterbed!" Eugene heard her say. Sue, in one of her moods, had said to him earlier that he had a low opinion of himself. He chuckled at that, feeling confident that he was the absolute hottest number on the Lower East Side. He repeated to himself, "Anything goes," adding a "man" as Nelson would, "anything goes, man," and he rolled, making waves in the bed. Its seams strained as he got up and went to the phone that Charity held out for him. She unzipped him as he made arrangements with Paolo to come to his studio.

1970, New York

Eugene beamed at the sight of the Atlantic. He had learned what hustling was, and what a bagel was, and now, finally, after being in New York for a year and a half, he was at the beach. He had talked Nelson and Moody Sue into taking the train with him. The three of them treated the trip like an expedition, even though it was only a long subway ride away. They considered themselves city people, and Sue made it clear that people who tried to tan were "plastic." The previous summer, when Eugene could have gone to the ocean on a few occasions, he was too drugged or busy with nightlife. There was an exciting perversion in him that enjoyed avoiding the sun and the weather and the California attitude, as Nelson had called it, after living all of his life in full view of the big sky of the Midwest. He ran down the beach, stripping to his briefs. Nelson and Sue shouted that he should go in, even though it was only April and the water would be cold. He did, feeling uncaged and overwhelmed by the full sound of the waves, running in as he'd seen in movies and on television, surprised at the strength of the undertow, falling quickly into the surf. He came up fast, his eyes burning from the salt, his mouth spitting out the water, not knowing, having been used to the pool at school and the freshwater river. He was shocked completely, baptized into the bigger world, he thought, cold and salt and loud and dramatic, even seagulls hovered, just like in the media. He emerged from the Atlantic, a new seasoned man, his white underwear sticking wet and transparent to his ass and molded to his inverted cock. He looked down at himself, shy about what was showing, and then saw the big grins on

Nelson and Sue and he hooted loud, as Nelson had taught him, "Let go, man, just pull it from deep when Jerry Garcia hits the first chord," and he clomped over to the blanket they had laid out, like a sea monster with long big strides. He said, "Well, I am now a surfer."

Sue, wrapped in a sweater over her long skirt and twenty strands of beads and peasant blouse, looked up at him and daringly said, "I can see your dick."

Eugene wrapped his towel around himself, turning from her sight.

"And I can see your cute butt, don't be so prudish."

Nelson, the handsome street-smart aspiring actor, was jealous of Eugene's show of emotion, prowess, daring, and flex, and quickly undid his bellbottoms and ran down into the surf, screeching an "I love life!" screech equal in volume, if not sincerity, to Eugene's, jumping into the freezing surf in his underwear. He came out quickly, shivering, running with as much screech back to the blanket.

"You two ought to see yourselves," Sue said, trying to light a cigarette in the wind. "You're both shriveled up, look at your dicks! You're going to catch your death, too. Doesn't that hurt?"

"What?" Eugene asked, hiding behind his towel, June's towel, that he'd always had, striped brown and aqua.

"Doesn't it hurt to shrivel up?" Sue smoked, her double chin hiding her neck, Eugene noticed, from the way she was squatting on the blanket.

Eugene looked at Nelson, who was also hiding behind a towel. Nelson shook his wet head, "No," and then Eugene said, "It only hurts from the salt."

Nelson took a handful of sand and slapped it on Eugene's wet back. Eugene jumped, dropping his towel and chasing after Nelson, running after him heavily in the sand, laughing and calling to him to prepare for the consequences of his attack. They ended up back in the water, wrestling and dunking each other despite the frigid waves pounding at them. Eugene swallowed ocean in his fits of laughter. He pulled Nelson's briefs down and Nelson fell under and Eugene managed to get them from his legs. He ran to shore and wadded them up and threw them to Sue at the blanket. Nelson jumped on Eugene's back cursing him, and the two young men fell back into the waves.

"Get'm back for me, man!" Nelson demanded, holding Eugene down with his foot and covering his cock with his hand. He was no longer kidding around.

Eugene agreed, seeing Nelson's embarrassment, and feeling like he'd gone too far, possibly, wondering if what he'd done had shown a queer bent. He shook his head fast, like a wet dog, and plodded out of the ocean, feeling salty and rushing and vibrant, even though Nelson was mad.

"He won't come out till I give him his underwear," Eugene dripped over Sue. "Nobody's around, I don't know why he's so mad."

Nelson stood waist-deep waiting as waves shoved against him, knocking him toward shore. "Come on!" he yelled. "I'm freezing!"

"Boy," Sue said, "you guys sure are hung up when your dicks are little. Nelson runs around naked at the apartment all the time."

Eugene walked slowly, deliberately teasing Nelson. Nelson seemed so sweet and edible and defenseless shivering out there. Eugene stopped the thought, calling himself a pervert. Sue watched Eugene's wet ass and she sucked deep on her cigarette. Nelson yelled, "Throw'm!"

Eugene threw, poorly, missing Nelson, forcing the naked young man to chase them into the shallow. Eugene saw, for a second, Nelson's dickhead, and thought he should look away or Nelson would get angrier.

In the sunlight, Eugene's long hair was drying and blowing in the wind, a red and dirty blond, a "dishwater blond" June had called the color. He was long and strong and freed from the city he'd been wearing for eighteen slum-gray and psychedelic months. Sue saw him fresh again, like when he'd first appeared at her door. Nelson saw him as a threat, turning from him to pull on his underwear.

"Fucking raisin dick," Nelson said, coming ashore toward him.

"Truce?" Eugene said, raising his hands in surrender.

"Truce," Nelson agreed. "My balls feel like they're in my stomach."

"I think it's a miracle, dicks are," Eugene said, keeping a safe distance from Nelson, not quite trusting the truce, "how big they can get and how small they can get."

An older man in a suit called from the boardwalk, "Hey you two! No swimming till June! Stay out of the water!"

Nelson stopped in the sand and shouted back, "What the fuck are you lookin at, you fuckin faggot!"

Eugene hated that Nelson had yelled that. He had just been feeling close to him. His face became serious. Nelson misread the look and told Eugene that there was no law about swimming at your own risk, and the man was just trying to get them to come up closer so he could get an eyeful.

"He's been up there watching us horse around, I saw him," Nelson said.

At the blanket, eating one of Sue's Twinkies, Eugene asked Nelson, "Why do you think that man was a faggot?"

"Because, man, you can tell, you know, he was getting his rocks off sighting the boys and the boys' toys. Just like Taylor."

Eugene looked away and muttered, "So what."

Sue set her book down and wrapped her arms around her knees and turned her head to Eugene and said shyly, "Eugene is in love with you, Nelson, don't you know that? Remember the Fillmore?"

Eugene looked surprised and then, knowing there was no way what she was saying could be possible, broke out a hard laugh, as real as he could make it, although he felt like he'd been kicked in the head from left field. Why had she said such a thing? That night at the Fillmore had never been brought up.

Nelson laughed too, because the idea of being in love was not something two men could be, but he played along, since one of the games these three roommates played was "daring perversity," which Nelson considered part of his improvisational acting practice. "Hey, you can't blame the guy, right? Eugene?"

Eugene looked through a tight screen, smiling.

"Anytime you want to eat my big dick, man," Nelson said, touching his towel which covered his lap, "it's yours. Balls too. I go to sleep at night with one wish, man, that you'll come over to my bed and tuck me in and spread my ass and fuck me up the rear till your hot come shoots into my insides and then your pretty-boy Kentucky tongue can lick me all over while Sue fingers herself and watches from the keyhole, right?"

"Fuck you," Sue said, returning to her book on Lancelot's Elaine. She was into the Arthurian legend.

Eugene was staring out at the waves, but they were no barrier from Nelson's attack.

"And you'd crawl around for me, man, and your bone would jump at the sight of me and you'd try to get me down, but it would be a fight, cause I'm the real man, here, man."

Eugene looked over, then back to the Atlantic.

"Hey, man, don't look so serious, so tender with your sad eyes, I'm just improvising. I got nothing against faggots. Shit, I'm an actor, but I do have to say that I wonder sometimes about you, man, doing those films, dicking Mr. Taylor, and those people you hang out with, big deal, Warhol. He's a pussy. I mean, let's face it, you are bordering on the queer world. Don't take it perse."

Eugene stared out at the ocean, imagining the curve and Europe beyond, and he wished that Sue had not come with him, since she had a way of baiting them, and a way of hitting a true nerve and Eugene thought of her as fat, and jealous that neither man was interested in her for sex. He knew that she knew there was some truth in her little joke, and below that, he knew that he was in love with Nelson. He was so slick and cool and self-confident, even his hair, straight cut and drying, fell right into place after each gust of sandy wind.

Finally, after Nelson had talked himself into feeling he'd gone too far, and had hurt Eugene more than he'd intended, Eugene turned to him and said, "Nelson, you know what gets me? How come you can come up with such things? What do you do, memorize *Screw* magazine? It just sounds like you sure have given a lot of thought about what queers do." Then he hated himself for saying that, as he saw Nelson stop grinning. "I'm kidding, Nelson, I guess the three of us could drive each other crazy with all our kidding. I promise I'll never pull your underwear off you again." And he hated himself for saying that. It was another attack.

Nelson threw his head back, as if he'd come to an abrupt stop, and he laughed, "Man, sometimes I think you either dropped one too many tabs of acid, or you need to drop a hell of a lot more."

Sue said, "There's something I'd like to say, if you two would stop for a minute, and that is," she cleared her throat and took a deep breath, "there is only one more cupcake. Do you guys care if I eat it?"

Eugene shook his head, "No."

Nelson said, "You need your sugar, go ahead."

Eugene wished he was back in the city. He felt sticky, sandy, and cold. He was glad that his old girlfriend, Katherine, was going to be visiting. She was coming in from Berkeley that week. They had gone together in Ohio, till Katherine was forced to move out to her father's house in Oakland in her senior year. Her parents were divorced and her mother said she couldn't handle her daughter's crazy ways any longer. She'd said, "The further you are from that trashy Goessler boy, the better," but the distance did not stop them from writing to each other. Eugene believed that when Katherine was sent away, he'd put his heart on hold, and now, soon, she would be with him, and the confused emotions he'd been experiencing would smooth out and fall into line. He imagined Katherine with him at the ocean. They would finally make love and roll passionately in the surf.

1972, New York

Eugene wasn't a street hustler, he insisted. He was a superstar-stud for hip, rich, and influential men. He did it for the money, true, but he said he was a student of life and was learning about the "otherworld." He took a course in theater at The New School and a course in film through the Millennium Film Coop. He posed for photographers, who inevitably, no matter how on the up and up they claimed to be, got him down to a posing strap, or nothing, with each additional line of coke. He took Charity's advice, which was, "Get it while you can, cowboy, cause one of these days you'll look in the mirror and know it's time to move on."

That day came in March, when Eugene stopped by the apartment to pick up his mail and change his clothes. Katherine's letter was waiting. It sounded inviting, but he was feeling too good to consider it. Things were starting to happen for him. He was supposed to start work that day on a "real big-budgeted art film that will be shown in Europe." He was to be paid a thousand dollars. Charity said, "You are on your way now, cowboy. Europe. Next thing you know you'll be in Paris!"

He pocketed the letter in his clean jeans and left some cash with a note for Sue, "to cover costs. Today I start a new movie and there's more money coming." He snorted a line of coke and ran to the subway, where he caught the train to Brooklyn. He reread the letter on the train. Katherine described her new life in the woods. She wrote about the garden and the rustic cabin and the river. She said she was getting to know her new stepbrother, Scott, whom she had just met for the first time, when her father

39

remarried in Oakland. She said Scott was a kindred spirit and had quit UCLA to travel to India and Tibet. She said he had no use for the material world. At the end of the letter, she offered Eugene a place to stay, "if you ever decide to quit New York and get your head together."

It seemed like Katherine was living on another planet, especially from his vantage point, standing over a drunken woman passed out and reeking of urine. She was under the only readable map. It was a dim, foul world on the Canarsie Line compared to Katherine's letter.

He walked to the warehouse studio where the film was to be shot. On his way in, Tex Houston, another cock star, was walking out, obviously pissed.

"Hey, Houston," Eugene said, blocking his way, making the air between the two striking young men momentarily the most valuable airspace in Brooklyn. Houston cracked a smirk, and then accepted a handshake, the "peace-brother" double-touch kind.

"Hey, cowboy, I wouldn't go in there if I was you. The shit's hit the fan."

Eugene laughed, "No, I've been hired. I'm supposed to be here for La Mondo Films."

Houston's eye twitched and teared. He covered it with his hand, and laughed, "Fuck, cowboy, why do you think I'm out here in this slum? I don't have to go looking for work either. They hired me too, man. We're just fuckin meat, man. El Grande got busted last night. The backers pulled up stakes. And guess who's left standing in the middle of nowhere with their thumbs up their asses?"

Eugene insisted on going in to hear for himself what was up. Possibly there was only a delay. Wouldn't someone have tried to call him? Houston begged a cigarette and said he'd wait, so they could ride the train back to Manhattan together.

Inside the warehouse, across an empty garage, he saw two men in suits, arguing in a glassed-in office. He checked himself quick, making sure his hair was pulled tight back and his jeans hung right, and then he knocked on the metal door that had a red star painted crudely on it, some of the paint running like blood halfway down.

"Get lost! The party's over!" one of the men yelled, with a tough thug accent.

Eugene knocked again, feeling he deserved some explanation. One of the men looked out through the grimy glass. Eugene heard him say to his partner, "It's another one of the queer boys." The door opened.

Eugene introduced himself and said, "For your information, I am not a queer, and I'm not a boy, and I think someone could have at least had the guts to call me. I thought this was a legit . . ."

"Get outa here, you fuckin fag!" the shorter of the two said. "We got a clock tickin on our own asses. You think we're gonna call . . . fuck, do you believe this guy?"

Eugene felt a surge of fury through his chest. Houston was right. They were just meat. A joke. He stepped toward the men, daring to scrape some sort of apology from them. "Yeah?" he shifted his tone to sound tough, "Yeah?"

The two men laughed together at the trembling bravado displayed by the "cowboy."

Eugene put up his fists, "Come on," he challenged them, taking another step in, "y'fucks. You think we're just meat. I want money for coming out here. I could have made fifty bucks easy today."

The larger of the two, who stood as tall as Eugene, said, "Look, kid, get lost, we got enough trouble. We don't want to hurt you."

Eugene was shaking. "Then give me some money."

The short man unzipped his trousers and pulled out his cock. "Suck this and I'll give you five bucks."

Eugene tried to laugh, but his mouth's muscles were tight. "Fuck you," he said between clenched teeth, and he reached down and wrenched the man's balls, "let your fucking buddy here do you . . ." He had the man falling, writhing in pain toward the file cabinets the men had been emptying. Then he felt the weight of a brick on his skull and saw stars just as he had when he was a kid and dove into the school pool, hitting his head on the bottom. His legs buckled under him as he was spitting, "You dirty fucks . . ."

The tall one tied Eugene's hands behind him with a cord as the short one kicked him in the crotch shouting, "You fucking pervert!" Eugene's head was exploding in pain. The wind was kicked out and up his throat with blood and he yelled, "Houston! Houst . . ." and was punched in the jaw by the short man.

"Stand him up," the tall one said as they lifted Eugene from the floor, heaving. "Stupid kid. Just what we need here, Tony, a smart-ass faggot."

"They want it," Tony, the short one, grunted.

The two men walked Eugene out of the office, and let him drop to the concrete floor of the warehouse.

"I'm not through with him," Tony said, taking off his coat and tie.

The tall man said, "Tony! We gotta get outa here! Man, you are a fuck!"

Tony knelt over Eugene and undid his jeans, unzipping him. Eugene was coughing and gagging blood. He opened his eyes as he felt the hand on his balls and saw the knife in the short man's hand.

"Hey studboy," the man spat when he caught sight of Eugene's eyes, "I'm about to do you a favor and take you out of action for good."

The tall man lit a cigarette, laughing, "Tony, cool it."

Eugene's wrists burned as he struggled to get loose. He couldn't even kick with his jeans gathered above his knees. He pleaded with the tall one, "Let me outa here!"

The knife was a switchblade. Tony dangled it loosely for Eugene to see, pointing down to his exposed genitals. "Tough guy, huh?" the short man sweated and joked. "Don't seem so tough now, do you, ya pussy."

Eugene shook his head and cried over toward the tall one, "Please let me outa here!"

The tall man walked over and pulled Tony to his feet, "Leave him like that, man. We got to get the rest of the papers and split, man. Play your games later."

"Hands off me, Krone, the fuck nearly pulled my nuts off."

The tall one, Krone, led Tony back to the office. Tony spit on the floor and turned to look over in the dim light at the young man squirming.

"My jacket," he said, and walked back to Eugene. He bent down to pick it up and said, "Say your prayers, cowboy."

"Tony!"

Tony gave Eugene a kick to the ribs, tearing the "cowboy's" denim jacket. Eugene doubled up on his side.

When both men were back in the office, Tex Houston appeared from the dark and knelt down, untying Eugene's hands, "Man, why the fuck did you come in here? Shit."

Eugene pulled up his jeans and they ran out. Eugene didn't stop till he was blocks away, where he collapsed on a bench next to a Hasidic Jew, who closed his paper and silently hurried away. Houston caught up to him.

"What the fuck happened?" he panted.

Eugene coughed, "I asked them for money. Then I tried to get out. That little guy, what a fuck!"

Tex Houston wiped Eugene's face, "That was Anthony Rizzoli, you asshole. He's one of the moneymen. He's a big deal. I hope he doesn't think I had anything to do with you. Fuck."

The two young men took the train back to Manhattan. Eugene's pains were rattled by the shaky ride. He ran the scene through his mind over and over. What happened. What he should've done. How he was lucky to be alive, yet in the foul tunnel, broke and aching, his life seemed to have burned out. Tex Houston combed his dark hair, and then offered the comb to Eugene.

"Man, I can't believe you fuckin hauled off and hit Anthony Rizzoli, Jesus, cowboy, wait till everybody hears about this," Houston raved.

Eugene retied his hair and tried to see his face in the glass of the subway window. His lip was cut. He sat down next to Houston, "Thanks for coming in."

"Hey," the handsome man chuckled, failing to pull off a stab at humility. "As long as they don't find out I was in on it, I'll say, 'You're welcome.' "

Houston got off first and said, "Stay cute, cowboy. Catch ya later. Max's maybe." Then he shot his finger at Eugene like a gun and made a clicking noise with his tongue.

Eugene hurried to his apartment, depressed. He was relieved to find that Sue had not been home. He took the money he'd set out for her and tore up the note he'd written, so naively, he thought, about all the money he was going to make. He snorted a line of coke and took a shower, then left again to see Charity. He had a cut in his scalp from whatever the tall man had hit him with, and he walked slowly, wondering if he should go to St. Vincent's to find out if he had a concussion.

"Houston told me . . ." Eugene started to say at Charity Ball's new big cheap space on West Broadway near Canal Street that she called a loft.

"Houston! Houston's a prick. Prime asshole. Nothing he could say would interest me, cowboy."

Eugene persisted, "Houston told me that I never would have gotten a grand for the movie. They say that to everyone. He told me that that Anthony and his partner are dope dealers and . . . he said I am out. For good. He said they control it all." He shuffled about the loft tugging behind him at his ponytail.

"Houston's full of shit. Don't believe it! They're small-time," Charity said, taking the pan of boiling water from the hotplate and pouring two cups of instant coffee. She wore a long silk green robe, and without makeup and a shave, looked like a red-haired man without eyebrows. She opened the window and March blew in to the dusty area she called the kitchen. She grabbed a carton of milk from the fire escape and closed the window again, saying, "Brrrrrrr, how can you go running around without a heavy coat, honey?"

"They could've called me," Eugene paced. "Fucking Canarsie train hell. I thought you said it was such a sure thing. Those fucks."

"Calm down, cowboy. That's show biz. You didn't do anything stupid, did you?"

"Yeah! I went there! That's what Houston meant about me being 'out,' I started a fight with that Rizzoli guy. They hit me with a fucking leadweight on my head and threatened to cut off my balls."

Charity looked up to her enamel ceiling. "Oh, cowboy, how stupid can you be," she sighed heavily, and then sipped her white coffee, holding it with both hands, imagining the scene over in Brooklyn. She giggled, "Houston too? The both of you?"

"No, he was outside."

"Oh, cowboy. Poor cowboy. And I bet you even powdered up your six-shooter for the director."

He grabbed at his crotch, making a big handful, slyly smiling, with added relief that he was still intact, not seeing that Charity was ridiculing him. He always felt Charity was hot for him. He liked her attention. With her, he could admit to being an exhibitionist because she dared him to love himself. He could let himself own up to the most exaggerated feelings he'd have, feelings that he usually denied or called fucked up. With her, he *was* a stud. He was clever about it, too. In the *Oxblow Incident* he had improvised a line he used often, when he said to the sheriff and the barmaid who were taking turns sucking him, "Eat it and weep." In his three and a half years in New York, he'd developed a real needy habit for that attention. It wasn't just the grand that he was frustrated about losing out on.

"I'm always impressed, cowboy," Charity said, pinching his ass. "I hope you didn't get hurt too bad. You got to take care of yourself." She circled him, checking him out from head to toe. "You carry yourself so well, such a tough act. Paolo loves you, honey. They all do. And now this, taking on one of the schmucks, my God, you'll be a hero."

"Don't call me 'cowboy' anymore, okay?"

"Touchy, touchy. You're just having a bad day." Charity patted his crotch. "How about a little grass?"

Eugene jerked away as her hand reached up to feel his forehead for a fever. Her nails were chipped blue and bitten.

"Oooooo, pardonnez-moi, cowboy," she teased.

"I mean it, Charity, I'm no cowboy."

"But one hell of a stud, right?" She reset her hand on his forehead. "Maybe they really hurt you?"

"Yeah, they hurt me. Fuck. They could've killed me. I keep running over it. I hate all this. I'm sick of it. This isn't good for me anymore. Don't you ever want to can all this superstar crap? Just get out of it. Be real?"

Charity laughed, "Be damned, cowboy, I'll ungird my loins forever if you can tell me what's real." She took a joint from her robe pocket. "Light, bigboy?"

He took a match and flicked it one-handed with his thumbnail. It was a move Nelson had taught him.

Charity smiled and inhaled deep. "And you say you're no cowboy. Honey, with moves like that, you sure act the part."

She was right, he thought, all his moves, the way he dressed in worn jeans and Western shirts, the boots. Walking into Max's or some party, he deliberately strutted, legs bowed slightly, as if he'd just gotten off a horse. "You know, Charity, you're the one who got me into this cowboy thing. I'm from Ohio."

She passed the joint, "If the shoe fits wear it, honey. Do you think I was raised in a pink nursery with ruffles around? You know better. Now lighten up, cowboy. You are so serious today. It's all just a big party, cow . . . honey, go check out my wardrobe for a new look if that's what's bothering you."

Eugene was so fidgety he reminded himself of Nelson. He scrutinized Charity as she closed her eyes to inhale the joint he'd passed back to her. "What am I doing here?" he thought, "with a man who thinks he's a woman, getting doped up in some slum in the middle of more slums, sashaying about town like some ballroom sheik, pretending to be so together when I'm totally fucked up." He remembered being on the concrete floor of the warehouse, seeing the knife, seeing the deranged eyes of Anthony Rizzoli. He knew he could be stabbed, be left there to bleed to death, balls or no balls, it wouldn't matter. He remembered feeling in some way pleased with himself because he had stood up to the men. He had drawn a line. He felt that he had become a man, or at least tipped the scales toward manhood, and the shame was that he would bleed to death as payment. He could see there was no reasoning with the switchblade, but reason lit a cigarette and watched. There was his only hope, and he pleaded to be let go. June untied his hands. No, Tex Houston untied his hands.

Charity passed the joint. "Here, honey."

He noticed the droning rumble below the floorboards caused by the hundreds of sewing machines in the sweatshop below Charity's loft. "Sounds like they've increased the volume down there," he smoked and passed the joint. "It would drive me crazy."

Charity shrugged and threw her arms out fliply. "You get used to it, like anything else, though sometimes I swear I can hear whips being snapped and think I hear someone yelling, 'Row faster, row faster!' "

Eugene couldn't shake his troubled thoughts, no matter how deep or long he inhaled Charity's grass. He and the transvestite superstar each sat in rolling office chairs and pushed themselves with their feet across the wooden floorboards. Charity said that she was thinking of using some of the money she had left from the sale of Alex's Porsche to produce her own film. Alex was a rich kid who had committed suicide. The subject of that money had come up because she had sold the Porsche to Anthony

Rizzoli's brother. She said she would definitely have a part in the film for Eugene.

"It would be a kind of *Prime of Miss Jean Brodie*, but I would be the teacher," Charity envisioned, "and my girls would be boys, and what I teach would be definitely higher education, and I'd bestow a few masters too."

Eugene was lost in his sullen thoughts. "Kids I went to school with are now college graduates, and where am I?"

Charity backbit, "I see you love my idea, honey."

Eugene apologized.

Charity said, "And how many of them are in bodybags on the news?" picking up her feet for a brief ride.

"Yeah," Eugene brightened a little, "that's right. At least I didn't hide out in college to stay out of Vietnam. I was going to go to Canada. Remember when I first met you and I was worried because I was 1-A and you said, 'Go queer,' and then they had the lottery and my number came up so high . . ."

"Mmmmm," Charity spun in her chair, "a hot number, cow . . . honey. God, you were so innocent. And look at you. Morose. What is it? You don't really want to go to college. You really are a case for Doctor Feelgood today, cowboy."

Eugene sneered.

"Sorry," she bowed, "I meant cowpoke. Is that better? I know! Let's do a couple lines of coke!"

Eugene nodded, then slumped in his chair, stopping the rolling game. "Still, when I think about it, all those guys have degrees in something, and what have I got to show?"

"How to strike a match one-handed?" Charity suggested.

"Yeah, that's about it," Eugene allowed her remark to weigh in.

"Honey! I'm kidding! Really, you are a real drag today. Look at you, so woe-woe-woe-is-me, and meanwhile *Fish* is playing at midnight shows in London and your balls are hanging on walls in Paolo's big show! If you want, I'll give you a degree from the School of Hard Knocks just for standing up to those thugs today."

That's true, Eugene thought to himself. He knew the streets of New York. The real world. Not like the plastic weekend hippies who came over from New Jersey to wear beads and walk up and down St. Mark's Place, and then run back to study on Sunday nights. How many guys from Bishop Miller could say they ate with Andy Warhol? One acid trip was worth a whole semester of something.

"And everyone thinks you're swell," Charity said, having decided to add "swell" to her vocabulary as an adjective. "I can't believe how fragile you tough guys are. Ouch, ouch." She scraped a set of four white lines on her hand mirror.

"Fuck you," Eugene said. "Don't you ever get serious?"

Charity sighed, then snorted, stumped by the wall between her and the cowboy. "Only the little things do I get serious about . . ."

Eugene said skeptically, "Yeah, sure," anticipating another "superstar's words of wisdom" coming. He snorted his two lines.

"Like when Woolworth's is out of my shade, or it gets so cold my milk freezes, or when they expect me, Charity Ball, Lucy's younger, redder, and funnier sister, to actually wait in line. Honey, now that's serious."

"Forget it," Eugene said, wiping his nose with his hand and pushing his chair away from her.

"Hey!" Charity demanded Eugene to look over, sounding really fed up. "You look me in the eyes, man, and you tell me, Charity-sex-change-or-no-sex-change-Ball, about tough times. You tell me about feeling bad about yourself!" Her voice had dropped to male huskiness. "You whine about it, slobber about wasting away! Honey, you're wasting my time and your time, if you expect me to take you seriously. I decided long ago to come to the party, and no matter what, have fun, and sometimes that's twice as hard as feeling sorry for myself. Do you hear me? It's your choice, honey! You are a superstar if you want to be! Heaven or hell, honey! It's all up to you. It doesn't matter in the least to anyone else."

Eugene felt his pocket for his cigarettes and touched upon Katherine's letter. He withdrew it and scooted back toward Charity.

"Cow, honey, are you listening to me?"

"Yeah, I heard you, and I know what you're saying," Eugene muttered, "but, you know that old girlfriend of mine who came here that weekend? Well, I got this letter from her today . . ."

"The Miss America?" Charity snickered, still male.

"Yeah, Katherine. She's Moody Sue's cousin, you know the

story, and anyway, she's living in the woods in a cabin out in Sonoma County, and it sounds like paradise."

"Ahhhhhhhhh," Charity got the picture, returning to her higher range, "so that's what's tripping you out. The call of the wild."

Eugene said, "I've never been to California."

"And you're thinking of becoming Natureboy." Charity fit Eugene into a new costume.

It wasn't such a bad fit, Eugene thought. "Yeah," he said, "run around in the woods and become one with Nature. Imagine."

Charity saw Eugene's face had lifted. She saw his decision was made, although he didn't know it. She realized she was saying good-bye to her "cowboy," maybe for good. He always did have too much sense about him. She smiled and said, "Far out."

"No, really, Charity, maybe this is what I need to do. To get away from this scene. New York. All the who's-doing-what-with-who-and-for-how-much. I'm always stoned. I don't know what it's like to be straight anymore. I can always come back. Sometimes I feel scared to come down."

"And does this Katherine expect you to be her old man?"

Eugene blushed an "aw-shucks."

"Does she know about your tastes?"

"That's just it! I don't know my own tastes!" Eugene realized he was going. "I didn't lie to her, really. She's cool. And all this can be put behind me, see?"

"I see," Charity smiled, "We'll have to have a party for you."

Eugene wrote Katherine and asked for specific directions to the cabin. He explained that he was going to hitchhike across country and estimated he would get there sometime in May. In April, he boxed all of his albums and books and his winter clothes, and stacked them out of the way in the apartment. He gave Moody Sue and Charity Katherine's address.

He played a song he'd practiced at the going-away party Charity threw for him upstairs at Max's. He gave his guitar to Nelson. Everyone promised to miss him. Moody Sue, who had gotten into astrology, said she had done his chart, and he was in a "regression." A lot of people said they envied his going on the road. Charity was excessively flamboyant and giddy around him, and he felt that she had already pulled the shades between them. "I'm not good at writing," she said to him, "but I expect to hear from you, natureboy. Send me a shot from the Garden of Eden, honey."

He took the bus to Harrisburg, Pennsylvania, and then extended his thumb at an entrance to the Pennsylvania Turnpike. He stayed on River Road for two days.

1953, Ohio

Eugene was born in Covington, Kentucky, but late in 1953, when he was three, he and his family moved across the Ohio River, to Cincinnati. His father, Melvin, had a job at a foundry there, and the Goesslers rented a house, high on a hill, seventy steps up from River Road, west of the city.

"No wonder the place has been empty for two years," Clara panted, carrying four-month-old baby Frankie in her arms. "I knew I should never have trusted your judgment, Melvin. Only you could get hoodwinked into renting a shanty way up here! My lord, I'll be a prisoner. I'll never get out. Only you, Melvin, could find such torture for us. Someday you'll get what's coming to you, you old hillbilly!"

Melvin looked up to the woman carrying on and said under his breath, "You're the one who wanted a house, I was fine and dandy right there in Covington, right on the bus line." He was a tall forty-one-year-old man, with a light complexion that was worn and sweating and bristly from not shaving for two days. He was strong from physical labor, but his gut protruded and he would pat it proudly and say it was his keg of beer. He had a vain streak in him, going back to his days when he played amateur triple-A league baseball and got a lot of attention. He combed his light hair back and greased, which made it seem darker and shinier, and he thought he still looked like Gary Cooper, as Clara had said when they got married back in 1940 before he went off to the war.

Melvin and Barney, a friend with a pickup truck from the foundry, rested at the fortieth step, taking a breather with the heavy horsehair mattress.

51

"Maybe she's right," Barney said, wiping his brow with a handkerchief. "This ain't the easiest house to get to. What was it, Goessler? An old lookout for the Indians? Maybe for that there Underground Railroad when they was freeing the colored?"

It was a warm November afternoon, and both men stripped off their sweaty shirts, hanging them on the bushes near the steps, revealing their pale white skin below their necks and above their elbows.

"Ahhhh," Melvin drawled, "that woman is never satisfied. She could have a big gussied-up mansion and she'd find something wrong. I do the best I can, what else can I do?" He looked around toward the train tracks that ran parallel with the river and the road. "Here comes something!" He stopped to listen, holding up his arm. Then his tall frame and muscular arms folded as he took in a long deep breath and looked out, satisfied at the fine view they would have. He had forgotten about the train. It was a happy surprise for him. A whistle sounded. Then there was a metal rattle way down road, then a rumble and chug.

Then the wail of Clara, overseeing from the rickety porch. "Oh, my lord in heaven, Melvin Goessler! Is that a train? Is that racket a train? Right down there? Melvin! Your soul is a mean one! Lord, what did I do to deserve this?"

"What?!" Melvin turned, squinting up to her. "Can't make out what you're saying, woman!"

The train passed. The sound syncopated off the hill. Seven-year-old June and three-year-old Eugene stood down at the bottom of the steps watching it pass before them. Eugene had never seen a train before. He held June's hand tight. It was so loud and fast and dark, blocking the sight of the river they had just been seeing. June called him a fraidy-cat. The train ended. There was a red caboose at the end, and a trainman waved at the children, who waved back, and Eugene was no longer afraid. He liked the word "caboose," as he heard June exclaim over and over how the man had waved to them, and it had been red, and it was a caboose.

Barney picked up an end to the mattress and heaved-hoed, as did Melvin. Clara stood tight-fisted and red with anger, shaking her tight curled head, moving her tight lipsticked lips that she had made up in case there were neighbors to meet. There were no neighbors. "He's enjoying my misery," she muttered. "I knew this was too good to be true. Him saying how we would have a home of our own and a place for the kids. No more apartment and noise from the trash in the apartment above and no more worrying about having people over. I can't ask anyone here to this shack." She hated Melvin's grin as the two men passed her into the house. "Put it in the bigger bedroom, Melvin!" The baby, Frankie, gurgled at her volume, and Clara swayed back and forth, noticing the give in the floorboards beneath her feet. "Good Lord," she said to the baby, "I married Satan."

Slowly, June and Eugene climbed the steps, one at a time. Eugene had heard the yelling about the number of steps, "*seventy!*" and he counted, one to ten, then eleven, and then he called out all kinds of numbers, knowing that he should save "seventy" for the top step.

"You kids watch out now," Melvin said, tugging June's blonde ponytail as the two men passed them going down to the pickup.

June held Eugene's hand. He saw a ladybug.

"Bug!" he exclaimed.

"Oooo, don't touch it, Eugene, it's a good-luck bug," June warned, tugging the little boy.

Melvin yelled for the kids to move aside as he and Barney lugged the big Emerson television by. Eugene saw Barney's foot step on the ladybug. It went from an orange and black dot to nothing. Barney farted. June giggled at the wheezing sound of it.

Melvin said, "Christ, don't let Clara hear you passing gas. She's about having a fit already."

"I can't help it," Barney explained, in panting grunts. "She's the one who made us wieners and beans for lunch," and then he felt his grasp slipping from the side of the television, "Whoa! Melvin! Whoa!"

The two men caught the Emerson's front legs on the edge of an irregular slate step near the top. Steps fifty-seven to seventy were slate slabs, twenty to fifty-six were cinderblocks set into gravel on the hill, and one to nineteen were made of wood, built on a cedar stringer that crossed a sewage creek, down at the road, leaning up onto the hill. The mahogany-veneered leg snapped, but they saved the television from dropping, possibly losing it and the two children still climbing below them.

From the porch, Clara screamed, "There you go! It's ruined! The one decent thing we own!"

Melvin was grateful that they had only lost a leg. Barney tried to make it clear that nothing was his fault, he was only there to lend a hand. June stood still on the step below, letting go of Eugene's hand. The sun was veiled briefly by a cloud. Eugene continued climbing without his sister's help.

"I'll glue it back good as new," Melvin said, touching the jagged stump of the television leg.

"Sure you will," Clara moaned. "Tell me another one, Lucifer."

Melvin took the broken leg and thin slice of veneer and set the pieces gingerly out of the way under the porch. He would show her, he decided, he would fix it. Hell, he was still making time payments on it.

He decided to yell, under such pressure, "You kids stay off the steps now! We pertinear knocked you over! Now get up here! Come on!"

Barney lifted Eugene onto the porch and motioned for June to hurry on up.

"Come here, Eugene," Clara said, calmer, taking his hand, and holding Frankie in her arm cradled against her chest. "Come on, June, you should know better than to dilly down there while your daddy's moving. Come on inside and see our new house."

As June passed her father, he gave her ponytail another tug, and she ran a little faster up the porch steps, afraid of being teased and teased, as so often happened, till she became hysterical laughing, and Clara would slap her and berate her father.

Clara held the screen door open. "I'll make some purple Kool-Aid, June, and we can pray your father doesn't keel over till he gets everything up here."

1958, Ohio

Red-blond burr-head Eugene played trucks with his friend, white-blond burr-head Bobby Schneider, in what they called the woods, a cluster of trees between the river and the railroad tracks that paralleled River Road. They made roads in the dirt and loaded the trucks with stones and smaller cars and built their own busy city. Bobby lived down the road in a house of two stories. He was Lutheran and lived with his mother. Bobby's parents were divorced. His father lived in an even bigger, newer house, out near the Delhi Country Club. Eugene considered Bobby rich. He had his own room, a new bicycle, a train set, a piano, and a dining room that was never used.

"It don't matter one darn wooden nickel," Melvin explained to Eugene one day after the boy came home crying about being poor, "if them Schneiders got every toy and gadget, boy, because the Lord says 'blessed are the poor cause they got a big house waiting for them in heaven!' "

"So do they go to hell?" Eugene asked his father.

Melvin held the boy's shoulder and said, "Shoot, they ain't Catholics so I imagine so. That's one thing you got that they don't, Eugene."

Eugene asked his third-grade teacher, Sister Adele. She said, "Only Catholics are the true Christians. Martin Luther was possessed by the devil." She told him that all Protestants had to be prayed for and even if they led good lives, they would not get to heaven, but they would be let into Limbo, which was like the front porch of heaven. Eugene asked her if someone in Heaven would be allowed out onto the porch to play with someone in Limbo, and she said she thought not.

In religion class, Eugene learned that any Catholic could baptize a pagan, and then they would be allowed in Heaven. Eugene decided he had to save Bobby's soul.

"Hey, Bobby!" Eugene called from the cold river, standing knee-deep in his underwear, "I dare you to come in and go under!"

Bobby laughed from the riverbank, "I thought you wanted to play trucks over in the woods!"

Eugene moved out deeper, trying to not act cold. "Chicken?"

Bobby laughed at that. He was older and stronger and taller and there was nothing Eugene could do that he couldn't do, and better. If he owned the game, he always won it, somehow, and he considered Eugene his. His slave. His little brother. His audience. "I ain't chicken! I just don't want to!"

Eugene's teeth were chattering, and he saw Bobby picking up his clothes on the bank. He knew better than to yell for him to stop, because then the boy would surely throw them in the river. Eugene went under and thought, "The devil is in him."

"Hey, Yew-Geeeeeen!" Bobby sang, holding the boy's shorts out over the water with his arm extended.

Eugene ignored him and yahooed over the "fun" he was having, diving under and keeping his back to the older boy.

The word "chicken" burned in Bobby and he yelled, "I'll come in if you give me your red truck!"

Eugene stopped playing and looked at Bobby. "But that's my only good one!" Under his breath he cursed Satan for being a wheeler-dealer.

Bobby explained the details. "You can still play with it and take it home with you, but it's mine whenever I want it. Deal?"

Eugene thought about it, but not for long. He was freezing, and according to June, the bomb could drop any minute, and then the truck wouldn't matter at all, but Bobby's soul would. "Okay," he said.

Bobby started to undress, saying his mom would kill him if she found out he went in the river. Eugene came closer to the bank, running "Hail Mary" through his head, nodding a bow, as he'd learned in school, at the word "Jesus." Bobby tiptoed into the mud and squealed at the cold. Eugene chided him, saying it wasn't so cold.

The two boys swam around, yelping and trying to push each

other under. Then Eugene dared Bobby to splash him. Bobby did, and with big gushing handfuls of water, the color of milky coffee from the kicked-up mud. Then Eugene retaliated, splashing him back, dousing the boy with the river and saying as fast as he could, "I baptize thee in the name of the Father, and of the Son, and of the Holy Ghost, Amen!"

"What?" Bobby laughed, hearing only the "Amen."

"Nothing!" Eugene laughed with relief, "I was saying a prayer I learned in school, that's all!"

Bobby splashed him heavy, and Eugene ran out. Bobby chased him, and they both fell onto the warm grass, giggling and shivering. Eugene watched Bobby closely to see if he seemed any different. Bobby said, "What are you looking at me like that for?"

"I'm not," Eugene said, although he couldn't pull in the satisfied grin that seemed to say he knew something that Bobby didn't.

They took off their wet underwear and put on their dry clothes and hung the wet briefs on a tree branch to dry. Then they went to the woods to play with their trucks.

As they pushed the trucks along one of their roads, Eugene asked Bobby how he was feeling.

"What d'ya mean?"

"I don't know," Eugene said, thinking that a few times he'd seen a sort of halo around Bobby, but it might have just been the light hitting him through the openings in the overhead trees. "I mean, do you feel like maybe going to Mass with me and my family tomorrow morning?"

"Huh? Don't be dippy. Why would I do that? We're Lutherans."

"Maybe," Eugene smiled, "and maybe not."

"No maybe about it, you dope. You sure are getting stupid today."

Eugene was experiencing the euphoria of religion. What drove men and women into jungles and into hardships beyond imagination as missionaries was what he was feeling in a small way, the self-satisfied knowledge that he was right, he had the answer, and although he had to forfeit his truck, he would be given credit for saving a soul from the devil. He couldn't but giggle and hum about it as he pushed the "borrowed" red truck up what they called "Turd Hill."

Bobby was getting mad. Eugene was acting so big, like he had a secret. "I want the truck now," he said, snatching it from Eugene as he was rolling it down the other side of Turd Hill.

"Why?" Eugene whined. "You got all yours!"

"This is mine too, remember?" Bobby snickered. "A deal's a deal."

"You act like such a baby," Eugene said. "You're spoiled."

"Yeah?" Bobby said, sauntering back to his trucks with the red one. "Well, you're just jealous."

The smile had finally left Eugene's face. That truck was a high price to pay, he thought. All he had left were old beat-up ones that he even let Frankie play with. He tried to offer it up and be happy anyway. It was spring, and school would be out for the summer soon, and at least he had wheels on all but one of his trucks, and he was Catholic, and . . . and . . . and he saw his red truck being pushed full force into the tree trunk by Bobby and he yelled, "Hey stop it, you brat! You'll break it! That's not fair!"

Bobby laughed, butting the truck's front again and again into the tree. "It's mine and I can do what I want with it."

Eugene threw one of his little metal cars at the boy, yelling, "You baby!"

Bobby threw it back, hitting Eugene in the head, just missing his eye, but cutting his eyebrow.

Eugene cried out, holding his head, and ran over toward the boy and began kicking at him till Bobby threw him to the ground. They punched out at each other and rolled around, but soon Bobby overpowered Eugene and straddled him, sitting on his chest. Eugene's face was covered with blood and he had to keep his one eye shut.

"Let me up!" he cried.

Bobby slapped him. "First say who's the baby."

Eugene saw the devil in him. Sister Adele said that the devil was almost as strong as God. Bobby had Eugene pinned. He tried kicking with his legs, but they couldn't reach Bobby's back. Eugene's blood trickled down the side of his head. He saw Christ nailed to the cross. He muttered, tight-lipped, "You are."

"You are!" Bobby screamed. "You are! You are!"

"You are!" Eugene said again, getting slapped. He had the devil straddling him, he realized. He prayed to Jesus to overthrow the boy. He cried, "Get off me, Bobby, or I won't be your friend anymore!"

"Not till you say that I'm not a baby and that you are and you tell me what the secret is."

"No!" Eugene swore. He could never tell. That would ruin it. Sister Adele had said that only the ignorant could be baptized that way. The savages, the pagans, and the heathens.

"You say it, or I'll hit you again and throw your truck against the tree so hard it'll break in a million pieces!" Bobby spat, having verified that a secret did exist. "Just say you're a baby and what the secret is, and I'll let you go."

Eugene tried to reason with Bobby. "I can't tell. It would ruin it, but it means that we can always be friends, even if the bomb drops!"

"Friends don't keep secrets," Bobby said. "You're a big liar!" And he slapped Eugene again.

Eugene tried with all his might to squirm at least one arm free from Bobby's thigh vise. He tried to hold back his tears, but they poured from his eyes. Their run down his face weakened him more and the blood ran into his mouth and he blew out a geyser of babyish boo-hoo-hoos.

Bobby ridiculed him. "Look at such a big baby!"

Eugene descended into the vast sea of hurts. He felt the poverty in his soul. The senselessness and illogical messages he'd been taught. He wanted to help Bobby, just as Christ would. He wanted to be rich so that his mother would be happy and they would have a happy family like the ones on television. He wanted, most of all, to go to heaven when the bomb dropped. June had really scared him. His fear of God was second to his fear of the bomb. He felt so weak. Just like Clara had said after he'd been pushed down by June and had come running in the house crying. "She's just a girl! Stop crying, you weakling, or I'll give you something to cry about!" Then Clara had chased him till she caught him and spanked him till he stopped crying. She left him on the floor and he left his body and fell asleep in the soft arms of Jesus. He cried for everything he didn't know. Why was the world going to blow up? Why did Jesus die? What was everything? He was scared of the devil holding him down, trying to force him into sin.

"Say it, big baby!" Bobby yelled over Eugene's sobs. "I'm not even hitting you. Just say the secret and I'll give you the truck."

"You're not a baby," Eugene sniffed.

"And what's the secret?"

"Nothing. There is no secret."

Bobby was exasperated. He had to extract something from the bloody boy, so he forced Eugene to say, "I am a big baby and Bobby Schneider is a hundred times better than me and will always be," and with that, Bobby rolled off Eugene and both boys lay panting heavily on their backs in the dirt.

Eugene wiped his face with his shirt. He thought he should hate Bobby, but he didn't. He felt satisfied that the baptism was safe and although he had lost the fight, Jesus had won a soul. He walked to the river to wash his face and get his underwear. He threw Bobby's in the river and watched it float away. When he returned to the woods Bobby was playing as if nothing had happened and whined, "It's not bleeding that bad, Eugene, why do you have to go home?" He said that if Eugene stayed and played longer, he could have the truck back. Eugene then thought that God was starting to take over in Bobby, and Eugene saw for a second a dim halo around the boy's white-blond burr haircut. The bleeding didn't stop though, and Eugene soon went home, with his red truck, and Melvin drove him to the hospital, where he was stitched up.

2007, Brazil

Eugene celebrated his fifty-seventh birthday at Octavio's family's coffee plantation in Brazil. As always when the two men were together, it was timeless and perfect and on a plane of life that the physical world exhausted. They sat in chairs on the terrace overlooking the north pasture. Octavio was reading and translating aloud for Eugene, a review of Eugene's *Goessler/Goessler/Back/Forth*, which was printed in the *Liter Rio* magazine.

"Goessler queerly tells of aluminum Christmas trees that strain the imagination, and why for?" Octavio translated. His black hair and beard glistened a reddish light in the southern light. He had dark skin, tanned from years of sun, receptive skin from Greek and Portuguese parentage.

Eugene laughed.

"Oh why they take you to task so, my sweetie fidalgo, for so much aluminum!" Octavio laughed. "So word to word."

"I don't know," Eugene sighed. "Possibly they cannot make the connection. They're referring to the *Clara Poems*, correct?"

"Uhhhh," Octavio said, scanning the words, leaping between the Portuguese on the page and the English in his mouth, "da, da, dee, da dee, so he reaps from the forest of aluminum trees, da, da, uhh, here! He says, '*Clara Poems*.'"

Eugene sipped his cool drink and sighed again, shrugging a "some-get-it-some-don't-get-it-and-it-is-what-it-is" shrug. He heard Clara, his mother, shriek a twangy toucan birdcall. She made a far better bird than mother, he thought.

Octavio sat the review aside on the terrace rock and leaned into Eugene. "Hey sweetie, it is not a bother, yes? You do not care of praise still?"

The bird flew off and Eugene kissed Octavio's strong veined hand. "Me? No, I don't care about that review. I was thinking of Clara as a toucan. She deserves the life of a bird, I think. No, I don't care about reviews. At this time, after all the years, the metaphors for every day, I only find them fun. I like to hear how words trip up like pebbles in shoes, or like a net in the river. They come to my garden. They come to my garden, and think what they see is what I see, what I planted. They see a weed and raise their eyebrow skeptically, and I know. I know it is not a weed. It is a birdbath."

Octavio held his hand. Eugene pulled him close and whispered, "The *Clara Poems* are dedicated to all the victims of victims of victims of victims of victims . . . and the two men drifted off into a chant that sounded like— "Vic-tum-uff-vic-tum-uff . . ."

1961, Ohio

Clara had saved all the Christmas cards the family had received over the years, and kept them in a box on the top shelf of the closet in the girls' room in the house above River Road. Clara and her daughters shared the girls' room; Melvin and his sons shared the boys' room. In the eight years that the Goesslers had rented the house, very little had been done to improve its condition. Melvin painted the rooms once, but the leaking roof caused the walls to peel, and he claimed it was pointless to repaint till the landlord did something about the roof. Clara claimed he always found excuses. She said she was ashamed to have anyone come up for a visit.

"You can't ask people to climb all them steps, and what do they get up to? A shanty! A hillbilly shanty!"

The outside clapboards were peeling paint, and the porch was rotting, precariously perched on the steep bank that dropped down to the road. In the winter, from the living room window and the porch, there was a view across the river to the rolling hills of Kentucky. In the summer, the view was overgrown. The living room was large and covered with a linoleum rug patterned with floral bouquets. A hall connected it to the big kitchen at the rear of the house. In the hall, there were three doors, one to each of the bedrooms, and one to the bathroom.

When Clara got pregnant with Debbie, she begged Melvin to ask for a raise from the foundry so they could afford a bigger house. He said they were lucky he had a job at all. He insisted, "We'll make do. The Lord will always provide."

After Debbie was born, Clara could be heard yelling, "Now

you stop pawing at me, Melvin Goessler! You're drunk and stink like an ol' polecat! This is just how we ended up with Debbie, you dirty pig! You let go of me now, I'm in my change of life! Why don't you go to the boys' room and pray to your Lord for some money!"

And the kids could hear Melvin slobber, "Clara, you, you are my dreamboat."

Eugene heard her muttering to herself, alone on the couch, watching the *Tonight Show,* as Melvin farted in the bed opposite his and Frank's bunks. He heard her say, "Can't have a decent minute of peace around here, coming up to me all drunk and lovey-dovey, acting like I'm some kind of queen. Hmpf! Over the hill, buddy, over the hill. Does more sinning in one night than I've done in my life."

Because of his father's drinking, Eugene felt that Clara was the lesser of two evils. He would argue with his sister June about who was better. She would say, "Poor Daddy has to put up with that woman and all her complaining. She's never satisfied with nothing," and Eugene would counter, "Poor Mother is nuts because Daddy drinks the paycheck and gives what's left to the Church because he's so shamed," and June would say, "He gets drunk because she drives him out of the house with her yelling and he's got nowhere else to go but to Stogie's. She's said so herself, Eugene, that she could fly off the handle any minute." But he still favored his mother. He felt sorry for her, and she had made it clear to him that he was her favorite child. Clara confided in him. She told him that she thought Frankie was stupid and slow, just like his daddy. She said Debbie was a mistake, a change-of-life baby. She called June a tramp and a juvenile delinquent because she stayed out late and kept company with older boys with motorcycles. She said Eugene favored her side of the family, not Melvin's. She said he was smart and handsome and had class. She'd said the same thing to each child, leading each one to believe that they were her favorite.

Clara would pinch Eugene's cheeks when he was young and she was dressing him. She would tenderly fondle him and say in sweet light sounds, "Honey, your skin is so smooth, and your eyelashes are so long, and your eyes are like beautiful emeralds, they don't belong on a boy, they should be on a girl. It's too bad

June didn't get your eyes, and your little behind is so cute. You are just my perfect baby doll, honey."

In the dead heat of August 1961, when the bees and flies were circling the rooms, and the Ohio river was steaming like hot milked coffee, Clara decided to get the box of Christmas cards down from the closet because, "before you know it, it'll be time for all the ads, and then the next thing you know, it's Christmas."

She sat on the couch with the box. She held out a card. "Eugene? Eugene? Don't you think this one's awful pretty?" The card fluttered in the wind from the fan. She repeated his name till he turned from where he was lying on the floor and looked up and nodded. He was almost under the coffee table, watching *The Three Stooges* on the Emerson. Where the leg had been broken, and "of course never fixed, only promises from the saints," Clara had arranged garlands of artificial flowers around the base to hide where it was setting on blocks of wood.

"You sit too close," Clara said. "And watch your toes, Eugene, they're right near the fan. God help us, we need all our toes."

Eugene heard her somewhere in his head, but he'd learned to lose himself into the television. He was a skinny eleven-year-old, with a shaved burr haircut that he unconsciously ran his hand over as he watched.

Clara continued, "Why don't you turn that junk off and sit here with me and help me look through all these. Your father is no help. Look at him staring out into space on the porch." She was making piles of cards and speaking as much to herself as to her son. "And look at that, the selfish man sits right in front of the window so he can block any breeze that might come up here through the trees. Melvin!" she raised her voice somewhat, but no one heard her. She laughed to herself, "Guess it's my own fault for sending him out there, but Lord knows, it's too hot for all of us to be in the same room eating up what little air this fan blows our way. He could at least move out of the way. Melvin! Melvin! See that? He don't hear me. I think he's losin his hearing since he got that transistor radio plug. Melvin! See, Eugene, he don't hear, and there ain't no game today. Melvin!!"

Eugene was bothered by her increased volume and pitch that even he could no longer block. He crawled across the linoleum rug and swatted the window screen behind his father's head.

"What?" Melvin jumped, startled.

"Mother wants you for something," Eugene muttered, walking on his knees back to his spot, collapsing as if he'd made an enormous effort, between the television and the fan.

Melvin tried to see in through the screen, and called in, "Now what?"

Clara yelled, "Stop hogging all the air! That's what! Move out of the way! Always thinking of yourself!"

Melvin shook his head. He could see her sitting there with Christmas cards. In August! And now she wanted him to stop breathing.

"*Move!*" she screamed, booming so loud Eugene jumped. "Are you losing your hearing?! You're blocking the window!"

He scooted his chair and said, "Why didn't you say so?" to himself. What a crazy woman she'd turned out to be, he thought. She had once been attractive to him, and he had his pick. All the girls were crazy for Melvin Goessler, the baseball pitcher. He had his choice and now look, he thought, she was overweight and sloppy and her hair was falling out from all the dye and from always being pulled so tight in bobby-pinned curls all round her head. The only time he ever saw her hair combed down was when she was going out for Friday night bingo at the church or for Sunday Mass. He shook his head, remembering what a looker she'd been, a healthy farm girl from Ludlow, Kentucky. "Well," he sighed long and drawn, "what's done is done. I just offer it up, what else can a man do?" Then he closed his eyes tight, trying to remember what he'd been pondering over before Eugene had given him such a start. Something troubling. The foundry. He had heard that someone new had been hired to work full-time. He was still on split shifts and wondered why he'd been overlooked. Then a breeze made its way, rustling through the leaves up to the porch, and he leaned back and took in a deep breath. He thought of the heat in the foundry. "They must be sweating like pigs right about now," he said to himself, laughing a bit. "Maybe come winter, I'll see if they'll put me back on full-time."

Inside, Clara heard Melvin mumbling. She laughed to herself, "Listen to him out there, talking to himself as if he'd lost all his marbles." She felt so hot and sticky.

"Eugene!" she yelled, using the voice that always cut through television, "why don't you go play with Bobby or go find your

brother. Lord knows he's probably drowned himself in the river.
How anyone could swim in that dirty old thing is beyond me."
Eugene remained immobile, but said, "I will when this is over."

In December, Melvin carried a very thin scrawny pine tree
over his shoulders up the steps with Eugene following behind
him, trying to help. Each time the boy reached up to the stump
of trunk, it would bounce higher. Eugene was giddy with excitement, but frustrated that he wasn't tall enough to bear any of
the holiday burden.
"Get the door," Melvin said, letting the boy run up onto the
porch before him.
Clara opened it from inside, where she had been waiting.
Eugene yelled, "Let me! Let me!" and the tree was brought in.
Clara moaned, "That's it! What a stick! And look at that! All
over the floor! Needles! It's dry as a bone, Melvin!" She slammed
the door behind them. "It's so ugly I'll have to keep the drapes
closed so no one sees."
Melvin caught his breath and half-laughed, "Shoot, Clara, nobody can see way up here from the road. You're always saying
that. It'll fill out once you pretty it up."
"Guests will see it, you idiot! Look! It doesn't have any
branches!" She shook her tight pin-curled head in disgust. "I
ain't asking no one here, no siree, Melvin Goessler, you've ruined another Christmas before it's gotten going."
Eugene grabbed onto the trunk, as if to share the blame with
his father, or to shed some of his exuberance into the tree, and
he sang, "It'll be all right!"
But Clara was not listening, she was reeling. "Melvin, they
saw you coming a mile away, I swear, and they said, 'Now here
comes a sucker too pickled to know a pine from a thistle,' and if
you tell me you paid money for this I'll kill you!"
Melvin looked at Eugene and insinuated, with his hand circling like a dizzy bird at his ear, that the woman was crazy. He
drove the tree into its stand and said, "Boy, you hold it straight
while I screw it tight."
Eugene pleaded, "Really, it'll be all right. It smells good,"
bending a branch toward his mother. "Mmmmmm, smell it?"
Clara recoiled as if it were poison, and folded her arms tight.

"Leave me out of this. All along I said I wanted one of them aluminum ones. You knew I had my heart set on one, Melvin, so you thought, 'I'll show her, I'll get her good this time,' didn't you now? And you, Eugene," she looked away from his desperate attempt at lifting the spirit, "you should be ashamed of yourself. I thought you had more sense. Didn't I tell you to watch your father? I thought you were the smartest of the whole bunch, and look at what you bring your poor mother! How dumb can you get?"

Eugene whined, "It's not that bad."

Melvin said, standing up, "There now, she's ready."

Clara sighed her defeated "why me?" sigh and sank to the couch, refusing to look at Melvin, too. "Don't look at me to help. My Christmas is ruined."

"Now, Clara . . ." Melvin said.

"Don't you, 'now, Clara,' me," she muttered bitterly.

Melvin and Eugene opened the decoration box that they had brought in from the girls' room closet before their expedition to get a tree. They untangled the lights. Debbie was taking a nap. Frankie was being punished for acting up earlier, trying to open the decoration box, so Clara sent him to the boys' room, not letting him go with his father and brother. He listened at the door, rolling his truck back and forth, biding his time till it felt safe to join the fun. June was down on River Road straddling her boyfriend's motorcycle. When Melvin and Eugene had passed her with the tree, she took one look at it and said, "Uh-oh, Daddy, Mother's gonna have a fit."

Melvin and Eugene spread the lights across the linoleum rug. Clara heaved a forlorn breath. They both looked over at her. She shook her head again and cried, "If it wasn't going to be my dream aluminum one, you could have gotten one with more than three branches."

"There you go exaggerating again," Melvin said. "You'll like it, girl. You always do. Just offer it up."

"I offer everything up, Melvin Goessler! Don't you tell me what to offer up! Why, I have a mind to throw you and your dumb boy down every one of them 'offer it up' steps out there. Now you get it lit before the baby wakes up. Little Debbie should be surprised while she's young. Lord knows the sweet times don't last. And you remember this, Eugene. Nothing ever works out nice like they say it should. It's all penance."

Melvin asked her which side she thought should face the room. She laughed at him, "It only has one side . . . bad." She thumbed through the *TV Guide*, ignoring them as they clipped on the lights. Eugene caught her looking up from the magazine and saw that she was stifling the urge to advise them where to set the lights. She said to the boy, "The most decrepit tree in Hamilton County. Even the colored have better."

Eugene asked, "Do they look right?"

Clara prided herself on her decorating touch, and it was all she could do to ignore him.

From behind the tree, where Melvin was attaching the last strand of lights, he muttered, "She wants to sulk, boy, so let her stew in her own juices."

Clara threw the *TV Guide* at the tree. "I am not sulking! I'm mad! You don't know what it's like, you good-for-nothing drunk! Frankie is so ornery. He carried on all the while you were gone about how Eugene always gets the best. You know, Eugene, I have a mind to punish you too for this sorry sight."

Frankie listened closely behind the door at the mention of his name. It didn't sound like all was forgotten in the fun yet.

"And that Debbie was screaming bloody murder not wanting to take her nap. She acts like a baby and she's three! She wants water. She wants a blanket. She has to go potty. Always something. And June! That girl has her head screwed on backward, I swear. Always singing and dancing and primping till someone honks for her, then she flies out of here without her coat as if she's going to the ball and all she's doing is showing off down there with them hoods who got only one thing on their mind!"

"Plug in the plug, boy," Melvin said.

"And then you bring this twig up here to torment me. With all the money you spend at Stogie's I could have gotten one of them clean modern aluminum ones they've been showing."

Eugene counted, edging the plug to the outlet, "One . . . Two . . . Three! Dah-dah!" He looked at his mother and saw a slight delight crack her grimace.

Melvin stood back and admired it. "It's shaping up. Now come on, Clara, it'll die soon enough."

"From the looks of it, I'd say it's been long dead, no doubt left over from last year," she hmpfed.

Eugene unwrapped ornaments. He found his mother's favorite, the one shaped like a fat elf. He held it out to her across the coffee table, "Here, Mother, you put this one on the tree, and look, there's still some needles in the tissue paper from last year's tree."

"Last year's was a beauty compared to this thing," she said, taking the elf by its hook. "Each year they get worse and worse." She examined the elf closely. It had been her ornament from childhood. Then it had seemed magical. Now, it seemed dumb. "And see this? The paint is all cracked and chipping away," she said, bitterly. "I don't know why I ever saved it. The same ornaments year after year. On the aluminum ones I saw at Sears and Roebucks, they have just one color ball. All red, or all gold . . . real classy," she dangled the elf from her finger, "it's such a shame the way your father makes us live. I just don't know anymore."

Frank yelled from the boys' room, "Am I allowed to come out for just one minute to see?"

"No!" Clara yelled back. "You are being punished!"

"Ahhhhhhhhhhhhhh!" Frank whined.

Eugene ran to the boys' room, pushing the door right into Frankie.

"Ow!" he cried to Eugene.

"Shut up, you big baby," Eugene said, whispering. "She's getting better, but she still might fly off the handle."

"Well, I want to come out and help too!" Frankie whined.

Eugene took a wrapped package from under the bunk beds and said, "Offer it up!" as he slammed the door and ran back to the living room.

"Here, Mother, this is a present for you for the tree."

Clara set the elf on the table and took the gift, almost smiling, saying, "Eugene where'd you get money?" as she untied the ribbon and undid the paper. She read the box out loud, "Angel Hair. Angel Hair? What is Angel Hair, Eugene?"

Melvin asked, "Angel's hair?"

Eugene enthusiastically grabbed the box from Clara to show his father, "Look. It shows here on the picture how it makes it look like heaven and clouds all over the tree. I got it at Bess's."

"I don't know," she said to Eugene, "is it fresh? Everything Bess sells is stale, from the day one."

Eugene laughed, "Fresh? It's fake stuff, Mother. It says, 'Fiberglass strands.' It's not real hair from an angel." He opened the box. "Maybe it'll hide the bare spots." He pulled the clump of shiny white fibers out and raved, "It's like cotton candy!" He placed it on a branch near a red light and raved, "It makes it pink!" He pulled another clump and stretched it where branches should have been.

"Slow down, boy," Clara said, "we ought to hang all the ornaments first."

She had said "we." His gift had saved the day, he thought. She stood up. She tied her Christmas apron around her waist and hooked her elf to one of the top branches. Eugene pulled out more and more angel hair. He laughed. There was no end to it. His voice got higher as he squealed, "It's like spaghetti!"

"Stop, Eugene, I said wait," Clara scolded him

"You heard your mother, boy," Melvin said, stepping out of Clara's way, "you let her have her way, now." He headed for the kitchen for a beer. He would let them do the rest.

"It's like snow!" Eugene sang out.

"Can I see?" Frankie cried from the boys' room.

"No!" Clara shouted at both boys.

Eugene said, "Just a little more, up here." With a handful he reached up and bumped Clara's elf, knocking it from its hook. It shattered on the floor.

"Eugene!" Clara screamed. "Look what you did!" She grabbed him by the neck and slapped his face. "It's broken! All those years and you broke it! You are the devil if ever there was one! Go to your room before I kill you!"

His face stung from her slapping. He pulled away from her, crying, his voice cracking, "I didn't mean it! It was an accident! You even said just before how it was old and cracked!"

Clara furiously swung her arms at him, "I said get out of here you devil! I'll get the goddamned belt! Get! Melvin! Where the hell is your father?"

Eugene threw the box of angel hair that he was still holding at his mother and ran to the boys' room screaming how much he hated her.

Clara, having broken his spirit for his breaking her elf, started laughing. "Go ahead and cry, big baby! Curse me all you want!

But as long as you're in my house, buddy, you play by my rules! Melvin!"

Melvin came down the hall apprehensively, holding a beer.

"There you are!" Clara asked. "Don't act like you weren't hiding while I do all the yelling. I want you to beat those boys."

He said, "It's shaping up real pretty."

"Oh shut up. Look at the floor. Eugene broke my elf. You missed it, of course."

Melvin turned to go back to the kitchen.

"No you don't, buddy. You stay here and help me."

She kicked the box of ornaments in his direction. He set his beer on the table and stubbed out his Lucky Strike. They could hear Eugene crying from the boys' room and a roar from a motorcycle down on the road.

"I want this done before Debbie wakes up," she said. "Here," handing him a red ball printed with bells of white shine, "put this near the top."

Melvin gingerly hung the ball, making sure not to step on the broken elf, "There, that high enough?"

Clara nodded and handed him another, "That Eugene thinks he's so cute, and he's got a mean streak in him. Take that there angel hair out."

Melvin tossed a clump to the floor, then hung another ornament where she directed, then discarded another clump, and then complained, "This stuff is itchy."

"It's from Bess's," Clara laughed sarcastically, "what do you expect?"

She studied the tree, deciding where the next ornament would go. She had read in the paper that the right way was to have the large ones at the bottom and the small ones at the top. She unwrapped each one, and Melvin hung each one.

Finally, Melvin could not contain himself and said, "I am itching like crazy. Look at my arm, it's breaking out in a rash from that there angel hair."

Clara, exasperated by another whine, said, "It's your own doing, Melvin Goessler. I told you all along I wanted an aluminum tree."

In his top bunk, Eugene cried into his pillow. He cursed his mother and his father and reached for his tablet to mark down how many curses he'd made so he could confess them. He tearfully scratched out the rhyme he had written for the Christmas card he was going to make his parents. He decided he would make one for his father, but not his mother. Then he heard Melvin yelling in the bathroom, washing his arms, "I'll wring that Eugene's neck for bringing me this itch!"

From the floor of the boys' room where Frankie was playing with his trucks, he sang up to his brother, "Boy, you are really gonna get it, Eugene."

"Shut up," Eugene said. "You're a shit," and then he made another mark to confess. He had stopped crying. Anger did that for him. He decided to make each parent a card, but he devised hidden messages.

The verse for his mother read:

Christmas
Love
And
Riches
Are
In
Store.
Merry Christmas
Ever more
And Happy
New Year 1962!

The verse for his father read:

Merry Christmas
Eve And Day.
Love Is
Very Very Nice They Say.
It
Never
Is
Said
All
Summer Long. But In Winter We Sing
Happy New Year
It Is
Time For Song!

He felt very clever. He forget for a while that he had been sent to his room. He decided that the two verses were only venial sins, not mortal, because neither Melvin or Clara would figure out what he had really said.

1963, Ohio

June Goessler married Mack Hoffman in the rectory of St. Joe's on a Saturday evening in late October. Melvin and Clara were the witnesses. Mack's family disowned him, and would have nothing to do with the wedding. He didn't need their consent, though, because he was nineteen. June was seventeen. The doctor told June that the baby was due in early April.

"At least the boy's Catholic," Melvin said to Clara as they drove to the ceremony.

"Some Catholic," Clara grumbled, tired and wanting everything to be over. "See what kind of Catholics his folks are, they threw the hood out."

"But he's doing right by June," Melvin said, "and they sure act happy about all this."

Clara held her hand wide open over her face as they sat at the traffic light, in case someone might see her dressed up and figure out where she was going. "Of course you Catholics can be happy-go-lucky. Just sin, sin, sin and then la-dee-da to confession and sin some more. It's a crime."

"You're one too."

"Only by marriage, Melvin, so don't throw that in my face."

June wore an orange dress and an orange pillbox hat, "like the kind Jackie wears." Mack wore a green sharkskin fabric suit and the polished Cuban-heeled shoes that June loved. His dark hair reeked of hair cream, and Clara kept a perfumed hankie to her nose during the brief ceremony, to avoid his "stink."

Eugene, Frankie, and Debbie waited at the house on River Road for the wedding party to return from the rectory for a

75

wedding dinner. They wanted to go, but Clara insisted, "This ain't a real wedding. It's an emergency room operation."

"I think Mack is really tough," Eugene argued with Frankie.

"Uh unh," Frankie said, "Mother says he's poor white trash and only wants to sin on June."

"She didn't say that to you," Eugene scoffed.

"But I heard her yelling that to June."

Eugene bragged, "His convertible is cherry," because he had gotten a ride in it with the top down even though it was cold. "And I bet he'll take you for a ride, and they're going to live right over Bess's, and that is really neat."

"But he got disowned," Frankie said.

"So what?" Eugene laughed. "He's not a kid like you. And the way he combs his hair like rock 'n' roll is tougher than nails. He'll be my brother-in-law."

"Mine too," Frankie said, but remembered another thing he overhead. "Mother said June might die from having a baby."

"She did not."

"She did too, and she said they might have to get out of it."

Eugene hit him on the shoulder. "You dope! Once you get married you have to stay married, if you're Catholic. It's not like Bobby Schneider."

"No, stupid," Frankie said. "They would have to get out of having a baby."

"Why would they go and do that? June even said she didn't care about quitting school, and the doctor said she was good."

"But the baby'll be a retard cause of their sins."

"I bet Mother *did* say that," Eugene laughed.

"Uh unh, fink," Frankie stuck out his tongue. "Daddy said."

The house smelled of pork roast. Clara had put it in the oven before they left for St. Joe's. Eugene was told to check on it to be sure it didn't burn. He and Frankie were also told to set the table. The two boys sat in the kitchen, drawing cards and coloring them to give to June and Mack. Debbie came in wearing a dress and asked them if she looked pretty.

"You look like a sweet, sweet girl," Eugene said, and then winked at Frankie, and said under his breath, "not at all like the whining brat that you are."

Frankie laughed. Debbie twirled about the kitchen watching her dress move. Eugene warned her to stay away from the cake that was on the sinksplash decorated with two bells. Clara had made the icing orange to match June's dress. The bells were blue. Earlier that day, in the kitchen, Eugene and June were sitting at the table while Clara iced the cake and she'd turned to them and said, "If this cake didn't turn out good, it's not my fault, my heart just ain't in it. I'm so ashamed of these goings on."

"Oh, Mother," June sighed, having heard the same pitiful line for a month. "I'm happy. I love Mack. You should be happy. It's what God wanted."

"Some God," Clara hmpfed at the sink, "my daughter the tramp sitting there telling me about God, now ain't that something. June, sometimes you're a riot."

June ignored her and asked Eugene if he liked her nail polish.

"That's right." Clara mixed powdered sugar and blue dye for the bells. "Act like I don't exist. I'm just a slave around here. I have a mind to slap you one last time, girl, and knock every roller off that smart-alec head of yours!"

"Mother!" June snapped, surprising Eugene with the loudness of her voice. "I've had so much shit from you, now just stop it!"

Eugene cringed.

June continued, standing up, waving her fingernails to dry. "And don't you ever listen? I am happy!"

Clara held the wooden spoon out like a sword, dripping blue sugar on the linoleum, "Don't you cuss in my house!"

June screamed, "Like mother, like daughter!"

"Why you little tramp! I was married to your father for six years before I had you!"

Eugene was amazed at how brave June was. She was not backing down, she didn't even seem threatened that Clara might fly off the handle. He caught his mother's eye and looked quickly back to his drawing pad.

"And in front of your brother!" Clara screamed. "How dare you talk to me like this while I'm slaving over your wedding cake!"

Eugene slid lower in his chair.

June yelled, "Oh, leave him out of this!"

Clara swung the spoon toward June.

"Don't you dare!" June screamed. "My nails are still wet!"

Clara stared eye to eye with her daughter, and then lowered

the spoon and turned her back to them and said, "God forgive you, June, that's some way to be acting on your wedding day."

June blew on her fingertips, and smiled to Eugene, "Wedding night."

"Whatever you say, miss big shot," Clara stirred. "I'm going to tell your father that you cussed in my house."

"Go ahead," June said, self-satisfied and sitting back down at the table across from Eugene. "I'm sure he'd like to spank me one last time." Now she was showing off for her brother.

Clara was silent. Eugene wrote, "You sure told her!" and showed the note to June. June silently pointed at him and then flexed her arms out like a strongman, implying that he could stand up to her too.

"Damn!" Clara bellowed. "Now look! I made the clanger too long! Bells don't look like that! I swear I'll be glad when this day is over and you're out of this house and shacked up with that hood."

"So will I," June sang.

Eugene tried to explain to Frankie what he had seen happen that afternoon right there in the kitchen where they were coloring.

"June said 'shit on you' right to Mother's face, and she didn't hit her or anything."

"I bet," Frankie scoffed.

"Really, it was so tough the way she was and I think it's cause she's getting married and Mother can't tell her what to do anymore and so I think that we should remember that. Don't use black, Frankie, it looks too sad. Use the bright red, but not my red."

"Here they come!" Debbie screeched from the living room. "Here they come!"

"Shit," Eugene said, gathering his pens and crayons and paper from the table. Clara had warned him that she expected the table cleaned and set when they returned from the rectory. Frankie gathered his stuff into his shoebox, and then ran their things into the boys' room. "Help me set the table, quick," Eugene told his brother.

The tablecloth had been set out on a chair. The two boys were spreading it out when they heard the front door open and Melvin said to Debbie, "Now don't you look all prettied up! Look at little Debbie, Clara, how pretty she is!" From the kitchen, it sounded like Melvin was in good spirits. Eugene and Frankie came down the hall to the living room. Clara was wearing her expensive dress that was covered in flowers and a bucket-shaped hat mostly pink. Melvin was in his suit. Eugene asked where June and Mack were.

"They went to the drugstore to buy flashbulbs and film," Clara said to Eugene. "Did you check the roast and set the table?"

Eugene nodded. "Well, how was it? Was it a good wedding?"

Melvin stopped swinging Debbie's hand and looked over to Eugene. "Boy, those two said 'I do' faster than jackrabbits in spring."

Frankie's clip-on bow tie was crooked, and Melvin pulled him over to straighten it to his collar, "You boys look real clean for a change. And something smells good enough to eat!" Melvin was whistling, almost exuberant. That irritated Clara.

"Your father acts like there's nothing to be ashamed of," Clara said to Eugene for some sympathy. "He even called that hood his son over at St. Joe's."

"Now Clara," Melvin said, "for once you are gonna shut your mouth and let us have a peaceful doings. June tells me she's pretty happy, now, and ain't that what counts? You promised in the car to let it rest."

She walked down the hall to the kitchen. Frankie and Eugene followed her, explaining how they still had to put the plates and forks and knives out, but weren't sure exactly where she wanted them, on such a special occasion.

"Where do you think?" Clara scolded them. "You two would put the plates on the chairs I guess?"

Eugene thought that was funny. Then Frankie smiled, and then even Clara smiled, and found herself saying, "And you'd put the forks upside down under the tablecloth," and they laughed out loud at their mother's joke, "and you'd put the spoons all in front of your father's place since he's such a slurper," and Eugene and Frankie were giggling so hard that they were hitting each other, "and you'd put the knives by June so she could cut her hood's food, and you'd put the saucer by his plate cause I'm sure he's never used one, he'd probably think it was a baby's plate!"

"And what about the cups?" Frankie cried.

"And the salt and pepper shakers? Where would we put those?" Eugene wiped his eyes with his sleeve.

"Oh, I don't know," Clara sighed, removing her hat tenderly. "Maybe we won't use cups tonight, we'll slurp out of the saucers and make June's greaser think we're all pigs!"

Debbie came running in, "What's the funny thing? What's the funny thing?" And that made the three of them laugh even louder, Clara catching her breath and saying, "Lord aren't we giddy, I don't know why. I don't know why we're laughing, Debbie, I don't know. Now, listen, little girl, you take my hat, and be careful, real careful, and you go sit it in its box on my bed in our room."

Melvin came into the kitchen smiling, "Well what's so god-awful funny in here?"

"Mother was being so funny," Eugene said, still giggling with Frankie.

Clara smiled at Melvin, and then her face dropped, "You hillbilly! Put your suitcoat back on, and put your shoes on, Lord! Melvin, I swear, you are worse than the kids sometimes!"

He turned and retreated to the living room, and she continued to yell, "First you tell me to have a good time and to have peace, and then you turn around and do something just to get my goat. I swear you are mean to the core sometimes!" But even her yells had lost their threats, her laughter could still be heard by the boys, within her familiar rampaging hollers. This day was a revelation to Eugene, he thought, as he stood in the kitchen, confident that Clara was not seriously troubled, and that they were all safe.

"Here they come!" Melvin yelled, tying his shoe, hearing the footsteps on the porch. "Here comes the bride!"

Clara was looking at the roast. "For such a hush-hush thing, he sure has a big mouth," she said. The boys giggled and ran down the hall to meet their sister and their new brother-in-law.

"Here comes the bride!" the boys and Melvin sang.

June entered, barefoot, carrying her orange high heels, "I broke my damn heel on those steps!" Her hair was dyed light blonde and she wore white lipstick, and Mack followed, panting from the climb. He'd removed his tie and left it on the front seat of his car. Eugene thought his hair looked especially black and shiny.

They shook hands. Mack said, "Yep, we've gone and done the deed, Eugene, your sister caught me."

Frankie kissed June.

"Which one?" Melvin asked, about the steps.

"Down at the bottom," June said, kissing Eugene. "Mack was teasing me and I tried to get away."

Clara appeared with an apron tied over her floral dress. "Your father won't fix anything, you know that," she said, seeing the group of them clustered by the front door. Debbie pushed past her and ran open-armed to June.

"Debbie!" June sang. "Now don't you look pretty? See, Mother, I told you that she could dress herself." She kissed the little girl and said, "And now this is your big brother-in-law, give him a kiss."

Mack stooped to peck and said, "You look tough, kid, wanna go on a date?"

Debbie giggled.

Clara said, "Everyone stay in here till I call you, dinner will be on the table in a few minutes. Put the televison on."

Mack showed Eugene how to use his flash camera. Melvin put on his favorite Saturday night show, *Midwestern Hayride*. June told Eugene to make sure her feet weren't in the picture. Melvin told Mack to pull up his fly. Frankie giggled. Eugene took the picture, and told them to say "cheese."

"Stand in front of the drapes!" Clara called from the kitchen. She claimed they were the only "nice" things in the living room.

"They are!" Frankie yelled.

Melvin took a picture of all of his children and Mack. Then he called for Clara to come in for a picture.

"I'm busy!" she yelled. "I can't be two places at once!"

Melvin told June to go get her mother and to bring a couple beers for him and Mack.

June went to the kitchen. "Mother, come out for just one picture," she said, opening the refrigerator.

"No," Clara said stubbornly, "you all go and have your fun, and don't go getting beers before supper."

"Mother."

"No."

"Mother! Please just one picture, you look so pretty tonight," June said closing the refrigerator empty-handed.

Clara turned from the sink where she was mashing potatoes, and muttered, "If that boy can't wear a tie on his own wedding day, then you can leave me out. I never."

"Mother!" June clutched the back of the apron, untying it. "I don't have shoes either, now you're coming out there and you're going to show off how nice you look."

Clara let herself be led to the living room, saying under her breath to June, "I'm just trying to keep this private, no sense the whole world seeing our shame and taking pictures of it."

Mack and the three kids were staring at the banjo player on television from the couch. Melvin was in the chair tapping his foot to the music. He saw them come down the hall. "Here she is! The mother of the bride!" And then to June he asked, "Where's our beers?"

June shook her head and motioned for him to get up and stand by Clara.

"Mack, come here by Mother and Daddy," June directed, "and Eugene, make sure you don't get my feet again."

Mack moved to stand next to Clara. Clara looked at June. June told Mack to stand next to Melvin. Eugene told them to say "cheese." Clara smiled and then left the room, calling Eugene to come help her. In the kitchen she told him, "At least with that hood on the end, he can always be cut off the picture."

That night, June and Mack left to go spend their first night in their new apartment on the top floor of Bess's. The store was on the ground floor. Bess lived on the second. She offered June and Mack the dilapidated space on the third floor if they could fix it up. "It's not much, honey," Bess had told June, the girl she'd seen grow up over the years, "but with some paint and elbow grease, you'll have a place of your own, and still be near your folks."

Eugene and Frankie were lying on the floor watching the Saturday night scary movie, and Melvin and Clara sat on the couch.

"Real good meal you made, Clara," Melvin said.

Clara stared at the television in her nightrobe.

"And real good cake. June liked it, you could tell."

"Mmm-hmm," Clara said.

"So, I guess they are sleeping right now in their new home,"

Melvin continued, having his eighth beer of the night. "Sure wish we could've done right by her and given her something."

Eugene adjusted his hand so that it covered his ear. He didn't want to hear Melvin drunk and rambling. He wished that they would both go to bed instead of sitting up and falling asleep on the couch.

"Ooooo," Frankie moaned, "yech! Did you see that, Eugene? It just smashed that guy flat!"

"And to think," Melvin went on, now watching the screen, "you will be a grandma and I will be a grandpa."

Clara spoke, folding her arms tight, "You'd think his folks could help them out. Maybe show their face. It's a real slap in the face for poor June, like she wasn't good enough for their boy or it was her fault."

"They'll come around, you'll see, once the baby is born they'll be around, they just don't have your gift of understanding."

"I hope you're right," she sighed. "I smell trouble, though, and I think June has gotten herself into one big trap. That place they are in over Bess's isn't fit for pigs and that silly June is so giddy about curtains, you know I never did think she had both feet on the ground. I'm sure that she got knocked up cause of that. She doesn't have a sensible bone in her body."

"Well, at least the boy was Catholic," Melvin said.

"Ahhhhh!" Frankie and Eugene both screamed. "Ooooooo!" and they rolled around the floor, having seen the monster's face for the first time.

"You two quiet down or next thing you know Debbie'll be in here too," Clara said.

Melvin swallowed the last drops from the bottle and set it on the coffee table. "You heard the father say that they were forgiven by the Lord by getting married. Now what if he'd been a Protestant?"

"Some Catholic," Clara said, "taking advantage of June's silly nature."

In November, June let Eugene feel the kick movement of the fetus inside her. Then she let Frankie feel. Then Clara dried her hands with the dish towel and she felt, and said, "Lord, June, let's hope there ain't no complications, you being so young." Eugene wanted to ask how exactly the baby was born. He felt that he should be quiet. His friend Bobby had told him that babies were squeezed out like turds. June had said that Jackie Kennedy had her babies cut out. That seemed to make more sense.

The next day, President Kennedy was assassinated in Texas. Eugene and Frankie were let out of school an hour early. They stopped at Bess's store. She came out from the backroom where the televison was set, wiping her eyes.

"Your sister is up at your house, boys. She was pretty upset about it."

Eugene was still hoping that it was a mistake, that somehow what the nun announced over the P.A. was wrong. Frankie worried that all Catholics were going to be shot. He stayed close to Eugene all the way home, and then ran up all seventy steps.

June and Clara were sitting on the couch staring at the television, drinking Cokes and sniffling. Eugene looked at them and knew that it really was true. The Communists were taking over. He dropped to his knees in prayer before the television and said the Hail Mary as fast as he could.

"Move!" Clara yelled. "We can't see with you right there, Eugene!"

Frankie sat down next to June. She held him close and he made sure that he didn't touch her belly where the baby was hatching. Eugene scooted on his knees backward, feeling a gray sad world even in the safety of the living room. After he'd said enough prayers, he laid under the coffee table, watching the recounting, detail after detail. Sniper. School Book Depository. He pictured the assassin in a library. He hated Lyndon Johnson because it was obvious to him that he now got to be President, so he had the motive. June said, "Poor Jackie, I just can't stand it." Clara said, "Something's going on that we don't know. Maybe Eugene's right about that Johnson. Who is he anyway? Or maybe Frankie's right and they shot him because he was Catholic. Lord knows there are a lot of jealous people out there."

That night in bed, Eugene put his pillow over his stomach and covered himself with the blanket. He cradled the pillow like June cradled her belly. He wondered what it would be like to have something moving inside of you, like swallowing something still alive. He looked down to see his snoring father. Melvin's gut rose and fell, bigger than June and bigger than his pillow. Eugene wondered if Jackie Kennedy had scars from having babies cut from her. He wondered what it would be like to be riding in a convertible and have your head shot. He wondered if Jackie would sleep. He laid back on his mattress and sadly moaned, "Oh Jack, oh Jack, why'd you have to go to Dallas." Melvin rolled about in his bed kicking the blankets, and then he farted. Eugene pulled his blanket over his head and removed the pregnancy pillow. He curled into a fetal position and wondered what it would be like to be inside a belly. He tried to remember being in Clara. It seemed impossible, but it was true. He wondered why such a miracle was kept so secret. He tested the air in the room, sticking his nose out from under the covers quick. It was awful. He lay still, wishing he had a room of his own, and then apologized to Jesus for being so selfish. The smell was nothing compared to having your head shot off for no reason. He would uncover his face, and endure the smell of Melvin's farts as an offering up for the soul of the dead President. He took a deep breath. Then he decided to switch his intentions, thinking how everyone must be offering things up for the President, and meanwhile Jackie was left all alone. Clara had said, "Just when she got the White House looking real nice the way she wanted it, she'll have to pack up and move, poor thing." He offered his stink endurance for Jackie. He took another deep breath and coughed. He put his hands on his chest, folded, like a dead saint. He was a corpse. He was the dead President in the morgue. He would be buried in the cold ground. Everything was completely different. If only it had rained all day in Dallas. Eugene hated Dallas. He hated Texas. He saw the glowing crucifix on the wall above his head. Jesus suffered more than the President, he thought. The nuns said that no one could ever suffer more than Jesus did. Sister Aloysius had said, "All the suffering in all the wars was equal to one drop of Jesus' blood." Eugene thought one of the worst sufferings would have been being stripped in front of everyone and trying not to let them see you cry or be ashamed. He thought that maybe the Johnsons would let Jackie live with them since it was a mansion, but then he decided that they would probably resent each other. His head was full.

The week before Christmas, "such a sad one for the Kennedys," as Clara put it, she went to the closet in the girls' room and took down the Christmas card box and brought it to the kitchen table. She had decided that it was time to cut the old saved cards for decorations and gift notes. Melvin had been gone all morning, and Clara had a "hunch" that he had gone out to buy an aluminum tree for her, "Now that everybody and their cousin had one."

Eugene felt he was to old to play "cutouts." He felt he was too old for a lot of things since June had gotten married and he'd become the eldest at home. Clara insisted he join her and Frankie and Debbie at the table.

"Ahhhhhhh, come on," he whined from the couch in the living room.

"Eugene," Clara called, stopping her shrill hum of "Little Lord Jesus," "Eugene, you always do the best cutting. Now you come in here. It ain't the same without you. It's not right for you to be watching television and breaking our tradition."

Eugene trudged to the kitchen, thinking what used to be something he looked forward to each year now seemed really stupid and childish, like kindergarten, but his movie was over and nothing good was going to be on for a half hour.

Clara gave him a pile of cards and told him to pick out ones that could be cut so the names of the senders would be removed. "Your father always says to throw'm out, don't he," she said, "but each year we always do something nice with all the Santas and things. I think I'm right." She found one and held it up for the kids to see. "Look at this cheap one from Bess. See how cheap she is, and you know what," she hunted through another stack, finding the same card, "I thought it looked familiar, see, the same card from 1961. No wonder we never used it up, on such flimsy paper. I bet she got these from the bottom of the barrel, and her, with all her money she makes off you kids. Cheap. No class."

Eugene yawned and reached for the scissors to cut the card he had given Clara two years earlier with the hidden message written in it.

"Eugene close your mouth or cover it, and leave them cards alone. Your cards stay on the special stack for my television display. Cut up this one from Aunt Wanda and Uncle Ralph. They always have to show off and send the real fancy ones to rub our noses in the dirt."

Eugene put his back and cut up his aunt and uncle's. Sometimes the special ones were used to fill up a line if there weren't enough new ones. Clara liked to string them across the living room wall, corner to corner. She told Frankie what to cut, and what to give to Debbie. Debbie got the throwaways, like both of Bess's cards. Clara said she didn't want to save it, even for filler. Clara was jealous of how close June had become with Bess now that they lived in the same building.

Frankie proudly held up a card that he'd made for his parents in second grade. "What are you gonna do with mine?" he asked.

Clara smiled, "Oh honey, that one's so messy. Why's that one still around? We can give that to Debbie to play with. We only want the real pretty ones, Frankie. You just don't have a way with art. See? Yours is all covered with old dried paste."

Frankie pulled the card close to himself and shook his head, "No." Debbie reached for it. "Stop it, Debbie!" he yelled. "It's mine. I made it!"

"Uh-unnnh," Debbie singsong whined, "Mother said."

Frankie said to Clara, "You saved Eugene's. His is handmade."

Eugene reached for his hidden-message card, more than willing to tear it up, showing Frankie "it's no big deal," and also relieving his worry that one day Clara might figure it out. "Here, Frankie, see!" Eugene said, about to tear the card.

Clara snapped his hand. "No! I told you that one stays, Eugene. Now, Frankie, you don't have the talent that Eugene has. You play ball. Eugene is an artist, and that's that."

Debbie reached for it. "See!"

"Get your mitts off it!" Frankie screamed.

"Mine!" Debbie screamed back.

Eugene looked at Frankie and said, "Just give the little brat the card, it's no big deal."

Frankie's face was so red with hurt he gave Eugene the finger.

"I saw! That's dirty!" Debbie yelled, still grabbing at the card.

Frankie burst. "No! It's mine!" He switched hands away from her grasp. "If she gets it she'll just tear it to . . ."

It tore in half. Clara was concentrating on her cutting and humming. Debbie scrambled under the table screaming with fear.

"You shit!" Frankie cried.

Clara hummed louder, and sang out, unmoved by their screeches so far, "Now, now, you two, I don't want no cussing."

Eugene said calmly, trying to force his voice as deep as Mack's voice, "Frankie, grow up. It was just a piece of paper."

Under the table, Debbie was kicked by Frankie and she screamed and then tried to bite his leg.

Frankie kicked her again, but missed and kicked Eugene's shin.

Eugene said, with a growing threat in his voice, "Fraaaankieeeee, you better watch it."

Debbie tried to squeeze out from under, but Frankie grabbed her little foot and she fell, but pulled Frankie off his chair and onto the linoleum floor. The kitchen shook.

Eugene looked at Clara, who was remarkably oblivious to all of this. He thought he was seeing a miracle. She had a slight smile on her face and a hymn on her lips. He felt a thud on his toes, "Ow! You two, that's my foot!" he yelled, then reached down to slap at both of them.

Debbie pushed her way out and ran down the hall to the girls' room and slammed the door screaming and screeching higher and higher.

Frankie chased her and stood at the door to the girls' room and yelled, "I hate you! I hate you! You little shithole!"

Eugene looked at his mother, who continued to hum and cut the intricate jolly Saint Nick. He yelled toward the hall, "Shut up you babies!"

Clara sighed, and set the scissors down on the Formica; the cries from both children were breaking her concentration. Finally she yelled, "Listen you two! You're gonna get what paddy shot at for Christmas if you don't stop this minute! And Frankie, you should know better than to pick on a little girl, she's just a baby!"

Frankie stopped pounding on the girls' room door and yelled toward the kitchen, "That was my card! I made it! I hate you! And I hate you too, Eugene!" And he slammed the door to the boys' room.

"Look at this one," Eugene said to Clara, showing her a Nativity scene that had a sugary coating wherever there was supposed to be snow, hoping to distract her from the screams.

She saw the baby Jesus reaching up to Mary. She wondered

where Melvin was, and if he really was going to surprise her with an artificial tree, or maybe he was down at the saloon. Wherever he was, he wasn't there to see how bad the kids were acting. She sighed and tried to hum, and then scooted her chair back so that she could see the clock on the stove.

Eugene asked her if he should cut the Nativity one or put it on the special stack. He wanted to keep her calm. He watched her lips, and then her brow.

Clara scooted back to the table and said, "I wonder if June is coming up for dinner tonight. She said something about going shopping with the hood I think. You know, she's yet to have your father and me down for a meal, and she's been there two months now." Then her face changed, and her body stiffened in the chair, and she howled, "Will you two shut up this instant!"

Eugene jumped in his seat.

"I'm going to count to two!" the woman screamed. "And then I'm coming after you with the belt! One! Two! That does it!" She stood up and marched to the nail where she kept the belt. It wasn't there. She turned to Eugene and screamed, "Where's the belt?!"

He shook his head and wanted to warn her that she was flying off the handle, but he couldn't speak.

The kitchen trembled with her voice, "Where's the goddamned belt!!"

Eugene searched the kitchen with his eyes. He searched his memory for how June had stood up to Clara. Clara had even asked him to remind her the next time she started to fly off the handle the day she came back from confession. How did June do it?

Clara opened and slammed the cupboard doors and the utensil drawers. Debbie's cries seemed higher and louder. Frankie's had stopped altogether. Clara came to the table and Eugene backed himself against the wall. She picked up the scissors, then set them back down and went back to the empty nail, and then back to the drawers.

"I am going to beat the living daylights out of the two of you! I swear! Where the hell is the belt!"

Frankie opened the boys' room window and quietly lowered himself down onto the frozen side yard. He crept around to the front of the house with his blanket and crawled under the rotting front porch to his hiding place. He shivered with chills of being caught. He prayed.

Clara again eyed the scissors. So did Eugene. They both made a grab for it and she got it.

"No!" Eugene screamed, scaring himself with the power behind his voice. "No Mother! Put that down!"

Clara held the scissors like a knife. She looked at him with mad eyes and heaving breasts. "Don't you tell me no, mister! Don't you tell me no!"

Eugene jumped from the chair yelling, "I didn't do anything! You've got the scissors, not the belt, Mother! You're losing control and flying off the handle!"

She came toward him, "I've had just about enough of all of you!" And she lunged across the tabletop stabbing at the air, knocking the cards onto the linoleum. "Look at what you made me do! You devil!"

Eugene tried to figure which way to run; she was between the kitchen door and the hallway arch. She plunged the scissors again at him.

"No!" he screamed. Scared tears came to his eyes. "You don't really want to hurt us!"

She smiled crazily, trying to see which way he would move. He wouldn't get away with it. She knew all the tricks. She teased him, making him sway with the direction of the scissors.

Debbie cried louder from the girls' room. The cold December afternoon wind blew up from the river and into the open window of the boys' room. June climbed the seventy steps slowly, her pregnant belly emerging from her coat at each rise. She'd gone shopping with Bess, and had bought Mack a Christmas present that she wanted to wrap, and then she would probably stay for supper. Frankie saw her as she neared the top, through the old latticework that ran around the base of the porch. June looked up. She heard Eugene screaming, "No! No!" Frankie called out to her in a loud whisper, "June!"

She stopped at the top step. Her blond hair was set with empty juice cans.

"Here! Under the porch!"

She approached him, panting from the climb.

"Mother's really really mad again and wants to beat us," he said, as she looked at him through the wooden slats.

Just then, Eugene made his move, and ran down the hall through the living room, and came bursting out the front door screaming. He jumped off the porch. He caught a glimpse of June as he landed and took off down the seventy steps, yelling, "Get out of here!"

Clara appeared at the door screaming, "Come back up here you little jackass! I'll kill you if you ever come . . ." and she stopped and lowered the scissors at the sight of June.

"Mother!" June stood with her hands on her hips. "What is going on?"

Clara smiled at June. Eugene had made it safely down to River Road and turned to look up. He saw his sister was about to go up on the porch and Clara was standing in the doorway. Through his tears he cried, "Oh God, June, don't go up there, she'll kill your baby!"

Clara spoke, "The boys were acting up again. What are you doing here so early? Come up here and get in out of the cold." She held the door for June. She motioned with the scissors, "We was making decorations."

June looked down to see Eugene panting on the road, and then back to her mother. She shivered at the thought of Clara actually attacking Eugene with the scissors, she shivered because it was a real possibility. She asked again, "What were you doing? Chasing him with the scissors? Shame on you!"

Clara shrugged and tried to laugh, "Oh, come on in, it's freezing out here. You just wait till that baby's born and you'll know my aggravation. Come up here, girl. I'm not going to bite."

"Where's Daddy? Is he working?"

Clara backed into the house, still holding the door open. She could see Eugene way down the steps staring up and she stepped in enough that he couldn't see her. She felt guilty for a moment. "I guess I flew off the handle. I should never have had kids so late."

June came up onto the porch.

Clara noticed the bag. "What's that?"

June entered the house, describing the fuzzy fake sheepskin carseat covers she'd gotten Mack for Christmas. She took the scissors from Clara and held it out the doorway, waving it for Eugene to see.

"That's it," Clara bemoaned. "Make it out like your old mother was going to kill her kids, June, but you just wait and see."

The door closed on the cold afternoon. Frankie crawled out from hiding and motioned for Eugene to come back up. Eugene looked down the road to Bess's store. He wanted to live with June. He thought how lucky she was to have gotten away. He started up the steps, thinking he would talk to June about living with her and being a babysitter. Frankie rocked from foot to foot with his blanket wrapped around him at the top of the steps.

"I hid," he said to Eugene.

"You whiner!" Eugene scolded him. "You couldn't shut up could you? You made her fly off the handle. It was just a piece of paper, but you had to scream your head off!" He panted from the climb reaching his younger brother, "She was going to use the scissors because she couldn't find the belt!"

Frankie grinned, "I threw it into the woods last week so she couldn't use it anymore."

Eugene pushed him, "Well, dope, you better go find it or she'll kill us next time. I mean really kill us."

Frankie pushed him back, "Well, it's way up down there in a tree, and I don't know how to get it."

Eugene didn't push him again. He realized that poor Frankie would have to fend for himself when he moved in with June. He felt sorry for his little brother and put his arm around him, at first scaring Frankie who thought he was going to be hit. "Well, we'll go down to the woods and try to get it some way."

"I'm scared," Frankie started to whimper.

Eugene held him tight and said, "June's here and we'll be all right."

Frankie heaved and started crying, "I hate mother! I hate her so much! She hates me! I wish she was killed by a sniper!"

The release of tears was contagious and Eugene fought to hold out from bawling. "We got to remember that she is off her rocker, Frankie, and we got to be careful not to get her mad, and maybe someday if Daddy gets money everything will be better," and then Eugene started to cry. He didn't believe that there would ever be a lot of money to make things better. Melvin was a drunk. The only hope was to get away. "You know, Frankie," he cried, "you got to always be ready for it, cause someday I won't be around and you'll have to be on your own."

Frankie stopped crying enough to say, "You don't ever take my side! You don't watch out for me! I'm the one who thought to climb out the window and hide."

Eugene withdrew his arm and went up onto the porch, "Okay, wiseguy, but I'm just telling you to be careful and stop whining around her cause she's nuts. They're both nuts."

Frankie stood shivering and heaving wrapped in his blanket. "Are you really going in?"

"Yeah," Eugene said. "It's cold. June's here."

Frankie went up onto the porch with trepidation. He said, "You know what mother told June? That she had kids too late. What's that mean?"

Opening the door, Eugene said, "It means we're runts." Then he saw the Olds pull up.

Melvin honked from down on River Road. Eugene held the door open and watched him take a box from the car and start up the steps. Clara yelled from the kitchen, "Either in or out, Eugene! Close the door! It's freezing!" Her yell was almost lighthearted. He closed the door, choosing to remain with Frankie on the porch waiting for Melvin to come up.

"Wonder what Daddy bought," Frankie said, wiping his tears with his blanket.

"I bet it's an aluminum tree," Eugene said, hoping, thinking perhaps it would change things.

1968, Ohio

In Eugene's last year at Bishop Miller High School the cold weather wore on and on into what should have been spring. Katherine had written to him from her father's in California, sending the letters to his friend William's house, because Clara could not be trusted. Clara swore that she did nothing to encourage Katherine's mother to send her daughter out West, but Eugene didn't believe her. He avoided being home as much as possible, and worked after school and on Saturdays for a construction company near the school. He worked in the company's yard, scraping down the wood forms that were used to set foundations, learning to carry heavy weight on his shoulders. The men who worked there would come in from jobs with a truck loaded with forms, and he would have to unload them, lean them against the wall, scrape any dried cement off them, rescrew any loose screws, and then oil them down so they would be ready for the next job. The men were burly types with foul mouths and big opinions and Eugene was the brunt of their talk because he was young and sweetly handsome and had long hair. They ridiculed his youth, jealous of his strength. It seemed they had an initiation rite of some sort and they prodded him to join their talk. He had made the mistake of saying that Martin Luther King's assassination was terrible, and he never heard the end of it. They called him a nigger lover. He hated when the trucks came in because till then he was mostly alone and the work was simple. The workers were the real tough part of the job. But he saved money, and by Robert Kennedy's assassination in June, he'd already saved over eight hundred dollars. After graduation, he worked full-time and went out on jobs, learning to erect the forms and break them down after the concrete had set. He wanted to leave Ohio and go to California or New York, and the only thing that stopped him from leaving was Frank and Debbie. He told his mother that he wanted to go away to school and she wouldn't hear of it. She said that he should stay in Ohio and be the man of the house and that if he left, "they might as well bury me, what with your father dead, and your sister dead, surely I will die of heartbreak." He felt trapped, and the only thing he could do, he thought, was to keep working and saving money till the time was right. Clara threatened him, saying he could not legally leave home till he was eighteen, so he set a target date of August 2, the day after he turned eighteen, to leave. And to justify leaving, "deserting," which was the word he'd taken to using also, to justify "deserting" he decided that he would go to school in New York. That is, he would *say* he was going to go to school. He sent for school catalogs and made sure they were left around the house for her to find. She had no idea about how difficult it was to enter these schools, and he had no intention of applying to any of them, but he thought somewhere in his plans for the future that he might try college.

Frankie and Debbie were still so young, Eugene thought, but he wasn't much help with them anyway. They all fought with each other. With Katherine gone, Eugene began to hang out more with William and William's friends, the Crowd. They'd go to Mount Adams where the crowd hung out, and they'd smoke grass in the park and look out over the city and listen to Jefferson Airplane. Most of them were actors' apprentices at the Playhouse in the Park, and for a while he was tempted to join that group and stay in Ohio, "just move away from home, but not so far," but that really didn't stay long, that feeling. The guys, one in particular, Kevin Meyer, was very flamboyant and witty and openly queer. He made passes at Eugene and forced Eugene to push him off, in which case, the Crowd thought Eugene was violent, and when he tried to explain that he wasn't into kissing men they all taunted him and said he was hung up. So he said if it meant that much to Kevin, he could go ahead and kiss him, but he didn't like being treated like a girl. Kevin kissed him, pushing his tongue into Eugene's mouth, in front of the eight core members of the Crowd, and then pretended to faint.

Eugene turned red, but took their initiation rite in stride. He always remembered that kiss, because in the brief moment when it happened, there in the park outside the Art Museum, he smelled roses and felt the rough chin of a male who was twenty years old and had done acid over a dozen times. He felt something that bordered on excitement, though he never could have admitted it, especially after punching him to begin with, in front of everyone there on the steps of the museum.

"There," Eugene said, his lips stretching across his teeth, still trembling at the confrontation. "Now will you all lay off me? Kevin got his kiss and I didn't hit him."

"You tongued him!" Leslie squealed at Kevin. She was jealous. Eugene's punch to Kevin had confirmed his masculinity, and he would be hers before a week was out. Eugene was one of sexiest men in the Crowd, and he had proven to her that she would not be refused when she made her move on the newcomer.

"And it was a sweet dive, if I do say so myself," Kevin announced, patting Eugene on the shoulder.

Eugene laughed and moved to the steps, away from Kevin, but not obviously away from him, and Leslie made room for him to sit next to her. It was Sunday and there were people going to the museum, and the Crowd sat on the steps making comments about each conservative person approaching the museum. Eugene thought the Crowd was so clever and witty and sharp. They would ridicule someone who looked fairly normal to him, and by the time the man was passing him on the steps, he'd become a former marine in Vietnam who'd massacred helpless people, who'd voted for George Wallace, and was going to the museum because his wife said it would look good as if they had culture.

Kevin took to calling Eugene, and since Eugene was rarely home, Clara took the calls and confronted Eugene one day. "I don't know what kind of fruitcake that boy is, but I don't get what he wants with you, Eugene. He sounds like Liberace."

"He's an actor," Eugene said, feeling surprisingly defensive of Kevin, "and he goes to U.C. He's fun and works at the Playhouse, and he's very bright, and I think he has a crush on me."

"A what!?!" Clara screamed, following her smug son to the boys' room door. "A boy has a crush on another boy? What are you, crazy? You talk so crazy."

Eugene turned grinning to her, and looked deep and solemn

into her face, and held her by her shoulders and said, "Queer, mother. Kevin is queer. And he has a crush on me."

"Don't talk like that round me, mister bigshot, don't start dirty talk around me just because I'm a widow!"

Eugene let her wriggle from his grasp. He scared her with some of his remarks, and he enjoyed that. When he was feeling confident and smart about his life and especially as money amassed in his savings account, he became more and more blunt with Clara, almost daring her to understand the world he lived in. He no longer feared her, and tried to explain to Frankie and Debbie when he was alone with them that the best thing they could do for themselves was to get some kind of job in the summer and after school and save money so they could leave home. To him, the closer it came to August the more at ease he felt around Clara and the more honest he got.

"Well, you tell that fruitcake to stop calling this house, Eugene, or I'll call the police and have him arrested!" she yelled at the closed door to the boys' room.

Eugene had slammed it in her face, and had immediately turned to the closed door and blatantly rubbed his crotch up against the wood and mumbled,"Yeah, Mother, a fucking queer, going after my dick, this dick right here, right on the other side of the door from you. Yeah, Mother, he wants to eat me and kiss me like a woman."

"And I'll tell him that if he ever lays a hand on you that you'll knock him out cold, Eugene! Don't you worry, he doesn't know just how strong you are!"

Eugene opened the door a slit, so that his nose and lips could be seen in the hallway, and he said, "I can take care of myself. I won't let him rape me."

Clara tried to push the door in, screaming what a foul mouth Eugene had, but he had added a lock two years before that was impossible for her to open, and he let her bang away and curse and cry and he stood on the other side of the door and jerked off, closing his eyes and fantasizing being sucked by Kevin in front of the Crowd, who had all at one point or another made sexual remarks to him. He was surprised that he gave off such a sexual scent, considering he was so inexperienced. Bobby had told him years ago that girls sensed if you were full of come, and that's why it was good to jerk off, otherwise you would scare them away, overwhelming them with the threat of so much cream. And Eugene thought that the Crowd was very sensitive to how much cream he had. He could not admit to himself at that point, there behind the door, how sensitive he was to their sexuality, but he ached for their attention, and he came all over his jeans. Then he told himself that he was especially thinking of Leslie when he came.

William, Eugene's friend from Bishop Miller who'd introduced him to this sophisticated group of "artists," had always been a target of Eugene's fantasies. They shared the same gym locker in school and often lingered too long in the showers acting silly with each other, and although they never owned up to it, after Katherine left for California in 1967, William sort of became Eugene's date. They'd drive up to Mount Adams and drink beer and smoke cigarettes and sometimes grass if someone had some, and although Eugene was new to the Crowd, and most of them were a year or two out of high school and either attending art school or the university, they accepted Eugene. He learned that he was very funny, and on dares he would do things to get laughs from them. William got jealous when he found out that Eugene was hanging around with the Crowd without him, and one Sunday, in Eden Park, he confronted Eugene, who was sitting with his feet in the lake, waiting for everyone to show up.

"Hi," William said.

"Hi," Eugene said.

"I thought you might be here. I called your house and your brother said you had been out all night."

Eugene slowly withdrew his feet and fell back onto the grass. "Yeah, we were all kind of drunk and I stayed over at Leslie's apartment. She kicked me out so she could study her lines. She has an audition coming, and, no, we didn't screw."

William adjusted his beads that were tangled in his collar. "Yeah? Good for her."

Eugene squinted up to him. He stood there in big bellbottom jeans and looked forlorn, as if he had something eating away at him. He wore wire-rimmed glasses and had made the most of his hair, combing it so that it looked as long as possible. William's family would not allow long hair in their house. He was already accepted at the Catholic college, Xavier University, and so he was forced to abide by their rules as long as he was going to be living at home. Eugene and the others in the Crowd found this choice of William's to be his downfall. They had all coached him on how he should get out from under their rules and had encouraged him to avoid Xavier since it was so conservative. "That college has never allowed one protest march." Eugene saw a sadness in William's face. He asked him what was wrong.

"Do you really want to know?"

"Sure," Eugene smiled, "tell me what's up."

William sat down on the grass. He lit a cigarette. Exhaled, then said, "I think you could at least call me and invite me to join you. I'm the one who introduced you to all these people, Eugene, and now it's like you don't ever bother to call me. I think you just used me to get to know them."

"That's not true, William," Eugene said, trying to understand why he kept hearing Leslie's tone of voice mimicking William. She'd say, "He whines all the time and is such a mama's boy and afraid to be free. He's a drag, really." Eugene tried to see William for the friend he was and not for what the Crowd seemed to think. After all, they'd had good times together, going to movies, bucking the trend of dating, daring to go out on a Saturday night to the college district even though they were still in high school. "That's not true at all, Will, it's just that I can't call you and arrange stuff, you know, I mean, Kevin called me last night and said they were all going to go to the Blind Lemon, and if I could be ready in ten minutes, he'd pick me up, and I was still dirty from work, so I jumped in the tub and ran down the steps and dried off as we drove, and there's no way I could have called you. I think Frankie was on the phone, because he grabbed it as I was hanging up from Kevin."

"Kevin drove all the way to River Road? That's so far out of the way," William said. "He lives in Clifton."

"Maybe he was just in the neighborhood or something," Eugene guessed.

"I don't trust him," William said. "He's really weird, don't you think?"

"Yeah," Eugene agreed, knowing that's what William wanted him to say, but added, "but he can be pretty funny, once you learn to not take him too seriously."

"What about the kiss?" William asked, having heard about it, but not having seen it.

Eugene reddened, especially embarrassed because he and William had come close to intimacy on a few drunken nights. He looked out over the lake and said, "It was no big deal. The Crowd dared me, really, because I had punched him earlier for always getting so close to me, and they all came at me with, you know how they get, real dramatic stuff, 'Oh my god, he touched me! I'm no longer a virgin!' and shit like that and so I had no choice but to prove to them that I wasn't hung up."

Eugene brushed his hair from his forehead with his hand, and quickly caught William's eye. He smiled. William smiled. Eugene sighed. At that moment, he realized how much he cared for William, how much he needed to be able to talk to him and be close to him, and he felt the urge to lean over and touch the young man. Kevin would have. Most friends would have. He didn't because he was too afraid of how the touch would be interpreted, not only by William, but by his own conscience. In his head he told himself that he was fucked up.

"I'm sorry I ever brought you up here," William said. "We used to have so much fun, just the two of us. And now that school is over, I never see you."

"Fuck," Eugene said. "I work every day."

"Not today," William argued.

"Yeah, and here we are."

"Yeah."

They sat on the grass silently smoking cigarettes. Eugene felt uncomfortable. He wanted to tell William how confused he was, about leaving Ohio or possibly staying, and about Kevin's kiss. He dared to think that William would somehow know something more. Know what he should do. Instead he said, "I don't know why you don't move away from your family, William. They really got you tied to them, don't they?"

"You're still at home."

"Not for long. As soon as my birthday, I'm leaving. I'm going to New York. Katherine has a cousin who lives there. Remember the last letter? Her name is Sue, and Katherine said she's a hippie, and I can probably stay at her crash pad."

William seemed surprised although they had talked about moving away for a year. "You really are going to do it? Really Eugene? In August?"

Eugene acted confident. "Yeah. Of course. And I think I'll try to go to some school that teaches theater. Maybe I should try to be an actor. Leslie said I'm a natural."

"I bet she did."

"What do you mean by that?"

"Nothing," William sighed, removing his glasses and cleaning them on his shirt.

Eugene mimicked him, saying, "Nothing," sarcastically.

William put his glasses back on and said, "She probably meant it, don't get me wrong, but she has a way of telling every guy she likes that they have natural talent . . . she told me that once."

"Well, even if she didn't mean it," Eugene defended his decision, "I still would like to give it a try. I know that theater people are fun and they don't take anything seriously and I'm all for that, fuck, I have to go to some school, or I'll end up in Vietnam."

"Yeah, you have to go to school, Eugene."

"Or I'll go to Canada," he said, sitting up.

"Would you really do that?"

"Sure," Eugene said, daring to be confident. "There's no way I'm going to go kill somebody. I'm into peace and love. Tell that to the priests at Xavier."

"You're mad at me for deciding to go to Xavier aren't you?"

Eugene took a long slow breath and fell back onto the grass again. "You want the truth, William? Do you really want to know what I think?"

"Yes," the young man said, looking at Eugene's dirty toenails.

"I think you're chicken to leave home and you're chicken to stand up to the Catholics and tell them to fuck off and you like to think you're real cool, but you let your parents tell you how long your hair should be and what school you should go to, and . . . well, I think you're chicken."

"And I think you're jealous," William blurted out. "I think . . ."

"Jealous!"

"Yeah, I think you wish you had applied to Xavier and that you had a goal and a plan and that you had somebody you had to obey. You said so yourself that your mother is a hillbilly."

"Fuck you."

"And you told me your dad was an idiot."

"Shut up, William. I can say that. You can't. He's dead."

"And I think you're a chicken, not me. You won't go anywhere, I bet. You're all talk. At least I know that I have a future!"

Eugene laughed. He realized how wrong William was. He realized, there at the lake, at that moment, that he was going to leave, no more doubts about it. He saw himself gone from Ohio, in a new world, on his own, in his own future, and William had pushed him into it. He leaned over and kissed William, just as Kevin had kissed Eugene, on the lips, full, sticking in his tongue as a shocker, and laughing, he said, "Thank you, William, thank you. You are right. I have no future, my dad was an idiot and mother is a hillbilly witch and I'm getting out of here!"

William wiped his mouth and adjusted his glasses on his nose, and started to laugh. "You're crazy, Goessler. Crazy. Why'd you go and do that?"

Eugene stood up. He wanted to leave immediately, but figured five more weeks would be bearable. He started running across the grass in wider and wider circles, feeling freer than he had since he could remember. What was it? A decision? A slap? The truth? Whatever it was, he lost his inhibition at that moment. He thought of June, dead. He thought he could feel June running with him near the lake.

William remained seated in the grass, laughing at Eugene's euphoria. Struck. He never realized how much Eugene meant to him till then. He still tasted his kiss, and did not hold it against him. Eugene's voice echoed up the hill toward the Playhouse and down the hill toward the river and out over the hills of Kentucky and across the lake and against the walls of his eardrums and he yelled, "Goessler? Are you flipping out?"

And Eugene ran close to him. Like a freed spirit, he sang, "I am gone!"

2012, Panacea, Florida

"All the little deaths," Eugene thought, sitting in the sand outside bungalow #4, "all the choices, the moves, the dares." A part of him, the part that was echoed in Lola's blue eyes, wondered if he would really go through with this ultimate move. The way Lola had looked at him up in Massachusetts when they were saying good-bye had within it a doubt. He himself had thought on the flight to Tallahassee, "Can I do this?"

He took the stack of pictures he'd brought out from the bungalow and burned one at a time. There was a picture of the Crowd lined up along the outdoor stage in Eden Park in Cincinnati. He remembered William daring him to leave Ohio. There was a picture of June and Debbie and Frank from June's wedding. He watched their faces melt. "Of course I can do this," he thought. "All of my life I have dared to live. I have enjoyed the pleasure of Eugene Goessler. I . . . I . . . ." he looked out into Apalachee Bay. It was June, his sister June, young, surfing by and waving. He waved back, but coughed at the sight of her through the smoke of the burning photographs. "I do only one thing," he said, "change. That is all there is."

"Eugene!" June yelled sweetly. "I dare you!"

1972, Ohio

Clara was, after the first hour of tears and kisses for her boy, again complaining about how much he looked like a hippie, and how ashamed she was for the obvious waste of his life in New York. "One look at you, Lord, and people would think you was raised in some loony bin." Frank, who was nineteen, was working for the same construction company Eugene had worked for, and going to a technical night school. Fourteen-year-old Debbie reminded Eugene of June.

He walked with Debbie along the river, and asked her who she was.

"What do you mean?" Debbie laughed.

"Well," Eugene explained, "I don't know you, really. You've changed so much since I left. You've really grown up. Do you know how much you look like June?"

She giggled like a little girl, "I guess so. Mother says that sometimes, usually when she's mad."

"When isn't she mad?" Eugene said, and they both laughed deeply.

They looked out over the water. Eugene asked, "Do you remember the fire?"

"Sort of," she said, awkwardly, "but Mother says . . . uh . . . I don't really remember, I guess."

"Mother says what?"

"Oh, nothing, Eugene. Did you think the Valentine I sent you was funny?"

"Mother says what?" Eugene would not let the matter drop.

"Oh . . ." Debbie sighed, " . . . uh, just that, you know, that

June got what was coming to her . . . or something like that. We don't listen."

"The witch," Eugene muttered, looking down river and wanting to light a joint or snort some cocaine suddenly. "Hey. Listen to me, Debbie. June was the best. Don't listen to Mother. Nothing she says is right. Nothing. She is completely and totally crazy."

"I know," Debbie's voice rose in pitch, as if to say, "I'm not a little kid." "Frank tells me that all the time, too, you know, when she starts flying off the handle and stuff," she reached down to the tall grass and ran her hand tenderly along the tops. "I wish you lived here, Eugene."

"No you don't," he laughed, " 'cause if I did, either I'd be in prison for murder, or Mother would be committed to Longview. Being away from her, Deb, makes it that much clearer how fuc . . . uh, nuts, she is. You just have to hold on a few more years."

Eugene left the next day, getting a ride as far as the Indiana border with Frank in his Mustang.

"Sorry I can't stay and wait for you to get a ride," he said to Eugene, "but I work."

"Yeah," Eugene said, letting the dig slide, "I wish I could've spent more time with you, brother. I hope you've got the facts straight."

"Shoot," Frank said, still sleepy-eyed in coveralls, "ain't no big deal."

Eugene felt such a distance from his nineteen-year-old brother, who looked just like Melvin's old baseball photographs. The night before, in the boys' room, which was now Frank's room, Eugene lay awake waiting for his brother to come in. He wanted to talk. He'd snorted the last of the coke that Charity had given him as a going-away present, and couldn't sleep. The room was definitely Frank's. There were baseball trophies along the bureau, and posters of Raquel Welch and Pete Rose on the wall above Frank's desk. On the table between the two single beds (the bunks had been dismantled soon after Melvin's death) were three framed snapshots. One of Frank in his high school baseball uniform with his arm around his girlfriend, Stephanie. One of June's wedding with Melvin grinning and holding her hand. The third was a picture of Eugene from the Bishop Miller track team. Eugene thumbed through one of Frank's high school annuals, then took his notebook from his backpack and tried to write what he felt being back in the old house, in the old boys' room: "I am on another planet, but it's very familiar ground. I feel like there's this heavy trip hanging on me. I got out. They have no idea what the real world is like beyond Ohio. Mother drives me crazy. When she yelled before about me not having any underwear for her to wash because I don't wear any, she threw the bowl of mashed potatoes at me and it broke the handle off the kitchen cabinet. She keeps saying I am ungrateful. What should I be grateful for? Outwitting her? I'm grateful for that. I think my saving grace was the river. It was always there, no matter what. I talked with Deb this afternoon when she got home from school. She carries her books just like June did. She's got teats and wants to be a detective. I tried not to laugh. She is a soft bud. I yelled at Mother, "You should only know what goes on!" God, she is so sick. She has Frank wrapped around her finger and Debbie under her thumb. When she dies we should give her a hand, ha ha. Maybe it wasn't such a good idea to come here. I am so tired and I can't sleep. I felt so up when I left New York, and now I feel like shit. I couldn't reach Kevin, and talked to Leslie on the phone. She seemed so phony. I should have taken that ride through to Illionis with that salesman. I just nosed my last and feel like j.o.ing. I think Frank is avoiding me. He said his classes were over at nine, and it's past one and he has to get up early. He is so straight. He could make a lot of money in New York with his looks. Fuck, what am I saying? Oh well. Tomorrow at this time, I'll be on the road, free and easy, and I'll think back at th . . ."

He stopped writing as he heard the front door open. Frank came down the hall.

"You still up?" Frank said in his Ohio accent, where the word "wash" is pronounced "warsh" and O's sound almost British. "I'm sorry, Eugene, I got into a big argument with Stephie. We drove to Mount Lookout to talk, and you know, I guess, how women get, so wound up, and the next thing you know they're pawing at you." Frank slapped the sole of Eugene's exposed foot.

Eugene playfully kicked out at his brother, losing half his cover, and made sure that what was over him covered his mid-section where his cock had swollen. "So, little brother, you couldn't come home early to spend some time with me, huh?"

He felt the rush subsiding. It was odd, he thought, how when he wrote, concentrating on the words he was spelling out, he would get an erection, just like when he woke from a sleep. He once wrote that his cock "has a mind of its own."

Frank unbuttoned his shirt. His chest was muscular. His arms were tan from his construction job. He dropped his trousers and said, "Well, I told you, Gene, Stephie was crying and that just cuts through me like a knife and she knows it, but shoot, what could I do? Anyways, I'm here now. So tell me, what's the ladies like up there in the big city?" His shoes were, like Melvin's always were, on the front porch. He stood before Eugene in his underwear and socks. A beautiful man. Innocent.

Eugene thought how much difference a few years in the real world makes. He saw himself in Frank. He saw Melvin in Frank. "The ladies are great," he said, resting his head on his hand, checking out his brother's body as brothers could. "They're real 'lookers' as Daddy would say. You know you really have been working out, man. It shows. The ladies would eat you up up there." Eugene thought of what Charity would have to say about Frank Goessler, and he laughed to himself.

Frank flexed his arms out for Eugene. "Yeah, I guess there's something good about working all them hours at Confab, but shoot, I'll never be as tight as you."

Eugene whistled and kicked out at his brother's knee. "Who are you kidding, man, the most weight I've been lifting is my backpack. You look dynamite."

Frank laughed, "Shoot," and then felt oddly exposed, remembering what he'd heard about Eugene. He stopped showing off his body and looked away.

Eugene resolved to start taking better care of his own body once he got to Katherine's and cleaned up his act.

Frank sat down opposite Eugene. His grin had faded. He said, "So, you want a beer or something?"

"None left," Eugene continued to study him, sounding like his own accent was returning. "Sorry, man. I drank the three bottles that were in the fridge."

Frank removed his socks. "Well, that's just as well anyways, Gene. We've got to get up bright and early if you want me to drive you out to the interstate before I go to work. Shoot.

Oooooooeeeee, my feet smell ripe," he hooted, getting under his blanket.

Eugene detected a long distance between their two beds, and wondered if it was because he was stoned, or because Frank wanted it that way. "Mother flipped out tonight," he said. "She threw the potatoes across the kitchen and broke the handle on the cupboard. It was really bizarre. I'd forgotten in a way what fun it was to eat here. She blew my mind."

Frank didn't sympathize, but stared up at the ceiling, and mumbled, "I'll see if I can fix it for her."

Eugene continued looking across to his brother, looking through the lamplight that illuminated the three framed photos, over to his brother's head. He said nothing. What had happened? Did Frank accept her behavior? He wanted to shake him. "Don't become another Melvin!" He wanted to hold him and promise him protection. He wanted to tell him that everything would work out, but then he realized that Frank was fine. He no longer needed Eugene's support. Eugene thought, "Maybe it's me who needs to be held and told everything will be all right."

Frank felt Eugene's eyes on him and said, "Hey, you gonna get the light?"

"Yeah, sure," Eugene said, switching off into the dark and falling back, just like his brother, flat on his back.

It was quiet. There was only the sound of Frank's clock ticking and the cars speeding along River Road. Since the interstate had been completed, there was three times as much traffic down there. Eugene's eyes were wide open. He was too stoned to sleep. He took a deep breath and let it out slowly, feeling his stomach under the covers to see how tight his muscles were. The air seemed full of things unsaid.

"You thinkin' of marrying Katherine?" Frank asked.

"No."

"Bet she's still real nice," Frank said, remembering her from when Eugene dated her before she was sent to Oakland.

"Yeah, we write each other," Eugene said, "and she always asks how you are, but I don't think either of us are into that whole role-playing wedded bliss trip. Maybe we can live together. I guess that's what I'm going to find out." Then it was quiet again till Eugene asked, "How about you? Are you going to marry Stephanie?"

Frank turned to face Eugene in the dark. "Promise you won't tell Mother," he said in a whisper, "but Stephie and me are unofficially engaged." He sounded excited.

"Far out," Eugene said unenthusiastically.

"We decided that if I don't go to Nam, we'll get married when I turn twenty, so we got engaged, you know, so we would feel right about, you know, doing it."

"Fucking?" Eugene said. "You know, Frankie, we're big boys now and we can say the f-word. You mean you never screwed around?"

"I ain't like you, Gene. I ain't no hippie, if that's what you're getting at." He said the word "hippie" as if he were cursing.

"You think I'm a hippie?" Eugene asked.

There was an affirmative silence.

"And you think I deserted the family, don't you," Eugene continued, "and you think I'm some kind of freak, right?"

"Hey, hey, hey," Frank whispered. "Keep it down. Shoot, Gene, maybe you should think of somebody else for a change. We don't stop living just 'cause you decide to drop in. All I'm saying is I keep my nose clean. I go to church. I pay Mother room and board. Shoot. I may have to go and fight for my country and there's my big brother burning the flag I'm fighting for and doing all the drugs he can find and calling us folks pigs!" He caught himself getting loud, and settled back to a whisper. "Shoot, Eugene, I know you're my brother and you was good to me when we was little, but you're the one who left. Not me. I stayed and owned up to my duties."

Now the room's air was moving. Eugene defended himself. "I've never burned the flag," and then he laughed, that he could be arguing with his own flesh and blood brother over a war that even Republicans were denouncing. "Though, Frankie, wise up. Nobody is for the war anymore. Nobody. Right now they're just trying to figure a way out without too much egg on their faces."

"I'm a hundred and ten, Gene!" he whisper-shouted about his number in the lottery. "You lucked out."

"Listen to me, Frankie," Eugene reached out to dark nothing, "whatever you do, don't go to Vietnam and get yourself killed. You come out to California and we'll hide you till it's over."

Frank laughed. "Why, I'd never do that, Gene."

"Really, man," Eugene conceived a new brother. "It's a big

world. We could see it together. I know ways to make money fast if we need it. Remember how we'd sit at the river and think of where it went? Well, little brother, it goes places! Really. Come with me, now. We could drive your Mustang. We'd have fun!"

Frank continued to laugh. Eugene was always such a big talker and dreamer. The reality of his notion was absurd, though. He couldn't leave his job and his school. Having endured the broken heart of his mother after Eugene left, he couldn't leave Debbie to that. And there was no way he could leave Stephie. Even Clara had changed her tune about her and told him, "for once somebody nice comes around." There was no reason to leave Ohio. It made no sense. "That's your dreams," he said, "not mine. Mine's to make a good life and raise a good family and have a big house with no steps. A ranch style with a double garage."

"Jesus," Eugene moaned.

"Bet that's the first time you've prayed to the Lord in a while," Frank said.

Eugene sat up. "Man, you sound like fucking Melvin! Do you hear yourself?" He lit a cigarette. "Frankie, you're freaking me out. You've bought the whole thing, haven't you? Man," Eugene had to laugh or cry, "I'm just blown away this time, Frankie, it's like you've given up, man. You've blown my mind, fuck!"

"From what I hear, it's not only your mind that's been blown."

"What are you talking about?"

"Nothing."

Eugene was shocked. What was he saying? How could Frankie know about what he did in New York? The only person he'd seen from his past was Katherine and she was living in Oakland when she came to see him. There was no way he could know what he was implying. "Just what the fuck do you mean, man?"

"Don't worry," Frank said almost paternally, "I'll never tell Mother."

Eugene's heart was pounding and sweat poured from his upper lip and brow. His ears were ringing as if he'd been punched in the head again. He was thankful the room was dark because he knew he reeked of guilt. He told himself that there was some strange mixup of words going on. Then he defended himself saying, inside the noise, "It's no big deal. It's cool. Love. It's not like I'm the only guy who's ever hustled for a few bucks." He demanded from Frankie, "You never will tell Mother what?" There was silence from Frankie's side, "Tell her what, man?"

Frank took a big breath and said, "Well . . . well, it's like this. Stephie's aunt lives next door to Katherine's mother up on Backbone Road, and when Katherine stopped to see her mother after seeing you in New York, she told her mother that you'd gone queer on drugs."

Eugene's mind worked quick. "Yeah? And you believed that? Man, why didn't you ask me about it? You said so yourself. 'Women are crazy,' and dig this, when Katherine came to see me, I was seeing this beautiful woman, Andrea Superstar, and Katherine was real suspicious, so I told her I was with a guy."

"Why?"

"Because . . . damn, I figured she wouldn't be as jealous, and that kind of thing goes on in New York all the time. Really," he laughed. "Some guys do it for money. Real easy money."

"And you let her think you were queer?"

Eugene took a deep breath, relieved that the story sounded plausible, and Frankie was buying it. "Hey, I was in a corner. It was real crazy, and it was no big deal. I mean, even if I had done it, so what? No harm done? A few extra dollars. And Katherine can be real uncool sometimes, because believe me, little brother, you know me, and you know that when we did it, she had no doubts about my sexuality. Jesus."

It was quiet. The air was empty, deflated, exhausted in the room. Eugene waited to hear how his story sat with his brother.

"Shoot," Frank said. "I guess I was so mad at you for leaving here that I wanted to believe you had gone to hell."

"Yeah," Eugene sighed, now feeling like a hypocrite. "Well, I don't buy the hell thing anyway, Frankie. I know some queers who are fine people. In New York, people don't care what you do in your own bed. It's not like the fucking Catholic bishops who are jerking off in the confessionals when they hear something that turns them on, and then turning around and condemning the sinner."

"I pray for you," Frank said.

"Thanks," Eugene said, getting out of bed and lighting a cigarette, so that for one flash of fire, Frank saw his brother's tall body, naked and sweating, "I'm going out on the porch for some fresh air."

"Like that?" Frank asked.

Eugene said, "Yeah, this is exactly how I was instructed to dress for the big party. Didn't you get your invitation, little brother?"

"I don't get it," Frankie said. "You're a weirdo, Gene, a real weirdo."

Eugene left the room and went out to the porch and smoked and rocked in the old aluminum chair and unconsciously played with his balls while he listened to the traffic through the trees and thought, "I'll never sit here again."

When he returned to Frank's room, he saw the clock glowing 3:34 and heard his brother rustle. He got in bed, feeling an overwhelming sadness.

"Wish you was staying longer," Frank said, half asleep.

Eugene said nothing.

A few minutes later Frank said, "Nitey-night," just like Melvin would have, and Eugene felt the lump in his throat crack and rise to tears, and he said, "Yeah, nitey-night, little brother."

Out on the interstate, Frank had stopped the Mustang, and the two brothers hugged awkwardly. Eugene patted the rusted hood and said, "Take care of Deb."

Frank said, "I'm going to refinish it," about the condition of the car's body. Then he got back in and made a U-turn and yelled back to Eugene, "Marry Katherine!"

1972, California

Eugene hitchhiked from Ohio to the cabin Katherine's father owned. She and her stepbrother, Scott, were living there, getting into nature. Her father had married Scott's mother in Oakland. Dora, the new wife, helped convince Katherine's father to "let the kids go find themselves, you can't say you ever use that old property." Katherine had dropped out of Berkeley. Scott had dropped out of UCLA and had just returned from India. The cabin was on forty acres of woods and fields and had the Clear River running past it.

"Oh, Eugene," Katherine said when he arrived, "you look so wasted."

He had been on the road for twelve days, including the stay in Ohio. He was dirty and thin and exhausted. He was jittery and overwhelmed by all the events of his journey. He had used up the cocaine Charity had given him in New York way back in Ohio, and he was worried that he was cracking up. Katherine swore he could pass for thirty.

"Come with me," she said, leading him down the path to the river.

Katherine had changed. She was no longer the modern teen beauty from Ohio, and she was no longer the pretty coed she'd seemed like when she visited him in New York City. She was now "natural" in bared feet, full auburn sunned fuzzed hair, sunburnt skin without makeup, and a loose white gauzy dress that was embroidered with vines and flowers and grapes on the skirt. He followed her. She seemed like Eve or an earth goddess, treading over the twigs snapping at her feet, pushing back green

113

arms of brush, and turning to look back to him with a demure knowing smile, as if she knew how to fix him up. He felt the interstates fading away, becoming gibberish in his head. He wanted to cry, as if he'd been lost and had finally been found.

At the river, there was a little sunny clearing spread with a blanket and clotheslined with a few towels and a pair of cut-off blue jeans that Eugene assumed were Scott's.

"We do our wash here, on the rocks," Katherine said, pulling her dress off. "We call this the grotto." She stood before him naked; her entire body was tan. "There's a deep part over there," she said, wading into the river.

Eugene checked himself, self-conscious at being dared to strip. He laughed at how confused his morals were. He had practically survived on nudity back in New York, and yet, there in the broad daylight, he felt embarrassed. He pulled his boots off. They stank. He took off his shirt, then his socks, and then with Katherine calling for him to come on in he pulled down his jeans . . . no brief/figleaf. Into the river he sank, his arms up, the water cold, and his feet sinking in the muddy underwater bank. "Fuckin' California!" Eugene splashed, waking up, coming to, feeling like he'd found Eden.

They came out dripping and fell onto the blanket. He told Katherine that he wanted to sleep, afraid that her strokes along his back were intended to arouse him. They had never fucked. Even on her trip to New York, where he'd planned to show everyone, including himself, that he was totally heterosexual, it hadn't happened. So far, in his life, he'd fucked four women, but not Katherine. She was, in his mind, "the one." And because of that, he was scared. In New York, he couldn't get an erection with her, and blamed it on being too drunk one night, when they'd come in from a long night at Max's, and the next night he blamed it on drugs and the fact that Nelson and Moody Sue were in the apartment.

"Sleep, baby," Katherine purred, squeezing his long wet hair.

When he woke up, he was alone, naked on the blanket, out of the sun, looking up at the shimmering light on the trees reflected from the little rippling river. Eugene stared. He recounted scenes from the long trip. He heard Frank's accusations. He saw the waitresses, so honey farmed and smiling in Iowa, and remembered feeling his cock harden at the thought of fucking either one of them, they were twins, out in the cornfield. He saw the truck driver from Missouri, the sky, the gravel at the rest stop, the "hey Joe, where you goin with that gun in your hand?" come-on. That truck driver. The come that burned like poison when the guy drove off, leaving him without the promised ride. He replayed the scene, swearing it was not his scene anymore. "For money, or in the films, for art maybe," he had said somewhere in Nevada, "but for a fucking trucker hick, never, never again."

He heard Katherine's laugh, off somewhere. He heard the exotic sound of the sitar. He realized he was unconsciously playing with his balls, rolling them in his hands, something he'd done since he was a kid in the top bunk on River Road. They felt like shelled hard-boiled eggs. Paolo Certiano, the famous avant-garde photographer in New York, had taken a series of what he called "eggshots" of Eugene's balls. Black and white close-ups. Eugene's eggs were in six of the series at the exhibition. He had written to Katherine, telling her his balls were hanging on Fifty-seventh Street, and he'd included copies of the raves. Paolo would snort cocaine and eat deviled eggs during shoots. "He's an egghead," Andrea Superstar had said to Eugene. Charity called him Snowbird. Paolo would say, "Charity, just remember, snakes lay eggs too."

Eugene's balls had always been a comfort to him. When he'd fucked, both women and men, he would reach down and hold them tight, then let them go, feeling them slap against the skin. There, under the trees, the trucker's rough face returned to him, and the dark feelings and the release of lust with him in the truck.

He found himself jerking off, shooting off, remembering how weak and torn he'd felt when the man had forced himself up his ass, and now, recoming, he dug deeper vows, "No way, no way will that ever happen to me again."

Tainted, drugged-out, and spent, Eugene tried to understand why the memory of the trucker who fucked him remained so vivid, turning him on. He couldn't peg it. That was all in the past. He whimpered slightly, there alone in the nature he'd sought out, lamenting how sexually screwed-up he felt. He'd come all over himself. He had done exactly what he had sworn he would never do again. The only way to appease his torment, he swore, was to let himself get tied up with Katherine. Fuck. Settle down, safe.

Eugene felt he was at the threshold of a new life for himself. He had made certain resolutions on this trip: He would stop relying on drugs to make him feel good. He would seriously practice the guitar, if he could find one. It made no sense to bring the twenty-dollar one across country with him. And he would straighten out his head about sex. In New York, he'd been told that his reputation was that of someone who would "do anything for money, and not a lot of money." "I didn't argue about the price," he explained, "because, man, I was getting off on it." He had tried to get listed with a legitimate talent agency, and get work doing commercials or ads or a role in something, but his reputation from the underground scene surfaced before him, and no agency would take him on.

"Once you've been shot shooting or being shot into, cowboy," Charity told him, "you are dead to Madison Avenue and the bigshots. Consider yourself lucky."

Eugene climbed the trail, away from the river, away from his thoughts of the long hitchhike, away from his sooty past, toward the light. The sound of the brush and trees and twigs and bees seemed loud. He no longer heard the sounds of the sitar or Katherine's laughter. He saw a brighter sky up farther, and hoped that there he would find the woman and her stepbrother. He felt the soft mulch on his bare feet. He had the idea that he might be lost and that the reason he no longer heard them was that he was walking away from their sounds. He decided that he would at least get to the top of the trail. He stopped to listen for something human. He heard the river trickling and birds tweeting. Then he saw, at the top of the hill, at the crest of the trail, a figure appear, lit from behind, coming down toward him. It had to be Scott. It wasn't a woman. He saw long blond hair, not Katherine's long brown hair, and the man was carrying an odd-shaped case, a sitar case, he decided, and Eugene made out more features as they approached each other. Scott looked so Californian, like a hippie surfer, he thought, seeing Scott's tan against his white gauzy loose pants. He wore no shirt. His chest was brown. His hair was blond straight and swaying with his steps toward Eugene. He was as tall as Eugene, barefoot, and wearing a bell on a band around his waist. He had a blue feather tied to some strands of hair near his ear, and a big white smile that grew as the two men neared each other. He had penetrating light blue eyes that made Eugene briefly look away, as if he were noticing too much of someone he was passing on a New York street.

"Eugene?" Scott said, extending his free hand, and then setting the sitar case down and extending the other.

"Scott?" Eugene said, moving to shake his hand, but being pulled into a hug.

"Welcome."

Eugene's bare chest pressed against the sun-warmed chest of the Californian and he could smell sandlewood incense in his hair. Eugene's hair was hardly blond compared to the lightness of Scott's. He awkwardly maintained the embrace, as if it were some sort of challenge as to who would let go first, proving who was most open and loving and hip and Eugene kept thinking, *surfer*. He felt so much like a New Yorker. Like he was out of his element. Like he was an artist and a talker and a reader and not a dreamy sunburned sleepwalker. Thinking that made him confident enough to let go of Scott's shoulders and step back.

"Thanks," Eugene said, taken by the natural beauty of Scott, there in the green light, the transcendental surfer in such exotic flimsy sultan pants. They were held up by a colored rope. "Is that your sitar?" he asked Scott, referring to the case.

"Yeah," he smiled, "I'm learning. I was in India. You hardly look like the pictures Katherine has shown me."

Eugene took that to mean that he looked awful, just as Katherine had said earlier, that he looked thirty. "It's been a long trip," Eugene explained. "I must have fallen asleep down at the river. It's beautiful here."

"Yeah," Scott bent to pick up the case. "I'm going to catch some sleep myself, now. It seems we have all left time behind, you know? Katherine is up in the clearing. I'll see you guys later. Welcome, man."

"Thanks," Eugene said. "I'd like to hear you play."

"You will, sure thing," Scott said, heading down the trail.

Eugene was flustered. He watched Scott's back muscles and the fall of his pants over his rounded ass. His hair was like cornsilk hanging down his tan spine. He seemed so healthy to Eugene. Katherine had mentioned in a letter that Scott had no use for the material world, and Eugene thought, with a defensive smirk, "I bet he owns that sitar," and then he ran his fingers through his own messy tangle of blond hair, trying to bring it to order to look better for Katherine. He ached for some cocaine to lighten him up.

The clearing was burning in the May sunlight. Katherine was sitting on a blanket in her white cotton dress, embroidering the hem of its skirt, which was pulled up, exposing her unshaven legs, showing a light brown down. Her hair seemed lighter and curlier and longer as it blew in the touches of wind, much different from what he remembered down at the river. He stood for a moment, looking, as his eyes adjusted to the light. She seemed so peaceful and graceful and familiar. He felt relieved to be there in so much green, in so much light, and he said to himself, "I've made it."

Katherine looked up and waved, covering her upper thighs with the skirt, "Eugene Goessler, come-eer!" she sang out, with still a midwestern accent.

She watched him walk across the field in his jeans. His shirt and shoes were down at the river. He was pale and thin, and his eyes seemed sad, not at all the funny light she remembered. He seemed unhealthy, but she would remedy that.

"Howdy," Eugene said, with his thumbs hitched in his belt loops. He knelt and touched his lips to hers in the kind of "greeting kiss" he'd learned in New York. "What a green spot!"

"By July it'll be brown," Katherine said. "You slept for hours." She made room on the blanket for him to sit. "Poor baby, you look so tired." She touched his face, which was not pale, but burnt from standing on the highways. His eyebrows were blond-red and freckles crossed his nose. His green eyes were puffed from sleep and they closed at Katherine's sweet touch. He wanted to bury his face in her and make the rest of everything disappear.

This was salvation, he thought. She would help him get straight, in all ways. Maybe Charity was right when she said he might end up her old man and never return to New York, and maybe his brother Frank was right when he yelled at him at the Indiana border to marry Katherine. He nuzzled his way toward her breasts.

"Your hair is a mess, baby," she said, cradling his head. She picked through it with one hand and petted his brow with the other. "Did you meet Scott on the trail?"

"Mmm-hmm," Eugene said, not wanting to talk. He remembered when they would go to the drive-in in Ohio, and fall asleep in each other's arms. They never had "gone all the way," but Eugene swore to himself that that event would soon be history.

"Isn't he fantastic?" she stroked.

"Mmm-hmm."

"I told him all about you. About all the fun we had in Ohio and how we were so crazy and unlike the rest. I only met him a few months ago when he got back from India. His mother, Dora, God, she's such a trip. She's really into my dad. And she adores Scott. My dad thinks he's another goddamned hippie, but he acts like he likes him. Maybe for Dora's sake. He thinks I've turned into a hippie too, ever since I quit Berkeley, but I just let him go on. He thinks God knows what is going on out here. Probably thinks me and Scott got something going, but I think he was glad to get rid of us. He said he didn't want any rent, but Scott and I decided to pay him fifty dollars a month, you know, to prove a point."

"Mmm-hmm."

She took a deep breath as he did. "Oh, Eugene, I was so glad when I got your letter. I really was so worried about you." She sighed, and then said softly, "When I visited you and saw how you were living and all those crazies you had me meet, God, it was like you were gone. Like you were a different person."

Eugene spoke sideways at her breasts. "You thought I'd gone queer. Frank told me."

"Your brother Frankie? How would he know anything?"

"He said you told your mom, and his girlfriend's aunt lives next door to your mom."

Katherine tried to remember. "I don't know what I said. I guess I was pretty upset when I visited her on my way back to Oakland. She never liked us being together. Remember all the stuff she accused us of doing? As if we were screwing around all the time, and I would say, 'I only wish!' "

Eugene felt guilty for not screwing Katherine. It was him, not her. He somehow felt that it wasn't just him being hesitant, but there it was, even back then, she was wanting to fuck. He wondered if he should try right there in the clearing.

"So I probably said, 'See Mom, Gene has gone off the deep end and doing everything you've suspected of us, and he's even having sex with men for favors.' "

Eugene pushed himself up to her lips and kissed her. She tasted salty and smelled of sandalwood. "What made you think that?" he kissed her again.

"Sue told me. She said you were a hustler. She seemed to think it was no big deal."

"Moody Sue," Eugene said, thinking how out of place she would be in a field.

"And I think she wanted to hurt me. She's always resented me and my looks, I know that. She's really so overweight. Even as a child she was heavy. It's all that sugar she eats. For all her reading, I don't think she's ever read a label of ingredients. Our families were never that close, probably because New Yorkers think they're so much better."

Eugene resented Katherine's tone of voice. He wasn't surprised that Sue had said something like that, but he found himself almost missing her, almost delighted that she had said no big deal to Katherine. So Moody Sue, he thought, was the cause of that hellish night back in Ohio with Frank. He laughed. "She does love her sweets."

Katherine made some distance between their faces, and looked into Eugene's eyes for the truth. "Well? Were you?"

Eugene was remembering Charity for a second. "Yeah, I guess, a little, you know, for the money. It *was* no big deal."

"You mean you had sex for a fix, like an addict?" Katherine wanted to clarify.

"Yeah," Eugene agreed. That sounded true without being a denial or an acceptance. "Really, does it matter? I just don't like hearing that I'm a queer from my little brother."

"Well, I was worried about you, Gene. I really was. Those so-called friends of yours were so spaced out, but I guess living in such a big mess of a city does it to you. It was depressing there."

Eugene was resenting more and more Katherine's obvious judgments. She seemed so prudish, but then he remembered her stripping naked at the river, and that had made him feel prudish. She was only saying things that he'd told himself over and over. The city was disgusting and the people were all burnouts. He tried to get back down to Katherine's breasts where he'd felt so comfortable. "Let's not talk about New York for a while," he said, feeling like a little boy pretending, and he told himself that that was all right to feel.

"You're right," Katherine started stroking again, "that's the past, and you're here now, and you need to forget. I have a great book for you to read."

Eugene pressed with his head, "Mmmmmmmm."

"It's so high. It'll really help you. Scott gave it to me. *Be Here Now.* I just know it will help you, baby."

Eugene could hear her heart beating.

"Are you falling asleep?" Katherine spoke softly.

"Mmm-mm," Eugene uttered into the embroidery, "I just feel so good and quiet. I would like to sleep for a week, right here, with you."

Katherine kissed his ear and whispered, "I love you, baby, you are so handsome and strong. You'll get better."

"I love you, too," he whispered.

"Mmmmmm," Katherine smiled, "I've waited for so long for you to come to me."

The eucalyptus trees shimmered in a breeze that crossed the clearing. Hills were visible for miles. A jet stream was visible miles up from a plane passing from Anchorage to Los Angeles.

"Look at that," Katherine said, pointing to the white line that divided the blue sky in half.

Eugene rolled his head to see, squinting in the light. "There are people up there drinking coffee and reading magazines," he said, "and eating nuts."

They adjusted themselves so that they could both lie on the blanket, facing each other, holding each other, and Katherine sang, "naptime," and it sounded just like when June would make him play house with her when they were little, and she would always sing, "naptime," and then "wake-up time," and Eugene said to June in his head, "California, June, look where I am."

They put their heads together and kissed. Katherine said, "Welcome to the first day of the rest of your life." Eugene had sold the poster with that saying in Patchouly, the head shop on St. Mark's Place. He was very cynical about posters and their love and peace messages. He always pictured them in a weekend hippie's bedroom in the suburbs. He hated his reaction there on the blanket, judging Katherine, and he kissed her again, accepting the new beginning with her tongue. Then his fear of sexual performance surfaced, and he wondered if they were about to fuck, and what passion he was feeling in his mouth turned to a yawn that he fought, but had to release.

"Oh, baby," Katherine whispered, "let's sleep. I don't want to rush anything anymore. You're here, and that's all that matters."

"Wipe out," Eugene said, "that's California talk, right?" He yawned big and freely and for a moment craved cocaine, knowing if he had some he would not be tired and he would be one hell of a horny stud.

Katherine yawned and held Eugene at his jean button, her fingers dipping into his trail of pubic hair. He jerked at the threat that she might explore deeper, hoping to find a hard cock aching for her, and he tried to send a signal to his cock to be alert. He felt that if he hadn't wasted his come thinking about the truck driver, he might be ready for her. He yawned again.

"Hang ten," Katherine smiled, and closed her brown eyes and maintained her hold on his jeans.

He relaxed. He saw her eyelids move. She was a natural beauty, he thought, no makeup, no hairstyle, just her tan skin and long lashes and full pink lips that held the slightest smile, a smile he felt responsible for. He closed his eyes, telling himself to cool all the thoughts and let go.

He dreamt that June was surfing. She waved to Eugene. She was in a beach party movie and the surf was a backdrop, she was really just tilting back and forth in front of the camera. Paolo Certiano was the director. He yelled for June to shake her teats and wiggle her ass and "show us what you've got!" June looked frightened and Eugene told Paolo to leave her alone. Paolo said, "One more shot, cowboy," and he pointed to a white line of cocaine that was set on a mirrored table, "you do that and let me do this," and he grabbed at Eugene's crotch, trying to shove his camera down his pants. Eugene said no, but was laughing, embarrassed that June was seeing this sort of behavior, and he tried to figure some way that he could snort the coke, push Paolo out the way, and save June from being exploited. June screamed, "Help me!" and Paolo held him face down on the coke mirror. June was being stripped. Eugene struggled, not wanting to spill the coke. She screamed, "Help me Eugene!" and the table shattered and Paolo fell through the floor and Clara came in with her hands on her hips and screamed, "All right! That's just about enough! Now both of you are going to get the belt! Look at this mess! You are the worst children on earth, I swear to God!"

Eugene opened his eyes to the setting sun. He was so thankful that it was only a dream. Katherine was sitting up, embroidering, her back was bent over her skirt. He reached out to her and she turned her face to him. She was a skeleton. Her face was a skull with slivers of flesh hanging like wash on each bone. He screamed and ran to Route 101 South. He ran crying, having nowhere to go. He knew he couldn't go home and he couldn't go back to New York, and he couldn't stay in California. He ran with the traffic, thinking he wasn't hitching correctly because no one was stopping for him, and then he was at the ocean. The highway was gone and he was in hot burning sand. He was thirsty. June ran past him with a surfboard, wearing a little yellow polka dot bikini. He called to her, "June! You're all right?" She laughed and kicked a splash at him. He called, "You're not hot?"

"No, silly, just drink this," and she waved her arms out around her displaying the ocean.

He knelt down at the communion rail that lined the beach at the surf's edge.

"Drink this and remember me," she said, surfing by.

He bowed his head and it went under water. He drank, swallowing and swallowing, wanting to swallow more and more till his thirst would be quenched forever. Everything would be fine, he realized, there was so much water to drink. He lifted his head and saw June surf by doing a handstand. She'd prided herself on handstands when she was a little girl.

"Come on, Eugene! You can do it!" she sang to him from the surfboard.

"I can't!" he whined like a little boy.

"Then catch this," she said, throwing him her baby. "Eugene! Catch the baby!"

He ran along the sand as the baby sailed slowly through the sky. June screamed, "The baby! Catch him! The baby!"

Katherine shook him awake. He had been mumbling and panting and sweating beside her. "Baby, baby, it's all right, you're just dreaming."

He could hear her familiar voice, but was afraid to open his eyes, afraid that it was a ploy to get him to look at her horrible skeletal face. He covered his eyes with his hands. "This better not be some sort of mind-fuck!" he ordered the unconscious. .Then he opened one eye at a time, seeing gold light between his fingers.

Katherine petted his forehead, brushing back the sweat-wet strands of hair, and soothed, "It's okay, baby, everything is fine."

With his eyes only permitting gold light to reach them, he asked, "Are you dead? Am I dead?"

She laughed, "Awww, baby, we're alive. More alive than those poor souls in the city, and we're together now. It's fine, really." She ran her hands over his chest, through the curly hairs and round and round his nipples. "Such a sweet man," she whispered, "I'm here for you."

He peeked through his fingers. Katherine had flesh. She was smiling and her skin was radiant. Her brown eyes watered as they caught Eugene's. She had the comfort and unconditional love of the Virgin Mary emanating from her face. He dropped his tense arms to the blanket and heaved a sigh of relief.

"God, what a dream," he said, then a laugh rose, a delight at the reality of being in the field, in the clearing, even if it too was a dream, it was breathtaking. "I was gone," he said, falling back to the blanket and seeing the full sky. "Look at that!" he pointed up to light-years away where blue was born.

"What?" Katherine asked, looking and seeing, not even another jet stream.

"The dream . . . the blue . . . uh, I don't know how to say it," he said, feeling dry, needing water or something.

"Are you thirsty?" Katherine asked, touching his lips with her finger.

"Mmm-hmm," Eugene said, feeling like he was falling for her, maybe for real.

At the cabin Katherine and Eugene and occasionally Scott would play at talking hillbilly talk. Eugene had tried to eliminate his accent during his first year in New York, but it was easily recaptured. The drawl of his Kentucky parents was as familiar as his teeth. Katherine, who had lived in Ohio all of her life till she was seventeen, had an ear for the sound of Kentucky.

She would play Lulubelle to Eugene's Zeke. If Scott joined them, they made him be Junior, the idiot chile, so he rarely joined them. The first weeks that Eugene was there, he was torn between his need to mate with Katherine and his denied attraction to Scott. Somehow, Eugene felt that all of his encounters and affairs in New York could be considered sowing wild oats if he could settle in to an affair of the heart, with Katherine. He was drawn to Scott, and therefore spent those first weeks trying to ignore him.

One morning, as light was pouring through the little window up in the cabin loft, Eugene woke with a throbbing hard-on. He rolled on to Katherine and entered her dry, waking her. She pushed him off, angry, telling him he was unfair. Then she fell back asleep. He climbed down the ladder and went outside, sweating with despair at his futile attempt. He was getting deeper and deeper, worried about his sexuality, telling himself it was a case of do or die. Then he would hear Charity's voice telling him to "Relax and enjoy the party. Water finds its level when it's not dammed or tampered with." He shook her from his thoughts and pumped water from the well for the garden, even though it wasn't his turn. He heard Frank's accusation. He really loved Katherine. He knew that. So why was it that he could not fuck her?

Later in the morning, Katherine appeared at the garden.

"It was my turn to water," she said.

Eugene brushed the sweat from his face, leaving a streak of mud from his hand in its place. His face was red from the sun. His hair was golden. Katherine smiled. Their eyes met and diverted, like opposed magnets.

"Are you pissed at me for this morning?" Eugene asked.

"No," she said, looking at the green tomatoes.

"You're sure?" Eugene felt his heart breaking in sad kicks as he held himself back from falling to his knees in tears and begging for her to understand him, as if her understanding would somehow rub off on him.

"Why shucks, Zeke, I'm jest a happy-go-lucky farm-girl. I don't need your molly-coddling. Hell, all us mules go in for that dry humping."

Eugene tried to smile. "You *are* mad, aren't you? I'm sorry, Katherine. I don't know what came over me." Here, he could have been honest and told her that in desperation he didn't want to pass up one of the few erections he'd had with her, knowing that they were both wanting to do it. Instead he lied and said, "I was just so hot for you, I had to take you. I lost all sense."

"Well, now, Zeke, maybe come next time, you'll let me in on your intentions while I'm wide awake."

Feeling stronger having lied, he buried his name and became Zeke. "You come right here now, Lulubelle, and give me a smack. I deserve it."

"I bet you'd like some smack," Lulubelle said as Katherine, then Katherine was buried and Lulubelle started to chase Zeke with the pitchfork, taunting him, "I'll stab your butt, Zeke! I'll tell them revenuers where yer still is!"

Zeke ran down the trail and fell against the cabin. Lulubelle caught him and stuck the pitchfork in the dirt near his feet. He felt his cock harden. He saw it through his cutoffs. He looked up to Lulubelle and slyly broke into a grin. "Looks to me like the sausage needs to be put in the old smokehouse, Lulubelle."

Lulubelle swayed and smacked her lips. "Oooie, Zeke, I was jest a hankerin for some fresh farm sausage. " She lifted her dirty skirt, showing her cunt and ass, dark-haired and tan. She danced from one foot to the other, still holding him captive by the power of the pitchfork. Then Zeke caught her by the arm and spun her closer and said in a low-down and dirty voice, "Woman, I've a mind to have you right here, next to the house, you tauntin and teasin me like that."

"What about the idiot chile?" Lulubelle asked, wetting the leg she straddled saddling Zeke.

"Junior went to town early, dreamboat."

Lulubelle laughed.

Zeke was being fed by the men in Eugene's early life. The men he'd met that Melvin worked with at the foundry, or bowled with, or drank with, or went to Crosley Field with to watch the Cincinnati Reds games. They took their women and screwed them. At least that was what Zeke was feeling. A real man had the power to make any woman wet. Those men back in Ohio had no doubts. No worries. They were always ready to fuck.

Zeke pulled Lulubelle with him into the weeds, laid her down as she undid his cutoffs, letting his cock bounce free. He sweated and entered her. She was wet and moaning. Somewhere in his senses, he smelled the stale beer of a saloon. He said, "You like this, don't you girl? Huh? Answer me, woman! Take me. You want me. I give you the time of your life, don't I?" Lulubelle moaned and scratched and wriggled and squirmed beneath him.

"Oooooo, baby!" Lulubelle shouted. "Come on, you Kentucky stud!"

Genuine heaves and spasms began to take hold of Zeke's persona as Eugene felt come rising. He held back, laughing, relieved of all his doubts, till Katherine's moves brought him to release. He yahooed, proving the past was the past. "I love you, Katherine," he whispered hot in her ear.

Katherine looked into his eyes. They both cracked into joyous laughter, having finally overcome years of waiting. The spot where they did it would be holy, they decided.

1962, Ohio

"You have a choice," the book, *Catholic Youth: Take the Hard Road*, read. "You can pray to Jesus Christ or you can prey on girls. You can build a strong body at the gym, or you can sashay about the dance floor like a ballroom sheik. You can join the Legion of Decency, or you can join the Legion of the Damned. You can go to heaven, or you can go to hell." The book was distributed to all seventh-grade boys. It was the church's version of a facts-of-life directive.

Eugene liked the photographs of the musclemen, oiled and flexing in brief swimming trunks, pressing younger bodybuilders of lesser definition above their heads in place of barbells. This was the ideal, according to the book. The next page was a drawing of a gang of spindly pimply teenage boys kicking their legs like chorus girls, with cigarettes dangling from their lips, and empty bottles that read "alcohol" strewn at their feet. Under the drawing was the caption, "Cha-cha-cha in Satan's dance hall."

The chapter on "pastimes" juxtaposed the same weightlifters photographed in their trunks sitting in a semicircle listening to the best-built man reading passages from the New Testament, and on the opposite page there was a drawing of girlie magazines, rock 'n' roll records, and whodunit paperbacks, all floating in what was labeled, "Satan's Slop Bucket."

Eugene and his friends paged through the book hunting for any mention of "sex." All they found was the rule, "No kissing or petting till you are twenty-one, and DO NOT TOUCH YOURSELF."

For weeks after receiving the book, Eugene refused to let June use him as a makeshift dance partner, as she usually did before she went to dances. He also started lifting weights at his friend Bobby Schneider's house.

1972, California

In the cabin, Eugene, Katherine, and Scott read by kerosene lamps and candles. Scott was reading *The Tibetan Book of the Dead* in a brittle old wicker chair beneath a black-and-gold poster that read, "Today is the first day of the rest of your life." His long fine golden hair and his dark tan shimmered in the amber light. His legs hung over the side of the chair, and his toes moved involuntarily back and forth as he read. Katherine was sprawled across the beat-up couch, with two kittens sleeping on her stomach. Her hair was dripping wet from washing it in the bucket. She was reading *Stranger in a Strange Land* and eating avocado slices from a plate on the floor. Eugene was sitting on an Indian blanket that covered a mattress, leaning his back against the wood plank wall of the cabin, wearing only cut-off jeans and no underwear, so that one of his balls protruded out at his thigh. It didn't matter. He'd been there two months and had lost his self-consciousness about being naked, or belching, or farting, or announcing he was going to the outhouse to take a shit. He was reading *Be Here Now*. It was a hot night. Inside the cabin, it was quiet but for the occasional crack of dried wicker under Scott's ass, or the thud of a broken spring under Katherine's ass, or the frequent cough of Eugene, who felt he'd caught some sort of cold, although Katherine suggested that it was his body's way of eliminating all that New York pollution and junk.

Outside, the forest was throbbing. The crickets and cicadas and nightbirds chanted. The moon was a sliver of egg white. The river rippled over rocks, Eugene could hear it. He set the book

129

down and turned his ear to the wall. He took a deep breath and closed his eyes and listened. This was the life. He wanted to be like this forever.

Scott yawned big, stretching out his arms, the book hanging from one hand.

"What did you just read?" Eugene asked him.

"Why?"

Eugene sat up from the wall, "Well, you know Katherine's cousin Sue, Moody Sue, who I lived with, once told me that when you yawn and you're reading or listening to something, it's usually because you didn't get it. You just yawned, so I . . ."

Katherine sighed heavily from the couch, "That's ridiculous. Eyes get tired. Ears get tired. Sue's an idiot."

Scott yawned again, and then laughed on top of it. He said, "If I yawned every time I didn't get something, I'd be yawning all day and night."

Eugene yawned, trying not to, then Katherine yawned, laughing.

"See," Scott said, trying to find what he'd been reading in the book, "ignorance is contagious. Here, Eugene, this is what I read, uh . . . 'O son, whatever you see, however terrifying it is, recognize it as your own projection.' "

All three yawned in unison and then laughed, and then said, "Far-fucking out."

"Shoooot," Katherine said as hillbilly Lulubelle, "I reckon that's devil talk."

"Yep," Eugene said as hillbilly Zeke, "I think Junior, the idiot chile, has been readin highfalutin books cuz he's been hitting the moonshine."

"Yesiree," Scott said, acting goofy, and not sounding hick enough, more cowboy.

Later that night, Scott suggested they all sleep out under the stars on blankets. Katherine lay in the middle. They held hands, staring up at the stars, and talked about space and death and how good it was to be away from "civilization" with all of its politics and deceits and trips. Eugene wondered if the three of them would have sex. He had his arm over Katherine's shoulder, and Scott's head rested on Eugene's hand. He could feel Scott's warm breath on his fingertips. Although he'd been sleeping with Katherine, Eugene found that he was still very drawn to Scott. In his head, he was formulating his theory of bisexuality. He wanted to make a sexual move, but was afraid that Scott would think he was queer, and that Katherine would think he was queer. Sex ruined the night, Eugene thought. Why couldn't everyone just be free?

Then Katherine-Lulubelle said, "If either of you two gents would like to tetch my boosums, yer more than welcome to."

Eugene was still in his cutoffs and Scott was in his white drawstring pants, but Katherine was naked, holding a blanket that she lowered, exposing her chest to the stars. Eugene watched Scott's hand move onto her left breast. He walked his fingers up to Katherine's right breast and laughed self-consciously.

"Don't worry, Eugene," Scott said. "Katherine is my stepsister, not a real blood sister, so it's okay for us to, you know, touch."

Katherine laughed, "But Dad would think it's terrible, mmmmmmmmmmmm, you know, according to the Church, he's not married to your mom, Scott."

Eugene felt jealous that she was responding to Scott's caresses and not his, and he wondered if Katherine had lied to him when she said that she and Scott had never slept together. He moved to suck on her breast, cupping it in his hand and letting his tongue barely touch her swollen nipple. Now she was responding to him, he knew, as her leg rubbed against his.

Scott began kissing her left breast and licking her other nipple, and the young men were head to head, catching each other's eyes momentarily. Katherine moaned and encouraged their legs to cover hers. Scott reached his arm over to Eugene and he began to run his hand up and down Eugene's back. Eugene released a sweet sigh, thinking that it was Katherine's hand on his back, and then he realized it was Scott and he felt embarrassed, as if he'd been too pleased. He started to worry how far they would go, and if he would mimic every move Scott made. Would they both fuck Katherine. Was Scott jealous of Katherine and him? What was sex, anyway? He wished he could stop thinking and let himself go. He stopped sucking on Katherine's breast and announced he was going down to the cabin to get some grass and the pipe. Scott looked up at him, grabbing his hand, and told him to bring the body oil that was on the shelf by the drysink, and before he let go of his hand, he said, "Hurry back, Eugene, we want you."

Eugene looked at Katherine for a reaction, but her eyes were closed. He ran down the trail in the dark, excited and scared, feeling his heart pounding. For the first time in weeks, he wanted cocaine. His ears were ringing. Scott had said he wanted him. Free Love! This was what he'd been trying to tell Katherine one day after they had made love. They were down by the river in the late afternoon. He had overcome his fears and had made love from start to finish as Eugene, not Zeke or anyone else. He was holding Katherine and feeling very pleased and he smoked a Marlboro. Katherine said she wished he would give up such a stupid habit. "How can you inhale smoke, when you could be inhaling all of this clean air?" He told her that he thought she was too opinionated and Catholic. With his new sexuality firmly rooted with her, he felt confident enough to stop condemning his past. He told her that he thought bisexuality was the highest state. Not that he was bisexual, but that it seemed like it was something to consider. He suggested to her that the animal she said he was had many sides, and that the animal she was was afraid to experience anything other than the accepted standard. They didn't really argue, but there was a confusing back-and-forth sentencing that left her feeling like he wasn't satisfied with her, and left him feeling like she was a strict Nature freak, but she got to choose what was "natural." Now she was up on the blanket, and Scott was up on the blanket, and he would join them for a "natural" orgy. He found the body oil that Scott had asked for, and ran out of the cabin and up the trail.

When he reached the blanket, he found Scott's lean ass flexing and pressing into Katherine. Her legs were spread wide, accepting her stepbrother's cock in her. He felt angry that they hadn't waited for him, and then he felt intimidated by Scott's obvious prowess and lust. After all, Katherine was a beautiful woman and it was only his hangups that had kept them petting for years. Scott was a real man. He had no insecurities, he thought, and he was seizing the opportunity to make love to her, with no doubts about it. Eugene also felt betrayed by Katherine, who had only that afternoon implied that they were lovers, and here she was letting her stepbrother fuck her in front of him. Was she proving that she could be free? And did Scott really want him? Or did he want only the body oil to add to his own manly performance? He was tempted to go back down the trail and leave them to their lovemaking. He felt his head pounding and heard his ears ringing over the sound of their panting. He remembered what Scott had been reading earlier. Was all of this his projection? The sight of them doing it was starting to excite him. He stood closer, struck a match and lit the grass in the little stone pipe. The flash of light caught Katherine's eye.

"Oh, Eugene, come down here, baby," she moaned.

He remained standing, wanting more prodding, feeling like his slot was already filled. What was he supposed to do? Rub her forehead as she was fucked? He had imagined something else. He thought that they would explore each other's bodies. He would touch Scott in front of Katherine, and it would be so natural, instead, he was gone a few minutes and there they were assuming the standard position, humping like missionaries. And what Eugene wanted to deny was that his real jealousy was not that Katherine was giving herself to Scott, but that Scott was giving himself to her, and not to him. He hated that he was so jealous, and immediately felt hatred for the Californian wiseass. How dare he! Katherine of course thought that Eugene was jealous of Scott, and said, "Come on, baby, I love you, come down here with us." Scott slowed down and turned his head to look up at Eugene.

"Hey, you're back," he said, pulling strands of his long blond hair away from his mouth, "drop your shorts, man, and come join us."

Eugene shook his head, "No," like a sulking boy, and took another hit from the burning pipe. Katherine reached over and took hold of Eugene's ankle and told him not to be uptight.

"I'm not," Eugene lied, feeling her hot hand rub his leg as high as she could with Scott on top of her.

"Let go," she said, "be free, right?"

"Yeah," Scott said, stopping any further gyration in her, and reaching up to Eugene for the pipe, "we all love each other, man."

Eugene gave him the pipe, and Scott's arm deliberately rubbed Eugene's chest and he lightly punched the Levis button on Eugene's cutoffs.

"Off with'm," Scott smiled his big white teeth, and he put the pipe to his mouth and sucked deep, thrusting himself into Katherine so that she went, "Oh!" and he laughed without letting

out the smoke, and Eugene was impressed by his sexual authority. Scott gave the pipe to Katherine and grabbed Eugene's hand
and pulled him down to the blanket.

"Comeer," he said, letting out the smoke in Eugene's face.

Eugene was kneeling next to them. Scott thrust into Katherine
as she sucked the pipe, and he grabbed Eugene by the back of the
head and pulled him to his face and placed a wide open wet kiss
on Eugene's lips. Eugene momentarily wanted to pull away, but
the sensation was overpowering, the warmth of both of their
bodies and the taste of passion on Scott's mouth pulled him into
their heat. He let Scott's tongue into his mouth and thought,
"Fuck you, Katherine, I don't care what you think."

"Hey, baby," Katherine grasped Eugene's arm, and he thought
she was trying to stop the queer kiss, but she was passing him
the pipe, and she was smiling and looking at him with love in
her eyes and acceptance, and then Scott thrust and her look
changed and then crinkled into a wider smile, and it infected
Eugene and before he could put the pipe to his lips, he fell
toward her and kissed her deeply, setting the pipe somewhere on
the ground. He felt Katherine's tongue darting about and his
tongue dug into her mouth and he felt his cutoffs being unzipped, and he stopped kissing long enough to help Scott get
them off his legs. Scott touched Eugene's cock and he looked at
him and said, "Mmmmmmmm, nice." And Eugene's cock jumped
not so much at the touch as at the sound of Scott's "mmmmmm."
It seemed so real, and not at all wrong or queer. Eugene dropped
back to kiss Katherine, and he felt Scott lead his hand toward
Katherine's cunt. He felt Scott's veins and the moist lips of the
vagina, and the silk wet heat of the moves in and out. He felt
Katherine's tongue and then Scott lowered his head to theirs and
he joined them, kissing, and Eugene wanted to scream with joy
at such delicious moves. He started coming, and pulled back
from them for a moment to get control.

"God!" he cried.

Katherine and Scott laughed, as if they were accustomed to
the action, and again the thought crossed Eugene's mind that
they had done it before, before he'd arrived on the scene. He
squeezed his cock, painfully letting the come subside. And he
rolled back to them, rejoining the kiss and feeling Scott run his
thumb over Eugene's cockhead. Scott pulled him by the dick up

onto Katherine with him, and he moved so that Eugene could try to enter her with him still in there.

"Ow!" Katherine cried out.

"Relax, just relax," Scott said, "let all of your muscles relax."

Eugene was worried about hurting her, but also had little subtlety in his penis control. He remembered the truck driver fucking him and how he screamed in pain, and how within seconds the pain had turned to heat and the heat to pleasure and the pleasure to passion and how he found himself shoving up for more despite his conscious disgust for the act, there in the cab of the truck at the rest stop in Missouri. Katherine took quick gasps of air and thrashed her head side to side. Her dark hair was wet with sweat and flying all over her face. Eugene, with the help of Scott's hand, slid in, along the shaft of Scott's cock, into Katherine, and he was on fire. The three of them lay there still, all gasping and panting, shocked at their accomplishment. The pulsing between the cocks and the quivering spasms in Katherine's cunt were all they felt. Eugene and Scott waited for Katherine to make the first move. As she relaxed into the stretch, she pushed up ever so slightly and again gasped for air. She spread her legs further out and up, and Eugene and Scott each held one over their outside shoulders. Scott was sweating so wet that her leg kept slipping, and each time it slipped, their two cocks would twist inside of Katherine and the three of them would moan, and then laugh, and then cry with pleasure.

Their heads met in a kiss of tongues. Katherine initiated the moves down below. At first Scott and Eugene moved, thrusting in unison, and as that smoothed out, Scott skipped a beat and pushed in as Eugene pulled back, like counterweights. The excitement of Scott's penis running along his own and the hot wet contractions of Katherine's cunt sent sparks and chills through Eugene that only took him further into abandoning any thoughts or consciousness. They became one pulse. The three of them on the floor of the earth, soaring through the dark stars, electric and playing sweet music. Katherine's hands held each of their necks. They churned and growled and licked each other's faces. Salt and hair and tears and then the first of the spasms started in one of them, triggering one after the other and higher and higher gasps and cries. Their voices echoed through the fields and trees. The river sang out for them, gushing and gushing always from then on, as it had been always before. The hot river ran and Scott shot in and Eugene could feel his seed as he shot in and Katherine grabbed all of it, scooping up into her blood their young and powerful passion.

"Yahoo!" Scott howled.

"Yahoo!" Eugene howled, pulling to his knees, out of Katherine.

"Yahoo, hoo, hoo!" the three of them howled, and fell upon each other, laughing and stinging from such a glimpse of life.

In the light of dawn, when the sky was ripening like a peach, Eugene opened his eyes and remembered the passion. He felt a hum in the air, a pink hum that he had usually felt when he was high on pure cocaine. He looked over to Katherine, who was sleeping deep, the blanket twisted up between her legs and over her breasts. Her fingernails were dirty and her hands held the blanket tight. Her brown hair was full of leaves and bits of weed and twigs and tangled glowing almost red in the light. Eugene thought, "And she spent so much time heating water to wash it last night." He smiled. He loved her for being so open and free, and then he looked over to Scott, who had rolled completely off the blankets and was sleeping on his side naked with his back to them. His back! Eugene's mouth opened in awe at the sight of his back, slightly bent, burnt from the sun, his angel's wings must have been freshly cut, he thought, his ass was so smooth and rounded and small like a boy's and his legs stretched out into the weeds, straight and layered in muscle from walking through India, and his long feet pointed out, one big toe twitched. "This is heaven," Eugene whispered to himself, and a flock of birds flew over his head and he fell back asleep with the rising light.

When he woke again, he was sweating in the heat of the overhead sun burning white on him and his mouth was dry and he felt cuts in the soles of his feet. He must have cut them running on the trail, he realized. Katherine and Scott were gone. Two of the blankets were hanging on the line that stretched from the cabin to the big redwood. His cock was hard. He remembered the night. It had been the most sexual night of his life, he thought, and definitely the most honest. He was in love. With two! And they could all live there for the rest of their lives! His heart was full. "Oh, Frankie," he prayed into the hot Califor-

nia light to his brother, "get out of Ohio! There's more to want
than a double garage! And yes, I have had sex with males, but
now I am in love with two gods! June," he repeated her name
over and over starting to cry, "June, June, June sweet sister, help
me keep this feeling, because if anyone can, you can see my
happiness."

"Eugene?" Scott called from the cabin. "Are you up yet?"

Eugene sat up and said to himself, "My love calls," and sang
loud, "I am now!"

His own voice rang in his head and he laughed, thinking of
what he had yelled out at the top of his lungs, "I am now!" and
the book he was reading.

Scott appeared at the trail, wearing his white drawstring pants.
Eugene covered his cock with his hand and smiled at the blond
Californian, feeling an odd embarrassment that maybe he was
the only one who had gotten so off as to be in the throes of love.

Scott walked closer and leaned down to him, reaching out to
touch Eugene's tousled mess of hair, and said deep and sweet,
"Good morning, beautiful."

Eugene rolled backward, laughing with relief, revealing not
only his hard-on, but his ass and his joy. There was no guilt in
this Eden.

"What?" Scott smiled, kneeling down to be closer to the
laughing man. "What'd I say that's so funny, beautiful? Look at
you, so happy. Finally. I think this is the first time I've seen you
so happy."

Tears were streaming from Eugene's green eyes and freckles
were dotting his nose from the direct sun and his hair seemed
more red than gold and he leaned over and kissed Scott's teeth
and said, "I love you." Scott was like a sun god, a surfer Christ,
emanating love from his eyes and smile, and he verified by his
tickling attack under Eugene's arms and playfulness, trying to
slap Eugene's ass, that the night had been no illusion. Eugene
twisted and laughed, fighting Scott's "say-uncle" touch, feeling
like an innocent baby, and a god himself.

"Yeah?" Scott teased, straddling Eugene's waist and holding
his arms out and pressed onto the blanket. "Yeah? Well Katherine and I love you too."

Eugene had a vague memory of being held down by Bobby
Schneider, and felt a drop in the heart that Scott would include

Katherine in his feelings. Eugene knew that Katherine loved him. Why did Scott put it that way? He pushed and kicked and rolled Scott off him, and into the weeds that were flattened from the other blankets.

"Hey!" Scott yelled, surprised at Eugene's aggression, and not wanting to get his white pants dirty. "Enough, beautiful, we're going into town today, I don't have any other clean pants, let up!"

Eugene sat on Scott's smooth chest, his balls resting on his taut stomach and his cock still extended, like a gun pointing in the Californian's face.

"Eat me and I'll let you up," Eugene said, half laughing and half serious.

Scott eyed him and reached out to Eugene's ass, to push him in closer, and he licked his lips and said, "A nibble, that's all, Katherine's waiting, but you are so juicy," and he kept his eyes looking up so blue to Eugene as he slowly licked and took in a few inches beyond the bulb.

"Hey you guys!" Katherine called, coming up the trail in a clean long dress and a rope bag over her shoulder. From the trail she saw Eugene's pink ass being squeezed by Scott's big tan hands. "Hey! Scott! I said wake him up, come on, we've got to get . . ." and then she saw that they weren't just horsing around and Eugene's cock popped out of Scott's mouth as Katherine came into view. Scott wiped his mouth and Eugene rolled off him and back into the bright light and onto the blanket. Scott sat up.

"What were you guys doing?" she asked, looking from Eugene to Scott and then back to Eugene, blocking the sun.

"Playin around," Eugene said, covering his crotch with his hand, while at the same time Scott said, "sucking him off."

Katherine tried to smile, although she was tempted to call them disgusting, but they were "free" she repeated to herself, and they were so handsome there on the ground, and she remembered the night and she shrugged her gut feeling away and said, "Come on and get ready, we've got to get into Graton. Control yourselves, boys, till we get back and then we can all play."

Eugene was embarrassed. He looked quickly at Scott and then away, searching the weeds for where his cutoffs could be. He felt as if he had been reprimanded by his mother. Except Katherine did not fly off the handle, but she still had that "I'm disappointed in you, you've let me down, shame, shame, shame" look about her, or maybe, he thought, that was his projection.

"They're down on the line," Scott said. "Everything was wet from the dew."

Katherine had continued up the trail, past the garden, to where her Chevy was parked. She called back, "Be sure to bring your I.D., Eugene!"

Then Eugene remembered what was going on that day. They were all going to Graton to apply for food stamps.

"Oh, that's right," he said standing with Scott, "I forgot about going into town today." Scott reached over, rubbing Eugene's sticky dickhead, and said, "Later, beautiful." Eugene brushed Scott's back and whacked his butt with spanks to remove the dust and green. He didn't tell him that they were stained.

In the food stamp office, they put down on the application that they were farmers. On the way back up into the hills, they shopped for kerosene, soap, and Joy Jell, which Eugene explained came in flavors and certainly must also be sold out West. By the time they reached the cabin, it had started to rain. It was Scott's day to haul water from the well to the garden, and so he started singing "Truckin" since the fates were on his side. Eugene was disappointed that the health food store in Graton did not sell Joy Jell. Katherine was still bothered by what she had seen the two men doing earlier, and then at the mailbox on the road, Eugene had received a letter from Sue in New York, and he didn't open it as they drove up onto the land. He said he wanted to read it alone. She resented that, too.

They ran through the pouring rain down the trail and into the cabin. Scott and Eugene built a fire in the stone fireplace. Scott had taught Eugene how to build a fire. He had been surprised that the "country boy" didn't know how. Then Eugene climbed the ladder up to the loft where their mattresses were set, separated by thin walls of wainscoting from each other, but all three open to the heat rising from the fire. It was cooking up there, so Eugene crawled back to the end of his mattress and opened the little window and opened the letter from Moody Sue, and read by the light of the fading day, the rain dripping in, streaming

over the sill, and onto his legs. It felt cool. The stationary was
pink.

July 11, 1972

St. Mark's Place, New York City

Dearest Cowboy,

Are you happy? Your postcard was welcomed because we were
all wondering if you made it across country in one piece. Nelson
was here for three days late in May and he is back on tour with
Godspell, still weird as ever. And Charity Ball called and said she
got a card from you. He sounded weird as ever. Or is it "she"?
Charity said to say hi if I wrote to you and to tell you to beware of
women with marriage on their minds, whatever that means. Lots
of calls for you, and I tell them you've gone out, like Kerouac, *On
the Road*, to find yourself. Have you? I'm doing great, of course. I
was working at Brentano's, but now I'm taking summer classes at
the New School and my parents are helping me out. That's the
least they can do. How's my cousin? Has she changed or is she
still uptight and straight? Tell her I said hi. I don't think she likes
me because I'm not into fashion, but maybe she's seen the light?
Don't let her read this, okay? I'm not into Old Britain anymore,
I'm now reading about the thirties in Hollywood and I'm thinking
of having my hair bobbed. I hope McGovern gets the nomination.
I wear his button. Well, New York misses you. That Italian guy,
the photographer, has called a few times for you. Let me know if
you're coming back soon. I'll be your agent. I'm thinking of giving
up chocolate if Nixon gets reelected. Love, Sue (Moody and blue
without you) P.S. I think I've lost eight and a half pounds.

The fire crackled down below. Eugene reread the letter. New
York seemed like another life. He took a deep breath and sighed,
looking out into the rain into the dripping gray-green land,
smelling the wet and the smoke and the tea Katherine was
brewing. He wished that everyone he knew back there could be
in California, to see what real life was like. He crawled to the
edge of the mattress that was open to the room below. He saw
Scott, back in the old wicker chair reading, his legs dangling
over the arm. He watched his belly breathe and the creases in
his tan inflate and deflate. Scott seemed so calm and trouble-
free, content, and he wondered if Katherine could really accept

him loving both of them. Katherine came into view carrying a mug of steaming camomile tea. She climbed two rungs and handed it to Eugene.

"Well," she said, "how's Sue doing? Still pigging out?"

"Don't say that," Eugene's smile faded, "she's a good friend, and she said to say hi to you, and she said that she lost weight."

"Good for her," Katherine said, disappearing back to where the table was.

Eugene took his notebook and answered Sue's letter:

July, 1972

Graton, Sonoma County, California

Moody Sue Hey! I was so glad to get your letter. That's why I'm answering it right away. I'm straight now, not straight in a suit and tie, but straight, no more coke, no acid, and no hustling. God, I was tripped out back there in New York. You should see me now. I am getting real tanned and I barely wear clothes (ha ha, pun intended) and Katherine is much looser. It's all such a trip. We have a garden and a rushing river and a field and last night we slept outside without sleeping blankets because it was so warm, and we became one with the universe. That sounds corny, but then, look who's talking, right? The hillbilly. Tell everybody that I miss them and wish they were here. I really do. This is so clean and right and I'm getting my head together finally, and I'm playing music with Scott, K's stepbrother. He has a sitar and two guitars and a mandolin. I'm writing lyrics to his music. Sue, I really think that he's the first person I've ever met that doesn't have an ego. He's just real cool and laid-back. Remember K said something about him having been in India? Well, it shows. I am learning from him, and fucking my brains out with Katherine. Tell everybody I'm doing good. Me too, blue cause you are faraway Sue, Peace, Eugene.

That rainy night, the three of them pulled the mattress in front of the fire and undressed and sat naked, passing the pipe. Scott faced the fire and Eugene and Katherine were on either side. It seemed religious. This time, it had been Eugene's suggestion. His passion had been awakened. He could safely be with a woman and a man, feeling love for both, the mother and the father, the normal and the wild. They sat quietly, inhaling and holding and exhaling, hearing the rain on the roof and feeling the heat from the fire. Eugene tried to sit as erect as Scott. Foremost in his mind was Scott's body, its beauty and power and perfect proportions, especially in the firelight. He was definitely supernatural. Katherine reached over tenderly with her arm and rubbed Scott's chest. Eugene reached over and daringly, before her eyes, stroked and petted Scott's blond cock. Scott closed his eyes to let himself feel their touches. He knew he had a great body, and he knew that both of them had been after him. He'd seen the looks. He'd been getting their vibes. He was freeing them to let go of their hangups and love with no inhibitions. He was afraid that Eugene was losing perspective, though. He'd noticed him looking and smiling and watching his every move all day, and he saw Katherine becoming jealous, and he'd decided that that was what she had to work through, to learn that she could not control people. He would be their teacher. He was two years older than both of them, and he had aligned himself with the higher planes of life, seeing the folly of mankind. They were both so hungry for him, he thought, wanting to suck his energy. Yes, they could have him. He loved them. He loved all mankind. Eugene started pumping Scott's half-erect cock, and Katherine lowered her hand down to his balls, and then under, fingering his asshole. She leaned in toward him and sucked his nipple, letting big taboos for her break through. *That* was not what a "woman" was supposed to do, to insert and to be interested in breasts.

Katherine was determined to be shocking to Eugene, and she was going to lavish as much attention on Scott as he did. She would make him jealous. She deliberately avoided making any contact with Eugene. She did think that Scott seemed pompous, just sitting there as if he were being worshipped, but then, she had felt that the night before. She'd gotten all the attention up on the blanket.

And Eugene felt like he was fighting for the best parts of Scott with Katherine, and that she was not being slow and sensitive, as only one male to another could know. He wanted to slap her hand away from Scott's balls, she was batting them about, and he was sure that was why Scott wasn't getting hard.

Scott felt two fingers in his ass. He wanted them to stop. What was going on? How could he have let himself be drawn into their desperate grasps? He wanted to say, "Hold it. Enough.

Something's wrong here." Eugene and Katherine were both tonguing and trying to suck his cock that flapped back and forth, and he hated them seeing him that way, limp. They were becoming cannibals! Greedy. He pushed back suddenly, their fingers uncorked, their tongues lapping the air.

"I guess I'm not into it," Scott said. He looked at them, the fire burning between them. They looked bewildered like pups, rejected. He took a deep breath and opened and closed his eyes to the firelight, and then said slowly and fatherly, "It's not easy for me to come down to the physical plane. To be in my body. This weight. I feel more like a spirit. You two go ahead without me. I'll watch."

Eugene thought, "I'm being too pushy, making too many moves too fast, and Katherine's being insensitive to this sweet god-man."

Katherine thought, "What kind of trip is Scott on? He's trying to lure Eugene away from me, flaunting himself for weeks, always making sure that Eugene sees him naked and chopping wood, or playing that sitar, acting like a Buddha. Go ahead and pull away, Scott, we don't need you."

And Scott thought, "Katherine is trying to make Eugene into her old man. He should be with me, not her. I can teach him. She gets in the way of his freedom because he is weak right now. And they both are closing in on me, expecting me to lead them and feed them with my body and soul, and all I want is to be the humble servant of the cosmic forces. I need space."

Nothing was said. Scott stood up, turning away from the light. He climbed the ladder, his smart ass rising like the host, and then, bending over because it wasn't high enough to stand up there, he looked down to them and said, "I hope you realize that you've ruined everything."

Katherine and Eugene looked at each other. She half smiled. Eugene looked troubled and whispered to her, "What did we do?"

Katherine was obviously not as bothered as Eugene was. She reached for his cock, as if they would start at it like nothing had happened. He was not interested, fearing that he had done something to hurt Scott, something that would kill the feelings he'd only allowed to be born the night before. How could Katherine be so nonchalant? It was her, not him, he thought. It was her fault that Scott had ascended. It was all so religious, and the fire was irritatingly hot, so hot, as if the stones themselves were burning.

"Leave me alone," Eugene said, scooting away from her touch.

Katherine leaned closer, whispering so that Scott could not hear her, "Hey, baby, he's on some fucking ego trip. Sometimes he thinks he's God's gift. I told you how his mother is, it's almost sick the way she idolizes him. Didn't you see how he watched himself in all the store windows today? He's probably pissed that he couldn't get it up."

Eugene hated what she was saying. She was mean, just like the way she called Sue a "pig." He whispered to her, "The way you were squeezing him, it's no wonder. It was like you were trying to hurt him."

Katherine whispered, "I hate this. Don't you see what's happening? Here we are arguing about the Zen god up there, and he's digging it, I imagine. Don't you see, Eugene? He's trying to break us up."

Eugene thought, "No, you're trying to break Scott and me up," but he didn't dare say that. Instead he stood up and said he was going to bed, alone.

Katherine said, full-voiced, "Hope you're happy, Scott."

Scott was lying on his mattress trying to cry, feeling like he was full of shit. Full of everything he knew to be wrong. His words reran through his head. How could he have been so pompous and call himself humble. He knew nothing. They were not his students. How dare he think they were. He would leave in the morning and go to Oakland, save up some money, and go back to India. He wanted to be able to love them, but he had to know they loved him before he could let go, let himself be vulnerable, let himself be wrong, or silly or open. He felt a tear, one little tear, and he hated himself for being so dry and calculating. He heard the heaves on the other side of the wall from Eugene's mattress. Such a crier, he thought. Such a sweet open crier, Scott thought, such a beautiful man, not knowing how much he is open, and so full of doubt for all the wrong things. Scott sighed, frustrated, and threw himself hard against the mattress in frustration at his blockhead, at his fight with himself. Why couldn't he let go? Why did he feel they had to see him only at his best? Hard, tan, and wise.

Katherine remained on the floor in front of the fire, and she stared, hearing Eugene's muffled cries and Scott's heavy sighs and leaded rustling about. She felt confused about Eugene especially. Scott was not the man she was attracted to. It was Eugene, and each step that she felt closer to him, she also felt that she had to understand so much. Why did he get up and go to bed? Why was he crying? Was he upset over her, or Scott, and if it was her, shouldn't she know that in her senses, if they really were in love? Shouldn't she know without words? She resented Scott's deliberate sexuality that he'd flaunted in front of her, and in front of Eugene for weeks, knowing that Eugene was open to experimenting, and knowing that Katherine was hoping for a permanent affair. She'd confided in Scott when she received Eugene's letter saying he was coming out to the cabin. She regretted ever having released her feelings in front of Scott, because she always felt that he judged her as a planner, a manipulator, and someone incapable of letting things just happen, and at the same time, she felt that he was jealous of her sure feelings about Eugene and about her love for him. Scott seemed to want what she wanted, if only till he knew he had it, to prove to her that she was just his equal or less, and then she felt bogged down by the contortions of the three of them and the fire needed stoking, and the men were up there sulking, so she stood, wrapped a blanket around her, and ran out into the rain to the woodshed for more logs.

Eugene was crying into his pillow. "Damn life and the tease of it!" He felt for one second he'd let himself really go, really loved both Katherine and Scott, and somehow even though it felt so right and so good and so perfect, the rug had been pulled out from under them. Was it his pushing? Was it Katherine's prodding? Was it Scott not really wanting him, seeing how queer things had become in one day? Or were all of those questions his own projections, his own thoughts or fears? He smelled smoke. Katherine was down there still in front of the fire, he was sure. He lifted his hand from the pillow and saw smoke, thick at the peak of the roof, three feet over him. He called to Scott, "Scott, do you see smoke?"

Scott didn't answer.

Eugene pounded on the wall, he knew the man was on the other side, he'd heard his cough and sigh seconds earlier. "Hey, Scott! Look up. Is that smoke?"

Scott didn't answer.

Eugene got angry. "Well, fuck you. Don't answer. I didn't do anything to you, man, so I don't know why you're pissed at me. You could at least say something, like 'leave me alone.' Scott?" Eugene coughed. He felt afraid and alone. Was he going crazy? He crawled to the end of his mattress and looked around the little wall to see into Scott's sleeping area. It was filled with smoke. He couldn't see anything.

"Scott!" Eugene screamed, and swung out over the beam and onto Scott's mattress, and there, way in the corner, curled in a fetal position, naked, practically sucking his thumb, was Scott. Eugene pulled him, "Come on, there's a fire or something, we've got to get out of here!"

Scott finally spoke, sounding deep and monotoned, "Get lost. And lay off me, you fuck. Keep your hands to yourself."

Eugene let go. He couldn't believe his ears. He couldn't believe that Scott would be so dead-sounding. Through the smoke, he couldn't really see if his eyes were open or closed, and then he realized that what he had heard was Scott's spirit, his sunken spirit. Scott had suffocated, succumbed to the smoke. Eugene screamed for Katherine and tried one last time to pull Scott by his legs, but they were deadweight, and repulsed his hands like a magnet gone round. He couldn't budge him. "Katherine!" Eugene gasped and coughed, and felt a flame run up his spine. Everything was burning. He was burning, and he thought, "Get out of here or die!"

He jumped from Scott's mattress to the floor below and ran crashing through the door and up the trail into the pouring night rain. He collapsed on the ground, gasping and crying. He heard the wail of a burning baby. He heard sirens and screams. He saw ice and snow. He thought, "This is it. I'm dying. This is no drug trip. I'm burned beyond recognition and I must let go. But, oh! I don't want to die! Not yet!" He thought if he concentrated on breathing, the sirens would reach him, but listening, he heard nothing but the crackling fire. No one would come way out there. It was hopeless. This was it. He cherished each breath he could muster, and cried for his futile attempt. Then he heard Scott's voice calling for him, and he thought, "At least Scott saved himself. He sounds alive."

"Eugene!" he heard, and then he heard Katherine's voice calling, "Eugene!" She was safe too. He was glad of that. But then he resented that he had not saved himself. He heard both their voices calling out. He felt the rain on his burnt flesh. There was no snow. It was California. It was summer. He opened his eyes and saw the dripping wet redwoods and mountain laurel wet and shiny, reflected from the blaze. Rain was so pure. Why did he have to leave the beauty of the rain? He took another deep breath, feeling his lungs seared. He coughed. He heard Scott and Katherine call his name again. They were close by. "Oh, God!" he cried, pitying them, for they would find his burned body, black and charred, flesh hanging from his bones.

"There he is," he heard Scott say. He was so sad that they would see him so destroyed. Then he saw Katherine's and Scott's faces dripping wet, leaning down toward him. They were like gods. They were both so glorious and holy, like the Virgin Mary and Jesus Christ. They were so brave, not flinching at the horrid sight of him, daring to touch his face with their palms, their tender loving touch, and he felt tears pour from their eyes to his and he cried, "Oh, I love you both and I'm sorry for everything. I want you to know that. I don't want to die, but . . ."

Scott smiled, and got within inches of Eugene's face and said, "Then don't."

"But I'm burned . . ."

Katherine started to cry, "Oh, God, he's cracked up!"

Scott said, "You can put every cell back together if you want to. You can choose to live."

"I do," Eugene swore, loving the bit of hope he was getting from Scott, that he could live on, if he reassembled every cell. But how?

"Look at me," Scott said, holding Eugene's head between his hands.

Eugene saw his eyes, full of love and water and light and rain, they were the Christ's eyes, pouring strength into his own. He felt life pouring into him, the power to put himself back together.

"God, Scott," Katherine sobbed, "he's flipped out, what can we do? Should I drive into town?"

Scott ignored Katherine as if she wasn't there next to him. Eugene didn't hear her words, only felt love from her side of him. He was mesmerized by Scott's eyes and thought, "He really is God, and this is a miracle and it's happening to me, he's healing me so that I can live."

"Now," Scott said, not moving his eyes from Eugene's, "I want you to look at your hand."

Eugene shook his head and cried, "No! The flesh is burned off and hanging like June's."

Scott said, "Is that what you want to see?"

Eugene said, "Ahhh, no. I want to live. I want to love and feel the rain and . . ."

Scott said, "Raise your hand to your eyes and look at it."

Eugene was terrified, but kept his eyes on Scott and brought his hand into view between their eyes. It was pink and fleshy and strong, it glowed with health. It was full of blood and power. Eugene's mouth fell open in awe of the beautiful hand, and it was his hand, and "Oh, life itself is a miracle," he cried.

"What do you see?" Scott asked.

"My hand, healthy. I feel it, it is full of love."

Scott said that Eugene could make his whole body that way, just by taking his hand and pushing all of the charred skin and flesh and bones and burns out of sight. He demonstrated with his own hand, putting it up to his arm, and then running it, as if he were washing with soap, and running it off toward the hand. Katherine was crying and kneeling next to Scott, and Eugene knew she was the Virgin Mary, and he said, "I want to thank dear Mary for loving me and praying by me. She gives me the strength of live and to love."

Scott said, "Push. Push it all away."

Eugene did, and saw himself healthy. His legs, his arms, his chest. The hairs weren't even singed. He would live. He was full of joy. He embraced both Scott and Katherine, and they held him in the pouring rain, and he remembered the cabin and cried out, "But oh, what about our cabin? Our poor beautiful cabin, gone!"

Scott laughed and pushed Eugene back so that he could tune in to his eyes again. "See for yourself. You can put it back together, too."

And Eugene looked down the trail. He could see that it was still there, no smoke, except for the smoke billowing out of the stone chimney, and a glow of amber light from one of the small windows. He sighed with relief. Everything was fine. And then he looked at Katherine. He saw fear in her eyes, and a knowledge that scared him.

"What? What is it?" he asked, fast and scared.

She looked down, wiping her tears, "Nothing. Just know I love you, Eugene."

Scott smiled at her. At that point they both knew that Eugene was under Scott's spell. He had brought Eugene back. Katherine had lost. They didn't know this consciously, but soon, Scott and Eugene would be sharing more and more time without her. She cried for Eugene's craziness, and cursed the rain and the mud and the dark.

They helped Eugene stand. He felt every muscle, every move, and he looked down at himself in awe. He was perfectly beautiful. Not a single burn or blister. And then he heard the voice of Katherine sound very familiar, as if nothing had happened, saying, "Let's go in out of this rain and make some tea." And Eugene thought of the look on Katherine's face, and he stopped them both and stood naked on the trail and cried, "Oh, my God!! I flipped out didn't I? There was no fire, was there? It was all in my mind wasn't it? A projection too, like in the *Book of the Dead*, right?"

Katherine smiled, relieved to have her Eugene back, and she nodded, not knowing what to say. "Just give out love," she told herself, trying to think like Scott. "We love you," she said.

Scott, on the other hand, said, "If that's how you want to see it, you can. How do you want to see it?"

Eugene held his head, shocked at how real it had been, and then heard what Scott had just said, and he said, convinced, "On some level it happened, crazy basement or penthouse. What the truth is, though, is that I want to live. I want to live."

Scott put his arm around Eugene's shoulder. Katherine put her arm around Eugene's waist, and they walked toward the cabin, and Eugene stopped them again and said, "I am alive! Wet!"

"Are you cold?" Katherine asked.

Eugene checked himself, first thinking what the word "cold" meant, and then seeing if it applied to anywhere on his body, and he shook his head and laughed at the power of suggestion. He hadn't felt cold till the word had traveled through him, and then the idea and picture of steaming tea seemed perfect. They went into the cabin. Scott opening the door, Katherine entering, then Eugene, and as Eugene went in, he turned and said to Scott, "I see God in you, despite your own doubts. You are perfect."

Scott reached forward and slapped Eugene's muddy ass, and said, "I see God in you, too." Then he let out a deep sigh, spent from such concentration.

Eugene was flying, thrilled with every smell and color and object, none of it burned. Katherine made tea, and he raved over the taste. "The best I've ever tasted!"

He and Scott played music in front of the fire. Sometimes the crackling of the heat would scare Eugene, and he would look into Scott's eyes and hear again, "You can make it whatever you want." Eugene made up chants and hoots to the music. Katherine sang along for a while, but soon fell asleep on the old couch, the kittens curled in her arms. At dawnlight, the rain had stopped and the sky was breaking gold. Scott and Eugene went down to the river.

"I'm not tired," Scott said. "I think I'm too high off you." He said he wanted Eugene to teach him how to cry, to open up. He said, "I love you, man. I think I loved you before I ever met you, just from the way Katherine lit up when she talked about you. You take risks, man."

Eugene kissed him. It was the tenderest kiss he'd ever given.

They fell together into the cold swollen river rushing from such rain, in love.

On Eugene's twenty-second birthday, August 1, Scott gave Eugene one of his guitars, and some pink dope. He cut Eugene's ponytail, and they buried it in the riverbank, and where they had dug, Eugene found a rock, and kept it. He said the ritual was his initiation into manhood and life, taking responsibility for every cell. Scott said it was his initiation into the collective unconscious, "into where music comes from, where there are no set words. Welcome to life, Eugene. The gods are with us. I know it."

They went up to the clearing with their instruments, to play with the gods.

2012, Panacea, Florida

Eugene ached to see the sun sink, he was so full of time for those few moments where the light was low. The vast sand could not be packed into the knapsack Scott had given him. He threw it out into the Gulf. "Whatever possessed us," he said, and then he threw his half of "their rock" in.

Scott had split the rock with a hammer before he left with the band for L.A. He and Eugene each had half. Eugene threw his half into the Gulf. Scott had already thrown his half into the Atlantic, in the Bahamas, two days before he died in 1985. In 1989, Octavio was on the beach in the Bahamas, a guest of Tonio, who was producing a recording of Brazilian jazz, at the well-equipped studio there, and Octavio found a halved rock and took it back to Rio with him.

As Eugene threw his half in the Gulf, Octavio, who was sailing with Tonio up the west coast of Florida toward Apalachee Bay to pick up Eugene, felt the earth was a string. A string wound round and round itself, all one string, and he thought, "What Eugene Goessler is doing is unraveling."

Unconsciously, Eugene knew all of this, as did the rocks, the bags, the strings, and all that was, collectively, tied to what was called the unconscious.

1974, California

Scott and Eugene lived on O'Farrell Street in San Francisco. Their apartment overlooked city center and the dome of the Opera House. They had formed their second band, The Dharma Bums, and were scheduled to play at The Boarding House on Union Street that night. The night before, Scott had been out in Oakland for dinner with his mother and stepfather, Katherine's dad. Scott heard stories about Katherine, whom neither he, nor Eugene, had heard from in over a year.

"Did her dad say she was planning a visit back up?" Eugene asked Scott as he wound the microphone cords and packed them.

"Nope," Scott said, adjusting his balls in his skintight suede pants, which had fringe running up the outer seams, "she called them last Thursday and said she was really getting her shit together, and said something about a therapy she was being trained in. But all this was through her dad, who thinks she's being held down there in Santa Barbara by a cult, so I had to take what he said and try to read between the lines."

"Poor Katherine," Eugene sighed, remembering their last times together. He told her, at the cabin, that he and Scott were "partners" and that he didn't want her as his old lady, and he hoped they could be friends. She said, "Sure," and that she had known for some time, but then the next day she drove off, and they found a note from her saying, simply, "Gone to Oakland." A month later, she drove back up to the cabin with her boyfriend, some guy from San Rafael who carved mandalas, and she seemed to be blissfully happy, although both Eugene and Scott suspected it was partially an act, since the guy acted as if they'd just met. She packed her things, taking the only can opener, all

152

three of the kerosene lamps, most of the pots and pans, and her clothes. As she was leaving, she told Eugene, "Tell Scott that he's responsible for you, baby."

Eugene called after her on the trail to the car, "What the fuck is that supposed to mean? I make my own choices! We're partners! He doesn't have power over me. That's your trip, Katherine!"

Scott and Eugene had started writing songs together at the cabin. Eugene played rhythm guitar and Scott played lead and sitar. They both sang, in strange harmonies, the strange lyrics Eugene wrote. While Katherine lived there, she would sometimes join them, playing a box for a drum and joining in the harmonizing, or singing out her own backup ooo's and lalalalas.

"She told my mom," Scott said, lacing up his deerskin shirt, "to say hello to us."

Remembering Katherine, Eugene regretted how the split had happened, and he felt that, in some way, he had been heartless. Now, a year later, he saw her in a different light. He remembered her last words to him. Scott did have the upper hand in most cases, and the way they were getting along the past weeks, he thought, "Katherine was right about him." He had been lured and compromised into Scott's world. At the cabin, it had seemed so clear, but now everything seemed muddled. The first band broke up because of Scott's insistence on rehearsing every day, and then he would call the rehearsal off at the last minute because he wanted to catch some other band, or he'd been out all night playing around. Both he and Eugene started drinking when they could afford it, and they smoked joints like cigarettes. Scott was dealing, on the side, and Eugene thought they might get caught by the landlord, since there was a constant stream of visitors to the apartment. Scott would say, "When you can come up with a better way to make bread, I'll stop." The sound of Katherine's name, there in their mess, was like a splash of cold water in Eugene's spaced-out face.

"I'm happy for her," Eugene said, "I hope if she ever comes up, that she'll get in touch with us. I mean, the past is the past."

Scott laughed in a way that Eugene hated. It had within its scrape a pompous, fatherly, oh-how-simple-like-a-peasant-you-are ring to it. "You've got to be crazy, dickbrain, you know how Katherine is. She'll never change. She had it bad for both of us and she couldn't stomach the fact that we got it on without her.

I know one thing, I don't want to see her, and I don't want to see you with her."

"She was hurt," Eugene said.

"Hey, man, I don't want to hear about it, okay? I should never have mentioned it. Now come on, Gene. Get ready."

Scott was a bastard, Eugene thought. He was on one "holy-fucking-major-ego trip," he said to himself. "One minute he's a humble peace-and-love-and-we're-all-in-this-band-as-equals, and the next minute he's dishing out orders and changing the order of the sets and stomping his feet till someone brings him a drink."

Scott looked at Eugene sitting with his arms folded on the couch. "Hey! Come on, you fuck! They'll be waiting for us down on the street!"

Eugene felt like he was seeing Scott for the first time in months, for what a hyper-agitated "rock star" he'd become. Scott was willing to sell his soul for a recording deal. He was constantly coming in with riffs he'd snatched from bands playing around the Bay Area, and he would say, "Hey, nobody owns music, unless it's pressed." Eugene laughed at him in a way he knew would irritate him.

"Fuckin Katherine, man!" Scott screamed. "Get over it, sweetheart! It's you and me, Gene, all the way. We are hot, man. We are tapping the source. We are gonna break. I can feel it in the air! Now get off your tight butt and let's get this equipment down to the street. I love you, dickmouth. Just ask my cock."

"Your cock doesn't know one mouth from the next, man," Eugene said.

Scott threw the guitar case across the room toward the couch. "Fuck you! What is eating you? This is no time to bring up all this shit. We got to screw our heads on tight and get high!" Scott dropped to his knees, performing a handsome plea. "Come on, Gene!"

Eugene stood up, charmed again, but this time, he thought, he would have it out with Scott, after the gig. He opened the guitar case and took his guitar from its stand and packed it in, not saying a word, as Scott walked across the floor on his knees till he reached Eugene, and started biting at Eugene's ass. Then Eugene turned and gave Scott some attention.

Scott unzipped Eugene's jeans, and Eugene said, "I thought we were in a rush."

Scott said, "Fuck'm, they'll wait. They can listen to the radio in the van and guess what we're up to."

As Scott sucked him, Eugene thought that he, and not Scott, was the liar, the one who was fucked up. He was the one who had ghosts triggering up the "pretty pictures of what the clean life should be, little lady, two kids, la dee da," and he was the one who put Scott up on a pedestal, and sure, the surfer god let himself be put there, but then who wouldn't? And from the time they left the cabin and started playing around, he'd been trying to knock Scott off. He wanted to say "I'm yours," and "I love you," but instead he thrust forward trying to fill him full, and moaned, "Yeah, hotshot, take it all."

A week later, Eugene missed a rehearsal because he was reading his poetry at an open reading in Vesuvio's coffee house across the narrow valley from the City Lights Bookstore. He told Scott that he was going to read all the "stuff you say is too out there to be lyrics."

He walked from North Beach back up to the apartment, feeling as if he'd been saved. He sang loud through the dead streets, words and noises, knowing there was no such thing as restriction. He had heard poets, some real, some phony, but when he read his pieces, he knew, just as he knew swimming, that he was on his own, out from Scott's shadow and editorial thumb.

"How'd it go?" Scott asked, as Eugene came in.

Eugene was surprised to find him there. "Great. I met some cool people, and I think they got off on my stuff . . . how was rehearsal?"

"Fucked as usual," Scott said, seeming somehow less than his usual big self. "Tony thinks we should tighten up 'Mercury' before we play it out."

"Mercury" was Eugene's most recent piece, and the band had already argued it to death. "Fuck him," Eugene said, opening a beer. "If I'd been there . . . you know, Scott, I don't want to force lines anymore, trying to make this crap sense."

"Oh no, dickbreath," Scott sighed, "don't start all that again. You can't complain if you don't come to the fuckin rehearsals."

"Why compromise . . . why? For a hit song?" Eugene sat down against the wall.

"Yeah. Do we have to go through this again, man? First you get a hit. Then you show'm you can make money. So bang. You got power. Then, slowly, you add more and more of what you want. Hit'm when they want you. We go from the inside out, Gene, or we'll never get in. I know it. Deep."

"That's just it. I don't want in. Fuck, you've managed to get the sitar to sound like a guitar. You've got your ears closed to me, and you're listening to that idiot, Tony, who thinks Fleetwood Mac is where it's at."

"Ah, the poet!" Scott belched and asked for a sip of the last beer.

Eugene tried to get through to Scott's head, "Yeah."

"Look, Gene, we were talking tonight, and that whole thing with the choppy poem between songs is fucked, and that Boris schmuck was dead. We'll lose it. I mean, who are we playing to? The dudes crossing the bay from Walnut Creek with Kerouac underarm? This is the seventies, dickass!"

"Well, why not? I changed 'cock' six times for you guys. Stick. Rod. Gun. Root, and then you said 'it all sounds too homo,' and I say, hey, take a look around."

Scott inhaled a joint. "Ziggy?"

Eugene belched, then offered Scott another sip. "Why don't you do your top forty and I'll do my cock six times and someday you'll come by my corner of the park and drop some money in my hat?"

"Gene, you're being a dick. You're a good singer. You write good stuff. Maybe you should lay low on the reefer. You're drifting away from The Bums."

Eugene imagined quitting the band, which he feared would mean quitting Scott, too. "Maybe, maybe not baby. It's being true to what I feel inside me, though. I like the sounds of yacking and clacking and racking and gagging and it's all chairs and items like in the Watts book, and fuck the books, Scott, the words we're doing are yours. You've made'm fit the band. You're smitten and bitten on the big-label bug, baby. I don't care about it, or why be badoopin and burgessin, fella, fella, fella?"

"Stop fuckin around," Scott laughed, passing the joint. "We gotta draw the line somewhere. You're East Coast nosy, Goessler, since I've known you, you think you got some wise bunk under you and that we got too much sun. You know that's all the ivy back there."

"And you with India? It's remarkable how you drop 'India' into an introduction."

"All I'm saying is, we gotta draw up a line, man."

"Why? Why lines!" Eugene was loose.

"Cause I'm a musician! I want to make a living at it!" Scott was loose too.

"And what do I want?" Eugene asked, acting goofy, making a face, and blubbering his big lips like rubber in Scott's face.

Scott pushed him back because Eugene belched an inch from his about-to-open mouth, "You dicklip, I don't know what the fuck you want. You fuck around onstage, asking for me to censor you, throwing out "Poontang!' in the middle of a decent lyric, ruining your own stuff, man, and then looking over at me with your doggie face and asking, 'How was that?' and then yelling out 'Who's got the comeshot?' over and over, and it's . . ."

Eugene was laughing, "Yeah, yeah, that's right . . ."

"And it's all too weird, man. Nobody gets off on it. Old Ziggler said we should stop fucking around onstage or we wouldn't be back. He said we should go over the bridge with that crap."

"Let's go!" Eugene toasted with the empty beer. "Let's close up shop and play for the babies at Berkeley who pant for the outrageous and stub butts all night and sleep all day and drink everything black."

Scott grabbed the beer can from Eugene and smashed it with his fist. "You're a fucking comedian, Gene! Why don't you go be a hobo?"

"And drink everything black?"

"Paint it black, dickhick."

In the morning, kicking through the garbage of the kitchen, they argued again, and that night, at rehearsal, Eugene told Tony to fuck off, and within two weeks, Eugene was out of the band and saying a you-sold-out good-bye to Scott. His North Beach poet friend Boris told him he could crash there for a while, but within a few days, Eugene convinced himself that he had to get away from the Bay Area, and he left, leaving his guitar at Boris's, hitching south on the Pacific Coast Highway.

"Here, Eugene," Scott said, handing him a canvas green knapsack, "you'll need this, I won't." He said that he wouldn't be needing it because he was planning to "fly from now on, and have roadies to carry my gear."

Eugene found a note in the pocket of the knapsack that said, "It is what you want it to be. Every cell. Love, Scott."

1974–75,
California/Mexico

Eugene left Scott and San Francisco and got a ride with a speed freak in a red Datsun. A tire blew on one of the hairpin cliff turns in Big Sur, and they came within inches of death. They had been listening to static on the radio, and Eugene was staring out over the turns, barely capturing his breath, before it was taken away again by the spectacle of the coastline. He was making up new words for "blue" when they heard a pop, then a steel growl, and felt the loss of control as they heard the blowout's roar, much too big for such a perky car, and the straining scrape of the brakeshoes that seemed powerless. Eugene thought, "We're going through," and then reached over to the wheel and shouted, "No!" to the driver, who for once was speechless. The Datsun skirted the guardrail that appeared around the bend, like a steel arm of God, saying, "Now, now, stay in line boys," and they wobbled to a stop in the gravel.

"Whoa!" Eugene screamed with joy. "We did it! Man!"

The driver was ghost-white, and his lips quivered, "Shit. Shit. Shit. Shit."

They both got out of the car, although Eugene had to kick his door to get it open, and the driver looked at the ruined side and started screaming. "You fuck! Look what happened because of the extra weight!" He blamed Eugene's one hundred and sixty-two pounds for causing the blowout.

Eugene was laughing and squealing out nonsense about everything being so beautiful when you think you might be losing it. "Hey, Jorge! We're alive!"

"And look at my car, it's ruined, and I don't know if the spare is any good," the driver, Jorge, said, folding his arms to himself. "What now?"

Eugene pointed to a trail that led down the cliff to the beach. "Let's go down there, to the beach, and count our blessings."

In December, Eugene crossed the border into Mexico, traveling with three lesbians from Los Angeles who were using him for "protection." "No one'll hassle us with a man at the wheel."

After hustling on Selma Avenue in Los Angeles for almost a month, Eugene had saved up two hundred dollars. On warm days, he slept in Griffith Park, and on other days he paid a dollar to get into the World Theater on Hollywood Boulevard, which ran three different movies. There was a cheap rooming house on Las Palmas that he stayed in twice, but he was saving money and hated shelling out sixteen dollars for a broken mattress and a dirty bath. When he felt low, he considered going back north to Scott, and he even considered starting his own band in L.A., but he knew that he really didn't want any of that scene, and he would talk to himself, pulling himself up, saying, "This is an adventure. This is your life, man, so dig it. You want this." He resented hustling, but it was quicker than getting a shit-zero job. There were times late at night, when he was avoiding the vice cops, playing exhausting cat-and-mouse games, that he couldn't see the difference between selling his body or Scott's selling out their music, and those were the nights he went with anybody. He loved being in Griffith Park. One morning, he saw two wild monkeys that lived in the hills, having escaped from the zoo years before. He cruised after bathing in the creek and sunning himself sometimes, always going for the best cars, and asking for ten or twenty bucks, depending on what the guy looked like. He only carried the green knapsack Scott had given him. He stowed his backpack in a cave up near the planetarium. He never did it for free, although he did meet a few guys that he spent the day with, almost friendly, but one night, one of the ushers at the Laserium show in the observatory let him in for free, for a blowjob. The usher wanted to suck him, too, but he said no, knowing he only let his cock out for cold cash. The usher wanted him to come home to Glendale, but Eugene again said no, because the guy had blow-dried hair, and wore jewelry, and seemed too swishy-disco, probably thinking he was being really wild to let someone into the show without a ticket. Eugene took advantage of the hot water in the restrooms, though, and he also pulled a wallet out of a girl's purse in the seat in front of his as she gasped at the stars and sang along with the Moody Blues. He took a ten-dollar bill, and dropped the wallet back into its bag, so he didn't count the blowjob as free. He would never have stolen from her if he hadn't overheard her saying about him to her friends, "Some people shouldn't be allowed in here, even if they can buy a ticket."

All along, Eugene had Mexico in mind as a destination of sorts, and as soon as he had the two hundred dollars he'd decided he needed, he made a sign saying "South," and within minutes he was offered a ride with the three lesbians, Belle, Tina, and Joey. They shared a house in Santa Monica. They were all in graduate programs at UCLA and they all said they were writers.

Tres Dykes Souse of Bordero was Eugene's first published piece. It appeared in the *Paris Review* three years after his ride with them. They were a breath of fresh air after his month on the streets of Hollywood. They were funny, and they were not interested in his cock, and they seemed trustworthy. Belle reminded Eugene of June. There was something about her smile, the way it turned up, but more than that, he realized over the weeks, it was her strength. She wasn't real butch like Joey and Tina, either. She was confident in herself, and dared to wear eye makeup even though the other two considered that hung-up. After an hour of ride with the lesbians, Eugene found himself singing along with them and feeling like there was never a doubt about his wanderings. He would never go back to Scott, and he would never go back to Selma Avenue, but he would always go back to Griffith Park. He painted a bohemian picture for them, telling them that he knew all the North Beach Poets and he made it sound like he lived at The Factory with Warhol when he lived in New York. They were grateful to have him along, whether or not he was a new generation Kerouac, he was a strong tall man, and they had been warned about the Mexican macho males, and how they harassed single American women.

Joey and Tina had planned the entire trip. They had a rented house in San Felipe, already paid for and waiting. They had the house till March. All three had taken off a semester to "experience another culture and work on our papers," although Belle said, "We want to have a blast."

By the time they reached the border (they had conferred in the ladies' room of the Chevron station in Calexico) they invited Eugene to join them for their stay at their house in San Felipe. "It was meant to be," they all agreed, as they were getting along so well.

San Felipe was a remote town, a hundred and twenty miles south of the border, on the east coast of the Baja Peninsula, on the Sea of Cortez, as Eugene called it, or the Gulf of California, which didn't sound foreign enough. It was a fishing town, with a long dock of trawlers, motorboats, and rowboats. The desert and mountains surrounded it, making it seem like an oasis. The house was south of the town on the beach, very modern, and nothing rustic and Mexican about it, or so it seemed. Once inside, Tina discovered that most of the electric outlets were "dummies" and that there was no hot water, "but soon, senorita, soon it will be," the caretaker explained. Their house was one of three built by an American man to rent out to American tourists. The rest of the town was poor and ramshackle, although a modern hotel was being constructed, and another was planned for a bluff overlooking a cove where the pelicans dove. Eugene was followed unabashedly by children with their hands out whenever he walked through the town, and the women who sold meats over an open fire, with a pig's head displayed on a stake next to their stand, giggled amongst themselves and called him "Heepie." The fishermen adopted that name for him, too. Some of the men were on the construction crew for the hotel, but most of them fished. Joey, who insisted on wearing men's coveralls even in the heat of the day, and therefore was the most hassled of the three women, said, "All these men do is fish, fight, and fuck."

Eugene wrote a Christmas letter to Ohio from San Felipe:

Dear Mother, Debbie, and Frank,
    I am alive and well and living south of Hell in a beautiful spot in Mexico and I hope you are watching the river for me and not regretting anything, because life is great and there's only today and you probably don't get it, but this is one bomba bomba chicabomba adventure and the Catholics here, all of'm are, carry

the plaster Jesus through their dusty streets and shower the crib with the few pesos they have. Just like you, Mother, they call me Heepie and I gave them all your address so they could write to you and tell you how ashamed you should be. "I am a seemple man, with seemple family," I tell them. And how are all of you? Did you put up a tree and fight? I'm sorry to miss that tradition. I am here with three women, and though you would never believe it, I am not living "in sin." I wish you were here, God, it would be fun for you to see beyond those blinders. Fun? I take it back. I wish you all a merry Xmas. There is no address for you to reach me, not that you would write. Well, I did like hearing from you Debbie, when you sent me that birthday card in San Fran last summer. Don't worry about me, and I won't worry about you. I'm close by in the brain, believe it or not, and I love you all.

Clara read the letter out loud at the kitchen table to Debbie and Frank and his new wife, Stephanie. Clara wiped her eyes when she finished, and said, "He's gone off the deep end now, and all we can do is say a prayer for his soul. It's a shame that he's not the child who died on me, cause he's broken my heart just the same. Such a rotten apple."

She started to tear the letter up, but Debbie grabbed it from her and explained, "I want to keep it, Mother . . . for the stamps."

In January, Eugene was hired to work with the construction crew on the new hotel. He lasted three days, and then was told to stay away, because he caused trouble, because he encouraged the men to use two nails instead of one for each wall stud abutment, and because he would strip naked when it was high noon and run down into the water, embarrassing the women who came by with their husbands' lunches.

Belle told him that he was welcome to share their food, and their money, as his had run out, and the fishermen said, waving their hand whenever he approached, "No heepie! No heepie! You bring the dogs with you!"

He returned to Los Angeles from Mexico with the three lesbians and a knapsack full of full notebooks. He had written and written and written, about pelicans and dykes and men who fish for life. He had spent many hours with Belle, talking and walking the beach. She knew all about writers. Who wrote what. Who knew who. She talked about Rubinstein and Snyder and Ginsberg. Sometimes he felt so ignorant, but when he was writing, he felt brilliant, and he told himself that it didn't matter if he knew who wrote what. He encouraged Belle to "find her own style" and then had to admit, he wasn't sure how that happened, "It just seems that everyone you mention was their own person, taking risks, not sitting around with history." Belle said she would, but "first I want to get my master's."

In San Felipe, Eugene had befriended a pack of wild dogs that roamed the beaches. They terrorized people, and were hunted down sometimes, and it was suspected that they were cooked and eaten. The dogs' leader, a large golden animal, would run with Eugene, and the other dogs would follow. He wrote about them, filling one notebook, calling it "The Dogs of San Felipe, Mexico." He wrote of how he had first spotted them, tearing up a mutt, chewing him to death in the rivulets of raw sewage that ran through the sand from the town down to the water. He grabbed a large stick and ran into the pack, trying to save the poor mutt but "he was a goner, and I should've left them to finish the job. I hated knowing I had interfered. The pack ran out into the desert, leaving me alone with the dying dog whimpering in the slop. I cried. There was something so pathetic about the mutt's one eye that was left, looking at me, as if to say, 'You fuck! Who the hell do you think you are? You know what you have to do, don't you?' And my stomach was turning, and I tried to leave, but each step I took away from him, he would yelp. I knew what I had to do. I took the heavy stick and raised it over the mutt's head, aiming for a precise blow, and I brought it down as heavy as I could, smashing the dog's skull. Squash! Mush! Gush! And I splattered both my legs with its blood, and I heaved and squealed and sat on the dune, the leader dog looking down at me. Each eye was different. His tongue dripped blood as he panted, and something was communicated between us," and from that day on, Eugene and the golden leader were companions.

Belle drove Eugene to Malibu where he could get a ride up the Pacific Coast Highway. "Heepie," she said, kissing him in the front seat, "you write to me, and when you get an address, I'll send you the pictures I took of you and the dogs. And you be sure and look up Rubinstein. Tell him I said you were worth it. He'll know what I meant. I hate this, go on, get going, now I know the party's over."

Eugene got out of the car and said, "The party's not over, Belle. Remember what my friend, Charity Ball said." He closed the door and moved to the gravel shoulder, and then yelled, "It's a come-as-you-are!"

Through Santa Barbara, Eugene looked out the window of the pickup he was in, but he didn't see Katherine.

In San Francisco, he went to see Scott on O'Farrell Street. Tony, the drummer, was living with him, but out. Scott gave Eugene a stack of mail, including a letter from Moody Sue, a postcard from Charity, and Christmas cards from Ohio and New York.

"Did you get my letters from Mexico?" Eugene asked him.

"Yeah, but I didn't write because I thought you'd be moving on."

Eugene tried to read Scott's face. His eyes were not as true as they were in his memory. Scott had chopped off his long hair, and he seemed more a student type, and less a surfer type. Eugene touched it. "What made you do this?"

Scott shook his head away from Eugene's hand. "Ahh, a few weeks ago. Time for a change. New look. My mom gave me three hundred bucks."

"Any news of Katherine?"

"Still being 'held against her will' according to the folks."

"Are you and Tony sleeping together?"

Scott got serious. "Why? You jealous?"

"No," Eugene lied. "I guess I think you can do better."

"Fuck you," Scott laughed. "He's too M.O.R., right?"

"So are you?"

"No. Tony's straight."

Scott cleared room on the couch that sat in the bay window and raised the shade, letting in sunlight and a view of the dome. "What about you? Meet any cute numbers in your travels?"

Eugene confessed his hustling in L.A., and said, "Either they turn out to be disco clowns or shadows," and then he said he was celibate in Mexico. "I met this one young man, Pablo, who worked on the construction crew of the hotel, and I saw him around the town, and we always looked at each other, but I wasn't about to come on to him. He had a wife and a baby, but he was very handsome, and I might have gotten to know him had he been single. He was sweet."

Scott let out a long sigh. Eugene was still so hung up, he thought, falling for a straight Mexican who was safely out of his reach. "That figures."

There was an ember of familiarity between them, and within seconds of sitting down on the couch, they were passionately sweating over each other in the sun, stoking old smells and moves till their friction caught fire, and they each squirted, then kissed, and then smoked cigarettes, and Eugene said, "I liked it better long."

They heard the key in the lock, and Tony entered, singing feyly, "Scottie!" He looked suspiciously at them on the couch, but only said, "How ya doin, Gene?" And before Eugene could stand to shake his hand, he'd disappeared into the kitchen.

Scott said, "Really, man, he's straight."

Then Tony yelled from the back room, "Dammit! Hey Scott! You fuck! You left the amplifier on!"

Eugene decided that his presence was the real cause for the current of tension, so he left, leaving his backpack till he found a place. He called Rubinstein, Belle's friend, and made arrangements to meet him at Turk's Cafe in Berkeley.

Bernard Rubinstein had a long brown beard and a short squat body. His head was wild and aware of everything going on in the cafe, and out the window, and it seemed as if his body was an afterthought. He introduced Eugene to other writers and poets as they drifted in, all eventually pulling up chairs to Rubinstein's table, checking out the new blood.

"What have you written?"

"What type of work do you do? Deadbeat?"

"What do you taste like?"

"Wanderer?"

In their own ways, they all came on strong to Eugene, sharing jokes he did not get, and dropping names and titles, and quoting lines, and getting rowdier and rowdier, and Eugene wondered if this was how they always were, or was it some sort of performance for his benefit. He briefly wished that he had a college in his background, and he told himself that they must've liked him, or they wouldn't be expending such a show of attention, so he relaxed, and tried not to judge them or be defensive when an obvious cutting remark was made, and he felt free to say fuck off, but never did.

He decided that his best bet for a bed was with the striking Israeli poet who seemed almost quiet, although his roaming eyes were loud and clear. They called him Yanick-the-dick. Eugene came in Yanick-the-dick's bed that night, smelling eucalyptus out the window. Yanick's place was full of books, and he was invited to hang around. Yanick ran a Zen workshop at the co-op. Eugene settled in, always keeping one foot out the door, but settled in nonetheless.

He learned that the writers sucked each other off in many ways. They used each other for language "spills," and they sang and chanted and mouthed so much that nothing was sacred. Nothing was sacred. Eugene grew a beard, and Yanick and Rubinstein called him pussyface.

Eugene saw Scott off and on. The band was moving to L.A. They had a contract. Eugene and Scott split the rock from the cabin. Where they'd buried the ponytail, by the river, they'd dug up the rock.

Eugene said, "Someday we'll match them up, and know each other, no matter what."

Scott said, about Eugene's beard, "I liked you better without it."

Eugene said, about the recording deal, "Make a monkey out of me, Scott."

Scott and Tony and the band flew off to L.A. Eugene's beard kept growing. He noticed that it hid the scars on his neck. He threw himself into working on the new magazine that he and Yanick claimed would "rip the lining out of the literary vests of academics."

1966, Ohio

Father Wetzel was dean of boys' Spiritual Health at Bishop Miller High School, and when Eugene was summoned to his office he went to his locker first and changed ties from the wild Carnaby Street tie Katherine had given him to the conservative black checked. He combed his hair as neat as possible, hoping he wouldn't be measured. Measurement involved a collar-to-ear hair ruler.

"Eugene, my son," the red-faced heavy priest said, swiveling in his chair behind his desk, with his hands pressed together, fingertips touching his thin dark mouth, "Brother Bob has asked me to speak with you about your faith, and your constant disruptions in his class."

Eugene shifted in the chair that faced the priest's desk. So this was it, he thought; he had been threatened by the brother, and now by a priest.

"Brother Bob tells me that you stood up and walked out of his class and in front of all your fellow classmates you called him a hypocrite. Is that true?"

"Yes, Father," Eugene said, "but . . ."

"There is no excuse for that sort of behavior here at Bishop Miller, Mr. Goessler. Now I know you have not had an easy time of it, but that is no excuse for such disrespect."

"But I would say it again . . ."

"Mr. Goessler!"

"I would say it again, he *is* a hypocrite! Brother Bob is piss . . . mad that I argue with him at all . . . everybody is . . . they moan when I raise my hand cause they're all hoping for study hall, and I . . ."

"Mr. Goessler, I will not allow you to be so insubordinate with me." Father Wetzel stood to show Eugene he'd better stop talking. "Now I want you to apologize to Brother Bob in front of the class."

Eugene stood, confronting the priest, standing taller and stronger, and full of anger, "No way! Not unless you hear my side. You're the spiritual advisor, aren't you? You've got to hear me out, Father!"

"Sit!" the priest bellowed. "You sit!"

Eugene lowered himself slowly to the chair. He saw by the clock that he would be late for swimming practice, which would mean he would have to swim laps when he got to the pool. He heaved a disgruntled sigh. They were all alike, he thought. Why did he even bother? They didn't practice Christ's teachings, all any of them cared about was discipline.

"That's better," the priest said. "Now, if you act like a gentleman, I will hear what you have to say, and keep in mind, Mr. Goessler, I too was once a young man with questions, and I've been around a lot longer than you."

Eugene said to himself, "Yeah, and you've got God on your side, right?"

The priest studied the young man's sneer. "Well? What is it Mr. Goessler?"

Eugene decided that this was it. He would open up one more time, but never again if the priest closed up and fell back into recitations of Church dogma. "Well," Eugene moved closer to the desk, "I think that the Catholic Church doesn't practice what it preaches. I went eight years to St. Joe's and I believed what I was told, and I had talks with Jesus and I went to communion and confession and . . ."

The priest smiled and raised his hand for Eugene to stop. "Talks with Jesus."

Eugene nodded.

"You mean you prayed to Jesus."

"I talked to him," Eugene said, "in my bunk bed, down by the river, even when I had something else on my mind, sometimes, I'd look up, and Jesus would be there."

"In your imagination, son."

"Yeah, I guess so." Eugene got the priest's eyes in sight, now if he could get through to his soul, to find out what everything was

. . . "What I want to know, Father, is, where do you get your truth? Why is the Catholic Church the 'true' church? What is truth? And, how can anyone have the power to judge anyone else? And what if . . ."

The priest smiled benevolently and condescendingly and rocked back in his chair a bit, and said, "Hold on now, hold on . . . uh . . . Mr. Goessler, one thing at a time . . ."

Eugene resented the man. His holier-than-him attitude and the eyes that had focused and now looked away made the young man feel that this man was no spiritual anything. "Okay," Eugene took a breath. "First off, I was baptized when I was a baby, and that was to be forgiven for 'original sin' right?"

The priest nodded with a slight tilt of reservations, but flicked his stumpy pink fingers for Eugene to go on.

"And then at six, I start learning the laws. 'Who made me? God made me,' and I trusted it. All of it. I lived in fear of the devil and counted my sins every night. A little kid! And all I ever got from Jesus was 'Love.' He didn't seem to be bothered with my behavior at all. He loved everything . . ."

The priest nodded and rocked.

"And at St. Joe's they would have these fund drives to send money to the missions in New Guinea and Africa, and there was all this gold and silver and stained glass and robes, and I thought, 'Shouldn't they sell all that stuff?' but I was just a kid then, and I figured that was the devil trying to get me. The nuns said he was tricky. You know, one nun I had told us that it was more of a sin to miss Mass on Sunday than to commit murder."

The priest's face seemed redder, and he seemed to be getting impatient, and he rocked a little faster in his leather swivel chair, and he continued to nod and look and then divert his eyes from the young man.

"And once I asked why no Negroes were at St. Joe's and I was told that they had their own churches in their own neighborhoods . . ."

"We have nine Negro students here at Bishop Miller," the priest said through his praying hands.

"And I started to say to myself, 'What if?' "

"What if?"

"Yeah," Eugene said, "what if this isn't the truth? Just what if? I begged God to understand that I was confused and just wondering, but what if it was true that rules were made up to keep the serfs in line, and you could buy a place in heaven from the Pope with enough gold, and what if Martin Luther had good reason to split from the Church? Look at Martin Luther King. Why would anyone name their kid Martin Luther, if he was not a good man? And then Daddy would say, 'Hitler wasn't so bad,' and . . ."

"May he rest in peace," the priest said, and then qualified his words, "your father, not Hitler. You must remember, Eugene, Cincinnati is a German city, and many people here had no idea of what Hitler was doing."

"They do now!" Eugene raised his voice and head. "Don't you see? These so-called good Catholics are bigots and hypocrites and hawks. They want to kill anyone who doesn't believe what they do, and they think they have Christ on their side, and I don't think I want to be part of it."

"Part of the Church?"

Eugene swallowed. He had thought it, but he'd never said it out loud, to a priest. His head filled with doom, and he felt tears rising, and he prayed to God to forgive him if he was letting himself fall into the hands of the devil, but he nodded, and said, in a low, nearly inaudible voice, "I've been sold a bill of goods."

The priest spoke, "Now, Eugene, what do you mean by that?"

Eugene regained his composure and sniffed, "Oh, that's something my mother always said about the Church, that they 'make it up as they go along, to whatever'll fit the bill.' I feel like what the Church is and what Christ said are two different things. My friend Kevin said the Church, the Vatican, is the wealthiest corporation in the world, and meanwhile, people are starving and dying and segregated."

Father Wetzel leaned forward and put his elbows on his desk, and his pointed prayer hands folded into themselves so that he could rest his chin on them, and he said, "You are having a crisis of faith, my son, but you mustn't feel that you are lost to the Church. You are questioning. That is good, but there's no reason to storm out of a classroom or hurl names. Brother Bob said he thought you were troubled, and from what you've said, I think he may be right."

"Well what are the answers!" Eugene interrupted the smooth-worded there-theres. "Is it true that Nazis were practicing Catholics? Is it true that . . ."

"Mr. Goessler!"

"That Jesus' words have been interpreted and reinterpreted to fit . . ."

"Mr. Goessler! Shame on your behavior!"

Eugene stood up and said, "Don't you judge me! How dare you think you can know my soul!"

"I will send you home!"

"I swear to God," Eugene cried out, "if I have the devil in me, then strike me dead right here! Because I think that Christ . . ."

"You are suspended!"

Eugene's face was tortured. "I think Jesus left your side a long time ago, Father, and you're all hypocrites!" And then, with his warm hand, turning the knob to the door to the hall to the unknown, he turned and said, "No, Father, Jesus has not left your side. I see him next to you, to your right, and he just told me to give up."

The priest's eyes glanced to his side, quickly, seeing nothing but trophies.

"And so I give up," Eugene said. "I will apologize. I will swim extra laps. Render to Caesar. Time is up, and whether you see it or not, Jesus just poured oil over me, like Extreme Unction, and your holy water will roll off me from now on."

The priest said, "Mr. Goessler, I want you to see the school psychiatrist."

1977, Colorado

Shortly after his twenty-seventh birthday, Eugene joined Rubinstein, Yanick, and Belle in a shared house on Euclid Avenue in Boulder. They were each studying and teaching at the School of Poetics within the new Naropa Institute, which had been founded by the Buddhist master, Chogyam Trungpa. Rubinstein gave classes in what was called the Jack Kerouac School of Disembodied Poetics. His class was called Word. Eugene put together a class called The Manure of Experience. One of the eight people who signed into that class was the tall woman who had designed the Naropa brochure, Lola Hampton.

"What do you want?" Eugene asked each of the students as they sat on the worn Oriental carpet in a semicircle in the sunlight on the second floor in an unused office that looked out on the mall in downtown Boulder.

When the question came round to Lola Hampton, she said, "I heard you were hung like a horse."

Eugene glared at her, at her large almond eyes and her devious small grin and her curled and twisted hair that was pulled up away from her long neck. Her lips were slick with a waxy balm to protect them from the mountain cold, and as they parted into a full-blown laugh, she added, "Well, you asked." This was a hip Buddhist-Western school, where there was no norm. Eugene was not shocked. He was confronted.

"Erect or flaccid?" he said. "Do you want inches?"

An eighteen-year-old young man from New Jersey said, "Both! Give us both!"

Another man, serious, and now dubious, wanted to know if Eugene was a practicing homosexual.

172

A young woman next to Lola Hampton said, "I don't see what this has to do with anything."

Eugene had lost any plan for the class at this point, and decided to take the advice he was about to deliver, that being, "Take the wrong turn. Take a chance. Spread out," and so on. He decided to undress for them. He undid his flannel shirt to the tune of their whistles. He bent to his boots, and had the young man from New Jersey pull them from his feet. He dropped his pants, and then his briefs, and stood before them, naked, a little cold, but definitely pleased with his answer, and he said, "Here I am," looking directly at Lola, "and as you could see, I prefer men to pull off my boots, but I don't mind being eyed by all of you."

Lola deliberately gawked at Eugene's cock. She seemed to be comfortable about his nudity, and she studied him closely, and asked, "Now, is that completely limp?"

The young woman next to her blurted out, red and fed-up, "This is repulsive! Obviously we have the male ego on display! Should we bow before your toy? This place is never going to get accredited at this rate!"

"That is not replusive," Lola said, pointing to Goessler's cock. She knew the woman, Nairobi, from a painting class at the University of Colorado. "That is what you get in life-sketching, Nairobi, right? So, just settle down, you silly lesbian. Now we know what the man is made of."

"I am not a lesbian!" Nairobi declared to everyone. "I am a new woman."

Eugene stood before them, five women and three men, and the truth was, the only reason four of them had signed into the class was because they had seen and heard of Eugene Goessler, and thought he was attractive. Lola sensed this, and selfishly wanted it out of the way. "See it, no matter how big a deal, right? And then get on with it," she said to Eugene that evening at Dot's Diner. She also told him that she felt as if she would know him for the rest of her life.

"I was wondering," Eugene said, "if you really think the cock is what the man is made of."

Lola blew western smoke over her eastern tea and said, "Look at it this way. This place is a fucking soap opera sometimes, and the one thing that buzzed about was who you were . . . that you used to be in the Warhol crowd . . . and in The Dharma Bums, and that you had this great body. I think a cock is as good as its keeper. I like to turn the tables."

"Well, we'll see who shows up next week," Eugene said.

"Are you kidding?" Lola laughed, throwing her arm out and hitting a waiter in the belt, "You scored. Word goes bzzzzzzzzzz. So and so is so high, bzzzzzzzzzzzz, so and so is fucking so and so and her husband is fucking so and so. I take it or leave it. It's like looking under a rock, these classes. You see what's there, and then either you leave it out exposed, or you cover it back, sometimes stomping on it. I love Allen Ginsberg, don't you?"

"I love Gary Snyder," Eugene said, shaking soy sauce all over his rice.

"Yeah?" Lola sounded surprised. "I didn't think you would say you 'loved' any writer. I heard that you were . . ."

"I love whoever writes the copy for *TV Guide!*" Eugene laughed, seeing Lola taking him too deep, too soon. "Try reading it out loud sometime and then Trungpa's 'The Manure of Experience and the Field of Bodhi.' "

"I don't read much," she said, "but I love skiing."

"White Rabbit" by Jefferson Airplane started playing through the speakers in the diner. Lola said she loved the song. Eugene thought, of course she would, being so tall. Then she asked him if he had a "favorite" song.

"Sugar Shack" was his answer.

"Sugar Shack?" Lola said, surprised.

"Sugar Shack," Eugene repeated, dead-serious and sure.

1978, New Mexico

Eugene felt an open channel of light lifting his legs and leading him to the highway. He trusted his moves, although he could not trust his thoughts. There were no tracks from the Indian's Jeep, no sign of their feet having ever made an impression on the white dust of the canyon floor. The heat of the sun reminded him of the heat of the water.

The day before, or what seemed like the day before, he had descended into the hottest of mineral waters within the caves of Indian Springs, in Colorado, knowing the handsome glistening Indian spread out nude on the rock slabs beside that pool was watching his every move. They had been eyeing each other in the dim primitive dripping silence of the cave for a steamy hour, till the other men, Rubinstein included, found their ways out to the lockers, or wilted toward the other pools, away from the charged air the two men were generating. Eugene's pores poured sweat. He lowered himself, dared by the Indian's black eyes. When his crotch touched the water, he gasped, and the Indian said, "Ahhhhhhhh, that's it, paleface." His voice was deep and slow and smoothing. "Redden your juices. Feel for me and I will salt you with the Mayan truth."

Eugene took swift short breaths as he lowered himself up to his chin, his eyes remaining fixed on the Indian's. "Salt me, then," he said, before his mouth went under.

"The green sea," the Indian said, "in your visions of this." He raised both his legs from the slab so that his feet were on the ceiling of the cave and his cock dripped silver onto his chest of smooth muscle.

Belle, who'd been down in the women's cave, and Rubinstein were waiting for Eugene up in the lobby of the old damp hotel that had been built over the caves in 1900. Eugene came up the creaking stairs from the locker room with a sheepish wet grin on his face and said to them, "You guys go on back to Boulder without me, I'm going to Taos with a Mayan."

"I told you," Rubinstein exhaled sighing to Belle. "It was apparent that we'd lost Eugene from our weekend."

Eugene said, "His name is Jesus lo Dichodicho. Dig it. He is taking me to a holy place. He has a Jeep and ancient come."

On the road, Jesus drove, and Eugene talked. He told the Indian about the Mexican he'd met in Boulder who was immersed in the ancient Mayan culture. Jesus would nod and hum, but said nothing, causing an uncomfortable tension in Eugene. He began to make up points. "They left on spaceships for lunch, and they're coming back for dinner, as we sweat out centuries of our heavy time, right?" The Indian hummed in tune with the Jeep's engine. Eugene stopped talking. His own words reverberated back to him as belches. Jesus laughed and stopped the Jeep as they approached the border to New Mexico.

"You drive," the Indian said. "You have tired me with your words of theories. Your words have nothing to do with you. All you do is spice your fine breath. You are funny."

As Eugene drove, Jesus reached over and put a dried mushroom in Eugene's mouth and kissed him. "Chew slowly, fine lips, golden man," he said. "*Charaqui maquo.*" The Indian began to chant and sing, deliberately slow for Eugene to follow and join him. He fed more mushrooms into Eugene's mouth, each time kissing the lips and saying, "*Charaqui maquo.*"

Outside of Taos, Jesus told Eugene to stop. "I will drive now, and your eyes will be covered."

Eugene laughed nervously. "Why? I have no idea where we are anyway. It's dark."

The Indian undid the bandanna around Eugene's head and blindfolded him, saying, "Trust me or stay here."

They drove on and Eugene repeated out loud, "I trust you. I trust you," as fear after fear rose in him of all the possible scenarios.

"Trust your self," the Indian said at one point.

"I trust my self," Eugene said, feeling tears. His stomach

rumbled and he felt a peach at his lips. He bit full into it, knowing he trusted everything.

When he came to, he was staked out, spread-eagled and naked, tied with leather straps and surrounded by four small fires. One was burning behind his head, one was between his legs, and one was at either side of him. The blindfold had been lowered and tied tightly around his mouth. Through the smoke he could see the stars. As he became conscious, he struggled to pull himself loose, and as he did, he felt a sharp sting to the soles of his feet. It felt like a bee sting in each of his arches, but he thought it might have been a snake, and he made himself perfectly still. He heard the sweet voice of the Indian say, "Trust the fires, poet. Trust the earth to hold you. Your animal needs soothing from inside."

Jesus Lo Dichodicho appeared, straddling the fire between Eugene's legs, his cock extended, tied in gold ropes. He wore toucan feathers in his black hair. His eyes reflected the flames, and Eugene was filled with lust, humility, and fear. He was afraid the Indian would burn. The gold ropes dangled so close to the tongues of flame. The Indian spoke, though his mouth was fixed in a slight smile. "Trust the fires." He knelt down into the fire and the flames disappeared. He lifted Eugene's ass, pulling him even tighter at the stakes.

When he came to again, it was full sun and he was freed. The Jeep and Jesus were gone. On his pile of clothes, Eugene found a playing card from a Reno casino. The ace of diamonds. Written in blood, it said, "You do not know, but you trust. Trust is close to what you would call electric. You gave me the instructions for the ritual. You will know now that you are an ecstatic being with the Mayan seed in your blood." It was signed, "J. L. Dicho, Mayan Croupier."

1979, New York City

Eugene returned to New York to direct one of his pieces for the New York Festival of the Arts. He stayed at the Chelsea Hotel, where the roaches were so big he could hear their feet. Viva told him that Charity was living in Greece with Charles, and Andrea had committed suicide. Tex was a male stripper in Brooklyn. Max's was dead.

Eugene went to see Sue Nieman, Moody Sue, who now lived on the Upper West Side.

"Cowboy! I thought you'd have your head shaved and be banging a tambourine!" she said, opening her door. The last time she'd heard from him, he had written a card saying he was going into the Rockies with a Tibetan Buddhist. "You look older, but I don't know about wiser . . . tanner . . . but then, the brain gets fried out West doesn't it?"

Sue was slimmer, and her hair was chopped short, still dyed black, and she said she had a lover, a woman, "do you believe it?"

Eugene said he wasn't surprised, and she seemed to resent that, and swallowed two white chocolate bonbons, one after the other. She was testing recipes for candy. She and her lover were going to open a candy business on Seventy-second Street.

"I know real quality will sell, hand-dipped, no crap," she said, offering one to Eugene.

He asked her if she ever heard from her cousin.

"Nah, let's face it, Katherine's a snob. She'd never get in touch with me. My mom said she was into some weird therapy. West Coast! And I think she lives in Seattle now. It rains there all the time, I hear . . . so it must do a booming therapy business."

She asked him what he'd been doing for the past seven years, but she didn't seem to be listening to his answer. He was talking about Berkeley, and she would butt in, "Oh, did I tell you? The guy who owned the building on St. Mark's shot some bum in the doorway and is doing time?"

He began to feel trapped by the hot sugary air in her small kitchen.

"And I heard from Nelson a couple years ago. He lives in Atlanta and runs a dinner theater, and get this, he has two kids! Do you believe it? I was sure he was gay. Surer than I was of you, Yew Jean."

He left her, and they promised to stay in touch, and he told her about the performance he was directing, and she said, "Yeah, that's a big deal isn't it? I'll see if Virginia wants to go . . . she's not real active."

He walked from Seventy-eighth Street down to Chelsea in the warm drizzling summer rain, thinking of how it was then, and how it was now. What was wild and avant-garde was now passé. Moody Sue was predicting, "Videos are the future," and he thought that the only real folly of youth was thinking anything was new. He realized that he resented Sue saying he looked older.

Back at the Chelsea, he looked briefly in the cracked mirror over the sink in his room, and said, "I'm twenty-nine. I'm nine. I'm ninety-nine." He pissed in the sink rather than go down the hall to the brown bathroom that reminded him of the crash pad he had shared with Sue and Nelson and the others when he first left Ohio.

The reviews were good. In an out way, he was hot, and he decided to stay in New York. He took an apartment, a tiny place, down on East Third Street.

1981, New York City

In Funicello's, a dim and un-redone oak-paneled bar, in what was now called Soho, Eugene Goessler drank with his friend, the sculptor Joe Bukovsky. Eugene had met Joe the year before when Joe's wife, Diane, was designing the set for Eugene's *Wordplay Wide* at Stage Nine in the East Village. Diane was very pregnant, and demanded that Joe deign to lower himself and help her.

"That woman controls me," he explained to Eugene at their first meeting. "She has me pussy-whipped, weepy. She says 'shit' and I'll be damned, but the next thing I know, I'm taking a dump. Boom!" He leaned his large slab of body back, causing the entire row of attached theater seats to move a few inches in a chain-reactioned effort to accommodate the big reputation he carried so loudly. "She said, 'You help me now, or your fat ass is sleeping in your studio from here on in!'" And he looked at Eugene as if he'd decided he was worth the look. He was, after all, an up-and-coming name, of sorts. He'd heard about him somewhere. "And then, Goessler, get this," he roared at what he was about to say, "she lays the clincher noose over my head, 'If I didn't have such a fat baby in me, I'd be able to work, and guess whose fault that is?' And, though I knew I was already undertow, I said, 'Hey, babe, you should have thought of that before, and kept your tail between your legs. Should've thought of that before you let the old Boxer up your Yorkie cunt!'"

Diane yelled from the stage, having heard Joe's lament, "Throw the fucking dog your bone, Goessler! Shut him up!"

"Yeah," Joe laughed, "gag me, Goessler, I hear you got your wires switched."

180

Eugene, who'd been listening in the aisle, approached Joe and planted a kiss on his forehead. He stood over him, directed his eyes to Joe's, and said, slowly and surely, "From the sound of this, I'm going to have to run a warm vinegar douche," and he pushed his hand into Joe's beard, plying his fleshy jowl, "into this."

Diane laughed from the stage. Joe pushed Eugene's arm away, but said with a sly grin, having to look up to the author, "Hey, I like you, Goessler."

In Funicello's, at the bar, Eugene told Joe how he was sick of living in his cramped slum-hole apartment on East Third Street. He said that he wanted space to rehearse pieces in, to hold workshops in. He said that he had been having dreams of large canvases and he thought if he had a big loft he might try painting.

"You and everybody else," Joe scoffed.

Eugene argued, "You know all the bigshots, Bukovsky. You could put out the word. I could set up that old printing press I got from Columbia. Just raw space, that's all, but big." He ran his hand over his short haircut as he spoke. It was less than an inch all over but for a braided tail in back. Joe had asked him, when he saw Eugene's head, if he had a bad case of lice, or had he "joined the ranks of the fashionable style set." Eugene expected as much from him. He himself had felt something had to change. "Hell, Bukovsky, I'm so crowded in that apartment, I cut my hair so I'd have more space. I'm serious. I was thinking of removing the fifty layers of paint. That would probably give me another square foot."

Joe shifted on his stool. He was imposing. He lifted weights in his studio to keep his bulky form consistent with his alcoholic bloat. His heavy brown beard was untrimmed, thinning out on his neck where his chest hairs took over the hirsute chores, cropping out of his flannel collar. He swallowed a Jack Daniels in one shot. The sculptor's hands were his soul's outlet, blunt sausage fingers, worn, knicked, and callused, but used to seeing with a feel, kinetic to shapes. His hands were his saving grace. Otherwise, Joe Bukovsky was simply an opinionated, dominating, boisterous bull, carrying a deck of gripe cards on any subject dealt, demanding to be heard, no matter how off-base, with his bass bellow of voice and heavy-footed stamp. In comparison, his wife Diane was witty, clever, and sweet-natured. Eugene imagined that Joe's sensitive hands had won her heart. His noise certainly hadn't.

"New Yorkers are patsies, man," Joe said. "You got to look under the rocks to find any space. Nothing's left. Forget it, Goessler. What you need is money." He guzzled his beer chaser, "Fucking light beer! Diane's got me and the kid on a diet."

Eugene's serious I-have-to-do-something-about-getting-out-of-this-hellhole-apartment-demeanor cracked. "Zak is only, what? Ten months old?"

"Hey, man," Joe pushed his empty glasses towards the bartender, "that's what I said to Diane. Come on! The kid's crying for food! But she said he's a little pig."

"Maybe he's got worms, a tapeworm," Eugene laughed. "Maybe you do too."

"Fuck you, Goessler, you keep your mind off my kid's worms, don't go getting faggy on me. Now, me," Joe's eyes twinkled at the amber pour before him, "I might have one of those mesquite worms in my gut."

Eugene smoked. "Zak is a little porker isn't he?"

Joe slammed his hand to his forehead with a brilliant meaty thud. He had a brainstorm. "I got it, Goessler! Stella Gold!"

A few heads turned at Joe's thunder, but most everyone there knew him. He'd become a fixture. Funicello's was where he could always be found. He claimed it was the only bar in Soho that was not nouveau, chi-chi, or chic. Wherever Joe lived, be it Chicago, Baltimore, or Madrid, he had always found a bar he could call home. He was "a barfly first, a boxing fan second, a sculptor third, a husband fourth, and a daddy fifth, though fifth and fourth might switch places."

Joe's suggestion for Eugene was that Stella Gold, the woman who directed his gallery career and owned three herself, was in the middle of renovating a six-story building in Tribeca, the new name for the area southwest of Soho, and he said that Stella had, on many occasions, indicated that she was interested in Eugene and in "getting to know him closer" and he said, "If you take her a few times for a ride, you know, grease the rusty plow, you can have your pick of floors in her building, and for a song, man. She can afford it. Believe me."

From the laughter Eugene started up, Joe's idea might have

been called a joker in Joe's deck. "Are you crazy?" Eugene smirked. "Do you hear what you're saying? You're the one who's claimed that Stella Gold's gynecologist is a dentist!"

Joe laughed, sort of, "Yeah, well, so she's got a bite between her legs, you know, you've had your johnson to the choppers a few times, Goessler, it's not that off the wall."

"I'd lose it," Eugene sighed, trying to seriously consider it.

"Don't say that, man!" Joe chided him. "Don't ever say that. You come to our place for dinner tomorrow night. I'll tell Diane. Hell, with what she's got me eating, there will be enough. Stella will be there. We're going over prices for the show, so she'll be flying. You can test the waters."

Eugene drank and shook his head, deciding there was no way.

Joe's king of hearts was dealt. "Hey, loverboy, wise up! This is perfect! You think of pleasing her for a few nights, and voilà, big loft, low rent. Believe me, man. It's waiting for you, all you have to do is play a little. She's hot for your ass, man, I know it." He leaned back so he could cross his arms, looking stern and all-knowing, looking into Eugene's eyes for an inkling of what was in the writer's hand. "You're serious, Goessler? You really think you couldn't fuck Stella Gold for a fucking loft!"

Eugene rolled his eyes at the announcement to the entire bar. "That's right," he swiveled on his stool to the other drinkers. "Women are out of the picture for me!"

Joe spoke softer, getting Eugene's turn, and broadcast, "Hey, nobody cares here. Now don't go saying that anyone is ever out of the picture, man. You are talking fag again."

"Bukovsky." Eugene was getting as pissed as he was getting drunk. "Hey, Bukovsky," he got the sculptor's eyes, "if I wanted to, I could, but I don't. I don't fuck around. And Stella is smart. What makes you think . . . ah, man, this is stupid. She knows my scene, Bukovsky. She's seen my dates."

"Stella doesn't believe in fags."

"Yeah, right," Eugene laughed.

Joe drank, playing a worthless two-card straight. "You know what I mean! She knows that anything can happen. Dicks are dicks and so on."

"What?"

Joe couldn't believe that Eugene didn't understand, "The candy! Everything has a price! Especially those decorator types."

"Joe," Eugene spoke, "listen to me, darling. I don't know what you or Stella think about fags, but just hear me out, okay? There's something in me that gets headier over males than females. If you put the handsomest man and the most beautiful woman, both naked, in front of me, and said, 'Take your pick,' without a moment's hesitation, I'd go for the man. I'd be pointing."

"Yeah, but I'm saying, 'Eugene, don't pick, take'm both!' "

Satisfied that his point was about to be made, Eugene acquiesced. "Okay, where are they?" He looked around the bar. "And I sure hope your idea of the most beautiful woman on earth is Stella Gold."

Joe defended, "I didn't say 'earth,' I said, 'the most beautiful woman in a six-story loft building!' Damn, what's going on, man? Have you joined the troops of the leather girls? You're talking like it's over. Bush is kaput! You're making me crazy! I'm starving!"

Eugene deliberately eyed a man entering the bar, sure that Joe saw. "What? I missed the last thing."

Joe called Eugene's bluff. "Nah, nah, nah, Goessler, you don't fool me. You think you're hot shit with the ladies. They've got their own sensors, and they know an available cock when they see one. I've seen you with that tall beauty, what's her name, right in front of that boyfriend of yours, what's his name. Before my eyes, man, you were sloppin choppers!"

"Lola," Eugene said, "and I don't know who the guy was."

"Yeah, Lola," Joe tried to file the name, "yeah, Lola, she does those fucking publicity stunts and calls it 'conceptual' right? Well, she's hot, man. A handful, right? And you're telling me you haven't laid her?"

"Right."

"Bullshit!" Joe shook his head, feeling the crest of all the drinks awash and overflowing. "Nah! Don't join nothing! You're too smart for that! Don't go fag! And, believe me, Goessler," he signaled for more drinks, "you know me. I don't condemn nothing. I say, do whatever you want. I love you, man. Hell, I had a couple of guys in my time, but nobody is closed up for good."

"Out of business," Eugene sighed, wondering if it were true himself. "Retired and . . ."

"A loft, Goessler! Just fuck Gold! I swear to you! Or forget it man, just forget it. I'm really disappointed in you."

Eugene noticed the New York *Post* on a barstool vacated by someone who'd had enough of Joe's close-proximity rant. It was draped open to a photo of Charity Ball, the superstar. He leaned over and read, "Warhol personality dies of cancer."

"Do you know that it's a fact that there's some chemical in the cunt that energizes the male?" Joe remembered from somewhere, and then saw Eugene reading. "Hey! Hey! Hey, man! Get your nose out of that rag!"

Eugene leaned back to Joe. He felt cold and sober. He heard Charity's quasi-Lucy's-younger-sister-eating-out-Ethel impersonation. What kind of friend was he? He always thought that someday he'd renew their friendship. "I knew her," he said to Joe, and downed his drink, tearing up. "To you, Charity."

Joe tried to focus. He saw Eugene's tears seeping out and over the lips of his eyes. "What?" he muttered, seeing Eugene gone grave.

"Charity Ball," he said, the W indented in his chin quivering in and out of control. "She was the one who got me into The Factory to begin with, way back."

"What, man?" Joe asked again, setting his heavy arm over Eugene's shoulders. "Hey, come on, what'd I say?"

Eugene thought of Joe as a pup. "Big bark," he thought, taking the paper to read the blurb. The *Post* questioned how much of a female Charity was. How far had he gone to be a she. And each time Warhol's name was mentioned, it was printed heavy bold. Eugene cursed whoever had had such "fun" writing the piece, and then thought, "Charity would actually like it, I bet."

Joe read bits, rubbing back and forth across Eugene's shoulder, as if he was trying to get the writer's blood circulating, or wake him up, and he saw "Andy Warhol, Warhol's films, Warhol's Factory, Warhol's entourage," and he muttered, "Fuckin *Post* rag, fuckin Warhol," playing into his queen of the clubs.

"Warhol's innocent," Eugene said, getting bothered by the heavy arm pushing him. "He's timid. Really timid. You know him."

Joe, hearing his friend's voice less shaky, removed his arm and took a shot and a beer, and said, "Nobody's innocent."

Eugene tore the photo and blurb from the paper and put it in his pocket, "All I'm saying is, they make it out like Andy controlled people, fucked them up, as if he had that kind of power. Any power he has was laid on him. He's a half-scared little bunny."

"Dig it," Joe argued. "Print, print, smack, smack, ten thousand bucks," he snapped his thick fingers, "like that. Get my drift, Goessler? Money, man. Warhol has the power of money. He arrived at my show like a feather, but man, remember the talk? Seemed every person there had had a heart-to-heart talk with him. He's his own concept."

"No argument, Joe," Eugene sighed. He was aware suddenly of other sounds in Funicello's. The sound of ice. The low drone of other talk. The trumpet solo from the jazz station, and two trendy women at the table behind them discussing what shades of pink were the vaguest. Eugene fluctuated from a swimming feeling to a floating feeling and imagined Charity dying, quiet, a sinking feeling.

Joe knew to be quiet.

"She was one unique soul," Eugene drank, heaving a long sigh and reaching up to where his hair was not there, so short, at least he had the braid, he thought. "God, she was funny. She would make an entrance and screech, 'Play Ball!' and you could feel the room lighten up. And she could kick ass, too. She once told me, in strictest confidence, that she was one of the stars on her high school football team, and made me swear . . ."

"Yeah?" Joe looked over from his drink.

Eugene felt so alive, just thinking of her, and then, at the bar, breathing deep as she'd always sworn was the best medicine, he saw the splash of rain starting to cry down Funicello's sign at the window, the sweet drops, the gold beer, the old warm wood, the glitter and gowns and gowns and acceptance of Charity, and he continued, "She made me swear to keep her boyhood secret. Like it would matter. God, she was so strong."

"Yeah?"

"To do that. To put your life out there. 'Have a ball!' She once told me, 'Hell, these idiots bought the ticket, but they sure as hell don't seem to be enjoying the roller coaster.' I should have made contact with her. I heard she had been living in Greece. She was outrageous. For a while there, after I had left New York in '72, she was like a Christ in my head. She loved life, and it rubbed off."

Joe placed his arm back around Eugene, and that meant, "Tell me. Talk and tell me about your transvestite Christ. Do your words. Show me who she was, why she shakes your chest and turns beer into water, sobering. Later we'll deal with Stella Gold," but what he said was, "Yeah? Well what?"

Eugene lit a cigarette, letting himself feel the sway from Joe's arm, the weight of his arm, rocking him. He said, "You know, one of the weirdest things, one of the nights I'll always remember, God, when I think of it now, it seems so wise, was . . . we were all at some uptown party. Maybe it was sixty stories up, a penthouse of that banker, the one with the Chagall collection, and Charity said, once, I remember, that we were like a string of lights that people liked to hang over their parties, or something like that. Everyone was stoned. The best stuff. That was the guarantee, well, it still is, isn't it? We'd go where the drugs were. Did you ever see Charity doing her Connie Francis in *Fish*?"

Joe frowned he didn't think so.

"She had this song, 'Where the Drugs Are.' I have to see it again. I'm in it, staring a lot, wearing a jock strap. Anyway, at this party, this young guy was out on the terrace threatening to jump. Everybody crowded out to watch, practically knocking the guy off the ledge. I remember someone taking pictures."

"Fuckin Warhol, man," Joe took another hot shot, cooling it with a beer.

"Andy wasn't there. Anyway, Charity was dancing inside, and I didn't know if she was jealous that the guy was getting all the attention or what, but she went over to the french doors and screamed that Onassis or somebody had arrived, and everyone moved, en masse, back to the party. The guy was crying, kind of whimpering, and I told him to come down. I'd seen him around. He was really fucked up on something, I thought. He told me to get away from him. He said I was evil. And Charity called me over and said, 'He does this once a week, cowboy, it's gotten to be quite the habit. Just go on in. I'll take care of this.' I did what she said. But I watched. She acted really pissed at him and screamed 'Go the fuck ahead and jump, Alex!' And she came in and locked the doors. He looked at her and spat. She pulled the drapes closed and told me the show was over."

"Did he jump?"

"Yeah, but wait. Not for a while. Charity stood guard at the drapes, and wouldn't let anyone look out, as if she had something cooking for us. Andrea said the whole thing was an act. Charity and Andrea were real bitches with each other. I was starting to freak out, and Charity swore that I should trust her and everything would be fine. She said she knew the guy, Alex, and he was a rich kid who had often threatened to take his life for attention. Andrea sauntered over and said she had called the police, and everyone started freaking out, planning to go to two different other parties, worried which would be the right one. Charity unlocked the doors and went out. He was still sitting on the ledge, but facing the french doors, not the long drop. People yelled, 'Bye, Alex!' through the glass as they left, and I saw him give Charity his wallet and keys and kiss her and tumble backward. I ran out. Charity hurried me back in and said, 'Let's get out of here, cowboy.' "

"He jumped?" Joe scoffed, pushing himself back on the barstool.

"Yeah."

"I don't get it, man."

"Neither did I," Eugene said, his face twisting with the memory. "I was scared and furious. I mean, she had told him to jump. I can still hear that, 'Go the fuck ahead and jump, Alex!' and I grabbed her arm, ready to fight, I mean she was strong, and as tall as me, and I said, 'You killed the guy!' "

Joe shook his head, "Fuckin Warhol."

"Warhol wasn't there!" Eugene insisted. "Just listen, Joe."

"Fuckin sickees . . ."

"So we're in the elevator, and everyone is worried about the police questioning them and we're all stoned and Charity has this weird smirk on her face, and she's twirling the keys around her finger and staring at me, and I'm staring at her. I remember feeling so betrayed. She had said to trust her, and I did. It was as if we were alone. Everyone ran out across the lobby. There were sirens and a crowd of people out in the street and cars were honking and Charity took my arm, and said, 'This way, cowboy.' And we walked in the opposite direction from the crowd, to a black Porsche, Alex's Porsche, and we drove down here to her place. And I remember crying and swearing that I had to get away from the whole sick scene, and she made all the lights down Fifth Avenue, I remember, and when we were at her place, she'd one of the first lofts down here, you know, she held me and I cried on her bare shoulder. I was scared. I started to flashback to this bummer trip I'd had, where I was burning. I thought Charity was the devil. I thought I was in hell, and pushed away from her, started to beat on her," Eugene was crying, and Joe held him still, "and then she threw me to the floor, as if I had no strength at all, and demanded that I shut up in a stern male voice. It was the voice of either God or the Devil, I didn't know, but everything stopped for me, and she said, 'Cowboy,' she always called me that, 'cowboy, Alex was tormented. He could not accept his life, and he was too confused to see how it didn't matter.' And then I said that he could have gotten help, and she shut me up with her look, and said, 'There is no end, cowboy. Some people go to a party and stand around like furniture. Why'd they come? Alex went to the wrong party.' She said, 'He wasn't having any fun.' "

"Did she keep the Porsche?"

"No." Eugene took a deep breath, disappointed that Joe was concerned about the car, but then his face bloomed into the memory of the car. "No, she sold it to this guy in Brooklyn. She said that she wanted the money to produce a movie or for a sex change, but I think she liked having a cock. She probably gave all the money away. When I left New York she gave me a hundred and a bag of coke. She was like that."

Joe borrowed a cigarette. Al Jarreau sang on the radio.

"So," Eugene slurred, feeling thickly drunk, realizing that Joe's arm was what was keeping him on the stool. He clinked glasses with Joe Bukovsky and lifted the shot, "Here's to you, Charity, thanks for coming to the party."

Joe said, "Are you coming tomorrow for dinner, Goessler, or not? You let me know, man."

1982, New York City

It was snowing as Eugene and Stella Gold walked together on Spring Street after a birthday gathering at Joe Bukovsky's loft. Joe had turned forty. Eugene was drunk. He held Stella's arm as she tried to walk without slipping in her high-heeled ankle boots.

"The blind leading the blind," Eugene said, sliding in the slush.

They were headed to Stella's six-story building in Tribeca "for coffee."

"I hate weather," Stella cursed, "I hate snow. I hate wind. It doesn't belong in the city. It should be regulated somehow."

Stella owned Gold Gallery, an art gallery on West Broadway, in Soho. She showed Joe Bukovsky's sculpture there, exclusively. He was under contract with her and could not show in any other gallery on the East Coast. Joe had informed her earlier that night that he was going to "take off for Europe for a while and rethink my life." She resented his selfishness. She resented that she hadn't been privately consulted. She felt that she had shaped Joe's New York success, as much as he shaped pieces, and she felt they were a team, and now, out of the blue, he was "taking off for who knows how long, Stella, I don't want any dates or schedules!" Possibly, Joe's wife, Diane, was jealous, Stella thought. Jealous of the article in *Art* that linked Joe and Stella as inseparable. Why else would Diane be so accepting of Joe's spontaneous decision? She was the one who always insisted he stay in New York. Stella held Eugene's arm tight. She would have to reschedule everything. She kicked ice and said, "He

190

owes me." Then she told herself to stop thinking about Bukovsky, the ungrateful sculptor who had New York at his feet, thanks to her, and now had made such a childish resolution to "expand." She didn't want to think about it. She wanted to enjoy Eugene Goessler again. She wanted to fuck with Eugene Goessler again. She wanted to seize passion and wring it dry. She would deal with Bukovsky tomorrow. Then she thought how close Goessler and Bukovsky were. She could have Eugene tell Joe just what a foolish risk he would be taking. He could tell Bukovsky how she had certain loyalties owed to her. She would lie serenely next to Goessler in the morning and tell him this. She would work it all out, but for now, she wanted to escape her thoughts and concentrate on getting laid again by the up-and-coming avant-garde poet. The experimentalist who was getting such ripe press. Goessler was hot. She knew it. She had a way of sensing who was on the verge. Goessler was even working with Bon Temps, the "new music" group, on a performance piece for the Brooklyn Academy of Music.

"I know Sandy Watts," she said to Goessler holding tight. Sandy Watts was the head of Bon Temps and hot in Europe. "He and I were like this when he was at Juilliard. Your piece and his music. It'll shake this town down."

"We'll see," Eugene said, thinking of Stella's tiny pointed feet so tip-toey fast next to his big brown wet shoes. "We'll see how it goes."

"Joe said the Rockefeller people are funding it," Stella said. "Of course, you know Joe. He says a lot of things. For all I know, he has some other gallery in Europe lined up and isn't telling me about it, or maybe tomorrow he'll say he changed his mind. What do you think, Goessler?"

"Beats me," Eugene said, ducking a big black umbrella. "Maybe he wants to get away from Diane and the porker."

"The porker" was Joe's child, Zak. He was a cranky child, and both Eugene and Joe believed it was because Diane insisted on dieting the toddler.

"But why open-ended?" Stella asked loudly. "Why so fast? He could have waited till I arranged for him to have a couple shows there, and make it work out for both . . . for his own good. You know what I'm saying, Goessler? You know that it all gets down to planning and presentation. He's being arrogant and foolish and inconsiderate and precious and goddamned pigheaded!"

Eugene realized that he was searching for a knob or switch to turn off the mouth that was walking, hanging, on his arm. The snow was so white and cold, and rounding off the brittle grime of the city, and Stella's voice was sharp and mean. He resented her tirade. Wasn't it nothing compared to the snow? He could have sworn she had had as many Jack Daniels as he had, yet she seemed completely sober and lucid.

They had slept together the week before, around New Year's. His memory was dim, but did recall her petite body spinning on his cock, and a resolve to "not rule out bisexuality for '82." Eugene had been cornered at a party by Stella. She accused him of avoiding her. She said she knew that Joe had told him about her attraction to him, and she was not accustomed to making the first move, but she had decided that he was the exception. She demanded an answer. "Was it just me, or is there a spark?"

At the same party, there was a writer from the *Voice* that Eugene knew. They had flirted with each other, but the writer said he was afraid to do anything about the attraction because he was still seeing his wife. Eugene decided to show the man that he too could go both ways, and before he finished his drink, Eugene found himself humpdancing with Stella Gold and nipping at her ears. Joe was there, and passed Eugene's back with a pat and a "way to go, Goessler." Eugene shoved him off. He'd decided that Stella was too shrewd a businesswoman to give away a floor of her building for something as fleeting as sex. No, his motives were far more passionate. As they danced, he began to feel excited over Stella's body. He wanted to nurse on her. He wanted to play, knowing he had nothing to prove. He knew his bent, but he didn't know his limits. Stella seemed like a challenge, and with the New Year as a push, and the eyes of the writer acting like he didn't see them, Eugene accepted. They left the party arm in arm and went to his apartment on East Third Street. They drank and teased and fucked. He didn't remember anything about it except that Stella seemed tender and almost sweet in the morning light. She had seemed soft to him, he remembered, as they walked through the snow. Now, she was stomping with her little feet, mad at Nature, and barking about

Joe Bukovsky and how he would be ruined if he didn't follow her plans for his career.

"The corporate buyer for IBM will be here next month and Joe should be here for that," she said, "and if Joe would sober up, he'd realize that he can't just take off like he was some free spirit. He has certain respo . . ."

Eugene pushed her against a brick wall. "Shut the fuck up, would you!"

Stella pushed him back. "What's wrong with you?"

"Nothing's wrong with me, except maybe that I've got you tied on my arm chewing my ear about this crap. Who the fuck cares! I thought you were drunk!"

She liked that. She liked Eugene's face when it looked fierce. She had no idea why he was bothered, but he was bothered, and she was the botherer, and she liked that. She threatened something. Why did he want her drunk? She loved his nose red from the cold, air fuming from his nostrils like an animal. The angry poet, she thought, she thought that was corny but she thought it was true. Males, emotional males, she loved them as much as she hated weather. She moved toward him, to either slap him or kiss him, she didn't know which. He pushed her hard. "Get outa here! Go count your money!" he yelled.

"Fuck you!" Stella smiled. "Fuck you. Fuck the fuck out of you. Go ahead and write about me, you fuck!"

Eugene laughed. So she was thinking, still, always thinking, "Oh, the poet, oh the emotional poet, will write this up and I'll be his words." He laughed, then knelt in the snow, grabbing her waist, shoving his face into her down-covered crotch. "Let me eat the pussy of Soho!"

"That's right, Goessler, now you know how it should be, you down there, knowing which end is up, you faggot!"

"Pluck every pubic hair and she's still a calculating cunt."

"Oh, fuck you!" she screamed, delighted and laughing, her voice high-pitched, her cunt feeling warm, with his head pressed into her coat, there in public, "a scene from a movie or better" she thought, on his knees, the poet for my sex, wanting it. "He looks like a cross between Sam Shepard and a Carradine!"

Eugene tore open her coat. Her leather skirt was no barrier, but her tights were. He shoved his arm between her legs and lifted her and himself as he stood. "Yeah, you fucking conniving bitch!"

Stella screeched with as much fear as she would have at an amusement park, catching a glimpse of the people passing on the other side of Spring Street and knowing they were thinking how wild the two of them were acting. Eugene knew that she was thinking that too. He set her down, carefully, on her little shoes.

He said low and soberly, "Oh, such a free spirit you are, right? Fucking can't let go, can you? Can't scream without listening to your own inflection, can you?"

He felt his cock hard. He wanted to fuck her. He really wanted to fuck her, and fuck romance and the rest. He had that with men. He wanted to plow her, take advantage of her. He wanted to force sounds from her shoving himself so far in that it would have to hit something vulnerable and force a genuine scream from her. He took her hand and forced it through his overcoat to his crotch, "This is going home tonight, lady, for once you will know passion!"

Stella was impressed and threatened and excited. She baited him, "Yeah? The queer delivers? I'll believe it when I . . ."

"Suck me, Fifi," he said, pushing on her shoulders to make her kneel. "Be the man you wish you were. Suck the queer, lady!"

"Fuck you, Goessler!" she laughed and ran. He chased her. She slipped and slid, squealing with self-conscious delight. Then she fell hard, on a patch of clear ice.

"My fucking heel broke!" she yelled.

Eugene laughed. He remembered something.

"It's not funny, you asshole, help me up!"

He saw she was saying, "No playing around, this is serious, I've actually had something happen that I have no control over, like the weather. This is not a graceful scene. I hate this. Get me out of this." He put out his hand and pulled her up. "You, lady, are going for a ride." He made her climb onto his back. They had eight blocks to go to get to her building. The snow fell heavier, Stella felt heavier. He called her deadweight. They passed a woman sitting in three coats in a doorway on Varick Street with a burning candle.

"Look at that," Eugene said, "how does that stay lit?"

Stella rested her head on his shoulder, her legs spread around his waist, she wondered if she was falling in love. She said, "My uncle invented the eternal flame you know. The flame on Kennedy's grave. He invented it."

Eugene thought, "She ain't heavy, she's an image. She's a ghetto blaster."

Stella lifted her head and asked him what was so funny. "He really did invent the fucking eternal flame. It's oil. It doesn't go out, even in rain and snow. I swear it's true."

"I believe it, lady," he sweated, "and I bet you think this is real cute, me carrying you like this, don't you?"

She didn't know what to say. She wanted to say, "fuck you," but she didn't want to limp through the snow, and she didn't want to admit that, yes, she did find it cute, because that tilted the scales, giving Goessler too much over her. She remained quiet, thinking he was strong and that he was warm, and that she was in the midst of a memorable night. She noticed the scars on his neck by his scarf. They were from some sort of burn, she thought, as they appeared and disappeared beneath the lamplights they passed. "What are these marks on your neck?" she asked.

"Acne," he lied. "I shouldn't have popped'm." He wasn't about to tell her about the fire.

"Doesn't look like acne," she said.

"Yeah, well you don't look like you weigh a ton, either."

"Ninety-eight," she said.

They reached the corner. She told him to make a right. He thought she sounded like she was giving directions to a cab-driver. He was so hot that when the snow hit him, before it hit him, within inches, his heat turned the snow to rain. He was soaked.

"Put me down, if you want," Stella said. "We're close. See the wreck with the dumpster down there, that's it, it's costing a fucking fortune to get it done."

He carried her to the front of the gray brick building and set her on the loading dock entrance. It was an old warehouse and machine shop, built in 1888. All of the other buildings on the block were still being used for some sort of manufacturing. Hers was the first to be renovated for living spaces. She unlocked the sliding wood bay door, and they entered a dark wide hall. She tugged a string and a bare bulb swayed ten feet over Eugene's head. There was a large freight elevator that Stella unlocked and entered, leading Eugene.

"This is safe?" he asked as she jiggled the switch to activate the lift.

"Would you prefer a ladder, darling?" she said. "There are no stairs between the third and fifth floors, we had to take them out."

The elevator scraped its way up. The cables growled black and greaseless up above them. Had there been light, Eugene could have seen their shaky strain, as there was no ceiling to the elevator, only the framework, and he was gaping up. "We" he thought, she probably had nothing to do with removing any stairs, she said "we" as if she was on the construction crew. He resented her money for a moment, and then realized that without it, she was the type that *would* be on the construction crew. He had to admit that she was a little dynamo. Everyone knew that. Even to be living on such a desolate block, in such a desolate building, took a certain amount of guts, he thought, although it was a very trendy thing to do, and he was sure that Stella would make it "the" block, and "the" building on the block. As it was, Joe wasn't the only person who'd talked about "Stella Gold's Building in Tribeca." Everyone seemed to know the progress of it.

"Step up," she said, pulling the iron gate open. The elevator did not quite make it to the sixth floor. She slid a large paneled door open and let Eugene in first. The light from the snow out the windows made the space seem blue. She closed the door and turned on the overhead spots. "Here we are," she said, removing her shoes and coat. She shook her black frizzled hair and tossed it like a salad with her hands. "Just drop your coat and take off your shoes, the floors were just sanded and they'll stain."

"Big," Eugene said.

All the walls were bare unprimed Sheetrock except for the sandblasted brick exterior ones. There was nothing in the space except Joe Bukovsky's twenty-foot-long "Nude Totem Reclining" and a graffiti-covered pair of IRT subway doors leaning against the brick wall.

"Homey," she said sarcastically, her voice echoing as if she were in a gymnasium.

Eugene removed his soaked shoes and overcoat and draped his

muffler around one of the totem's hands, then followed Stella's little black mini leather skirt around a wall to a carpeted room that seemed gray-to-colorless with the dim setting Stella set on the recessed lights.

"Get comfortable and I'll get drinks," she said, reaching up and kissing him a peck. "You don't really want coffee do you?"

"Are you kidding?" Eugene said. "After carrying your carcass, I need water, cold water, maybe with a big wash of Jack Daniels. And make yourself a big one, since you need your edges sanded badly."

"I don't get drunk, Goessler," she said. "I could drink you and Bukovsky under the table, and I would not be drunk. I consider myself lucky to have made the evolutionary leap beyond the power of alcohol."

Eugene laughed as she disappeared behind another gray wall. "I see," he said loudly, flopping onto a pile of big cushions, deliberately messing up their spontaneous free-spirited arrangement so that their zippers showed and they clashed in a pile, tearing the cover of *Architectural Digest*, which was nonchalantly set on a gray marble cube table, "and I suppose you are willing to prove it!"

She reappeared with two tall drinks, not reacting to his quick mess of her lounging area, knowing any reaction would only prove her casualness was only a "look." "Here you go, Goessler, bottoms up." She handed him a drink and dropped to the pillows to join him.

His drink was strong. He took hers and tasted it. It was straight firewater whiskey and it burned his throat. He dared her to down it fast.

"Cheers," she said smugly, gulping a third of the glass.

"Fifi," he said, "I'm impressed."

"I would have put more in yours," Stella said, "but I want to be sure you can get it up. If I'm to be your dog, Fifi, I'm going to need a tree to bark up."

That threat, at another time, would have given Eugene a scare, but he didn't care. He was too relaxed, too comfortable, too confident to worry. He was no longer trying to prove he was straight. He'd resolved that. He loved the male body, the male essence, the male configurations, he knew that as true as he knew himself, but he was in a dallying mood. He wanted to play beyond his boundaries. "A nice place to visit, but I wouldn't want to live there." Eugene felt both sexes carried electric, and for some reason, Stella Gold dared him to go beyond gender. If he had any fear of fucking, it was that he might enjoy it too much and get involved with her. He laughed at himself, because that was the remnant of his long-ago wish, and that of Katherine's, that he would "come around" to the "right" way. After he had fucked Stella earlier in the week, he was intrigued with the lack of memory of it. If she hadn't been there in his bed in the morning, he thought he possibly would have had no recollection. He remembered dancing, and he remembered Stella saying that he lived in a rat trap and that he was a slob, but sexually, his consciousness was dark. There was something about eggs and horses and rabies, but that was it. He reached over to her legs and stroked her tights, massaging her thighs.

Stella's legs went soft and she moaned, "Mmmmmmmm."

"Is that a real 'mmmmm,' or are you trying to help the faggot feel like a real man."

"Hmm?" she opened her eyes. "Don't start, Goessler, I know what you can do. New Year's was enough to show me that."

He withdrew his hand and dropped back onto the cushions. "You know, I don't remember much about that," he said, "are you sure you got the right guy?"

She didn't believe him, but played along. "Well, I can't say for sure, but there's one way to find out," she said, undoing his belt. "You know I am a visual woman. My eyes never forget what they see."

He took a drink from his glass and then put his hands behind his head and let her strip his pants and socks and underwear. He watched her face as she let her eyes eat his legs. He flexed his muscles for her and said, "Makes you hungry, doesn't it?" Her hand seemed small compared to most of the hands Eugene had seen cupping his balls. Her painted nails could be deadly, he thought, as she pulled his briefs down and off. His cock was hard and big and flopped back against his shirt. He thrusted a few times for her, letting himself strut the blood in his cock so that it pulsed before her eyes. "Recognize it?" he asked, swallowing at his own seduction.

"It's all coming back to me," she said, in a low sultry voice. "I think I'd know this face anywhere."

"Yeah," Eugene said, pulling up his shirt and arching himself up to her face, "and just exactly, lady," he said like a Brooklyn detective, "what did this perpetrator do to you?"

Stella caught his cock with her hand and held it still, pressing. Eugene pushed the muscles so that it throbbed in her fingers. A clear bead of juice appeared and Stella's thumb swerved over it, waxing the accused's head. "He took advantage of me," she whispered.

"Advantage of your free spirit?" Eugene asked sarcastically, pushing her away from his crotch. Her mouth went from moist lip licking to a growl as she looked away from the cock to its owner's lascivious smirk.

"Ow!" she growled. "Don't push me away."

"I want you to take my shirt off with your teeth," he said, "but first take off your tights and turn up the lights."

She smiled, liking his demands, and stood in front of him sliding her hands up under her leather skirt and began rolling her tights down. He waited till they slowly were bunched at her knees, and startled her with his yell, "No! Turn up the lights first!" She started to pull the tights back up, but he told her to leave them around her knees and to waddle over to the rheostat. She didn't want to. She didn't want to look ridiculous, caught with her pants down in a sense, but he insisted, "Look, lady, faggots got weird ways about'm, and waddling women gives'm that geisha look. Show me your butt while you're at it."

Stella laughed. "You schmuck, Goessler, you love this, don't you," as she tried her best to get across the carpet with grace. When she reached the rheostat bank, she moved the knobs so that the lights strobed dark to bright a few times, and she bent over, lifted her leather skirt, and mooned him. Her dark pubic hair extended into her crack.

Eugene laughed, "What a boy's ass you have!"

She removed her tights, holding the wall for balance, and then she pulled her hand-painted blouse up and over her head. Her small breasts fell into place, and Eugene was delighted with the sight of them.

"I forgot about those two," he said. "Come over here, Fifi, and give me sustenance. I'm the runt of the litter. The oddball, and you're the bitch."

Her skin was white and her ribs were visible and her nipples were pinker than her lips. She walked like a bride slowly over to him, with her hands folded in prayer between her breasts. She smiled demurely and shook her hair so that it fell forward over her left eye. She stood in front of him, her legs closed together, and she looked from his eyes down to his cock. He pulsed for her, and she seductively licked her lips, and then he lifted his legs and held his thighs with his hands so that his ass was spread and open, as if she were expected to smell him as a dog would.

She scraped a laugh from her bridal pose. "Goessler! What did you do that for?"

Eugene lowered his legs, but remained spread out, and he plopped his cock with one hand and his balls with the other, "Poetic justice," he said. "Now come down here and do me with your sharp little teeth."

"I'm surprised you didn't fart," she said, kneeling. "And stop playing with your cock."

He let his penis go and pulled her onto him, growling and moaning. "Come on baby, get my shirt off me, it's making me crazy."

She tried to bite the buttons but ended up using her fingers. He licked her teats and caught brief sucks of her nipples as she hung over him. The shirt was pushed aside and he sat up and moved his head under her skirt, fingering deep in her cunt and taking little nips at her vaginal lips. "I'd like to roll up that *Architectural Digest* and shove it up here," he said from under her skirt.

"Oh, shut up," she whispered, gyrating on his head like it was a bicycle seat. "Just eat and don't talk with your mouth full."

"Yes, Mother," Eugene slurped, letting the image repulse him. He nuzzled in deeper with a mad voracious tongue, and he gagged, "Oedipus, eat your heart out."

"You're disgusting," Stella panted.

Eugene's tongue dove and retreated and dove and retreated and he forced Stella's legs together with his thigh muscles, scooting closer so that his cock slid between her ankles. He gripped each of her butt cheeks with his hands and let every repulsion and turn of his stomach happen, feeling the loss of the cock, and the shock of the absent cock, and the deformity of the missing part, that he knew, at that moment, was the basis for the size queens, the men who worshipped the big ones, and the smaller the cock,

the lesser the attraction. Stella's clit became her cock. Her butt
was a boy's, her tight little body was mush, and he held her all
over him, thrusting his fun between her ankles.

She was dancing and she was panting and she was not acting
like she was moaning, she was moaning, deep guttural calls that
triggered deep sounds from him. He pulled her down, coming
out of her skirt wet and sweating, chafed from her hair, pulling
her onto his cock. There it was, in, and he held her so that she
descended slowly, squealing as it rose deeper and deeper. He
moaned and cried with the wet sea and she howled with the
invasion. With the freedom of howling, the pain wasn't pain and
finally their faces were leveled and their lips touched like flint
to stone and their tongues were beastly starved animals glorify-
ing the instinctual hunt without conscious reason.

Then what seemed too much was not enough for her and for
Eugene, and Stella began the gyrations that would pull his come
up and out and in, to her egg. They both realized this at once, in
an iron-doored slam of quiet. They both stopped panting and
breathing and friction. The heart of Eugene sent the spasm of
come out to sea to black-starred skies to a hammock of swaying
souls waiting for a cradle. They both opened their eyes and took
a quick sip of air. Then a gasp, then a shiver, then a laugh, a
knowing teary laugh.

"No," Stella melted. "No," Eugene spasmed again, uncon-
trolled, and they both spiraled down, round their necks, and
back to the bright lights of the gray-colorless casual area. There
was all color and the thickest twang of music.

Stella's spine tensed then relaxed. She held on to Eugene's
back, digging in with her fingers. His cock squirted one last spit,
and they kissed, "Mmmmmmmmmmmm." He felt her vaginal
muscles contracting around his spent dick, holding him in her.
He thought she should hurry and douche, because something
seemed to have happened, some song of impregnation. Some
conceptual truth. Or was he being imaginatively romantic? No.
He knew. She knew. Beyond consciousness, or behind it. Something had bit. Had they not known the destination? The timeless point where the seed and the egg met, winked, and pinged.
Stella went, "Mmmmmmmmmmmm," and then, "Mmmmm-
mmm . . . ?" wanting Eugene to come back from his thoughts.

She dug her nails in his back, and he cried, "Oww! You sweet bitch!"

He was done. She wasn't. He was there in her loft, his cock subsiding but held inside her by her tight cunt muscles and her ninety-eight pounds. Her leather skirt hid the sight of their joint venture. She let him fall back onto the cushions. She said, "I'm going to keep you in me as long as I can." The conception was warm and sealed.

Stella offered Eugene the fifth floor of her building. She said he was too dear to live in "that filthy hole the size of a hotel room." He said, shocked at her offer, taking another sip of her fresh morning coffee, that he couldn't accept the offer without paying "something."

She laughed. "Well, I didn't mean it would be free, Goessler, I'm no fool. Do you know what space like this is worth? I figured it out this morning while you were still sleeping . . . I'll give it to you raw, for eight hundred a month."

Eugene had recovered from the thought that his cock had worked a miracle, and he stared at the white snow piled on the window ledges and said, "Eight hundred?"

"But with a ten-year lease, Goessler. Ten years. You can't beat that, and it'll be fun having you live below me. Nothing serious . . ." she smiled, "but we'll know where we can find relief . . . if the need arises."

1983, Amsterdam

After Stella left with their baby, Jason, Eugene left New York for a while, having spoken to Joe Bukovsky, who begged him to "get your ass over here, man. I got a big studio and all the hash you want." Joe never admitted it, but he felt responsible for Eugene's turmoil. How was he to know that Stella would "get knocked up and keep it."

Eugene was thirty-three, "as old as Christ got," and sitting with heavier-than-ever Joe, in a cafe on the Leidseplein, a square near the Central Station and the Singelgracht. It was as if they were in Funicello's in Soho, Joe still complaining, but now he had a new deck, a European Art Scene deck of cards to deal with. He complained that the "frogs" were too "high-tech" and the "dagos" were too "rococo." "The Americans are pigs. Check out those two secretaries from Pittsburgh or Denver," he said, nodding toward an outer table. "They fuck it up for the rest of us, flashing their money. What are they doing here?"

Joe was not pleased with the way his adventure away from New York and Diane and the porker had gone. He had moved from Lisbon to Rome to Nice and now to Amsterdam. Stella had tried to put a show together for him in Paris or London, but she "didn't try hard enough. She could've pulled some strings, Goessler, I know it, and you know it, but she had one thing on her mind, and that was that baby."

"You are, in a sense," Eugene said, getting reacquainted with Joe's bombast, "Jason's godfather, Bukovsky. You and Stella and Stella and me. You should see him. He's a wonder, but you know what I mean, you have the pork . . . Zak."

They were drinking dark ale. Joe reached for Eugene's guilders

203

and Eugene said, "Got to watch it, Bukovsky, I am feebly broke, and too old for whoring, and being sucked off by some business-strasser leiderhosen ain't my thang, capiche?"

"I thought you'd arranged to do that piece at The Blue Nose?" Joe asked.

"There's no money in it, Bukovsky. All I'm saying is, I have to watch it."

They proceeded to get drunk.

Joe bellowed, "You don't know snow from hash, finger asshole, now when you see my wooden work, you tell Stella she owes *me* this time and a show, or I'm not coming back to New York!"

"Stella's in California," Eugene sighed, swirling his eighth ale, enjoying his paternal drama. "When I say Stella, I mean Jason, you know that, Bukovsky?" And then he saw the "man." "Is that the guy? The hashish man? We should buy some, Joe. What's the procedure?"

"Give me that!" Joe said, grabbing Eugene's money. He went over to the man and was handed a drug menu and brought it back to the table.

"Sixty guilders for so-so?" Eugene asked Joe. "Is that good?"

"Seventy-five for better is better, Goessler," Joe said, taking the menu back to the man, counting out the money and getting a bag.

They finished their ales and walked along the Leidsestraat. Eugene eyed all the transients hanging out along the cobble-stones, so many stares of hunger and sex and dope. They turned onto the Prinzengracht, the canal along which Joe had his studio. The poet and the sculptor smoked the hashish, and Eugene felt again the melancholy that came and went, a grieving for the son that was taken away, like a recurring cramp in his psyche. They sat on the wood floor, up one flight, with the large arched windows open to the canal below.

"I've missed you, man," Eugene said. "New York isn't the same without you."

Joe smoked more hash, and laid himself flat on the floor and said, "Talk to me, Goessler, tell me what's eating at you."

Eugene stood and then sat on the window ledge, and looked out. "I don't know. Sometimes I think I've missed the boat. I've been having these nightmares where I wake up in a cold sweat, shaking, and I remember only parts . . . my mother shoving bark

chips up her hole and complaining about splinters and June
being Venus being Aphrodite being Vanessa Bell and then being
just a dancer on a dance show rating records and chewing gum
and always denying to me that she's dead, shaking her peroxided
head, and I accuse her of falsifying the records."

Joe shook his head back and forth on the floor. He was going
bald at the top, Eugene saw.

"Youth," Eugene said.

Joe was drifting in a daze of smoke, quiet, for once, contented,
mustering some movement to show Eugene he was "listening,"
and not sleeping.

Eugene saw two young men entering through a red door across
the canal. They looked like they were up to no good. He imagined that they were shooting something up. "Give me a big
warm Dutch cigar to suck on. Shoot me out of hiding with a
slick World War," he sighed. "Anne Frank."

Joe spit a laugh. "No respect, Goessler."

Eugene turned from the window to see Joe flat-out, glassy-
eyed, staring up like a dead father on the side of a road. "Respect? The best I can get is a spelling bee from Aretha Franklin
out of that, sweetheart."

Joe didn't respond. He had a slow grin over his bearded face,
from hogging twice the amount of hashish Eugene had had.

Eugene turned back to the window. "I want to drink coffee
and smoke hash and never go back to New York, acting out
words, printing out words . . . Bukovsky! Don't you pass out on
me! You make your fucking stuff and sell it for so much and
squander it all and you've whined about it since I've known you.
Your big fat gut heaving. Big pork bellies futures for you, right?
Rising like a pregnancy and falling like a shaken cake in my
mother's kitchen, screaming not to walk heavy-footed. You
listening?"

Joe heard, but he was fuzzy, on a pillow of familiar sounds, not
particulars. Goessler had lost him a while ago, but he heard. He
heard Eugene's mixed-up accent that went from hick to New
York to general American, and all close, known, dear. He followed the crack in his ceiling, and then he gathered all of his
splattered consciousness together to say, "Spill it, Goessler. You
got stuff to say, say it. If I start in . . . I can't. My tongue is thick.
I only got ears. My mouth is a blanket and Amsterdam is flat,

like this floor, man, and you fight it, sitting up, spined. Relax. Just relax." Then he closed his eyes and rested his big hands across his hill of torso.

"If I had money," Eugene said, "I don't know. Maybe I'd like to own a place that would be a base. A home, though Lola says 'we're all just renting,' but you know what I mean, a security. I've never owned anything. If I had money, I think I'd write one word a day, till I filled a page, and then call my agent, and tell him to buy space in *TV Guide*, and run it." Eugene saw the two men come out of the red door. They walked in opposite directions. "They just shot up something. Cute Europeans in their American denim." He leaned out and yelled, "Dutch Master! Light me! Hey!"

Joe twitched at the noise.

"Don't you miss the porker? Zak?" Eugene asked, and stood up from the window, stepped over Joe, and walked across the studio to where Joe had sketches pinned to the wall. They were all studies of a nude woman, very bony, no head, dark dark heavy scratched bush, and long sagging breasts that looked like they were weighted down by the dark dark nipples that were drawn in fast heavy-handed spirals. He walked over to the wood chunks, the pieces Joe was carving into rounded shapes, the ones he wanted Eugene to rave about to Stella, as if he was on speaking terms with Stella, and he touched all the chisels and knives that were laid neatly on a rag, like surgeon's tools. Then he climbed the three steps to the small kitchen, holding on to the whitewashed wall for stability, and he decided to boil water for tea or coffee or something. He wanted to see steam. "Good hash," he said, filling the pot. He looked out and down to Joe on the floor, to the man he had no designs on, never did, but that of a chosen brother, a big loud pussycat.

He said, in a made-up Swedishy accent, "You truly are the leiderhosen, Bukovsky. Will you be wanting some hot bogen-bachten, big art svenslaka?"

Joe said nothing.

Waiting for the water to boil, Eugene read through a copy of *Artschpiel* and thought of fields of tulips and windmills and wooden shoes. "That's what you should be carving, Bukovsky," Eugene said, as the steam rose, hot, wet, old, air, "shoes and tulips."

1984, New York City

Eugene helped Lola Hampton perform her tone poem set to music and dance called *Mother Earth* at The Cube Club on Avenue B. Lola was a tall, blond-haired, blue-eyed Pennsylvanian. She was over six feet tall and had a model's body, a model's face, high cheekbones, big eyes, and full pouty lips. But Lola's mind was nowhere near a model's runway. When Eugene had met her in Colorado she was painting and writing. New, in New York, she seemed to have made some definite decisions about her "art." In three years in the city, she'd gone from street shows to the cover story in *Artnews*, sleeping with anyone interested in getting her ahead, and ahead to her was "known." She told Eugene, "I am here to be my art, all of it, and I am here to be seen and heard and watched, and I no longer deny it." He was convinced, offering to help her in any way he could.

He was on stage with three other men, all of them naked except for the flagpole twenty-four-inch plastic cocks they had strapped onto jocks. And shoes. Each man wore shoes. Eugene wore cowboy boots. One wore sandals (he was the Christ, Lola had suggested at rehearsal), one wore spats, and one wore women's high heels. Each man twirled slowly around a heap of flags. The men had a colored flag hanging from their plastic cocks. And from the heap, Lola rose. As she moved, the men began to chant in Esperanto, "Maturo Viro! Maturo Viro!" (ripe male), turning circles faster around the heap. Three saxophone players tooted short choppy discordant sounds from the side of the stage. Lola's head appeared, her hair chopped short and dyed pink. She looked around, her blue eyes wide with wonder, and she dropped back below the flags, then her head rose again, this time covered with maps rounded. Her head was the globe, and she stood erect and naked. Her tall body was made up with pink, and her pubic hair was shaved, so that she looked like a very long bony pink baby with breasts. Her nipples were painted aqua. She peeled the atlases from her head, revealing her face again, and discarded the pieces of map as the men continued to spin and chant around her like gears. She made abrupt moves and eventually had her arms reaching high toward the clamp-on spots that lit the stage. Her armpits were shaved, too. Then, as if she were going to yawn, her mouth formed an *O* and a small globe appeared, like a magician's egg, and she spit it out to the audience. They cheered. She screamed, "La rivere fluas de la montoj al la maro!" (the river flows from the mountains to the sea) and she went into a wild frenzied dance, kicking the flags at the men still turning, and scream-singing, "No murej! No murej!" (no walls!) She hooted and sang a long list, at times matching a sax sound. If a tip of plastic cock touched her she would shudder as if she had received an electric shock.

Eugene concentrated on his turns and chants and found himself transported into Lola's concept. How ballsy and strong she had become. How surefooted and big and clever. He was dizzy with the fun and freedom and knew she was a success. He could feel the electric she was miming, the excitement and frenzy building with the layers of words and sounds and moves. The audience, including the press, hooted.

Lola came to the edge of the stage and screamed, "Silentu!" and everything stopped. She began to breathe and pant and moan and slowly gyrate. Her naked cunt pushed out into the audience. Her voice echoed and scared and thrilled the audience in her birthing screeches. She spread her legs and the four men knelt behind her, their hands reaching up between her legs like starved children begging for something. Eugene found the tab and slowly pulled the deflated globe from her cunt. Lola reached up in one big joyous push and the saxophones let out a piercing rising and falling howl. The nozzle was pulled between her thighs and Eugene blew it up, so that the audience saw the withered flaccid earth grew rounder and taut before their eyes, between Lola's thighs. She tossed the beach ball earth onto the heap (there was not enough money to throw it away into the audience) and Lola and the four men all turned their backs, revealing their asses, and each ass pooped out a white Ping-Pong ball, exclaiming "La luno" (the moon).

1985, New York City

It was September, the best month of any month for weather in New York. Eugene walked down Avenue A to Houston Street, away from the complicated rehearsals of his word-poem, to be performed as a one-act play along with a Beck piece at La Dada Teatro de la Cité de Pomme, an East Village experimental theater. He passed a newsstand and bought a paper. He checked out all the covers of the porn magazines, but none struck him as worth a pickup. He turned onto Houston and walked crosstown and down to his loft. He climbed the five flights of stairs and once inside saw his tape machine flashing four messages. The first was from Lola, the second was from one of the actors requesting a private talk with him, the third was a cryptic message from Bukovsky saying, "Sorry, man, if you need me, call." And the fourth message was from Katherine. She was living in Seattle. She had three children and was married to a psychologist who taught at the University of Washington. Eugene hadn't heard from her in several years. He had sent her a copy of *All California, Sequoia, La Jolla, How Are Ya*, which had been published in 1979, because so much of it had to do with their time in Sonoma County. Over the years, as he went off on his own, away from Scott, he'd resolved his feelings about her and had made an effort to keep track of her through Scott. Her message was a kick in his chest. "Eugene, this is Katherine. I don't know if you know this, but Scott died of AIDS two nights ago. My dad called from Oakland just before. He and Scott's mom just found out. Call me." And she left her number and apologized for leaving the message on a tape recording.

He rewound the tape and played it again. It was deadening to him. He had known eight deaths from AIDS, and had written four eulogies. He had said, "One thing is certain, there's a lot of fashion on the other side, the spirits are decked out now," when he delivered one of the eulogies at the famous designer Claudio Antova's wake. Claudio had worked with Lola closely, and through Lola, Eugene had come to know him. Eugene had become numb to AIDS news, overhearing daily that so and so had tested positive or that so and so had lost weight and that so and so had gone macro. But Scott? Scott was the healthiest person he'd ever known. Even in their druggy days in San Francisco with their bands, Scott maintained a rigorous diet and exercise schedule, ridiculing Eugene's cuisine of peanut butter and canned rice pudding. Eugene knew it had nothing to do with eating or exercise or rigor. The disease knocked all of that out, like a salt truck on an icy road. If it was a question of maintenance, he knew quite a lot of people who should have kicked it. Snow was big and beautiful, and yet, one dispensed load of salt, and the beauty and white turned to gray wet slush, and all of the remedies or so-called vaccine attempts at best refroze the melt, and so far, only temporarily. But Scott? Eugene said his name out loud, staring at the phone. He had plans to know him down the road. He and Scott had gone their separate ways, but Eugene believed that in the long run, they would get together someday, in a cabin, by a river, and recount to each other their lives. Scott was Eugene's springboard. He had poured a special potion into him, telling him to "choose to live" and to "put each cell back the way you want it." Did he choose to die? Did the truck plow him down at his own request? Was there no stopping the overpaid street cleaners? He repeated Scott's name again, seeing his beautiful smile, his Californian hair and ease, his strut and posture, his grace. Eugene felt his tears rising and swallowed, and he felt the pressed sense of no time passing. Katherine on the phone. Scott filling his loft. The life he perceived was such a fucking illusion.

"Damn this!" he cursed, as he howled and moaned and cried into his hands and slumped to the floor by the phone. "Damn this game and these rules and all of it!" He thought of the last time he'd seen Scott, in 1983 in London. He'd come from Bukovsky's Amsterdam to meet with a writer, Spenser Wallace, and he read that Scott's new band, Ma Da Faux, was playing at a big trendy club there. He spent the next day with Scott, walking. There was a bond between the two men, although they were no longer mixing in the same scene. Scott was going on about how the group was fighting their label to produce stranger sounds, but Eugene believed that Scott was only saying that because he wanted to impress upon Eugene how he hadn't sold out to the system. Eugene didn't care one way or the other. The afternoon they had together certainly did not seem like a conclusion. He'd taken it as incidental, and had told himself later on that evening, as he headed back to Spenser Wallace's house in Harrow, that one day he and Scott would drop all of their words and outfits and markers, and reunite in the innocence they'd once known. Eugene felt guilty for not having said something to Scott, for not having said, "I don't care about who buys your records and how much money you've made," but instead, he'd deliberately kept quiet, almost letting Scott talk himself into the ground, and there was a definite satisfaction in that, feeling that he *had* kept more integrity than Scott had, or whatever. Eugene shook his head in tears, feeling so sad for himself and for his own guilt and mortality and swore he would make amends, make the effort, but for Scott it would have to wait. "There's still me stuck in time, Scott, but knowing you are transited into the light, it makes me want it that much more, and that much sooner, oh man, you *must* be able to read my heart and know how much I love you and how sorry I am for not being there with you, if only to plan our rendezvous. It's all projection. All cells. Oh God, you definitely are God now," and Eugene cried as he stood and went to piss and he cried as he dialed the phone to call Katherine, and he kept all the lights off in the loft, feeling that the dark was man's true state and that electric was a human folly. "Nature, you are breaking me!" he cried, hearing Katherine's phone ring on the opposite coast.

Katherine's daughter answered the phone and Eugene asked to speak to her mommy. He thought of how he had once envisioned Katherine and his family life, content and cozy. Katherine came to the phone. Her voice sounded so familiar, still maintaining the *o* so from Ohio.

"My Dad said that Scott was in the Bahamas and he overdosed," Katherine explained, sounding very factual and efficient, "and I called this guy we both knew in L.A. that I once met when I was visiting Scott and Jack, his lover, the one who used to play bass for him, and he told me that the truth was Scott had AIDS and when it got to be hopeless, he had planned this whole thing out, I guess, but when he couldn't take it anymore, he shot himself with an overdose of heroin, and Jack was there and I think the guys from the band, and they are flying his body back to Oakland. Dora just cracked up, my Dad said, you know how she was about her son. He was everything to her in a way, you know. And my Dad started in on how he knew all along that drugs would do him in and how all the money in the world couldn't make him respect Scott because he was always selfish and only recently sent Dora a check for ten thousand dollars. And he said that she cried when she got it, and not because she was happy, but because she told my Dad that what she wanted most was to have Scott visit her. He said she said she didn't want his money and . . . oh well, you know how they are, anyway, they have no idea why Scott really died."

As Katherine was saying this to Eugene, he kept picturing their days at the cabin in Sonoma, and how now the disturbing times seemed hardly weighted, and the time there *was* the Garden of Eden. Katherine sounded like a secretary to her former self. She asked him about his mother and brother and sister.

"Frank has a daughter, and Debbie married an accountant and they live in Indianapolis, and Clara lives with Frank and Stephanie. I really don't talk to them much, you know how it is."

"My Mom died last year," Katherine said.

"I'm sorry," Eugene said.

"She had cancer. I went back to Ohio. I drove by your old house on River Road. It's gone."

"Yeah, I know. Frank told me once when I called. What a place," Eugene sighed, feeling the tears dry on his cheeks, feeling thrown from a train. Hadn't he been troubling over actors' lines and the sounds of rolling *R*'s only an hour ago?

"And where Bess's was is an apartment building, expensive for Ohio, with little balconies facing the river, they were pretty nice."

Eugene didn't want to hear about Ohio. He interrupted Katherine, "Are you feeling anything? About Scott? I mean, didn't we have something there for a while? You sound so, I don't know . . ." He knew but didn't want to say.

"Cold-hearted, Eugene? Is that what you want to say? Well say it. I really think you're a fine one to talk. I wonder if you had found out about Scott, would you have even considered calling me? I think that for me to call you shows real maturity on my part. We were kids then. I thought I could change you."

"What makes you think that you're no longer a kid? Because you're a mother? I have a kid too, but hey, Katherine, I'm not denying my past. We had some ancient, beautiful, timeless days there. And aside from that, Scott is your stepbrother, and . . . oh, forget it, I'm sorry. I have no right to be going on like that." Eugene broke down and started to cry hard into the phone, sorry for Scott and Katherine and himself and lovers and for structures and for apartments being built on River Road and for time, which, despite its fiction, seemed the deadliest weapon right then. He wanted to hear Katherine call him "baby," and he knew that she would never, and Scott would never curl up with him in old age and he might never reach old age himself and all of it made him furious.

There seemed to be a hint of emotion in Katherine's voice, a ticket stub from an old movie, and she said, "We each have our ways, Eugene. I don't know. I guess a part of me will always feel that Scott came between us before we had a chance to really get . . ."

"Jesus! That's it isn't it? You still think that I was just swept away, as if I had no choice! Remember what you said? About him being responsible for me? How could you think that I didn't want him? You didn't know love, though you used it enough . . . when it fit your picture . . ."

She hung up.

He threw his fist against the wall and screamed, "Damn you! Damn you!"

The next day he woke late, having passed out from a headache, and he read the paper he'd picked up the night before on his way home from rehearsal. There was a brief mention on page six that Scott had died of a drug overdose and that he and the band were in the middle of recording a new album at a studio in the Bahamas. *People* magazine had a picture of Scott in its next issue.

Later that year, Eugene received a call from Scott's personal manager telling him that Scott had left him $25,000 in his will, but the will was being challenged by Scott's mother, claiming that he was under the influence of drugs when he wrote it. Eugene eventually received $19,000.

1972, Sonoma County, California

It was Eugene's twenty-second birthday. The bees droned in the dry yellow heat of the summer fields. Eugene and Scott sat naked facing the sunset. Scott played the sitar he'd brought from India. Eugene played the guitar Scott had given him earlier that day, down by the river, after he'd cut Eugene's ponytail. The music was perfect since they had both snorted a pink dope that Scott had also given Eugene. Katherine came up the trail from the cabin to the field carrying a tray of fruits and cheeses. Unbeknownst to her, she was gravity to the two young soaring men. They stopped music, watching the notes trail off into the sky like the tails of kites set free. Katherine looked at Eugene's hair and asked what had happened. Scott and Eugene looked at each other, sharing some deep doped inner notion, and they fell back onto the ground laughing.

"I don't get it," Katherine said, cracking a smile at their monkey rolls of crazed laughter.

Eugene saw her through the tears rolling out, but there were no words for him that had meaning. Every word that came to mind was a tickle at best. He reached with his arm outstretched to her. She hesitated, and then settled her full white skirt onto the field like a blanket, and set the tray of food before the two naked men.

1986, New York City

Eugene climbed the stairs up to his loft in Tribeca. The elevator was still out. Stella Gold, absentee landlord, was living in Los Angeles with Jason and her husband, Sidney Harris. She had hired a management company for the building, and they had promised that as soon as they had permission from the owner they would have the elevator fixed. Eugene stopped himself from cursing Stella, and climbed the steps as if they were the ones up from River Road.

"The first nineteen were wood," he said, breathing deep and hearing his voice echo in the stairwell, "then twenty, twenty-one, twenty-two . . ." The last syllable of the number became his exhale, and there was a long childish lilt to the sound, "twenty-eighhht, twenty-niiiiiiine, thirteeeeee," and the numbers came singsong and his thoughts drew Stella's well-made face laughing at his climb. He saw her deliberately not fixing the elevator because of his ten-year lease. The laugh from her sounded a lot like his mother's berating laugh. He shook that image free, imagining the looks on his friends' faces when they saw the toys he'd bought them for Christmas. He was carrying three shopping bags that switched hands unconsciously on each landing. They were filled with odd dolls and games and tin vehicles from Hong Kong. Within one bag, though, was a leather jacket that he'd bought himself. He had finally received the money from Scott's estate, a year after Scott's death. The money in Eugene's wallet and bank account helped him take the steps so buoyantly, capable of blocking both Stella and Clara from his thoughts. The word "flush" crossed his mind over and over since he'd read his balance at the cash machine on Church Street.

Once inside the loft, he dropped the bags and took off his old coat and put on the new leather jacket, hoping it would look good to him still. He had paid four hundred for it and all the way home he had argued with himself, warning himself to be frugal and practical, but then rationalized that Scott would have wanted him to buy it. There was something special about it. Thinking of Melvin wasting money on beer, he accused himself of buying two years' worth in one shot.

He stood in front of one of the three ten-foot mirrors he'd gotten from the dancer on the third floor when she moved. As a child, he'd been taught to avoid mirrors. "The devil is in them," Clara had warned. He was afraid of them in a deep way that provoked him into bringing them up to his space. He told Lola that he was going to "watch myself live."

"Like a bird in a cage," she said. "Now all you need is a swing and some little bells to peck at."

He loved the feel of the leather. It was soft brown sheep hide that had not been treated, so it still wore an animal's life visibly in its imperfections. He put his hands in the pockets and turned around as far as he could and still see the reflection. He said, "It's all backward." Not the jacket, that could be taken off and looked at in the flesh, but it was him, the man he was, the body he wore. That he could only see reversed in the mirror. "Then the opposite of the devil is what I am," he said, but not biting. He looked closely and said, "Ugly." He took the jacket off and threw it onto a stool. It hung dead-armed to the floor. He lit a cigarette and read the receipt from the store where he now felt he'd been coerced into buying it by the salesman. That wasn't true. He had to admit. From the moment he felt the weight of it and inhaled the smell of it . . . no, the jacket was wonderful, a wonderful gift from Scott. It was not the jacket that caused the aversion he'd felt looking at his image.

He put it back on, zipping it halfway, tucking in the tags. Before looking in the mirror, he adjusted himself, taking in a few deep breaths, getting comfortable and loose. He shook his shoulders and inhaled smoke, and then stepped in front of his reflection. The first sighting was great. He thought he looked cool and tough and not at all ugly. Like Melvin, he too had a Gary Cooper look with his hair flat back. He said, "I look neat," sounding surprised, and then he caught sight of his mouth saying that and smiling, seeing his lips stretch out, and the deep lines falling to his chin, and he thought his skin was "cheesy" looking. He saw the scar in his right eyebrow and the scar on his neck from the fire. He felt his head was misshapen, remembering back to grade school when the girl who sat behind him said, "Yech!" to his freshly shaved burred head, "Your head's all bumpy like mashed potatoes." Eugene looked away from the mirror disgusted and shouted, "Fuck! Why can't I like myself? What the fuck is it!" He reapproached closely, studying his face, almost challenged by it. He said to his self, "Why do you fight? Why do you hunt for trouble? What do you expect to see?" His eyes seemed distant and foggy. His forehead seemed to be as square as Frankenstein's monster's. "Without stitches," he smirked bitterly. "Yes, even in the horror of seeing the true me, I do draw the line and temper the monster." He hated his cynical humor. Was this where it was rooted, in self-loathing? "Yes, yesiree," he said, "this is a very expensive jacket and I wonder why the fuck I bought it. How do I justify it? Boy?" he mimicked his father's Kentucky tongue, "well boy? Yer darntootin that's a fine jacket but on yew it looks like shit, boy. Boy?" he watched himself, looking very much like the Melvin he remembered, then he looked like Frank, his brother, and then he saw June's face, and then he looked like the picture of the Aryan Christ Clara had hanging over her bed, and he sneered and made himself to look like the devil, meaning "Christ with a sneer." "Boy?" he repeated, "I hear tell yer real flush, boy? How's that make yew feel? Dead man's money? Feel yew deeserve it boy? Fat lips boy, that's what yewve got, like the colored. Must be some colored in yer mother's side."

Scott, Lola, Katherine, Rubinstein, and Charity had all said at one time or another, "You have beautiful lips," he argued with himself, "and I've had other people who were not insane tell me, 'You are handsome.'" He scoffed and fell forward, "Who the fuck cares what they think? What do I see?" He decided that he had to be completely honest, trusting his objectivity. In his green eyes, he saw such sadness, and then beauty, and then fear. He felt anger shoot him in the forehead between the eyes and his face twisted. He cried out, "OH COME ON, MAN!"

He liked that. He liked that look. The anger was not feigned. He threw out his arms, "WHAT IS ALL OF THIS?!" And the answer came from another voice, but through the same lips, "The physical world. The skin. The hide."

He was afraid of that voice. He let himself whine, "But it's just that I don't see myself right."

"What is right?"

At that question he laughed and said, "Good, yeah, now I'm getting somewhere."

He strutted around the space, swaggering like a cowboy, sashaying with his ass like a queen, kicking like a dancer, and trotting like an athlete. He ended up back in front of the same mirror, hoping to see a released soul, free from whatever had been, but what he felt was disappointment. He heard Clara's voice say slowly and venomously, "Who does he think he is? Just who the hell does he think he is anyway?"

Eugene blew smoke and stubbed out the cigarette on the floor, sighing, forlorn, and troubled. "A very expensive jacket," and again he unzipped it and threw it over the stool. "Fuck! Why does this matter? Why is it important? Is it such a big deal that I've let it screw up the whole day?"

He laughed, "The whole day? How about your whole life."

"This is ridiculous," he said approaching the mirror, determined to see a truth. He knew enough about himself to know that he was on to something. "I'll just stand here till I die, and watch it," he said. "Fuck the opening tonight. Fuck everything. What is the point of going around hating yourself? Obviously what I see is more than skin deep. HEY! YOU! Face it, I'm not kidding!" He screamed at his image, and then thought, "Oh, man and all the fucking false gods!" He heard the sarcastic singsong rising in his voice, noticing a sneer where his lips turned up. "FACE IT, MAN! You have to accept yourself, in every way!"

He stared. The longer he stared, the more thoughts passed by him. Somehow, he realized, he had never spent more than a few minutes looking directly at himself, without looking away. He thought of how "wrong" or perverse what he was doing was, and then how stupid that was, to think of right or wrong. Allen Ginsberg had said, "Let the peripheral happen, don't try to shut anything out." All these doubts and fears and questions were to be accepted. Eugene saw the stacks of big empty canvases stretched and lined against the opposite wall beyond his reflected face. He never did paint. He never ran a workshop out of the space. He did have a son. For a moment, he felt the irony of the consciousness, and then he saw the deep cracks in the white of the plastered wall. He saw the scar on his neck. He caught his eyes, and said, "Change." He saw lines in his face, some imagined, some already there, and he laughed, "Change. Change is going on whether I decide to see it or join it or not. The lamb is now a jacket. The boy is now the man is now the dead. Enjoy the change, in joy."

He wrote on the chalkboard that hung next to where he was standing, "In joy you buy a leather jacket . . ." The chalk broke and dropped to the floor. He said to his reflection, "Excuse me for a minute, I'll be right back." Down on his knees, he looked around, crawling on the dirty wood floor, seeing closely all the cigarette butts and scraps of paper and garbage running the distance of the loft. "What a mess," he realized, from his opened visualization. Just as a viewer leaves the dance noticing everyone's moves, he not only was confronting his physical image, he had opened up to seeing, even the mess he'd chosen to ignore for months. Sounding like Clara, he hollered, "Pigsty! We live like pigs!" He found a different piece of chalk under a table, a green piece, and he crawled back to the mirror, checking himself out crawling. "No wonder I feel so ugly," he sighed. "What that woman laid on us kids." He stood and wrote on the chalkboard, "Clara, feel the leather. I don't accept your guilt, only mine. I take on the animal's skin. I accept that. I have beautiful lips. You are the only you. An ecstatic being who has accepted the invitation to the party." He stood back and read it. He was tired, too tired to fight himself.

"Okay," he sighed at his reflection, "I give up. I love myself, and I am not ugly. Something is only ugly in comparison to something similar. I am the only Eugene Goessler. I have a choice. I can love myself or hate myself, and I choose to love myself." He laughed, seeing his face relax and turn sweet. "Ecstatic!" he cried, remembering the Indian's message on the ace in Taos, New Mexico. "I trust myself!"

1955, Ohio

June and Eugene draped white sheets around their necks and danced in front of the mirror that hung on the door to the closet in the girls' room. They pantomimed to the country songs that played from their mother's bedside radio. Eugene copied his sister's wiggle. She made fun of him and he exaggerated even more of a wiggle.

Melvin opened the door, coming in for Clara's radio. His was on the fritz and the ballgame was about to start. "Boy! What the hell are you doing? Dancing around dressed up like your sister! Boys don't play like that, and in front of a mirror! Are you a little girl?"

"No," Eugene said, full of guilt.

Melvin roughly pulled the sheet off the boy, knocking him to the floor. Eugene started to cry.

"Go ahead and cry, you sissy," Melvin said unplugging the radio. "What you was doing was a sin. Only sissies and dandies do that sort of thing. The devil's in them mirrors." He took the radio and left the room.

June reached down to her brother and petted his head and told him he had pretty doll-baby eyes. He cried louder. She then tried to cheer him up by dancing silly for him, freely twirling her sheet. That only drove his hurt deeper, seeing her having fun, loved by their father, and unaffected by the devil. He gasped for breath. It was all so unfair. He looked up and caught himself in the bottom of the mirror, his face red, wet, and twisted. He quickly looked away and felt a strong arm reach out through the mirror and lift him up.

1986, New York

Eugene pulled the boy through the mirror and held him in his arms, rocking him, comforting him, letting him cry. "It's okay, it's okay, just let it all out little boy. I'm here for you. I'm here, loving you, and you're going to stay here with me."

The boy cried, "But I'm bad!"

Eugene held himself even tighter. "Ohhh, don't you see? Daddy didn't know what he was saying. He was only doing what he thought was right. Mother, too. They didn't know. They were victims too, just like you, but now I'm here and I'll never let you go back there. I'm putting you in my heart."

"What about June?" the boy sniffed.

"She's already there, waiting for you," the man said, seeing himself in the mirror, overwhelmed at the pure innocence of the boy, and that the boy was him. "I want you to help me, little Eugene. I want you to keep me honest, and I'll keep you warm."

From then on, despite feeling foolish sometimes, and down-right ridiculous at other times, Eugene made a point of saying deliberately and directly to his reflection, "I love you." He did not allow himself to call the reflection a pig or a pansy poet or a pretentious hick, or any of the self-deprecating terms that often surfaced. They were lies. They came from a voice in him that had lost its power. That was over. Change, as dynamic as death, revealed itself to him. He would sometimes have to repeat "I love you" ten or twenty times before he got through to himself, but he always did. Somewhere, he felt, Scott had a hand in this revelation. It had to do with the jacket. It had to do with all the

221

deaths, and the reality that hate and anger were a waste of precious life.

He decided, later that week, to divide the loft, and rent out half the space to one of Joe Bukovsky's apprentices, Tom North. He gave Tom the canvases he'd never used, and as he was moving the three mirrors to his half, the framing came loose on one and Eugene found a king of diamonds between the silver and the backing. He had saved the ace from Jesus Lo Dichodicho, the Indian, and now he had the king. He tore off the backing of the other two mirrors and found a joker behind one and only dust behind the other. He built permanent framing for the three into the brick.

Eugene told Lola about his experience with the boy Eugene, and she said it sounded a bit schizophrenic and called him Sybil for a while.

Eugene told Joe that his mirror work was "an examination of conscience."

Joe said, "It smells faggoty to me, Goessler. Do what you want here in your own place, man, but if you start that shit in the mirror at Funicello's again, I'm going to sit a few stools away from you."

Eugene dared Joe to look in the mirror and say, "I love you."

"Nah, man, I know how much I weigh," he scoffed, and then changed the subject. "So how much rent are you going to charge Tom for the other half?"

"He's cute, isn't he?" Eugene smiled. "Of course everyone's cute, Joe, even you."

"Fuck you, man. You're starting to grate on me. Let's go. I told Diane we'd be there an hour ago."

Eugene put on his leather jacket.

"Whoa, Goessler, where'd you get the coat?"

"Four hundred bucks," Eugene said, modeling like a Sears ad, manly dull, for manly big gut Bukovsky. "I consider it a gift from Scott. The money from the estate."

"Hot, man. You look good, Goessler."

"Yeah," Eugene dared to agree, letting go of false humility one more time.

As he closed the door, he remembered where he'd seen a jacket like his. Melvin. His father had had a jacket, brown leather, soft and plain. He stood still on the landing, stunned at what was now so obvious. How could he have forgotten that jacket?

Joe yelled from below, "Goessler! Kiss yourself good-bye and hurry up!"

1963, Ohio

The Olds ran out of gas. Melvin put his bowling bag in the trunk and started walking along River Road. It was late. He crossed the railroad tracks that paralleled the road and climbed through the brush to the riverbank. He took off his old jacket and rolled it into a pillow for his head and lay down on the slope. He stared up at the stars and counted everything wrong with his life, everything seemed to have come to a head. He was being put back to part-time, June was knocked up, the Olds was empty, and he had bowled, as Barney had put it, "like a cross-eyed Jerry Lewis."

"Clara's right," Melvin sighed, and then belched out to the river. "Sometimes there ain't no justice." Then he laughed sourly, thinking he was going to be a grandpa. "Shoot, life sure is short when you stop to think about it."

Up the seventy steps, Melvin lugged the long day, feeling lower and lower as he climbed. He left his shoes on the porch and tiptoed in and down the hall to the bathroom.

Eugene heard him come in. He feigned sleep and continued praying for his sister's sexy sin. Mack Hoffman had put his dick in his sister. Mack was so tough, and now Mack was going to have to be Eugene's brother-in-law. He heard the toilet flush and his father belch. Sex was so exciting, he thought, and it was everywhere. For every person on earth, a dick had to cream in a pussy, even the nuns and priests and the Pope came from sex.

Melvin came in the boys' room. The full moon shone through the window, illuminating his sons. "June may be lost," he thought, "but the boys might be something." He touched Frankie's base-ball glove that hung from a nail over his head in the bottom bunk. "You got your daddy's arm," Melvin said to the sleeping eleven-year-old. Then he looked up to Eugene's bed. He saw the glow of the body of Christ whitish-green plastic hanging on the cross on a nail over Eugene's head. He made the sign of the cross. Eugene was a good boy, he thought, but too deep. Maybe he would be a priest. That would count for something.

Eugene pretended to be asleep. He felt his father's breath and smelled the beer. There were many nights that he would act asleep to avoid having to talk with the drunken man. He hated the smell of his father's farts, and the sound of the loud belches and phlegmy growls, but what he hated most was his father's irrational words that rambled on and on, especially if the man caught either boy awake.

Melvin swayed a little and shook the top bunk, "Are you awake, Eugene? Boy, do you hear me?" He shook Eugene's shoulders.

"Huh?" the thirteen-year-old muttered into his pillow, acting groggy.

"Boy? I thought so. You ain't that asleep. You hear about your sister getting herself in trouble?"

Eugene said into the pillow, "Shhhhhhhh, we're sleeping."

Melvin stopped shaking the bed. "I just wanted to say nitey-night, boy."

"Night," Eugene said, relieved.

"Nitey-night," Melvin said, belching.

Eugene listened to the rustling and shuffling of his father undressing and getting into his bed across the room. Melvin farted a long wheezing pitched fart, and Eugene pulled the sheet up over his head and sunk his nose as deep as he could into his pillow, knowing the stench would soon waft over.

"You wanna know what I bowled?" Melvin called from his bed. "You know, Eugene, somethin don't feel right. When I walked in the house, somethin just felt wrong."

Eugene said nothing.

"I bowled poorly, and I blame your sister what with all I had on my mind tonight. She always was a show-off, thinking wonders who she was, it's no wonder."

Eugene said nothing.

Melvin belched, "It's a hell of a thing. Your mother is all broken up over it, but she had an inklin that June was flighty."

Eugene said nothing, but was forced to take a sip of air.

"Hey boy! You ain't that asleep, now!"

Eugene rolled as close to the wall as he could and said, "School tomorrow."

"You're so smart, Eugene, shoot. You think I don't know about learning. We pay extra for you to go to the Catholic school, boy, so you can be smart. Your little brother would want to know what I bowled. You act awful high and mighty sometimes, boy, like you is better than the rest of us. Just know, boy, you come from good bluegrass stock, nothin highfalutin. Know your place."

Eugene whispered into his pillow, "Shut up, you hick."

"And your poor mother. For all her faults, God bless her, she's made a nice home for all of us, and look how your sister goes and gets knocked up prettinear stabbin your mother in the heart. Shoot, we don't have money to throw away on a wedding. She should have thought of that before she goes out giving herself to that boy, but you know June, I don't think she's ever had a thought."

There was a slowing drawl developing in Melvin's talk, and Eugene hoped he was drifting off to sleep. He tried to cover his ears, but the harder he pressed, the clearer and louder the rambling sounded. He tried to not make sense out of the words, but they always seemed to be saying, "We are poor and stupid and stuck." Eugene refused to accept that. He knew there was a whole world out there. He thought he could be a missionary. To the nuns, they called the missionary life a hardship, but he thought, "How could it be worse than here?" He thought he could be an artist, too, and live in a big garret and paint and have sex. He thought of everything he could be, and life excited him, and he refused to accept the fate Melvin's words dished out. He would not eat. He would not swallow. The only trouble he believed that could stop him from having a big life was the bomb. That was the only thing. And every plane that passed over their house on the way to land at the airport, was, for a moment, the one with the bomb, to Eugene.

"You listening to me, boy? I said, 'Keep your hands off your wiener.' You and your brother better say the Rosary to keep your wieners cold. I saw you growing up, boy," he belched, "the Goessler gun, shoot. Time goes fast, I remember when you were just a star in the sky, boy. God love the Catholics, they sure as hell got sex on their minds, now, don't we? But you know boy, they can't bowl as well as them Lutherans, the devil religion . . . something's wrong, I feel it . . . and your mother, your mother made me Swiss cheese for work and cried on the rye bread telling me the bad news. She means well. I know you and your brother hate her for yelling, but boy, you got to remember she's not quite right." He farted a long growl and toot. "Whooeee, them beer nuts get me going."

Eugene muttered into his pillow, "Shut up, you hick, just shut up."

"Ahhh, sometimes I don't know. Nothin works out right. Prayin don't seem to get through the clouds to the ears of Jesus. I prayed for your sister, boy. The river was mighty pretty tonight. The Olds ran out of gas." He grunted and farted again, as a train whistle blew. "Sounds like a train, boy. Boy? Something's just not quite right. What is it?" He trudged through the muddle of his night looking for what was wrong, and then he remembered, "My lucky jacket, boy! My jacket from way back when I played ball! I must've left it down by the river! Shoot."

The train rattled past the house.

"Well," Melvin sighed, "come morning I'll go down and get it, with all them stars it won't rain. Now you remind me, boy, to go hunt for it. That jacket was given to me by the mayor of Covington, Kentucky."

The train rolled on toward Indiana. The room was quiet. Eugene heard a brief snore and cough.

"You remind me, boy? Can't forget that, not that."

Eugene heard deeper snores. He uncovered his head and saw the glow-in-the-dark crucifix above him. He decided that June was lucky to be getting married and moving out. He heard a tug moan down on the river, hauling an empty barge upstream where it would be loaded with coal from Wheeling, West Virginia. He asked Jesus to forgive June for her sins, and to forgive him for his erection.

The waves from the barge lapped high onto the riverbank and carried Melvin's jacket out and down the Ohio River.

1987, Colorado

"**I**'m freezing," Lola shivered, putting on Eugene's jacket, and then stopping herself midway. "Are you sure you don't want to wear it?"

"No," Eugene laughed, "wear it, wear it if you're cold, but once the sun comes up it'll be hot, and you're going to have to carry it down the mountain."

They were in the mountains, about to climb to 12,000 feet from their rented cabin at 9,000 feet. It was 3 A.M. and they had just driven up Canyon Road from the Harmonic Convergence party that had petered out long before sunrise. The Harmonic Convergence was the beginning of the end of a Mayan cycle. At the party, on Sunrise Mountain, a painter had said, "It's the fuck, the conception of a new age, and in 2012 the baby's due, man as spirit." Lola had said, "I'm available as a holy receptacle," and the two of them had gone off to "converge." She told Eugene on the drive up that the painter had to be tied up in order to stay hard. "He stuck a goddamned crystal up me and squirted on the rocks," she laughed, drunk and swerving on the road, "and I think he thinks you and I are sleeping together, Goessler, and you know, the disease . . . some convergence, Jesus."

Eugene was taking it seriously. He knew Jose Arguelles, the Mayan authority, and he had vivid memories of his experience with Jesus Lo Dichodicho in New Mexico, and he had found a queen of diamonds in a prayer book in the pew at St. Patrick's Cathedral during the memorial service for Warhol in April. The card had a picture of Machu Picchu, Peru, on its opposite side. Then in July he interviewed the Egyptian healer-Modernist poet Paul Ankh Ka, who told him, "You are Mayan, one of them,

228

whether you know it or not. You are holding the cards, Eugene Goessler." It was a strange series of signs, and he did not tell anyone, especially Lola, who had called their trip to Colorado Hokum Pokum Up the Yup, to which Eugene accused her of becoming Goessleresque. Even that, Lola's ridicule, he was beginning to feel, was part of something true. He knew that if she hadn't scoffed, he would've.

With flashlights and wine, they set out for the 12,000-foot pass. Lola wearing Eugene's jacket and Eugene wrapped in his keepsake towel over his flannel shirt. The towel had been June's.

The trail was well marked, but the mountain at night was completely mysterious and overwhelming. Lola's humor and complaints became reassurances of reality as they climbed up above the timberline and the flashlights captured spirits in rocks and scruff foliage. The wind seemed to be deliberately helping them. Eugene counted sixteen shooting stars.

"I hope," Lola panted, "for our sake, the spaceships land and take us away, Eugene, because I'm not about to climb back down."

Eugene heard the wind say, "They've already landed," but he said nothing. They stopped to rest and opened the bottle of wine. They toasted the mountain. They toasted the earth.

"To the aliens!" Lola said, handing Eugene the bottle.

"To the universupials! Which we all are!" Eugene said. "Where nothing is alien."

"Tell that to immigration," Lola said.

As the sky lightened, their flashlights dimmed. It was perfect timing. The white of the glaciers became fluorescent, and with surer footing, they pushed themselves to the top. They collapsed onto each other laughing at their success, just as the first rays of the sun, like lasers, beamed red over the peaks. They held each other to stay warm and Eugene started to cry. Lola kissed him.

"I love earth," he said, "and I love you, Lola, and I love life, and I love myself," and he reached into his pocket with his frozen fingers and brought out the cards he had and held them up to the light, "and I love this game I'm playing, although I don't know the stakes."

Lola took the crystal that the painter had inserted in her earlier in the night from her pocket, and she held it up to the light and said, "Hey! Let me have it!"

Eugene sang out, "To the sun!"
Lola asked him where he'd gotten the cards.
He said, "It's a long story," and handed her a palm full of
water from the beginning of a river.

1988, New York

Eugene's thirty-eighth birthday was in two days, so Lola came by his loft with her latest lover, the ex-professional basketball player, Tobey "Too Tall" Thomas, to give Goessler a gift and drink a toast. She and Tobey were flying to Paris for a week, so she would miss Eugene's actual birthday.

"Could I open it?" Eugene asked. He wore only shorts because it was so hot, even with the air conditioner whining out his window. The other half of the loft, the side that Tom North rented for studio space, was sweltering.

"No, wait," Lola said, smiling slyly. "Open it on your birthday."

Eugene looked at her suspiciously, and then to Too Tall who shrugged an I-don't-know-anything-about-it shrug. Lola held on to the six-foot-ten-inch black man's arm and said, "Eugene doesn't trust me."

They had to hurry to the airport, so they quickly drank a bottle of champagne and Eugene made small talk with Tobey while Lola went to the bathroom to stuff the cocaine she'd bought earlier in her "pussy purse" just in case their bags were checked in customs.

"You do all those wild paintings out there?" Too Tall asked Eugene.

"No," Eugene laughed. He said that he let one of Joe Bukovsky's apprentices, Tom North, work in that half of the loft. He told Too Tall a quick synopsis of all his plans for having such a big space, including painting and setting up the printing press.

Lola came out packed and ready to go. She kissed Eugene and whispered, "I feel like a fucking cheerleader with him." Eugene

231

shook Too Tall's big hand and said, "The one word of advice I'll give you both is 'duck.' "

Tobey rubbed his forehead and laughed. He said, "We've got to go, I'm double-parked," and to Lola he said sweetly, "Come on, shrimp."

Eugene listened to Lola telling Too Tall about Stella and the elevator and Jason as they descended the stairs. Eugene closed the door and went into his half and picked up Lola's gift and shook it. The intercom buzzed. He pressed the button and Lola's voice said, "Goessler, put that package down!"

He set it on his desk, which was sixteen feet long and four feet wide, made up of two sheets of plywood laid across four saw-horses. The school-size chalkboards hung on the brick wall, and the mirrors were positioned around the corner nearest the window with the air conditioner, so that if he chose to, he could see three of himself.

He sat down on his bed and looked at the card from Frank and Stephanie that had arrived that morning. It was a "masculine" birthday card, showing two duck hunters in a blind with their shotguns aimed at a flock flying overhead. "Duck," Eugene said. There was no mention of Clara on the card even though she lived with Frank in his suburban house. He looked out the window where he could see a sliver of Hudson River. Soon, he thought, he would see none of it, as a building was going up that would block the view. The foundation was already poured. He sighed, feeling sad and hot. He went to the kitchen and made an iced juice-and-seltzer drink, and rolled the glass over his fore-head. "Duck," he said again, and then wrote the word in big letters on one of the chalkboards. He turned on his sound sys-tem, and played his "Clara Tape," which was a loop he'd re-corded on Joe Bukovsky's equipment of his mother's message to him, which she'd left on his answering machine in 1985 after reading in a local Ohio paper that he'd won the New York Poetry Award: "I am ashamed of you, Eugene. They said in the paper that you are a pervert and you write about it. I only hope you know how bad you are. I don't ever want to hear your name again. You are no longer my boy. You have put the final nail in your old mother's coffin. I never." Click. And then it repeated over and over. The voice took on an intoned musicality, layered well beneath the words. Clara's bitter whine and forlorn moan penetrated Eugene's subconscious. He heard the voice of the critic in himself, the judge, the liar, the cynic, and the sinner. This was the voice he'd absorbed as a baby, knowing no other. This was what he'd had to nurture himself on. The truth of that fact set in motion the gears of a drawbridge that had been raised for years. He let himself cross to his mother with compassion. The voice that held him and denied him in the same breath, became the voice of a poor little farm girl being fed Kentucky bible and fairytale babble. He heard the little girl's voice so full of fear of life and the unknown. Her voice became the voice of every soul encased, every breath squelched, blind to the privilege of life itself, the birthright of humanity. Like a big woman's dress on a tiny infant, the resentment and anger and hatred he'd held for Clara slipped off easily. It was no dress at all, it was a blanket. Love and innocence filled his heart as he forgave his mother. She was merely a victim of victims too. The little boy in him, that he carried in his heart, reached out and lifted the baby Clara from her sad farm and held her in his little arms. In the voice, looping for the thirty-eighth time, Eugene heard the defeated whine, the lashing tongue, and the dead moan of a loveless baby, finally comforted. These were the stages of death, he thought, the forgiveness, the letting go, the truth. He rocked himself back and forth and loved her to death.

"Duck, duck," he thought he heard, but then realized it was, "Knock, knock," and it was Tom North at the door to Eugene's side of the loft. Eugene turned the tape off.

"Yeah?" Eugene said, crossing to the door, coming back to the heat.

The door opened and Tom peeked in saying, "Yo, Eugene? Knock, knock." He held an electric fan. "See what I got?" He wore shorts and sandals and no shirt, revealing a sculpted chest on a short man's frame. He had a dark hair flat-top cut and a lot of stocky muscles to compensate for his five-and-a-half-foot height. He had wide brown eyes and a deliberate perfect set of teeth, trained in braces for years. "Sorry," he said, reading the lost look on Eugene's face, "I didn't mean to disturb you. I heard it's going up to ninety-eight tomorrow." He was wet with sweat and he eyed Eugene's drink.

There was only ice in the glass, but Eugene handed it to him. "You know, Tom, I really doubt if that fan is going to make much of a difference for you. I've had the air conditioner on full blast all day, and feel how hot it is."

Tom sucked on a bit of ice. "Yeah, well, I had to do something," he said, and moved into the space, setting himself on the arm of an overstuffed chair Eugene had found.

Eugene did not want to deal with Tom North. Tom licked his lips and looked a little too directly at Eugene. Eugene suspected that the young man was deliberately sweating, just as he was deliberately running the ice cube slowly over his well-made chest and spread-out thighs. "Uh, Tom, I'm really in the middle of something, so if you don't mind . . ."

The young man jumped to his feet, "Oh, sure. I'm sorry, Eugene." He handed him the glass and Eugene said, "Keep it." And Tom went back to his own space, with his fan and the glass and a slam of the door.

Eugene had felt uncomfortable around Tom ever since Joe Bukovsky told him that Tom "is after you." Eugene had laughed, but Joe went on to say that the young artist was "nuts in love" with him and had confided in Joe.

"Tom's a slut," Eugene said, trying to brush off the idea.

"Hey, Goessler," Joe had said, "all I know is that he's supposed to be painting my wedges so they can be assembled and he said he can't stand to work over at your place because he's all twisted about you. Man, you fucking faggots."

Eugene had said, "I don't want to know about it. He's a sweet kid, but he's a slut. I had to tell him to stop bringing guys up to the space. He said he was just showing them his work or something like that. He's a walking case, Joe, I know it."

"Who cares, Goessler," Joe had said, "all I'm telling you is, maybe you're queering on to the guy and don't even know it. He is a tight little bunny, right? And I think you better have it out with him, because I'm not getting my pieces done and it's fucking everything up."

Yes, Tom North was a bunny, Eugene thought, after the young man had left, and yes, he would have to have a talk with him, but not now, not the way he was feeling. Clara's voice was still resounding in his head and heart. Forgiving her or Melvin was something that usually freed him up, lightening his spirit, and instead, the only thing "up" was his cock, which, despite Eugene's prudence, had been enticed by Tom's overt display. He considered jerking off to relieve the fixation, something he had taken to more and more, going so far as to have a sizable stack of porn magazines. "I bet each man has within him, within his life, enough sperm to repopulate the earth. Its entire history. One man," he thought, rubbing himself. Then he thought of how numbing the porn had become. It reeked of a false air-brushed perfection which he suspected was some sort of balance to the subconscious library that carried all the hell of homosexuality and not a single copy of the homo-hero. "Surface," he said, and let go of his cock. He yawned. Maybe a "sleep-work" nap was the answer. "Sleep-work" was his practice that required his watching the approach of the fall-off into sleep, grabbing that moment, and speaking into his subconscious, filing new information. He believed the subconscious did not know judgment, morals, or proportion as the conscious mind did. He believed that no matter how much he resolved consciously, no matter how much he understood what motivated this or that, until he rid the subconscious of the base images, he would inevitably find his conscious clarity undermined. What was filed as base images? Original sin. Wars begetting wars. Suffering, conflict, poverty, wrathful gods, fate, torture, Hell and very select Heaven and so on. Why did man not learn from history? Since the fall from grace was accepted in the subconsious, man would always fall, no matter what he devised consciously to hold him up. He would fall till the fall was released from its file. Eugene's groundwork was filled with information from Melvin and Clara and the Church as well as the collective history of life, and nowhere in there was the birthright of joy and love, free, no strings, unconditional, his simply because it was always there, full. As he approached the sleep-state, he would say something like, "I now open and release all the words and images that have to do with sin and hate and poverty and victims and in their place I put the reality of love and acceptance, honesty and joy, all of it woven in the universal infinite truth that supports me unconditionally. I say the joy of sexuality is always pure and always reinventing itself. I put all of this in, not as a wish, but as a fact."

He eyed the birthday box from Lola and heard her voice go "ah-ah-ah." He smiled, remembering what Tobey had said to him while Lola was in the bathroom hiding the coke up her cunt, "I sure hope there aren't too many delays anywhere, or by the time we get to Montmartre we'll be snorting mackerel." He wrote on his chalkboard, "Duck to duck to coal to diamonds," and then he fell onto his bed, still trying to shake the image of Tom's sweaty chest, still trying to stop the sound of his mother. All of the lovers he'd had in the last five years seemed so convoluted. Why was Tom so alluring and abhorrent to him? He told himself AIDS could be in the promiscuous artist's blood, and then told himself that AIDS, cancer, and humidity all existed because there was no resolution for them planted in his subconscious. It was all so complicated, beyond words. Again he considered a dive into his porn.

1964, Ohio

Eugene walked along the river on his way home from his fifth week of classes as a freshman at Bishop Miller High School. The river was brown and high. He wondered if he was carrying his books like a jock or a sissy. When he was little, he'd been impressed with the way June stacked hers and carried them like a tray, but he had learned that boys carried them sidearmed, no matter how many there were. His wrist ached. He restacked them in the weeds, felt the sun on his back and decided to sit for a while, even though he was supposed to babysit Michael, June and Mack's son. A coal barge passed. He squinted to see it plow through the golden light. He wondered how diamonds came from coal, and decided to look it up someday. He wasn't about to ask Brother Templeton, who'd only that morning ridiculed him for asking too many questions that had nothing to do with biology. A catfish jumped. He said, "Oh!" and imagined swimming in such muddy water and then coming up for one brief glimpse of the bright life. He pitied the catfish. He lay back into the tall grasses on the bank and felt the sun on his face. He heard the ripples of waves lapping, reaching the shore from the barge that was well past. He thought of Brother Templeton's handsome dark moustache and clean fingernails. He saw the brother's black robe, his back turned to the class, and his dark-haired arm appeared as the sleeve fell when he wrote, "formaldehyde." Eugene heard a bee. He ached to glimpse the brother's entire arm. To lick the underside of his wrist where the blue veins showed. To kiss the hand that seemed so clean and pure. But then he stopped those thoughts, feeling so queer. He swatted the bee and scooted back, thinking the bee might retaliate. He heard the Beatles on a radio and looked over to the road and saw Bobby Schneider walking with his transistor playing loud.

He was about to call out to Bobby when he remembered that they were ex-friends. He watched him. Bobby saw him and gave him the finger. Eugene's spirit plummeted. He saw the end of their friendship. Bobby was a freshman at Delhi Public, even though he was a year older than Eugene, because he "stuck" in fifth grade. Their schools' football teams had played each other, and the rivalry seemed to be all they ever talked about since they'd started high school. And then, last Saturday, after Bishop Miller trounced Delhi, they ran into each other at Bess's. They each bought Pepsis and ran across the road. They talked about everything but the football game, and started walking along the railroad tracks. They were both tall and lean and could have passed for brothers. They were both trying to grow their hair and comb it like the Beatles. Bobby said that at Delhi there were no hair restrictions like at Bishop Miller. Eugene was tempted to bring up the lopsided football score. As he turned to Bobby, he noticed a color-printed thin catalogue's pages flipping in the wind on the train tracks right behind them. He stopped and picked it up. He had not seen it fall from Bobby's jacket.

"Look at this," he said, seeing men and a woman in underwear.

He paged through the ads. It was from a store in Los Angeles that sold men's underwear, swimwear, and pajamas. Eugene felt himself turning red and warm and erect all at once, and he felt a heady shock at the sight of the men almost naked, and, embarrassed, unable to catch his breath, he violently pushed the catalogue and Bobby aside and said, "Yech!"

Bobby laughed at him and stood as if it wasn't his. He sat down on the tracks and moaned, "Oh shit, did you see the girl's ass?"

As quick as Eugene had darted away, he darted back. His head was swimming with the fast images he'd seen. He hadn't really seen any woman, only men in skimpy suits. He sat down next to Bobby. It was full of something that made him feel more than hunger. He felt starved. He wanted to eat it. "Let me have it," he said to Bobby, grabbing the catalogue, "I found it. I want to see what it really is. Where'd it come from?"

"Who knows?" Bobby said, keeping one hand on it.

They paged slowly, from the beginning this time. There were

five male models and one female, who was wearing a bikini. To save face, he raved, "God, look at her teats! This is really sexy!" The girl in the bikini held a surfboard on one page, and the five men were gathered around her in what the print said were, "sun-n-fun posing straps." Eugene could see some of their asses and the outlines of their dicks. He was so excited he said, "Bobby, they're showing off their dicks, just like girls show off their teats!"

Bobby turned the page. The men were in bathrobes and the girl was wearing a little towel wrapped around her. Eugene was relieved. He felt that his raging lust was so loud that Bobby could certainly hear his thoughts, and they were all focused on the strutting, posing, daring men, who were brazen enough to let themselves be photographed like that.

"I'd like to pump off all over her," Bobby said.

'Me too," Eugene said, beginning to wonder who would get possession of the treasure.

Bobby suggested that the "fancy jockstraps" might be for bodybuilders, "like the ones they wear in all those muscle magazines." He and Eugene often lifted weights in Bobby's basement.

"Yeah," Eugene said, turning the page to the underwear, where before his eyes, he saw one male model wearing a black see-through pair of net briefs that exposed his dick and pubic hair if you looked close. Eugene swallowed hard and tasted the thick saliva he'd noticed whenever he'd fantasized about sex. He felt himself throbbing uncontrollably and thought he might be having some sort of attack, and then he felt himself shooting come into his underwear.

Bobby saw him flinch and jerk, and laughed, "You creamed in your pants!"

Eugene caught his breath and recovered. He said, "Teats." And he adjusted his blue jeans where he felt wet and sticky. He said, "I guess my man cells are just too strong."

Bobby looked closely at the page, and then at Eugene. "She's not even on that page, Goessler! Her butt's showing on the next page!" He pulled out his dick, not about to let Eugene think that he had any fewer "man cells," and he looked around to see if he could be seen from River Road, and then in broad daylight, in front of Eugene, he pumped himself till he shot cream. "Oh," he moaned, "I think I must have creamed twice as much as you did, Goessler."

Eugene laughed out of embarrassment. He tried not to look too long at Bobby's dick, so he looked around to see if anyone might be walking along the road. When he looked back, the boy was tucking it back in his pants and rubbing his hand clean on some leaves.

The next page was an order form for the Beachware Boutique, which Bobby pronounced "Bow-tee-cue," and Eugene laughed and said, "It's 'bow-teak' not 'bow-tee-cue' you hick. I know cause June's girlfriend works in one at the shopping center."

They both stood up and drank some of their cola, and decided to walk over to the riverbank where the sun was still hitting. Bobby carried the catalogue and Eugene wanted it. When they were both lying on their stomachs by the river, turning the pages, Eugene began to wonder if Bobby wasn't also excited by the men in the pictures.

"You've got that one *Playboy*," Eugene said, preparing his argument for ownership of the catalogue, "and they show a lot of teats, don't you think?"

"Yeah," Bobby said, wondering what Eugene was getting at.

"Well then," Eugene said, "I think I should get this one. You'll still have the best."

"I don't see why," Bobby said.

"Because I don't have any naked pictures!" Eugene argued, "and these aren't that naked, anyway, not like your *Playboy*."

"Well," Bobby said, "but you have to let me look at it whenever I want to."

Eugene quickly agreed.

Then Bobby said, "But you know what, Eugene? Maybe we should send away for one of those jockstraps. Maybe girls think they're real sexy."

"Maybe," Eugene said, stopping himself from imagining Bobby trying it on in Bobby's basement. He felt so queer. He said, "I don't know, they cost ten dollars, see, and it seems kind of queer."

"You calling me a queer?" Bobby said, getting to his knees.

"No," Eugene laughed, feeling Bobby should only know what "queer" felt like. "I just think that those guys are show-offs."

"Well," Bobby said defensively, "You're the one who's taking it home, so who's the real queer?"

"I want it for the girl!" Eugene yelled, "and if I had your *Playboy*, there's no way I would want this. If you want, I'll trade you."

"No way, queer," Bobby said.

"What are you so mad about?" Eugene asked, standing up so that he would be higher than Bobby, who was still on his knees in the grass.

"Because you called me a queer, queer!"

"I did not," Eugene insisted.

Bobby reached out and grabbed Eugene's legs and knocked him down, spilling both of their half-finished Pepsis and pushing Eugene into a roll down the riverbank.

"You fucker!" Eugene yelled. "Take the stupid shit pictures if you want'm so bad! You always have to have everything, Schneider!"

Bobby threw the catalogue at Eugene and started to leave. "I don't want it, queer. You keep it. You're the one who creamed on the page when the girl wasn't there." He disappeared over the bank.

Eugene yelled, "Takes one to know one!" And he picked up the catalogue from the grass and folded it so it would fit in his back pocket without showing. That was the last time he'd spoken to Bobby. He went home, feeling his pocket burning.

The sound of Bobby's radio faded. He wondered if he would ever talk to him again. The catalogue was hidden under his mattress cover on his top bunk. The bee returned, flitting at his face. "Get lost!" he yelled, and fell back down to try to return to the thought he'd been having before he heard the Beatles blaring from Bobby. A V of geese flew overhead, heading south for the winter. The sky was as blue as Bishop Miller High School's Olympic swimming pool, with a few thick cottony clouds floating in it. Eugene imagined Brother Templeton in the black net underwear. He felt that the only sin an adult could possibly commit was "sexual sin" and he thought that the worst sexual sin was to imagine a member of the clergy in those see-through briefs. He felt hot pressure in his forehead, and heard a pumping in his ears. He tried to recapture the "good river feeling" he had always been able to find there, but he felt so ashamed. In the sky above him, a list appeared, in his own handwriting, as if it were a slate. The list read:

Get to June's by four.
Give Bess two dollars when June pays me.
Look up coal and diamonds.

Then a blackbird flew through the list and Eugene said, "Oh!" and the pressure eased a bit, and he felt himself giving in to the riverbank. The ease passed over his school trousers and bared feet, over his shoes and socks that tipped the high water's edge, over the red tie that was loose at his neck, and over his brass hair that Clara called too long and that June called hay and that Bess called golden and that Melvin called beer-colored. Another V of geese flew over and Eugene stretched out as spread-eagled as he could, as if he were going to be drawn and quartered, and he took a deep breath and said the Act of Contrition, till halfway through it, he saw Brother Templeton in the sky wearing those black see-through briefs and he held up the football score and Eugene heard cheering and forgot the rest of the prayer, and instead added to his list, "Save money to send away for a 'posing' strap."

1988, New York

As the sunset dwindled over Eugene's sputtering air conditioner, he rolled his pent-up blue balls in his hands and decided to "get it over with" and jerk off and then do "sleep-work" till he fell off for the night. "I'm not going to think anymore," he said, "I'm not going to judge myself anymore. I'm not going to open Lola's gift. I'm not going to nuzzle into the bunny. I trust everything. I know nothing. I need a fucking release from this heat." He reached into the box near his bed and pulled out a copy of the porn magazine *Malemen*.

He turned to one of his favorite leathermen, Tony, a dark-haired Italian muscleman with a serious piercing stare, from the page. A caption that Eugene would have torn away had it not been printed across Tony's boots read: "He sees you. You see him. You know there's nothing you would not do for him. You fall to your knees and beg for his mercy." Tony told Eugene to "light a big motha-focka Marlboro, and do it fast!" Eugene lit a cigarette and positioned Tony beneath his bedlight, adjusting the beauty for the least amount of glare from the gloss. Tony said, "Now get hard and rub your big thick dick," and Eugene said, "I'll do it if you show me your cock." Then he turned the page, and there stood Tony, completely naked but for his boots. His cock was a salami. His chest was covered in black downy hair, and his nostrils were flared as if he was really excited. The opposite page had Tony in a black leather posing strap, and obviously not hard, and that disturbed Eugene because it threw his scenario off. There was no reason for Tony to get dressed. Tony told him to shut up and keep pumping as the cigarette was burning low. Then Eugene heard a knock on the door.

243

Tom North's voice said, "Eugene? Are you in there?"

Eugene jumped up, knowing his door was unlocked. He threw Tony into the box and pushed it under his bed. "What?" he said angrily, pulling on his gym shorts.

Tom appeared, coming around the corner of Eugene's big work desk, and said, "I was wondering if . . ." and he stopped, sensing he'd cracked glass again. "I'm sorry. Were you sleeping? I did it again, right? Shit. I was wondering if you wanted to go over to Funicello's for a drink or something, maybe talk."

Eugene stubbed out the Marlboro at his bedside, and sat down on the edge of the bed, because if he'd stood, his cock would have held out his shorts like a sail. He hated that Tom was there, barechested and sweet. He was tempted to jump on him. "Come on, man, I don't want to go out drinking! Does it look like I want to go out drinking? Why don't you think up some better lines?"

"What's eating at you, man?" Tom said, almost tempted to leave.

"Are you deaf? I just told you. I don't want to be bothered!"

Tom smiled, showing his great teeth. "So you don't want . . ."

Eugene thought, "I must be crazy. Here is this beauty with his beguiling brown eyes and muscled body in his paint-splattered just-so shorts and his go-ahead grin, and I'm throwing him out so I can jerk off." He felt a line of sweat run down his back. "I'm sorry, Tom. It's been a tough day." He smelled his armpits. "I'm not fit to go anywhere. Even Funicello's."

Tom shook his head, resigned, and moved out of the light, then he turned to Eugene and cleared his throat and said, "Can I ask you something?"

Eugene stood up from the bed. He felt his dickhead dripping against his thigh under his shorts. "Shoot," he told Tom.

"Well . . . uh . . . you know . . . uhm . . . well like when . . . two years ago, you let me start using this space and I helped you build the divider and . . . like I was seeing Marco then, remember him? . . . and, well, it's been months since we went our separate ways, and, okay, I'll just say it . . . one of the reasons we split up, was cause or you."

"Me?" Eugene acted surprised and oblivious to Tom's stare at his bulge.

Tom North laughed nervously in the shadows. "Yeah, you.

Don't you know? Don't you feel the energy between us, Eugene? Don't you know that I'm waiting for you to make a move. Didn't Joe tell you? Sometimes I can't work. I just hear you talking to yourself or on the phone or exercising or typing, and I can't stand that you're ignoring me. Sometimes I want to just barge in and jump on you and say, 'Look at me, man! I'm wait . . .' oh, fuck . . . maybe I've said too much . . ."

Eugene lit another cigarette. "Tom. Tom, I'm going to be thirty-eight in two days. You're what? Two years out of Cooper Union. What is that?"

"Twenty-four, but so what?"

Eugene paced, keeping his distance from the young man. He decided that he was having the "talk" whether he wanted to or not. "Okay, okay, Tom. I have to say something. I don't know what your motives are, and it doesn't matter. I want you to know that I'm flattered that you would want me, but I don't see it, man, not at all. I don't buy your excuse about not working on Joe's wedges either . . ."

"It's true."

"Well, whatever. I know myself, Tom, and I'm not into seeing anybody anymore. Not sexually, not with AIDS all over and frankly, from what I can tell about you, you are not careful."

Tom stepped back into the light. "You mean that's what's bothering you? Hey! There is safe sex, or no sex. I don't care. I want to know you. Be close to you . . ."

Eugene blew smoke and looked away from the possible sincerity in the artist's eyes. "Well, for me, I don't want a lover, and as far as friends, hey, you've got it. You probably see me more than anyone, having the space here."

Tom was rejected. He walked to the door and said, "I'm sorry . . . no, I'm not sorry. I really think you need to touch someone. We all do. But then who am I, right? A naive apprentice doing assembly work for the big guy, right? You know, Eugene, you wrote that eulogy for Catlin Dakota and said, 'These ripe deaths get the juices going,' and I think you don't even try, man, you don't even dig the squeeze . . ."

Eugene blew more smoke.

Tom closed the door, saying, "See ya."

Eugene was tempted to chase him, but instead fell back onto the bed, grieving for so many losses. He took off his shorts and listened to the air conditioner rattle on. Something was way off. Tom North, a man who easily could have been a paper doll in *Malemen*, had stood before him, offering real flesh and blood, and Eugene had blocked any notion, any taste, not even a kiss from invading his flat routine. He pulled the hair back from his sweating forehead. "What if I had asked Tom to strip for me," he thought, "not to touch, but to look?"

He took his notebook from the nightstand and wrote: "Tom North stood in show-off shorts before me, making an offering of himself. I was threatened. I saw danger and risk. I saw disease, trouble, and complications. Sweat drops from my nose and an old, old tear is mustered around my eye. I am so sad at this. He was here. Right here. If only he'd been a glossy shot, right, Goessler? Then you would have been at ease? These magazines have become too easy an out, and I inevitably come up empty. Haven't I performed enough dicklifts over those men? What is it doing to my psyche? God, all the way back to those men in posing straps! Then posing myself! Males stripped. Something about the three crosses. Wanting to be on the cross next to Christ, stripped. Charity, stripped, not a woman after all, exposed for what she was, a football star. I've filled my head with one hunk after the next and imagined perfect scenes, always under my control, always timed to the length of a smoke. I have a spectacular man at the head of my bed, no questions asked. I have him before me, directed, overpowered or overpowering, always the same, the same glint in the eye, the same hard gunpoint, and I can get him to move by squinting and blinking fast. Never a real touch. It's like passing a cafe and calling it lunch. I am so fucking hungry! They tease me. They say, 'See my pecs and lats and round tight ass. I have no faults, they've all been airbrushed away for you.' And I come and close the magazine and go away. No questions asked. No talk. What do you do? Do you smell? Is there a choke in your laugh? None of that bother, none of that heavy stuff . . . just paper weight. Enough. Enough. I want to shred the paper! I'm not condemning the art of the wank. Pump yourself dry, Goessler, but imagine Tom North. What I'm saying, is that it's time to let go of the easy image, so perfect and folded, and like plastic fruit, not fruit at all. Let lust in! Let go!"

He moved fast. He dumped the contents of the box on his bed.

First to go was Tony the leatherman. He kissed the glossy cover shot, and said, "So long you big lug." He tore him into strips that curled up like ribbon. He thought that he could use the box of scraps for packing something. He imagined sending a fragile "Pieta" reproduction to Clara, packed in shredded homosexuals. Or a crystal goblet to Stella in California, telling her that it was "packed safe, packed in proof of my health, so stop spreading fear about catching AIDS from me."

He said good-bye to Mark the Cowboy who reminded Eugene of himself when he'd first come to New York. He tore and tore so that no piece was whole. Some were dearer than others. How many seeds had been sown in such fallow ground!

As Eugene tore and tore, he felt lighter and lighter, having taken a step toward a new sexual life. As he carried the box of shredded men down the five flights of stairs to the street, he told himself that he was going to get his feet wet again, no matter how polluted the bloodstream was. He would be careful, but he was going to swim. He carried the box down the dark hot block. The empty street hummed with air conditioners. There was a dumpster in front of a new renovation project. He climbed up its side and threw handfuls, like ticker tape, over the piles of broken plaster lathe. A hot wind blew up the street and a few scraps went sailing up and out, like freed souls. He called out, "Butts to butts and asses to asses! Ducks to ducks and coal to diamonds!"

Tom North came round the corner and saw Eugene standing in the dumpster. Eugene laughed and explained, "I'm changing my ways, you bunny. I am alive. That is that, and from now on I am determined to live this body out." Tom took that to mean that Eugene was ready for him, and he walked the poet, arm in arm, back up the block and up the five flights and into bed.

In the morning, Eugene woke to find Tom making iced coffee and he resented it, just as he had resented Tom's declarations of love during their sweaty roll-around during the night. He realized that his heart was not in it, and said as much to Tom. The young man threw the tray he was preparing and stormed out of the loft. Crushed ice landed all over the gift from Lola. Eugene heaved a sad but relieved sigh. At least he'd been honest early in the game. "No more games," he said, crawling out of the bed and reaching for the wet package. He tore the wrapping paper off to find an old jack-in-the-box. He turned the crank and the toy played a tinny clinky tune till the hatch flipped open and a big cock popped up. Lola had removed the Jack-clown head and attached a rubbery dildo to the spring. Wrapped around the bobbing shaft, Eugene untied a folded pamphlet that contained plane tickets to a sexual ashram in Canada that Lola had talked about a few weeks earlier, much to his amusement. She had written on the pamphlet, "Pop your weazel, Eugene."

In September, outside of Quebec City, Eugene heard the guru say, "To practice sexual tantra, total truth is required. You and your partner must consciously see your movements as purification. You agree to share karma. There is no holding back. All fantasies are shared. All thoughts are shared. You will see the paranoia of lust dissolve and there will be no separation, no dance of the second chakra. Two become one in an act of worship to the universal God and the orgasm knows no owner. To do this, one must first become a monk and enter the self's cave and find the self's true heart."

1990, Massachusetts

Eugene, his open flannel shirt showing how warm the weather was for October, sat with Lola, hair dyed maroon, in the front seat of their rented Chevrolet, outside Widow Turner's Bed and Breakfast in Massachusetts, near Mount Greylock in the Berkshire Mountains. They had come up from New York for the weekend to get away from the city and to see the colors of the autumn.

"We have no choice," Lola said. "We are not going to find anything else, Eugene, so let's just pay her and settle in."

They had been given the widow's address from a motel manager, the tenth one to give them the "Nothing for miles, should have made reservations" routine. The widow's house was full of crocheted doilies and framed pictures of Christ, Mary, grandchildren, poodles, and Kennedys. And the widow wore a green eyepatch, explaining she had a "weakness."

"Truth is stranger than fiction, Lola," Eugene sighed. "This is not what I had in mind. I thought we would be able to find some remote spot alone, if only an anonymous motel, not some dear old lady's frilled crucifix house. She's wearing a fucking eyepatch! She'll probably want us to talk with her!"

Lola took the keys. "You'll get into it, Goessler. Let's give her the money and get a room before someone else gets here."

"I want a physical big stretch. A comeshot in the woods!" Eugene smacked the dashboard.

"Goessler," Lola said sternly, "am I going to have to go through this again? Just get into it. It's only a place to sleep. We'll unpack and then drive out to that field we passed."

"Look at the clouds, Lola," Eugene argued. "We're going to be stuck learning how to starch lace with the widow while it rains."

Lola, frustrated, got out of the car and grabbed her bag. "I'm going in and giving the old one-eyed Christian the money, and I'm going to the room, and you can stay in the car if you want, Goessler."

In a thin whiny flat voice, the widow took the money and said, "So you made up your mind, dear? That's nice. Better to have a room before the clouds break."

Thunder bowled through the valley, rattling the windows. Eugene followed Lola up the stairs, nodding to Widow Turner, who lifted her patch to get a bigger picture of the messy man, the intruder dirtying her pillows, he thought she was thinking, showing him her reddened eye. She snapped the patch back over her eye and said, "Tea at ten, checkout by noon," and slippered her way back to her parlor.

Lola and Eugene turned at the landing and five steps above saw a dark bearded man in black briefs dart past them down the hall to what must have been the bathroom. They both stopped. Eugene, having seen the sprint of the long muscular legs and the bouncing black bulge and the skin and male of the sight, sang out, "Chevrolet, Chevrolet! I take back everything I said, Lola. Was that a mirage? I think I love this place!"

Lola moved on up. "The widow's got herself a houseful now."

"I was a fool, Lola, to have questioned staying here in the lady's house. There's a goddamned poem peeing beyond that door!"

They could hear the stream of piss hitting the water as they found their room, "the blue one, dears."

Lola said, "We'll flip for him."

Eugene said, in the hallway, "Oh chevrolet, chevrolet and johnson, oh johnson shaking dry! A cathedral of Januaries, I genuflect to the widow's fine taste!" And he knelt outside the bathroom door.

"Get in here, Goessler," Lola whispered. "You're going to love this room."

There were statues, palm branches, and two duplicate prints of Leonardo's "Last Supper" around the room. Eugene threw his bag on the double bed and made the sign of the cross. "I think we've found the only bed and breakfast that has received the church's imprimatur."

Lola started to close the door, then had second thoughts and left it open, hoping to catch a glimpse of the man as he came out of the bathroom.

Eugene lay on the soft mattress and watched Lola standing in the doorway, fluffing her full maroon hair and adjusting her tight red denim jeans. She removed her blouse, exposing her skimpy pink guinea tee.

"God, we must be horny," Eugene sighed. "Look at how we're acting."

Lola dry-humped the air, causing Eugene to laugh, which prompted her to turn around and stick her ass out into the hall. She looked over to him and said, "After spending all those hours with you in the car talking nonstop about how you want to be completely and totally physical and sexual, of course I'm horny, Goessler . . ." and she saw Eugene's eyes move from hers to the hall. His smile closed and he fell back on the pillows laughing, as he had seen the man pass their door, looking at Lola's wiggling red denim butt. "What?" Lola gasped, standing up. "Was that him? Did he see me?"

Eugene nodded.

"Really? Oh, great. Well, maybe it looked like I had lost something."

"He got an eyeful, Lola."

She laughed tears so hard her face reddened despite her popular "white" look. She closed the door and jumped onto the bed with Eugene and they wrestled about, both of them, despite their ages (Lola was thirty-eight, Eugene forty), acting up as if they were naughty children, fully aware of how noisy it must have sounded to the widow crocheting or praying in the parlor below them. As the rain poured, they decided to take a nap, knowing that down the hall, a Greek god was sharing their roof.

When Eugene opened his eyes, it was dark. Lola was snoring and twisted in the blue bedspread. He entered the hall to go to the bathroom, and noticed a light and the door open to the bearded man's room. He peeked in, knocking lightly on the wood molding that framed the doorway. The man, Octavio, was reading in bed. He looked up from his book and smiled.

"Hello," Eugene said, "we're down the hall. We saw you before . . ."

Octavio uncovered and crossed the room, still in his briefs, as if it was a beach and he was wearing swimming trunks. Eugene wanted to scream, "My God, you're gorgeous! How can you walk around like that? And not expect jaws to drop in awe?" The man was almost as tall as Eugene, and he had a smooth muscular well-defined torso, and strong arms that reached out to shake Eugene's hand.

"I am Octavio Beneto," he said with a Brazilian accent. His hair was black and his beard was black, a nest for the pink lips that spoke so sweetly. His eyes were creased with wit, dark dark brown, and the lashes were thick and black so that the whites seemed brilliant. His entire being was brilliant to Eugene. The man was releasing words in Eugene's head like, "Mediterranean, Adriatic, Venetian, Apollo, and Chevrolet." From the grasp of his hand, he felt photographic, imprinted, and melting, and he was tempted to apologize for such shock, but at the same time felt the tender eyes were just as impressed, and the lips that said his name seemed to have said much more and long before and would again, and Eugene felt his knees weaken and all of his pores opened in that one touch of hands. Lightning streaked through the lacy curtains, briefly showing the mountain beyond the widow's yard.

"I'm Eugene Goessler, from New York," he swallowed, actually daring to show his excited nerves, lost in Octavio's eyes, "I, uh, I feel so strange . . ."

Octavio let go of Eugene's hand and motioned for him to come into the room, which was yellow, pastel yellow, with daisy-and-butterfly wallpaper. Octavio's back was as toned as his front. He turned to Eugene and said, "And the red woman? She is a friend with you, yes? A wife?"

"Lola," Eugene swallowed again, unable to pull in his smile, "she's a close friend. I am not married to anyone," he explained, without reservations, which seemed sacrilegious at this point, "female or male, and I'd . . . what are you, Spanish?"

"Brazilian," Octavio said. "She is very impressive, your Lola."

For a moment, Eugene thought that Octavio was interested in Lola and not him, that he had misjudged the feelings he'd felt, the power, which beamed from the man's face and he thought, "lucky Lola," but then Octavio added, "Of course to be with you, Eugene Goessler, she would of course be beautiful and impressive."

Eugene was flattered and relieved and laughed, sitting down next to the man on the bed, "Well now, isn't that the pot calling the kettle black?"

"That is a saying?"

Eugene was caught again by the warmth and truth and innocence and strength and surrender in Octavio's brown eyes. He searched, as if to say, "What is this? Where did you come from? Why am I so vulnerable and open and silly all of a sudden? I'm not a teenager and I'm certainly not looking for quick-dare-sex-risk. I am captured, willingly, wordless." "Yes, it's a saying," he said aloud.

"They burn teas two ways?"

"No," he smiled, wanting to call him by name, knowing he would, wanting to record every reflection and nuance in the words, the charm and the aroma of the man. "Well, in a way."

Octavio scooted back against the wall. "Would you like pot?"

"Sure," Eugene said, then realized whose house he was in as he was looking at a large gold plastic crucifix, and he added, "But what about the widow? Should we open a window?"

Octavio laughed at Eugene's concern, straining the marijuana within the lid of a case he'd taken from the nightstand. "The 'widow,' Eugene Goessler, has gone to evening Mass."

Eugene thought, "How lovely he moves, how familiar he seems," and he stood and announced he would be right back, that he had to use the bathroom, that was how he had found himself out in the hall to begin with.

Octavio nodded, licking the rolling paper. Eugene caught a glimpse of his tongue, just the tip, and he said, "Oh what a mouth you have," and then hurried from the room, embarrassed.

In the bathroom, Eugene held his cock and heard himself questioning his abandoned heart so thawed so fast. He looked in the mirror. He said, "I love you, and because I do, really love you, it is now time to let yourself go." For years he had practiced the "examination of conscience" with his reflection, and had learned to accept loving himself, but there in the widow's ruffled bathroom, at the vanity, he realized that he could now accept the truth, "Love is the most contagious of all the diseases."

Eugene returned to Octavio's room and found Lola, wearing her red teddie, sitting next to the Brazilian, lighting the joint. Octavio patted the mattress for Eugene to come and sit next to him.

Lola inhaled. "I was looking for you, Eugene." She slyly winked.

Eugene sat down near Octavio and said to Lola, "He's from Brazil."

Octavio inhaled.

"Rio," Lola exhaled.

Octavio passed him the joint. "And Octavio," he said, inhaling, hearing Octavio's name pass from his lips for the first time, as he felt Octavio's thigh touch his, "and Octavio said the widow's gone out to Mass."

Eugene, Lola, and Octavio Beneto went to dinner, stoned on Octavio's grass. Eugene suggested they leave a note for the widow, but Octavio said, "Oh, she does not lock the door. She tells me yesterday that the Lord is her lock."

In the rain, Lola drove the Chevrolet. Eugene sat in front, and Octavio sat in back.

"I was doing a demonstration at the university," Octavio explained, "on the powerful touch processes we have developed in Brazil, and I am not to be back in New York for three days so I decide to stay in the beautiful autumn here and I had to take the room at the widow's for each hotel I go to said with no reservations there was nothing."

"Touch?" Lola asked, looking at Eugene knowingly. "I love it. Perfect."

"Yes, touch," Octavio laughed. "Is that funny?" He grabbed the backs of both Eugene's and Lola's necks. His fingers were electric and powerful and then hot and gentle within seconds.

Eugene and Lola looked at each other and burst out laughing.

"I make you laugh with my hands?" Octavio asked.

"We're stoned," Eugene said, turning, his head pivoting in Octavio's hand, till he was within a seat back's thickness of the Brazilian's pink mouth, grinning, surrounded by a coal-black beard.

"That's not it, Goessler," Lola said, keeping her eyes directed through the slushing wipers to the unknown road. "On the way up from New York, Octavio, our friend Eugene here said, over and over, he had made a decision to, now how was it exactly, Eugene? 'Reawaken the incarcerated physical and sexual life, to touch.' "

Eugene said, looking at Octavio's eyes lighten and darken with the passing streetlamps, "I've been a monk, unwilling to take the risks of passion, and I've decided that it is time to parole myself . . . do you get me?"

Octavio kissed his cheek. He said, "You are atomic, Eugene Goessler, you are flesh as me, as this driving Lola. One god said, 'If we were steel, we could not love.' " He kissed his cheek again and said, "Yes, I get you. Do you get me?"

Lola said, "There are lights up ahead."

They found what they wanted, a cozy restaurant. Eugene spotted smoke billowing from a big chimney and bet correctly that that restaurant would be lodgelike. They wanted a table near the fireplace, so they chose to wait and order drinks in the bar off the dining room. Lola started to explain the drink she wanted, and before Eugene and Octavio could order theirs, Lola was behind the bar, showing Tommy the bartender her special mix of Grand Marnier, Drambuie, Kahlúa, and vodka. Lola was obviously interested in teaching Tommy more than her drink concoction. She patted the bartender's ass, told him he looked like a famous actor she knew, "No, not Warren Beatty, but as tall, and not as old," and she turned to Eugene and Octavio at one point and pretended to be lapping Tommy's ear for them.

"I think Lola wants the bartender," Octavio said.

"I think Lola's got the bartender. She works fast," Eugene said. "She wanted you, you know."

She had realized that Octavio was taken by Eugene earlier, when Eugene had gone to the bathroom and Lola had entered Octavio's room, and Octavio had excitedly asked her, before any introductions, who Eugene was, and if Eugene was inclined toward men. Octavio was delighted with her answers. She was delighted for Eugene, but she knew she would be on the hunt when they went out after finishing the joint.

"Hey, lady with the violet hair," Octavio called, "could I have a drink?"

Lola sashayed over to the two men with her hand fisted on her hip and said, tough, "The hair is maroon, doll. What's your pleasure?"

Tommy came up behind her and escorted her out from behind the bar, telling her that she was breaking a rule.

"I've been thrown outa better places than this gin mill, handsome," she said taking a stool. "Why don't you take a break and come have dinner with us?"

He said he obviously couldn't, and she asked when he got off, and he grinned slightly and said, "Not often enough," and the fey way he acted macho made her ask, "Are you heterosexual?" and he said that of course he was, and he asked her if she was, and she said, "Heterosexual is my middle name, Tommy," and she winked at Eugene, who knew her innocent act. The poor kid. What was he? Twenty, twenty-two? She said to the bartender, "I have another question, Tommy. You see, I have this need. It's really quite documented. Legitimate. You can ask these men here. I have this need to undress men taller than me. Naked. And then I have this need to have them lay down on the floor and guess my weight."

Tommy was flustered. He excused himself and went to the opposite end of the bar to take a waitress's order. The three of them watched his strut.

"Pronounced johnson," Eugene said to Lola. "Be gentle with the kid."

"You make yourself a date?" Octavio asked.

"We'll see," she sighed, sipping her drink. "I get this way when I'm hungry."

Tommy returned and Eugene and Octavio ordered ales.

"You are big," Octavio said to Lola. "You make his day."

"Now, if he'll just make her night," Eugene said, "it'll be tit for tat."

"Goessler, have some respect," Lola jabbed him. "Octavio's going to get the wrong impression of me."

Octavio asked, "Tit for tat is a sexual position? I've never heard of that."

Tommy set the ales before them and excused himself again.

"He's polite," Lola said, "I like that. Tall. Cute ass. Polite."

"And a pronounced johnson," Eugene said again, "a pronounced chevrolet johnson."

"How do you mean, 'chevrolet' the car?" Octavio asked Eugene, grasping his thigh.

"I feel the word. Shev-row-lay. It's music to me. It's what lips do when they swell. I've managed to use it enough to obliterate its metaphor. Such a sound wasted on a vehicle."

"Goessler is a verbal anarchist," Lola said, drinking. "And he had 'chevrolet' written before him on the visor driving up. All the sex talk and that word, I think it crossbred in the front seat of my car."

"You have fun with me," Octavio said, drinking, "but tell me of your sex talk, Eugene Goessler."

Lola laughed a dying note. "It is all so perfect!"

"Lola, drink your drink," Eugene jabbed, "the sex talk was just that, talk. . . . I am pent up. I am ready."

"Eugene, let me tell it," Lola said. "You get so serious."

"Yes," Octavio said to Lola, patting a there-there on Eugene's thigh. "Tell it, the sex of our Eugene, Lola Hampton."

"Jesus Chevrolet Johnson," Eugene sighed and drank.

"Well," Lola settled herself on the stool, "Eugene said he was ready for several tantra," she looked at him okaying her choice of words. "He said he was ready to trust his subconscious and let his heart out of the cave." She looked to Eugene again. "And he more or less said 'Fuck it!' He was aching for boundless passion."

"Ahhhh, passion," Octavio fingered his beard like a psychiatrist.

"Physical passion," Lola clarified. "And look who he meets, exotic dark and mysterious Mister Touch. It's perfect!"

"She's got us married," Eugene laughed, getting used to the hand on his thigh.

"You are funny, both of you, no?" Octavio said, and studied Eugene closely. "And you are red in embarrassment. You are new air for me after the week of university."

"Do you have someone in Brazil?" Lola asked.

Eugene shot an arrowed look from his green eyes to her blue eyes and jumped in, "Don't answer that."

Lola said, "See, he has designs on you, Octavio. He wants you without."

Eugene said, "Go ahead, now you must answer."

"Yes, a long-time love there," Octavio said, and added, "in Brazil . . ."

Eugene felt, for a moment, a sadness drape the hungry hollow he'd allowed himself to acknowledge, thinking sustenance would be coming, and although he was still filled with desire, he now judged Octavio as not needing what he was needing.

Octavio saw this and said, "In Brazil, Eugene Goessler, in Brazil, and he is family more than passion, my friend," and he touched Eugene's lips that had contracted, "and I do not lie."

Eugene was seduced. Honesty was the clincher. It was perfect, and of course he was not looking for a marriage, but he did whine silly, "I just would like to be the one with a girl in every port."

Octavio was lost, "A girl in every port?"

Lola explained, "Eugene is being greedy. First he's screaming out the sunroof how he has finally accepted the full physical force of earthbound life, and now he's playing in his chest of clichés."

Octavio finished his ale, not following anything.

"We Americans," Lola continued to try to explain, "are a cliché-ridden people without the simplicity of simplicity."

"Thanks Lola," Eugene finished his drink, "that clarifies everything."

Octavio shook his black curly hair, "I don't understand half of what you two say, but I don't think you do either, no?"

Lola smiled at Eugene, "It is perfect, Goessler. Octavio does not understand your words. Your fucking words are weightless with him. You'll have to use your mouth for other charms."

Tommy came down to their end of the bar and asked, "How are we doing?"

Lola said, "We love your New England accent. We love your use of pronouns."

He leaned toward her, flirting, "Let me make you your drink. Lola. On me."

She cooed, "*We* would love that."

"My pleasure," he said, turning to the bottles.

Eugene, still smarting from Octavio's existing love life, whispered to Lola, "I think we should ask him if he has a lover, or possibly a wife."

"GOESSLER table," was announced. Eugene and Octavio stood. Lola said she would find them, but she would wait for her drink.

Tommy asked Lola to taste his efforts. She said it was perfect, and then she asked him if he was married.

Eugene and Octavio arranged the chairs so that all three faced the fire. Eugene noticed how considerate and at ease Octavio was in the crowded dining room, thanking the hostess who seemed bothered that Eugene had moved the settings, and saying "Good evening" to the people next to their table, and even pulling out Eugene's chair for him and giving him a squeeze on the shoulder. Octavio was wearing a thick scarlet wool sweater that enhanced his black beard. What struck Eugene repeatedly to the heart, though, was Octavio's deep dark dark laughing eyes. They were eyes that loved and could easily love someone in Brazil for years, and love Massachusetts and women and water and fire and a forty-year-old paroled wordsmith.

"You take my breath," Eugene said. "You said you don't lie. Well, one of mine has been to tell myself that I didn't need anyone. I have not been honest with my body. With these hands," he held his hands up, "that need to touch passion. I acted, judged, and strutted, and that was my crime. I crave honesty, Octavio."

"We will have that, then," he said in the amber firelight, "we have that, then, honesty, yes?"

Eugene was tempted to explain further about his constant thinking during sex and his performance awareness, but it would have been gibberish. He said, "I'm ready."

They were as close as two men could be in a public restaurant full of New Englanders in 1990. Their knees touched under the table and they took deep breaths, smiling without control.

Lola arrived. "He has a girlfriend," she said very oddly, "dead."

Octavio stood to seat her. Eugene noticed all the diners looking at the striking Lola in her chartreuse tights and cheesecloth dress. He thought that their table was by far the handsomest.

"Kinky," Eugene said. "You asked him if he was attached? And he said to a dead girlfriend?"

She centered her drink on the butter plate and did not respond to Eugene's remarks. She was disturbed. "He said she was killed eight months ago."

"Killed," Eugene said.

"Who was killed?" Octavio asked.

"The bartender's girlfriend," Eugene said, and then to Lola, "What did you say?"

She twirled her Lola drink. "I asked him if I could have an olive."

"You asked for an olive." Eugene was not quite sure what to

believe, this was a stranger Lola. "He said his girlfriend was killed and you asked for an olive, and then what did he do?"

"He gave me two."

Octavio looked back and forth at the two and said, "This is another joke I am missing?"

Eugene shrugged, not knowing what was what.

Lola took a sip, then recentered her drink, "She was one of the passengers on that plane that was blown up in Chicago last winter."

"And you asked for an olive?"

"No! I said, 'Fucking asshole religious fanatics, give me a goddamned olive!' What else could I say?"

"What plane?" Octavio asked, seeing no joke.

"The one carrying the bishop who had released the list of clergy that had died of AIDS to the press. The bomb was planted under his seat," Eugene spoke contemptuously, "and they suspect the cardinal had something to do with it. You must have heard about it. Over two hundred were killed, God bless the Church."

"I don't know," Octavio said.

Lola's buoyancy was thwarted and Eugene blamed himself for being so flip to challenge her to find out Tommy's status. "I'm sorry, Lola."

Lola stared at her drink, then sighed, "Well, I hate these serious types. I'm not a nurse. He doesn't want to be with me."

Despite the flickering crackle and the sweet smell of foods, the table was silently gloomy, and then Octavio spoke, "But of course he wants you, Lola. You asked for one olive, and he gave you two. Yes?"

Lola and Eugene both looked at Octavio and started to smile, then they looked at each other and said simultaneously, "Perfect."

The waitress took their order. Lola said she would go to the bar for her own drink. The waitress frowned at that, but Eugene and Octavio diverted her into a conversation about the skiing in the area. When she left to get their chowder, Eugene noticed that Octavio's eyes followed her.

"Do you have women?" he asked Octavio.

"She is healthy," Octavio said, and then said, "not in my bed for years." He kneed his knee into Eugene's knee beneath the tablecloth. "Do you?"

Eugene said, "Not since my landlord," and he saw the confusion again appear on Octavio's face, and he apologized, "I'm sorry. It must seem like riddles the way I speak. I'm sorry, Octavio."

The waitress set three chowders before them and a basket of warm bread. Octavio reached for the iron poker near the hearth and was about to stoke the fire, but she took it from him and said she would get someone to do that and hurried away. They tasted their chowder, reading each other's eyes. Eugene said to himself, "moony and lovestruck and goo-goo eyes." He took his napkin and wiped a drop of clam from Octavio's beard. A youthful busboy in tight white clothes appeared to stoke the fire, and both men watched him bend to the hearth. Eugene thought, "Octavio would prefer that young thing to me."

Octavio said to the boy, "Thank you," and the boy's face glowed. Octavio said to Eugene, "What a flower."

"Mmm-hmm. Chevrolet lips and a pronounced johnson," Eugene said with a trace of sarcasm in his voice.

Octavio detected a break in the warmth, and felt Eugene's knee attempt to break the weld beneath the table. "What?" Octavio asked.

"What?" Eugene returned.

"You what," Octavio said. "Was it the boy?"

Eugene laughed and started to unwind a spool of excuses, and saw this happening in his head. He saw himself trying to thread a needle. He stopped the pile of words before they reached his tongue and said, "Honest, right? Well . . . well, I saw how you looked at that boy, and I thought you would prefer him to me."

"Would I?" Octavio laughed. "Or is it, would you?"

"No!" Eugene jumped. "I was just enjoying the sight."

Octavio took Eugene's hand, oblivious to what it looked like to the other diners, and kissed it. "Oh, my Eugene Goessler, you are sweetly stuffed. Let me tell you something. I love bodies. I love eyes and hands and even the lifted eyebrow of our waitress over there," and he kissed Eugene's hand again, ". . . and that boy has a lovely ass, no? And an angel look, no? And we both see that. We have that to share and I want to kiss each vein in your man hand."

Eugene was swept up and felt trust. In Octavio, and in metaphors.

"Boys!" Lola sang, appearing with wine and an entire bowl of olives.

Octavio laughed, "They should pay you, Lola. First you make the drink by the bar and now you serve our table."

Eugene saw the waitress bothered. He thought of all the rules in the world.

Lola was bubbly, "We had a serious talk for a minute and now it's set. I'm going to pick Tommy up and bring him back to the widow's tonight, which means you're to fend for yourself, Eugene . . ." Then she asked the waitress to reheat her chowder.

Widow Turner's Bed and Breakfast was a throbbing sexual gland that night. Lola and her bartender were in one room, and Eugene and Octavio Beneto in the other, and between them, the widow and the Lord.

Eugene and Octavio sat on the bed. Eugene was nervous, but determined to be sexually honest. He said he felt fucked up, and Octavio said, "Why say 'fucked up' when that is not it. You are physically shy," and Eugene laughed big at such a turnaround in wording. "Physically shy! That sounds almost appealing," and Octavio kissed him and said, "It is very appealing, Eugene."

"I am forty and physically shy," Eugene mused, "and I know I could pull some role out of my head to hide behind, but . . . you know, I do feel inhibited with the widow sleeping in the next room, I mean, that has nothing to do with being 'physically shy.' "

Octavio said he could be quiet then, and have a quiet night, if it bothered him. "We will have noise another night."

Eugene cursed the setting. Why here? With this man I'm so attracted to and wanting to be with and willing to take risks with? Why here? In this sweet old half-blind Catholic's sanctuary of crucifixes and crocheted proverbs and novena candles? Why do I have to not only be honest physically, but also deal with the Church? He whispered loudly, "But I don't want to be quiet. I don't want to hold back."

Octavio's dark eyes lit with an idea. "Would you like me to tape your mouth shut?"

Eugene laughed, but saw that the Brazilian was not kidding. He was opening his toiletry bag and removing a roll of wide adhesive tape. Eugene thought, "Uh-oh, here comes the kinky part." Was Octavio a bit too advanced for his fast-breaking?

"This way you could scream and it will be quiet," Octavio explained, smiling slyly in the evil lamplight of Widow Turner's ruffled shade. "Would this free you, Eugene?"

"Is there something going on here, Octavio?" Eugene was unsure of the stranger with the magic fingers. "Are you really out there? Just tell me."

Octavio twirled the roll of tape on his finger. "It is an answer, no?"

"Yes," Eugene said, "but let's put it with the rubbers, and use it only if necessary. I trust you, Octavio, but I want you to know, I can defend myself if I have to."

Octavio laughed at Eugene's reactions. He was far more honest than he realized, the Brazilian thought, and then he said, "You have no need to defend yourself with me. Already we are making love. It doesn't stop and start. It has always been . . . this love, this making love. You are funny."

Octavio was a master of acceptance. Eugene was opened, overcome, unhinged, and awed, as if he were seeing art. Art that revealed the sun and the stark. He said, reaching over to touch the man's eyes, "I am in awe."

"What is this owl?" Octavio smiled. "The night bird owl?"

Eugene laughed, remembering what Lola had said at the bar in the restaurant, that words would not be coming into play with this man. He kissed the Brazilian's lips. And he could have sworn he heard an owl hooting out the window. Octavio tasted male. He tasted like the smell of hay, kissing deeper, moving over each other, he tasted like the wet leaves out the window, and the burning leaves, and the man's mouth was smoke and tomatoes and a lion's den and sweet sap. Then, Eugene's head jerked back, shocked with a sharp stabbing pain, as if he'd been struck behind his eyes.

"Lay back," Octavio said, "put your gold head on my hot lap for you, sweetie."

He massaged Eugene's head, starting at the temples and pushing back through the blond beginnings of hair, through the shades of red and gold and brown, and over the skull he was cradling. Both men were still fully clothed. Octavio was in his dark scarlet wool sweater that felt like a cat to Eugene's cheek, and Eugene was wearing a dark green flannel shirt, his favorite, because he bought it in Amsterdam.

Octavio said, "Relax, feel my fingers and relax, let go to my fingers."

The pain was increasing behind Eugene's closed eyes. He continued to smile, though, because the touch was so tender and loving, and then he became angry with himself for smiling because he was in pain, and this wasn't a pleasure, and he was smiling because for all external reasons, this was supposed to be pleasurable, and the word "relax" triggered a tightening in his back and neck, and he realized how a direction called relax said to him, "You're uptight and fucked up, and incapable of relaxing," and he said this to Octavio, and as he said it, he replaced "fucked up" with "physically shy" and took a deep breath and asked Octavio what the word "relax" meant to him.

"Allow. Let in," Octavio said exhaling slowly, massaging the sides of Eugene's head. "Let your uptight be uptight, that is relax."

Eugene thought, "Maybe I need glasses, maybe that's what this pain is, this isn't the first time I've had this pain, pounding against the backs of my eyes. Maybe I have a brain tumor. Maybe . . ." and his thoughts stopped abruptly as Octavio's finger dug in on his temple and it felt as he were being stabbed in the head. He moaned.

"You tell me to stop if I hurt you," Octavio said. "We are getting something here."

"Is this touch therapy?" Eugene asked.

Octavio exhaled slowly. "This is you feeling behind your eyes where you have seen much that hurts. This is my, how do you say? Shovel? To unbury."

The pain became excruciating and Eugene twisted on the bed, fighting, in one sense, the confrontation of his ache, and in another, the force of fingers, and he mustered his resolve to see it through, hearing Lola's voice saying how perfect everything was and how Mr. Touch appeared when Eugene had decided it was time. He thought of his eyesight. He thought of the fire at the cabin and Scott directing him to push the destruction aside, to rebuild as he saw fit, and he thought of Ginsberg saying to let it all be seen, without giving any of it weight or significance, entering the peace of acceptance that is meditation. The fingers seemed to have entered his skull. His eyes felt as if they were being pushed out from the inside. The pain came in throbs, so powerful, and yet Eugene fought screaming, afraid of disturbing the sleeping widow. This had to stop, or he would have to have his mouth taped. And then, it seemed, the widow be damned, the scream was rising in his throat like vomit, and there was no turning it back, and his mouth opened wide, in a gasp and dry heave, but the sound was a whimper and squeal, that of a pup having its paw stepped on. The bed squeaked louder than his voice, from his thrashing legs and arms. His neck seemed to be stretching as far as possible, pivoting and tugging in jugular spasms, as if trying to escape any link with the head. His last conscious thought was, "Octavio is God."

Octavio's warm wool touch and cradle and his rhythmic deep breathing and his flesh-bone digging assured him he was safe to let go. He heard screams that were not from his mouth, and not from the house. He saw Clara coming at him, blustered and panting, spewing anger that was thick and visible. He was running. Round and round and round the kitchen table on River Road, and then down the hall and into the living room, to the Emerson, and he could make out her rant. She was screaming, "You'll go blind lying there so close to the screen you filthy pest!" And he was filled with hatred and pushed her with all his might away from him, away as far as he could, and then turned and dove head first into the television, crashing through the picture tube, through sparking black and white crystals, hearing shots from snipers and the bells of the Eucharist and then the crash and crack of metal and telephone pole. The bomb.

1966, Ohio

"E"ugene! Eugene! Did you hear that?" Frankie asked excitedly. "A crash of a car down on the road I bet!"

Eugene jumped down to the floor and said, "Daddy." He saw the empty bed across the room. They ran out to the porch. Clara came out, buttoning her duster, with eight-year-old Debbie in tow.

"Lord, it sounds like it's right down there, don't it," Clara said, although the only sound to be heard was crickets intoning all over the thick overgrown hill. "One of you better go in and call the police."

"What if it's nothing?" Frankie asked.

"Well, that's why I said one of you should call. You're just kids."

Frankie ran in, and Eugene started down the steps.

Clara yelled, "Eugene Goessler! You get back up here and put some clothes on!"

Eugene and Frankie were in their underwear. Eugene ignored his mother's call, and so did Frankie as he banged out through the screen door, jumping to catch up with his brother, and yelling back to Clara, "The phone's dead!"

"Get up here you two!" she screamed, letting herself consider who was not there on the porch, Melvin, and who would be a likely candidate for an accident. Debbie sensed the fear all around and grabbed onto her mother's hand.

At the bottom of the steps, Eugene heard two different cars screeching around the bend and braking. Then one nearly hit him as he stepped out into the road. It was rounding the bend in a wide arc to avoid a chrome fender that was twisted and driven, almost perpendicular, into the tarred pavement. The car honked loud and long and trailing off as it sped away, and the headlights momentarily blinded him.

Frankie came down from behind him, and saw the fender and said, "Look at that!"

Eugene recognized the Cincinnati Reds Pennant 1961 bumper sticker. He grabbed Frankie's arm and said, "Wait here." His head was full of "No!" and yet he knew around the curve, he was going to find the Olds.

"I'm going with you!" Frankie demanded.

"It's Daddy," Eugene heard himself say, also hearing Clara's voice up on the hill yelling for them to come back, and hearing another car brake to a skidding halt. Part of him was running back up the steps and into bed, as they neared the bend. They had started walking, but within steps, they were both running, scraping their bare feet, and not feeling a thing.

"Ahhhhhh!" Frankie screamed, seeing the Olds halved in the ditch by the leaning telephone pole.

Eugene held his brother's head away from the sight, and a brewing well of fear rose in his throat, so that he couldn't speak, or even cry like his little brother. Two men in a station wagon had already reached the wreck, and they were pulling Melvin from the front seat. There was no door. "Stay back!" one of the men yelled.

Eugene and Frank held each other and approached the Olds.

"Watch out for those lines!" one of the men yelled.

"Jesus," the other man muttered, "Jesus, Mary, Joseph."

"Daddy!" Frankie screamed, catching sight of Melvin's body, now on the ground.

"Daddy," Eugene said, somewhere in his head, and the word, "dead."

Clara had gone back into the house, to see for herself if the phone was dead. Then she went to the bathroom and washed her hands and looked in the mirror and said, "Damn you, Melvin, I ain't nursing another thing. Damn your sorry drinking."

Debbie cried that she wanted to go down to the road and see what had happened, but Clara insisted she stay up in the house with her, safe. "Your brothers will come tell us."

Sirens echoed along the road.

Eugene bent down over his father. Melvin's neck was broken.

his eyes were open, but he was gone. Eugene looked up and around, into the overhanging trees, and then out to the river, and then back to his father's blank face. Frankie cried onto his father's bloody bowling shirt. Eugene looked into his father's eyes and his mouth fell open as if he were going to cry out, but the only sound was the approaching sirens and Frankie's gasps, and he was sure that whatever was missing from his father's eyes was the soul.

There was a pulsing red light passing through the trees and onto the porch.

Clara started to go down the steps, holding Debbie's hand, just as Eugene and Frankie turned up from the road. She yelled, "Well? What is it?" And then she scolded Debbie, "Now just stop your crying till you know if there's something to cry about, girl."

Frankie ran ahead of Eugene. He was covered with blood, terrified.

"I told you two to get clothes on!" Clara said. "That's disgraceful, going out on the road in your under . . ."

"Daddy!" Frankie screamed at her, dropping on the step at her legs.

Debbie turned and ran back up into the house screaming.

"Now, now," Clara patted his head, "how bad is it?" Frankie sobbed, incoherent.

Eugene reached her, looking older than sixteen and bloodlessly pale. He wore Melvin's dead face on his, staring blank and through his mother.

She said, "I've got to go down there." She sensed that the worst had happened. Till then, she'd been held up by grudges and resentments of all the trouble Melvin caused her, but now she saw "dead" in Eugene's face. She shook his shoulders from the step above him. "Let me go down there, Eugene. What is it?" Her head was shaking, "No, no, no," as if her thoughts could suppress her instincts.

"Daddy's dead," Eugene said, releasing an immense moan that was deep and strong and forlorn. "The police are coming up here." And then, as he had to choose which word went before and after the next, to make that sentence, tears began to tumble out and down, and he felt his knees weakening in front of the woman.

"Melvin," Clara muttered.

Two policemen turned onto the steps and started climbing slowly, trying to see up to where they had followed the boys.

"You go get some pants on quick, Eugene," Clara said, "and stop your crying. You're the man of the house now, and you've got to help me. Take your brother, now, go on! And come back down here and talk to these men!"

Eugene hated her voice and her demands. He pulled Frankie up and they held on to each other as they climbed.

"Hurry up!" Clara said again, "You're the man, now."

Eugene cried, "Never!" and swore that he would not let himself get sucked into being another Melvin. He squeezed his eyes shut as tight as he could.

1990, Massachusetts

As Eugene's scream rose, rushing up to erupt, Octavio lowered his lips over Eugene's and inhaled, pulling, coaxing, taking it as a vacuum. It was dead quiet. He treated Eugene like a drowning victim, feeding fresh Brazilian air in to revive him. A flood of tears streamed from Eugene's eyes, and barges of concepts and judgments, and sins unconfessed forgave themselves down his cheeks as Octavio blew a sweet clear breeze over his river, smoothing the waves as if they were bed sheets, and soothing with his licking tongue. He felt the fingers withdraw and pet and pet his forehead and ears, and the pain was gone.

1991, New York City

Octavio returned to the United States in the spring. He and Eugene spent themselves over and over at Eugene's loft. Eugene could not remember ever having known so many perfect days. The phone would ring when it was supposed to ring. The sun would come out when it was supposed to come out. The Brazilian had opened him up, or at least helped loosen his lid. He strummed Octavio like a guitar, and Octavio plucked him like a harp. Eugene was naked, vulnerable, and full of acceptance for everything. They were babies and horses and gods.

"This has nothing to do with gender, does it?" Eugene said, as Octavio licked him like a dog, being a dog, a dog of the Latins. "It is pure. Accepting all. Copacetic poof. And . . . ohhhh . . . the ticktock, Octavio . . . the ticktock . . . the yours and the mine . . . I don't want . . . I don't want you to leave . . . I don't want to think . . . or speak . . ."

Octavio slid to Eugene's ear and said, "Accept that, sweetie. Accept all as perfect or nothing at all."

"Nothing to do with gender . . ." Eugene said again, and he closed his eyes at the silk smooth tongue that licked his eyelids, and he saw a drawbridge lowering across a dream river, and he said, as if possessed by his father, speaking in Kentucky tongues, to Octavio, "You are my dreamboat."

Octavio showed Eugene how to read a body like a book. "It is the history there in the cells. We tantalize them, tantalize, yes? Is that the word?"

Spent into sleep, their sleep was deep and sound and smooth and in the middle of their sleep, history shuffled its feet, blood pumped, and when they woke, more metaphors surfaced to be kissed and sucked and toyed with.

"I am Braille!!" Eugene shouted.

Octavio found a muscle in Eugene's calf that spoke to him. Eugene's flinching confirmed his find. "These are your treasures, Eugene Goessler, what is this here?" He chewed and brushed the leg with his beard and Eugene smelled the locker room at Bishop Miller High School. He smelled chlorine from the school pool. It was as if Octavio was pressing stubborn puzzle pieces into place. Eugene remembered the lust he felt back then, suppressed into swimming laps till cramps set in. He said, "Puppy." And they both laughed, and shared a pear and then a banana.

"Each time love is made," Octavio said, "there is a conception."

On the seventh day of his visit, Octavio's hair fell over one eye. He was straddling Eugene's waist, feeling the distance and the closeness of Eugene's cock behind him. It was Eugene's neck that he'd been kissing, and what had been sweet and circular began to feel square, and then rocky, and he kissed closer to the scars where baby Michael's burning had burned. Eugene shook his head, fighting the touch, then fought the fight, all of which generated a flash of arrows that directed Octavio to the scar. Here! Here! Here is the acute triangle splintering Eugene Goessler's heart!

Octavio pulled back, letting Eugene have his way. "You don't want me there, yes?" the Brazilian magician said.

Eugene smiled, knowing so much unsaid. Octavio was dancing on him. He was lean and dark and young and old. He would not force, unless force was accepted. His eyes read, "Take what you want, sweetie." Eugene said, "I'm afraid of that."

"Afraid of this red on your neck?" Octavio touched.

"Afraid of that. Afraid of what I want." He took a deep breath and thrust his cock up toward Octavio's ass. "Afraid of that, too. That I want to be in you."

For seven days they had plunged between everything else, but they had not entered each other.

Octavio's eyebrow raised as he felt the first touch at his ass. He looked into the sea-green eyes and broke into a smile. "You want?"

"Yes, I want," Eugene said.

Octavio suspected that Eugene had bolted from his neck, to the ultimate diversion, and so he suggested, "Both."

"Both?"

"I kiss your red neck and you go in me."

Eugene felt his erection melt. Octavio would not leave his eyes. He suddenly felt pinned beneath the man, and this was no ordinary man, this man read his psyche as if he had neon glaring out, "Break the Block!" and "I'm Lying!" Octavio seemed extraordinarily handsome, dominating him, glaring at him, and Eugene thought he was the devil, and thought, "He can be whatever he wants to be, no wonder." Octavio started to lean down toward the scar, as if he were a vampire. Eugene pushed him back, "TIME!" He wasn't going to contribute to the centuries of blood this man had thrived on.

Octavio settled back without a fight and said sweetly, "What?"

Eugene laughed nervously, feeling a thousand emotions activating, and as he was about to say what he'd been thinking he realized how ridiculous his thoughts were, how they conspired to prevent the acknowledgment of the truth. He touched his neck, and he jerked back, flinching from his own fingers, as if his fingertips were just-out matchsticks. "I'm afraid of here," he said to Octavio.

Octavio touched the lines that spread from Eugene's eyes. He tried to read the depth of what they were saying. Was Eugene's fear too strong? Should they let it be for now? It would be fine. The sun was hitting the bed squarely. He loved Eugene completely. He told himself that the poet knew himself completely, "He knows everything. He knows what to pursue. He knows the perfection of his lips and nose and eyes and chest and arms. He knows."

Eugene maintained his stare at Octavio, letting the dark eyes pour into him, and he brought his hand back up to the scar and slowly set his fingers, one at a time, onto it. Why was it so painful? Were all of their nerve endings exploding from so much touching? He recoiled, but maintained his touch, and his face contorted before Octavio, as did Octavio's watching his. Eugene felt as if he were being branded. Octavio put his hand over Eugene's, pressing it in, keeping it there.

"This is not the Widow's," Octavio said, full of pain, tearing up, from the sight of Eugene's twisted face, "so the scream can happen, sweetie. Let it go."

1965, Ohio

Mack was in Vietnam. He had volunteered after June gave birth to the baby boy they named Michael in April of 1964. He had been home for Thanksgiving after basic training in South Carolina, and then he left for Saigon. June and baby Michael spent almost every evening up at the house on River Road, and Eugene spent as much time as he could down at June's apartment over Bess's. He would stop there on his way home from school. He babysat Michael whenever June wanted to go out. He was the baby's godfather. He took his duty seriously. He would carry Michael around and point to things and say, "This is God." He loved to make Michael laugh. June would see him making faces at the baby, and she would say, "That is *not* God, Michael, that's your rubber-faced uncle." Eugene would also take him across the road to the river, all bundled up, and let him crawl around, especially when Mack was there in November and Eugene knew they wanted to screw before going to war. He told Michael that the river was God and the trees were God, and once, he whispered, "Since I'm your godfather, I hereby tell you to never get Catholic." Michael laughed.

The fire started in a frayed wire that ran to an electric heater Bess had running in the back room of the store, to keep the pipes from freezing. The front store heater did not reach the back on such frigid nights.

Earlier in the evening, there was an argument up at the house over the call Clara had received from Bishop Miller High School over Eugene's hair length. The dean had said that he was not to return till he looked like a boy.

June said, "It's not that long."

274

Clara cried, "What they must think! That we can't afford to get him a haircut!"

Eugene yelled, "There are seniors with hair as long as mine!"

Melvin left, "for a quick drink at Stogie's."

Eugene walked June and Michael down to Bess's and asked if he could come up, since Clara would not stop harping till she fell asleep. "Just let me stay till I know they're all in bed," he pleaded.

June said he would have to go back sooner or later, and that he would have to learn to let their yells roll off his back like water on a duck. She seemed so wise and secure, opening her own door, with her own key, and sitting on her own couch holding her own sleeping baby.

"Everyone acts like they have the right to tell me what to do," Eugene whined, "and since you got married, there's one less kid to yell at, and so guess who gets it. Never Debbie, 'she's just a little girl,' and Frankie never gets hollered at by Daddy because he's such a good ballplayer . . . so guess who gets it?"

June took Michael to his crib to change him and get him in his pajamas. Eugene stayed on the couch, and stared at the drawer in the chest across from him. It was Mack's drawer. His underwear drawer. When Eugene babysat sometimes, he would go through the drawer and get out Mack's jock strap and swimming trunks and try them on. He would pose in June's dresser mirror like the men in his catalogue. Mack was tough.

June washed her hair while Eugene stood next to her at the kitchen sink and talked about how bad he had it. She said, "Before you know it, you'll be gone." Then she said that her friend, Carol, was coming over the next day to take sexy pictures of her to send to Mack. She said she was looking forward to living on a base somewhere when his tour of duty was over, "maybe California or Hawaii." Eugene watched as she set her hair, rolling the dyed blonde hair up all around her head. He thought she was very good at it. He said he hated the thought of her moving away.

"Mother says you'll never really move away with Mack," he said, drinking the Pepsi she had given him.

"She'll believe it when she sees me waving good-bye," June said, looking at herself in a mirror on her lap.

Michael made a noise and June looked toward the bedroom door.

"They drive me crazy," Eugene sighed, and then heard a new song start up from the stack of 45's June was playing low. "I can't wait to move out of there and see the world once I'm old enough. Maybe I'll go to California. I could be an artist."

"You are good at drawing," June said, going to the doorway and peeking into the dark room. "You got all the talent, except for ball."

"Or maybe I'll learn to play electric guitar and have a band and live in England."

"England!" June laughed, "Now that *is* a touch farfetched."

"Or a surfer. I'm the best swimmer on my team. I wish the river had waves," he sighed. "All I know for sure is . . . I'm getting out of that house."

June saw the last record drop from the stack. "Oh, Eugene, let's do this one!" It was "Sugar Shack." Eugene and June sang along with the record turned up and the bedroom door shut tight, and danced around. At the end of the song, their heads were forehead to forehead, singing, "I gotta get back to my sugar shack," and then they danced away from each other fading out along with the song. They laughed at the thought of the Singing Goesslers, like the famous family acts that were on television, and they couldn't stop laughing.

"I could see us on *Midwestern Hayride*, maybe," June cried.

"Or *Amateur Hour*," Eugene cried.

And then it seemed that June wanted him to leave. She yawned and said, "I bet Mother is sleeping now, Eugene."

The thought of going back up there made Eugene blurt out, "Can't I just stay here on the couch tonight? Please!"

He sat down. She sat down. She crossed her legs and swung the one out, kicking the air. She folded her arms. Eugene mimicked her, trying to get her to smile.

"Mother and Daddy'll be worried where you are," she said.

"No they won't!" he begged. "They know where I am!"

"And what about school?"

"What about it?" he said, and then remembered that Melvin said he would take him to a barber bright and early and then to Bishop Miller to see if he passed the inspection. "Ahhh, I could get up real early and run home."

"I only have the kitchen clock, Eugene, and there's no alarm. Bess has my wind-up . . . look, this is silly. Just go home, and I promise you, if it's terrible for you tomorrow, tomorrow night we'll get the clock from Bess and you can stay here . . . okay?"

"You're right," he sighed, resigned to the heavy cold climb. "You've really got it made, June, you really do."

He stood and put his coat on and wrapped the scarf his new girlfriend, Katherine, had knitted for him for Christmas around his neck a few times. June started to run a bath, and then came out to kiss him good-bye.

"Ooooo," she said, touching his sullen chin, "you've got little blond hairs growing there, Eugene. You know, I know there are a lot of girls who think you are really neat."

"Yeah?" he acted surprised. "Do you think any of them have alarm clocks at their houses?"

June pushed him toward the door. "Oh, you conceited jerk!"

"Not after tomorrow," he said. "After my haircut, the only girl that'll think I'm neat is the witch up there on the hill who's dreaming up ways, right now, of how to ruin another day of my life."

June laughed, "Go on, you poor thing! It's over before you know it."

"Easy for you to say," he said, descending the narrow steps.

"Thanks for walking us home," June whispered loud, not wanting to wake Bess.

At Bess's door, he stopped to hear if she was snoring as loud as June claimed to have heard. She was. He looked up to June who shushed him and said, "Go on!" and they both laughed. Eugene honked, and then hurried the rest of the way down. He was going to tell Bess that he heard her the next time he saw her. He opened the door on the side of the building and crossed the crackling cold gravel parking lot. The night was black and clear and out across the road and tracks, through the stark trees, he could see the river frozen white. It had been completely frozen for a week, and he and Katherine and some friends had made it across to Kentucky and back the night before. He walked up the road to the steps. All the lights were out in the house. He hated the thought of the barber, and worse, going to school with Melvin. He told himself that if June made it, so could he.

Melvin was not home, although the Olds was parked down on

the road, so Eugene knew where he was, Stogie's. Frankie was
asleep. He climbed up into his bunk, and fell asleep holding his
balls with one hand, and his soon-to-be-gone hair with the other.

Sirens. SIRENS!

He rolled and jumped to the floor. Sirens wailed. "Frankie!
Wake up!" he shook his brother. His father's bed was still empty.

Out in the living room, the strobing red lights from the road
pulsed through the window glass making eerie black cracks all
over the walls from the bare tree branches. He could smell
smoke. It looked like fog on the road. Frankie woke his mother.
Eugene ran down the steps with a blanket wrapped around him
and his sneakers untied on his feet. He ran as fast as he could
toward Bess's. The gold light flames were shooting out over the
road. The street was filled with fire trucks. He ran past them.

"Get back!" a fireman shouted at Eugene as he pushed his way
through the men unraveling one of the hoses. He ran to the side
of the building to the door that led up to the apartments. "Hey
boy! Get away from there!" He didn't hear them call. What he
heard was June's screams. He heard her voice, but there was so
much smoke, he couldn't see where the voice was coming from.
Was she out? Inside his head, he was screaming with her. Where
was she? He saw the door crack open by a slice of flames. He
was thrown back by the heat across the gravel. Up on the hill, he
thought, where Bess's second-story windows were almost level
with the ground. He started to move in that direction, and then
he felt arms on his shoulders, pulling his blanket. "Come on!
Come on!" the fireman yelled, and said something about being
"safe."

"My sister!" Eugene roared, deep, and pulled himself free of
the blanket and took off running across the gravel into the thick
smoke, and up onto the wooded hill, through the thorny frozen
sticks that cracked brittle, in his underwear and sneakers. He
held to the incline with his hands, and sided his way to within
twenty feet of the back of the building. He heard June's voice
over the latest siren to arrive.

"June! JUNE!" he yelled over and over and over. There was
smoke spurting out at the eaves like incense at Benediction,
almost nothing, and there were no flames at Bess's two windows, or the kitchen window in June's apartment in the gambreled
peak. The window over her sink. Get to that window, he prayed.

"June! Go to the back! To the back!!" He held a treetrunk so he wouldn't slide down the steep icy slope. "To the back! Bess! June! To the back!!" Forever he heard his screams and June's screams, and then, for a second, nothing. At Bess's back windows he saw flames starting to lap at the glass, and then ignite the curtains. He scrambled along the hill till he could also see the other side of the building, the side that was not graveled, but overgrown every year with saplings and weeds. He saw a ladder appear toward the front through the smoke. He caught sight of the dormer window on the side, up in June's living room. There she was! He saw her hanging out, holding Michael outstretched in the air.

"JUNE! JUNE!" he screamed, and tried to climb down through the thicket. Sparks and falling burning wood were cascading down the clapboard siding. He saw briefly that the firemen were chopping their way back through the lot. She saw them. She yelled for them. She didn't hear Eugene calling from the back. Michael was squirming and crying. He saw her bring the baby back inside, and he yelled, "No! Stay there!" He slid down the hill, scratching himself all over his chest and arms and legs, and he continued to scream for June to come back to the dormer window. "They're coming back for you!" He screamed up to the window she had disappeared from. He was below the window, in the lot, yelling at the dormer. "JUNE!" Then he heard something blow up or break. Something crashed. He screamed for her again, and then she appeared, looking down, catching sight of him on the ground, his arms outstretched to her.

"Eugene! Eugene!" she cried. "Help me! Help me!"

He twisted in helplessness, trying to stretch three stories to her, seeing her eyes from so far, "JUMP, JUNE! JUMP!"

She disappeared again, and he screamed at losing her from his sight, and then she was there with baby Michael, and she held him out, "Catch Michael!" she cried, kissing the baby. "Catch him, dear God!" and she let go of the child. Eugene thought of what a bad catch he was. He thought how untrue that was. The baby landed in his arms, already broken and burned black on his face and arm, pink skin unraveling and hot. He held Michael to his shoulder and his neck was burned from the heat of the baby's smoldering sleepers. Smoke billowed between Eugene and the sight of June. He yelled, "I got him! Now jump!"

The fire truck was backing in knocking down the small sticks of trees. "They're coming June!" he yelled through the smoke. The firemen were bringing a hose around to the side. He heard more breaks and pops and each one sent an orange flame flying through the white clouds. Eugene held Michael tight and jumped from one foot to the other screaming for her to jump, choking on the smoke, wishing she would say something, wishing he could see her, and then a wind gusted and for a moment he could see the window.

"Eugene!" June cried, catching sight of her brother holding Michael down below. The fire was pouring out of the window with her. He screamed for her to jump. She was burning. Her hair was burning. She pulled herself up onto the window sill, holding on to the frame, and as she did, the entire window frame collapsed into the room and she fell backward with it, onto the floor, which gave way down into Bess's.

The fire truck's hose began spraying the side. Eugene stared at the empty burning dormer, not believing what he had seen, dead to the firemen's calls to him. He cried out June's name and held Michael against himself and rocked back and forth and the heat became so intense that he felt himself burning, and then felt a spray of cold, as water was falling from the hose that was over-shooting from the gravel lot side. He was led away to the front, and Michael was taken from him into an ambulance. Clara was standing at the barricade in her nightdress. Frankie and Debbie were at each side of her, holding on to her arms and staring wide-eyed at the burning building. Eugene saw Melvin, who had been drinking down at the saloon, crying on his knees in the road, "Save my girl! Save my little girl!" Eugene's eyebrows were singed and his neck was burnt red from Michael's skin and pajamas, but he felt nothing. He walked past his mother, and she looked into his eyes for some hope, but she saw horror and she screamed, "Don't you dare! Don't you dare say. . . !" and she stopped making sense. He walked away from the fire, bare-chested toward the railroad tracks. The trees that they called the woods were bare and twisted and red with the reflected fire. The river was ice-white but flickered pink. The sky was black. Eugene turned. Hoses were shooting water all over the building. From where he stood, he saw the entire roof collapse into the shell. He saw Melvin weeping in the road. He saw Frankie look-

ing back to him, staring at him, wanting to know. Someone
wrapped Eugene in a blanket. He sat down at the curb. He
thought he saw June's face in the flames of where the front
windows had been. She was calling for help. He felt the flames
climbing her spine and melting the rollers in her hair. He smelled
the burnt hair of the baby. He smelled his own burnt skin and
hair. Someone put something cool on his neck. June could still
be alive, he thought, and jumped up, leaving the blanket on the
curb, and he ran toward the barricade. None of them knew what
they were doing, he'd decided. He could find her. She was in
there, with Bess maybe, in a hiding place, safe. There was that
chance, he thought. He had to try, and he screamed bloody
murder as he was held back by the police. He kicked and cursed
them and collapsed to the road next to his father, who grabbed
hold of him and held him close and smelled of beer. Eugene
hated him for being so weak that he would do nothing but cry
on his knees in the street.

"Where were you!!" Eugene demanded in a deep frightening
voice, accusing his father, "WHERE WERE YOU? YOU DRUNK!
You drunk! You drunken lying shit!"

Melvin maintained his hold on the boy, letting him rant into
the man's chest, not hearing anything that he wasn't already
hearing from his own mind.

"You have no right! I hate you!" Eugene sobbed.

Someone resettled the blanket around Eugene. He thought of
Bess. Bess wouldn't let June die. She wasn't a witch. She wasn't
what Clara always said. And then he thought, "This is life. This
is what it is. This is life. This is the tragedy that Mother always
knew of. This is why she's so mean. This is why Daddy drinks.
This is why the firemen seem so feeble. They were trying to put
out the inevitable."

He passed out and was carried to an ambulance and taken to
St. Francis Hospital. Clara rode with him and petted his head
and prayed that everything would resolve itself somehow. Eugene felt June kiss him and she was holding Michael and she
thanked him for being so gallant and courageous. He tried to
hold on to her, but she slipped through his fingers and fell back
into the flames screaming. "JUNE!" he cried out. Clara petted
his head harder, her Hail Mary concentration broken, "For crying
out loud, Eugene, you'll scare the driver and he'll drive off the

road." She petted and petted and said, "It'll be all right," but her words lacked any conviction.

In the hospital, Eugene was sedated and he saw June again. She still held Michael, and she said she was going to Vietnam to get Mack. When he woke, his face and neck and arms were greased with salve. Melvin, Clara, Frankie, and Debbie all were standing around his bed. He thought they all looked very sad and concerned. He felt hot, and he liked being in a bed that wasn't so close to the ceiling. There was a crucifix on the wall opposite his bed. He closed his eyes so he wouldn't have to see it, or his family. They had it all so mixed up! How foolish they were, standing there talking and not making a sound. He spelled out the letters "F-U-C-K" and opened his eyes to see their reaction. Then he drifted back to sleep. He sang with June, and twirled Michael around in the air as the child gasped with laughter, like he was on a ride at a children's park. He talked to President Kennedy who said Texas was the worst state, and then Christ sat down with him on the couch, and he and Eugene watched television. Christ told Eugene that he knew the end to the story, and asked him if he wanted to know, but then looking into Eugene's eyes, Christ said, "You don't want me to ruin it for you, do you?" And Eugene said, "Of course not," and a feeling overwhelmed him of truth being possible, and fire appeared in Christ's face. They shared a bowl of potato chips and drank Pepsis and watched Eliot Ness carry a dead baby from a burning building and Eugene said, "Yech!" as if he was little, and Christ said, "Just forget it. Don't look. Change the channel."

When he opened his eyes again, he saw his Uncle Ralph and Aunt Wanda standing there. They smiled. He smiled back, but wondered what they were doing there. They were well-off and lived near the Delhi Country Club, and they never visited his family. Ralph and Melvin were always on the outs with each other. Eugene often heard his father say that "my brother sold his soul for the almighty dollar." Eugene didn't like his cousin, Perry, Ralph and Wanda's son, because he was always told that Perry was "never going to have a worry in the world because he'll get both butcher shops."

"Hello, Eugene," Aunt Wanda said. She was wearing dark red clothes and her made-up face seemed like a mask. Eugene thought she looked like Lucille Ball. He wondered if his whole family had somehow died, and he was now orphaned, and he was going to be taken to their house to live and be rich.

"Eugene, my boy, it's time for you to go home," Uncle Ralph said sternly. He had Melvin's accent, but he had backbone and discipline in his voice and Eugene wondered how much he would like having him breathing over his shoulder. He decided that he would leave them, just as he'd planned on leaving his own family, as soon as he turned eighteen. He didn't want to be a butcher, anyway.

Aunt Wanda's eyes started to tear up, and their wateriness surfaced ooze around all the dried powder on her face. Eugene remembered how his mother always said that "Wanda thinks she's a big deal." The woman leaned in closer to Eugene and said, "You were asleep for a long time. Now you have to come with us. Your sister's funeral is tonight."

He rode in the front seat of their brand-new Thunderbird that had bucket seats. The car smelled new and the heater worked. Aunt Wanda sat in the back and reached up, offering Uncle Ralph and Eugene each a mint. His uncle kept repeating, "It's a darn shame, such a darn shame. That place was a firetrap. Should have been torn down years ago. Such a darn shame."

Eugene tried to picture June dead, but he couldn't. There was no reason for her to be dead. She went to Vietnam. And Michael, he thought, he saved the little boy, he caught him, so he was definitely not dead, and then they turned onto River Road, and there was Bess's. Eugene bit down on the mint. It tasted like powder. Powder from his Aunt Wanda's compact that she had just snapped shut. The building was shimmering in frozen sunlight. The charred ruins were covered in sparkling ice. The hoses' dousing had formed a glass shell where walls had been, and behind the glistening, prismic ice, there was a black velvet core, absorbing all the light, the coal of wood that had framed the building. Eugene's eyes remained fixed, looking up the road through the rear window of the Thunderbird, as they pulled to a stop across the street from the steps up to his house.

Clara saw Ralph and Wanda climbing the steps with Eugene. She yelled in to Melvin, "Here comes your brother and his uppity wife and the place is a wreck! I told you we should have gone to the hospital to get Eugene! I know she's just dying to see how shameful we have to live!"

Melvin was in the boys' room putting on his suit. He was sober and sad and praying a prayer each time June's screams were heard in his head. That's what the priest who came to the house had told him to do. From now on he was going to follow the rules. He'd heard the priest say that the blessing was "in learning to love the strange ways the Lord works." He muttered as he tied his tie, "Shut up Clara. They paid the hospital bill, didn't they? For once shut your mouth and stop worrying what everybody thinks. They've helped us out."

Clara had drawn heavy curved eyebrows on her face, and rouged her cheeks very red. Her anger was her only way of grieving. She repeated over the days, "I just knew in my bones it would end up in tragedy, I just knew it! Did June ever listen to me? Never!" And she was angry for the waste of all those years raising her, "just so she could burn up with that Bess. I always knew that Bess was too cheap to ever fix anything. Faulty wiring!" And she would sniff, "Who I feel sorry for was that little angel, Michael, such a sweet thing. But it may be for the best that he's with his mother, because what kind of life would he have with that hood for a father." And she said, "They come out of the woodwork with their sympathy, don't they. Where were all these relatives when they was giving parties? We never got invited to anything, and now they all come up to say how sorry they are and get a chance to look around, looking for a free meal, no doubt, feeling that they can make up for what's already flushed down the drain. They can take their stinking sympathy and . . ." and she would work herself into a fit, her face swelling with blood, and finally she would burst into tears, and she would cry and moan and June's name would drip over her like rain and she would grab whichever child was nearest and hold them tight and make them promise to always mind her, and heed her warnings, because "I have a sense to the nature of things."

The night of the fire, while everyone was arguing about the length of Eugene's hair at the table, June was doing a load of diapers and towels in the automatic washer Aunt Wanda had *given* to Clara. "She thinks we're a charity case," Clara had smirked. June was going to come up for it in the morning, after her friend Carol took pictures. Eugene kept one of the towels, the brown and white and blue striped one. Clara used the diapers for dustrags, even though it broke her up at first.

1991, New York City

Octavio pressed his hand on Eugene's hand on the scar where the baby had branded Eugene a living soul. He was a survivor. He would live a life, here. Eugene had free passage across the drawbridge, a second birthmark, and a baby and a sister for guides.

The scar on his neck was nothing compared to the scar his ears were branded with . . . the piercing scream of June's soul, etching a channel of pitch that reverberated a chant, constant. As they pushed against his neck, the heat traveled up through his face, to his ears, the flames splitting, burning the bridge that traversed his conscious and unconscious eyes. He heard the screams ringing and saw the low chant of Octavio and the gods as light. Earwax began to melt from the heat, and then run. His ears were crying and the way was clear, to hear again that scream originate. It was from his own voice, the voice the same as June's, "AHHHHHHHHHHHHHHHHHHHHHHHHHHHHHH HHHHHHHHHHHHHHHHHHHHHHHHHHHHHHHHHHHHHHHH HHHHHHHHHHHHHHHHHHHHHHHHhhhhhhhhhhhhh for twenty-six years and a millennium and then some!"

It came up then, because there was room for it. There was acceptance of it. There was full frontal, strong back, open heart nudity. There was toying with fucking, which could be deadly in the new diseased blood spread, but love overruled death. There was that.

June's voice screaming to death had always been balanced with Eugene's voice screaming to life. It was his strength.

Octavio left at the end of the week. They slipped through each other's fingers time and again, accepting the separation, accepting the truth, together they were dynamite.

2013, Brazil

The man, white-haired and weathered by tropical light, squatted in the red mud bank of the wild jungle river wearing a rag of a towel. He heard an unfamiliar sound. It growled mechanically somewhere within the music of the rushing water. His head turned sharply back and forth, instinctively, to test the sound alien to him, to hear if it was threatening. It was not thunder. It was not a man-bird. The noise faded. A fruit dropped to his feet to be eaten. He made this sound, "Ahhhhhyersweetmmmmmmnectarahchurchychurchyoblowsteammmmmmdrop."

1993, Los Angeles/Brazil

Eugene's flight from Rio landed in Los Angeles, and he sent his luggage on to Oakland and took only his green canvas bag with him into the taxi. The sky was green. It was hot. The cab was stuck in traffic on Santa Monica Boulevard, so Eugene paid the driver and said he would walk.

"Walk?" the cab driver seemed to be questioning his sanity. "You'll fry, buddy."

He crossed Sunset Boulevard and climbed the hill past the sleeping guard and gate that stopped cars, but anyone on foot could easily go through, and on to Beverly Lane where Stella lived with her husband, Sid, and Jason. The house was a low ranch with a manicured lawn and a circular drive. Warning signs and "Keep Out" signs and "No Trespassing" signs were posted all along the streets. Eugene laughed to himself, because he saw how easy it was to get into the "restricted" area, and he knew he did not look like he belonged. He was bearded and his hair was long and tied back and he was wearing jeans and Octavio's well-worn blue shirt. He wondered if anyone looking out his window would report him. He thought that if he was questioned, he would show his wallet and his credit cards and the picture he carried of himself dancing with Caroline Kennedy that he'd cut from the paper in New York. It was taken at the opening of The Museum of Suburban Art.

He rang the bell. He had been scheduled to fly to San Francisco, or so he thought, and he would have to be in Berkeley in a few days, but because of the mix up in Rio, he decided to drop in on Jason, unannounced, before he hitchhiked for old times' sake up the coast. His agent had arranged for him to give a workshop at Berkeley. He rang the bell again. The house was very similar to the one he'd just come from in a suburb of Rio.

He and Octavio had been staying at the home of Maria Gustavo Breton, the noted Brazilian spiritualist. They had attended a dinner in her honor two nights earlier, and she had taken Eugene aside at one point in the evening and said that she noticed Octavio was giving off a very tender color that she had never seen from him, and that it had intensified when she saw the two of them talking in a corner. She asked Eugene if his love for Octavio was pure, and Eugene proclaimed, without a doubt, "He has my heart!" She said, "Good, that is relief. It *is* love then." She said she was worried because a very similar aura coming from a body could be interpreted as illness, or susceptibility to illness. "Those with the immune deficiencies show this color, a little paler, but similar flickering pink." Eugene asked her why they would be the same color, and she said, "Love is the opening, the vulnerable, the opening . . . I don't know how to say in English, it is wide . . . let go, just as with some disease, the let go."

Eugene looked across the room where Octavio was laughing and talking and holding his drink, and Eugene tried to see the aura for himself, to see what Maria saw. He caught Octavio's eye, and the handsome Brazilian in his white suit smiled big over to him, and Eugene saw, for a moment, a color, a pinkish color, like the light around a candle, and then one of the maids crossed the line of vision wheeling a noisy tray of sweet pastries over the terra-cotta tiles, and when he could see Octavio again, the aura was gone.

Later that night, in the guest house by the pool, Eugene asked Octavio if he was aware of his aura, and he told him what Maria had said, that it revealed "in living color! Love!" And then he added, somberly, "Or disease." Octavio, having had many drinks, laughed and pushed at Eugene for being so serious. "It is love," Octavio laughed. "You are my earth, Eugene Goessler! That is what she sees. Maria would know."

"But she asked me," Eugene said, "as if she wasn't sure."

Octavio fell onto the bed, dizzily silly, "Sure? What is this, 'sure'? How can color be 'sure'? Shhhhhhure!"

Eugene went swimming. Maria had scared him. There were so many deaths, and so many of the dead had been "sure" they were healthy. "No," he said, spitting water, "she saw love." And he repeated her words over and over under the hot black Brazilian night, there in the illuminated aqua, as he swam laps back and forth, telling himself that if he did fifty, everything was fine. He did a hundred and three, and pulled himself exhausted out of the pool. He entered the guest house through the wide glass doors, and found Octavio soundly sleeping in the bed, blatantly spread nude, half-hard and so dark against the white sheets and under the fluttering light from the aftershocks of aqua reflected on the white ceiling. Eugene stood dripping at the foot of the bed, staring. He had never known such captivation. The shimmering light into the room seemed to make the Brazilian's aura blue.

"You are full of life and health," Eugene chanted. "I love you with whatever love is, and do not want to weaken you by even one doubt."

He fell upon Octavio, rousing him from his drunken sleep, and began to lick him and kiss him all over. Octavio was shocked at the wet, but accepted the attention, and then with his hands in Eugene's dripping hair, he tightened, as he felt his cock being sucked, and he said, "The rubber, sweetie."

Eugene shook his head free of Octavio's hands and dove back down to the feast of persimmons and salt. Again, coming more awake, Octavio said, "The rubber. I will come in you if you don't stop," and he tried to pull himself away from Eugene's mouth, which was like trying to push away a plate of food when you're starving, which was like trying to avoid jumping in a waterfall when you're sweltering, which was like having the sunset before your eyes and closing your eyes to it.

"No rubber," Eugene said, looking severely up to Octavio's eyes, "I want you."

Octavio fell back, giving in, giving so in, so in to the deep tomatoes and bones and splashes, thrusting, all giving in one stab. Howl!

In the morning, Octavio asked Eugene, "Why?"

Eugene continued packing and singing and Octavio continued to ask "Why?"

"I wanted you in me," Eugene finally said, "no Trojan. Just you and me. I will be taking you back home."

"But there is the threat . . ."

"The threat? Of what Octavio? Disease?"

"Yes. We have always been doing the safe ways."

"I don't care anymore," Eugene said, "I wanted to taste you, and I did, and when I fly out tonight, I'll barely have enough of my own heart to pump blood. I got you and if you got something, I got it too."

Octavio laughed, putting on his yellow swimming trunks that vibrated against his dark tanned skin, "You are crazy, Eugene, the only thing I've got is a crazy man for my earth."

"Then tell me this," Eugene said, blocking the doors so that Octavio couldn't get out to the pool. "Since we've known each other, three years, and before that, have there been risks . . . have you taken risks?"

Octavio sighed long and low, seeing Eugene's trouble all over his serious face, and he suspected the confrontation had something to do with the impending separation. Each time they parted, there was some sort of passionate, dramatic, gesture. He thought, "Ahh, this is it." He settled down on the bed, knowing he would not be going into the pool for a while. "Okay, my friend," he said, "you have some bird biting on your nose . . . now what is it? You want me to say that I have never see anyone but you? I do not lie. There is Tonio. You've known of him since the Widow's . . . and you know we are dear friends . . . but I tell you, sweetie, it has been with safe . . . done safe . . . and you. You. What? What do you want?"

Eugene paced back and forth, still hearing Maria's colors and feeling the fear he'd felt the night before. "I know, I know, I know, I know. I just want you to meet with Maria, though, and have her check your color. Will you do that for me?"

Octavio grabbed Eugene's leg, stopping him from passing again, "You see me belly soft, Eugene, but that is because I am so much open with you. When you leave, I will close and be strong again. I am strong and safe without you."

"I'm not jealous, you know . . . you know that don't you?"

Octavio laughed, "Yes, I know that. I think you are afraid of Maria, not what she sees around me, but that she sees. She sees through. She knows no mistakes, and for you, I will have her look again, after you've gone . . . and now I see why you said, 'no rubber,' and why you got what I got. I see . . . you, crazy man."

Eugene knelt in front of Octavio. "I knew last night that as far as this life goes, I've met my match with you . . . and . . . well, I understood jumping on a funeral pyre . . . the lure of the flame."

"You are doing a play, no?" Octavio smiled. "What is this, on your knees so sweet and humble in love? You tell me anything in the world and I'll say it, and I never lie. You tell me to jump off the mountain and I will."

"Say you'll never lie."

"I'll never lie, Eugene, and I'll say this to you again, you make earth home."

At the airport, Eugene was informed that his flight was to Los Angeles and not San Francisco, as he thought he had made clear to the agent. He started to get angry, not speaking Portuguese, which made it impossible to argue out. Octavio took over, and after a long dispute back and forth, it seemed the agent was bowing to him, and Eugene momentarily thought that Octavio had persuaded the man to reroute the flight.

"You will go right from one plane in L.A. to another to Oakland, which is closer to Berkeley, no? This is good, no?"

"It's fine," Eugene said, already deciding to see Jason and send his luggage on, and hitchhike up the Pacific Coast Highway for old times' sake.

He rang the bell and knocked loudly on the yellow door that was framed in leaded glass sidelights. There were three cars in the drive, so someone had to be home. He stepped from the entrance porch and walked across the chemically green lawn, past a lemon and a grapefruit tree, both of which were burdened with fruit, some fallen and rotting on the ground. As he rounded the corner of the house, he heard music and children's screechy voices playing, and the sound of splashing. He heard a radio announce, "KROK, L.A., brings you one commercial-free hour of The Bushwackers!" Eugene came to a redwood fence and gate and looked over. There was a kidney-shaped swimming pool, and there was Jason on the diving board, and two other boys splashing about. On a chaise, nearer the house, glistening with oils, was Stella in a white bikini, motionless. A bird of paradise, thick and blooming, jutted out in front of Eugene's nose. He stepped back so he wouldn't be seen. Jason was yelling from the diving board, "Aaron! You motherfucker! Get out of my pool! Go home and swim in your toilet! You piss!" He was so much bigger than the last time Eugene had seen him. That was in 1990 in New York. He was seven then, and sitting the entire time they had together. Stella had allowed Eugene to join them for lunch at the Brasserie on Fifty-third Street. Then, his brown hair was stylishly shaved at the sides, and he sulked and whined and demanded cake first, and then eggs benedict and then he sent them back because "they just don't look right! Pisshole!" Now, he stood dripping and bouncing on the diving board, his body growing tall, and he glistened in the sun, tan, a little chubby in the belly, with his dark hair shiny flat to his skull from surfacing head-back.

Stella remained perfectly still, but her white lips moved. "Enough of that kind of talk, Jason. You know how I hate vulgarity. I'm trying to listen to this song."

"Aaron pissed in the pool, Mother!" Jason whined. "I saw him do it!"

"I did not!" the boy yelled from the shallow end.

"You did too!" Jason screamed, turning red in the face. "I saw it get yellow by you! We'll all get AIDS!" Jason wished that his mother would go inside so he wouldn't have to consider her.

"Jason," Stella's mouth moved, "Aaron knows the pool rules, don't you, Aaron? And I'm sure he didn't go in the water when the cabana is right here, right, Aaron? So why don't all of you stop yelling and play? See who can stay under the longest and keep quiet. I love this song."

She was referring to The Bushwackers' third hit, "Chewing My Fingernails," from their first album, *The Channel.* Eugene had just heard the Portuguese version down in Brazil, and it was interpreted as "Nervous Waiting."

A heavyset maid in uniform came out of the house and anxiously hurried over to Stella on the chaise. "Madam, there was someone ringing the bell and when I answered, there was no one there. Should I call the street guard?"

Stella moved her arm, which had been hanging limp to the stone terrace, bringing it up high enough to motion to the maid to go back inside. "Activate the perimeter alarm for a while, Angelica, and I'll keep the boys within the pool area. I'm sure it's nothing."

The maid nodded and retreated into the cool house. Stella told the children to stay near the pool because "the juice is on the fence," and then she said to herself, "She watches too many mysteries, always hearing things, twittering about like a nervous wreck. The woman *is* stress."

Eugene saw the beam box at the corner, under the eave over-hang, turn light blue. He backed further from the fence, till he could barely see over to the pool and Stella. He smoothed his hair back and tightened the rubber band that held it in a tail, and ran his tongue over his teeth, and then called out, as hillbilly as possible, "Do I smell bacon fryin, or is that Stella Gold over thar sizzling like a slab of pork in a pint-sized bikini?"

"Mom!" Jason screamed. "Someone is over in the side yard, by the fence!"

Stella was sitting up in the chaise and putting on her sun-glasses. "I heard, Jason, now be quiet, it's probably someone we know." She stood up, adjusting the elastic around her burnt thighs, patting her flat stomach, and picking up the pool cleaner pole for a weapon. She called for Angelica to come out, and she approached the fence. The boys watched her.

"She moves like Ophelia! She is a goddess! She is owed! She plays it safe! Tis the Trojan Woman!" Eugene emoted. "Be still my heart!"

Stella cautiously stood on her toes to see over the gate, avoid-ing the electric beam. "Goessler? Goessler? What the hell are you doing in my yard?!"

The three boys stood at the far end of the pool, dripping and worried. They might be kidnapped by terrorists. They were all rich.

Stella called out to Angelica, in a loud New Yorkese voice, unbecoming a lady, "Angelica! Turn off the system!" She seemed to be doing an exercise the way she was craning her neck and stretching up to see over to Eugene. She yelled to the boys, "It's all right, kids, there's nothing to be afraid of!" And then she and Eugene both saw the beam box blue fade off. She spoke in an aggravated hush, "How dare you come around here, Goessler, with no warning! How did you get past the gate?"

Eugene approached the redwood gate. "I walked past."

"Walked!"

Eugene laughed. "What is that? A dirty word in this town?" He took his sunglasses off and hung them on his shirt.

"Well, why don't you walk on out and leave us alone," Stella said, opening the double-locked gate to him. She almost smiled as he tried to see her eyes behind her dark glasses. "Don't get close to me. What are you looking at, Goessler?" There were some pools in Beverly Hills that were colored the same green as his eyes. "Sid'll kill me for letting you in . . . What are you looking at? Stop. God, you're unnerving . . . He'll be back from the studio any minute."

Eugene poured on whatever charm he could muster. "I want to see your eyes. You have beautiful eyes."

"Fuck you, Goessler. Save it for a fool."

He entered the yard. Jason recognized him and dove into the pool, mad.

"I stopped by to see my son," Eugene said, knowing the use of a possessive would bother her. "I'm hitching up to Berkeley."

Stella sighed. "Jason! Jason?" she called the boy, but her back was to the pool, so she didn't know he was underwater holding his breath. She stared at Eugene. The man who seemed to challenge her by existing. "Look who's here . . . for a minute."

"*Who* are you supposed to be?" Aaron yelled over to the unkempt man, as he would to the gardener or the maid, but never to his parents' friends.

Jason surfaced at the edge of the pool with snot running from his nose.

"I'm Jason's father!" Eugene announced, deliberately looking at his son.

"Bullshit!" Aaron laughed.

Stella said to Jason, "Well, say hello . . . show him that at least you have manners."

"Hi," Jason said as dejectedly as possible, and he did a backward dive, hoping Eugene would be gone when he came up for air.

"You're not Sidney!" the wising-off Aaron yelled.

Jason came up and pulled himself out of the pool and ran inside the house. Aaron and the other boy ran in after him, yelling for him. Stella accused Eugene of upsetting Jason.

"Cute," Eugene said.

"You're disgusting, Goessler. Did you see Jason's reaction to you? He's in there having a fit, I imagine, thanks to you. I can't believe you have the balls to just 'drop by' like this. Have you ever thought of the child?"

"You, Stella, of all people, know I have balls. You bore my fruit."

She halfheartedly slapped him.

He repeated himself, emphasizing the word "bore." "Like I said, you bore my fruit. You'd bore any fruit."

"Jason is not a fruit. We've seen to that. He's all boy."

They walked along the pool. Eugene said, "You certainly have become the proper moral prig in your matron years."

"Goessler, I'll have you arrested for trespassing."

Eugene laughed. Stella went to her table for a cigarette and adjusted the coverage of her bikini bottom over her ass as she walked across the stones.

Eugene said, "And I'll be reporting back to New York how Stella Gold really lives. You will be the first name on The Museum of Suburban Art's Honorary Achiever list. Where the fuck do you get off, lady?"

"I don't get off with you, that's for sure," she said blowing smoke toward Eugene. "And stop looking at me with that damn smile of yours . . . God! You're so perverse!"

He dragged an iron chair across the rocks till it was in the shade of the house, set his green bag down, and then pulled Octavio's blue shirt up and off. He sat down, exhaling as if he'd traveled far and had reached his destination.

Stella hid her eyes behind her glasses, dumbfounded. "What do you think you're doing?" Eugene was still handsome and strong and almost attractive to her, because he was so perverse. "Don't get comfortable, Goessler, because Sid'll be here any minute. You're not staying."

Eugene smelled his armpits, "I stink . . . how about a dip?"

"That is not a bathtub, you asshole. I'm serious, Sid'll kill me for letting you in here and upsetting Jason. He loves Jason. I imagine you can't understand that."

"How is Sid?" Eugene asked sarcastically. He'd heard from Joe Bukovsky, that Sid and Stella's marriage was as rocky as the terrace Eugene was trying to balance his chair on. "I heard . . ."

Stella changed the subject, as she caught herself, for a moment, actually glad to see Eugene. "What do you mean? Hitchhiking to Berkeley? You have money. I read your slang is in its third printing . . . or is it to 'slum with the real world'? That's it, isn't it? You're carrying a wallet full of credit cards I bet . . ."

Eugene laughed, "Slang?"

"Sorry darling," she blew smoke, satisfied that she'd deflated any hot glory of the road that he might be impressing himself with. "I didn't mean 'slang' I meant *Crap*, and to dedicate the damn thing to Jason. How dare you? People will read that."

Eugene ran his index finger over his lips. "Got anything cold to drink?"

They heard a scream from inside the house. Angelica came running out. "Madam! He's done it again!! Jason put Eugene in the microwave!!"

Stella ran into the house. Eugene grabbed Angelica's forearm and asked the woman who Eugene was.

She pulled away from the bare-chested man. "Eugene is Jason's hamster . . . was Jason's hamster. That's the third one. Poor thing. I have my hands full with that boy. He has a mean streak running through him . . ." and she stopped, realizing she was saying too much, to a very strange stranger. She hurried back in.

The radio played The Bushwackers' first hit, "In a Gyrogyroriverrondo."

Eugene finished Stella's drink, kicked off his boots, dropped his jeans, and dove into the pool.

1994, Ohio

Frank Goessler called Eugene and told him that Clara was in the hospital, very sick, and that he should come from Massachusetts as soon as possible.

Frank and Stephanie's house in Harrison, Ohio, was similar to The Museum of Suburban Art that Eugene, Lola Hampton, Joe Bukovsky, and Bernard Rubinstein had helped establish on Avenue C in the East Village of New York City. The museum was a three-bedroom ranch-style house, with an authentic recreation room in the basement, lawn ornaments on a lawn, and even a garage and driveway. It was built on a vacant lot owned by the city, and was funded through the Warhol Foundation and the Certiano Foundation for Photography. Set between tenements, the museum was perfectly out of context.

Frank's house was up for sale. They were building a "better, more up-to-date" house out in Oak Haven. Stephanie and their two children were not home when Eugene arrived in the car he'd rented at the airport. Frank said they were visiting her mother. Eugene refused Frank's offer to stay at the house, saying he'd already checked in to the Harrison Motor Lodge. To Eugene, who had not seen Frank in years, Frank seemed to look, talk, and drink just like Melvin. His baseball trophies were displayed on the VCR cabinet. There was a crucifix in each room, with dried Palm Sunday branches behind each one. And while they were at the house, Frank downed five beers. Frank made little sense to Eugene. Eugene made no sense to Frank.

At the hospital, Frank went in the room first to prepare Clara for the shock of seeing Eugene. Her last communication with him had been the call to New York that she had left on his answering machine. Eugene waited in the hospital corridor.

"Mother, you'll never guess who's here to see you," Frank said.

Clara Goessler was pale and shriveled, in a white hospital gown that made her seem little. She had an oxygen tube running to her mouth, to draw from when she felt breathless. Her eyes were glazed with film that made her seem blind. She guessed that it was Debbie down from Indianapolis.

Frank laughed, "Shoot, no, Mother, where's your mind? Debbie was here just yesterday."

In the hall, Eugene paced, feeling his hands sweating, feeling eyes on him from the nurses and interns, hearing their Ohio accents, thinking how odd it was to be there, and one particular thought recurred. Where was Stephanie? The kids he'd never seen? First Frank said they were at her mother's, and then a beer later, they were at the shopping center, and then later, he said they were at church.

"Which is it, Frankie?" Eugene had asked him, following his younger brother up the steps from the family room where Frank had proudly shown him their pool table.

"Which is what?"

"Where's your family, Frankie? First you say one thing and then the other, and I would have liked to have seen them."

Frank sat at the breakfast bar and opened another beer. "Well, shoot, you will, sometime, but Stephie and I thought it best . . . well, that we should, you know, just you and me, for old times, be together."

"Uh, Frankie, I think you're hiding something," Eugene suggested, clinking cans of beer, with no toast mentioned.

"Shoot, Eugene, little baby Melvin is too young to be around all this." He stood and said they should get going.

In the hospital corridor, Eugene thought, "They don't want me to infect their kids. That's it, Goessler. Dig it."

A nurse asked him if he needed any help, and he pointed to the door, and said, "My mother's in there. I'm just waiting."

Frank held Clara's spotted bony hand and said, "Eugene is here, all the way from Massachusetts, to see you, Mother."

"Eugene?" she muttered, and a smile crossed her drugged face, and then her eyes tried to focus on Frank, and her brow wrinkled like pleats, and her mouth dropped into a low pout, and she muttered, "He's no son of mine. He's shamed us."

Frank patted her hand. "Shoot, he's still Eugene. He's your own flesh and blood. That was all a long ways back, Mother. You got to see him. I know that I can't think of anything Tiffy or baby Melvin could do to stop me from wanting to see them. Even murder, and shoot, Eugene ain't no convict. People in the know say he's real good, made a name for himself. Now what do you say to that?"

Clara shook her head violently back and forth on the pillow, her white pin curls that Debbie had put up the day before for her squared off on her skull like a garden plot. "No. He's only here to put the final nail in my coffin, I know it. He deserted us and went to the devil. He had no right, leaving like that, after your father went and got himself killed. He had no right . . . always had a mind of his own . . . if only it had been . . ."

"He was on drugs back then, Mother, shoot, Eugene had a wild streak in him."

Clara sucked on the tube to catch her breath. In her anger, a little color had returned to her face. "Always had to do things his own way," she coughed, picturing the teenager and not the forty-four-year-old man on the other side of her door. "He shamed me to no end. I don't know why you brought him here, Frankie. You know how I am. You must be trying to kill me, too."

With the beers in him, Frank Goessler saw the past in a fog, and he kept saying to himself, "Let bygones be bygones," even though he still resented that Eugene had left them. First June and the baby died, then Mack was killed in Vietnam, then Daddy in the wreck . . . still, to this day, he thought, he couldn't drive around Deadman's Curve without thinking of him, and then Eugene up and left, good as dead, so selfish. "But, Mother," he said, holding her hand tight, "you always liked him when he was a boy, and I can't help thinking that somewhere deep inside you, your tail's a-waggin like a homesick hound dog, aching to see him."

In a low growling voice, the old woman said, "It is not!"

"Yes it is," Frank said, smiling, not willing to let her be sullen. "You always loved Eugene, whether you own up to it or not."

Clara sniffed the air. "Something stinks in here, Frankie." She tried to get enough of the smell in her nose to identify it. "Did you pass gas?"

Frank shook his head, "No," and sniffed the air, to help.

Eugene's voice spoke, "Maybe it's your own breath backing up in your face, Mother."

Frank felt Eugene's hand on his shoulder. Clara saw Eugene and closed her eyes tight, as if she was about to be dropped or dunked or hit.

Eugene continued, "Remember how you'd say that whenever one of us kids said we smelled something awful? Do you remember me, Mother? I am Eugene . . . Look at that, Frankie," he said leaning close to his brother at the bed watching their mother squeeze her face as tight as possible, "look at that. You look like a raisin, Mother, or a newborn baby pushing its way out of the cunt."

Frank disassociated himself from Eugene. There was no need for him to make fun of the old woman, and to use dirty words. "You are riling her, Eugene, and her blood pressure is already sky-high. Why do you talk like that?"

Clara was trying to pull herself into a knot, and the source of the smell became obvious. She had shit in the bed. Both Eugene and Frank saw the brown of it as she squirmed to get as far away from Eugene as possible. Frank hurried from the room to get an orderly to clean it up. He said to Eugene, "Let her be now."

Eugene was alone with Clara. She looked like a baby, a prunish newborn baby, with her hands fisted to her mouth. "You shit, Mother," he said leaning over her. The woman was turning redder from holding her breath, and Eugene remembered how little Debbie would hold her breath when she was punished, till she would pass out. "I'll clean you up," he said, going to the sink and wetting a towel. He reached over, pushing her soaked hospital gown apart. His stomach turned from the smell, and then the sight of her, curled on her side, fetal. He took a closer look, seeing her wrinkled ass for what it was, a wrinkled ass, a wrinkled shit-covered human ass, and the shit was shit, his mother's shit. He had been born from not too far from this shit-covered spot, a spot as real as lips or hands, but hidden from him since that birthday. He wrapped the wet towel around his hand and moved to wipe her.

At his touch, Clara twisted over onto her back and screamed,

"DON'T YOU DARE!" She sounded strong, and she had moved fast. Her eyes glared at him with hatred.

Eugene held the towel-wrapped hand up in surrender, and smiled, "Hey! You still can yell!"

She closed her eyes tight again and spoke in a low mutter, not about to please him with another show of strength, "Go away from me," she slurred. "Get out of my sight, you shameful polecat."

Frank came in with a candystriper girl who shocked Eugene with how much she looked like June. His jaw dropped and his smile faded. It was like seeing Melvin and June. The girl pulled the curtain around the bed, separating the men from their mother.

In a chipper sweetened teen voice, the girl could be heard saying, "Did we have an accident?"

Clara cried out, "Get him out of here! Get him away from me! He's the devil!"

Frank looked at Eugene, wondering what he'd done. Eugene motioned for him to follow him out into the hospital corridor. Eugene threw the towel in the sink.

"Look, man," Eugene said to Frankie, "she doesn't want to see me. She's as bitter as ever. It was wishful thinking on your part, Frankie."

Frank turned away from Eugene and said, "Well, I was getting her ready, when you just barged in and scared her with your dirty talk, Eugene. She was coming round to admitting that she wanted to see you. What the devil, Eugene, she could be dying."

Eugene was still trying to shake the thought that June was in the room with Clara. He said, "That may be wishful thinking on your part, too. She seems pretty feisty."

Frank blessed himself, "Eugene, don't you think that! I've done my best with that woman, let her live with us, make extra work for Stephie, and where were you? I'm only going on what the doctors said. Her heart is too far gone. Don't you think that I wish her dead! You talk so jackass funny about something so wrenching!" It was obvious that Frank had thought of the relief of having his mother gone. "Shoot! Why don't you take an interest in her welfare before you point fingers at me! I pray for you, Eugene. I pray that someday you have to face a tragedy like this, and then you'll know. I pray for . . ."

Eugene pushed him up against the ceramic white wall, "I

know all about it! Little brother! All the dying! You and your fucking Church know me, and my 'kind,' know all about the tragedy! Your Lord's way of mending our ways, right? Divine retribution, right? Let me tell you something, brother, I have seen the sweetest souls on earth die. The strongest, healthiest, clear-light souls ... men who your Church judge as being punished for their crimes ... that bitter woman in there has no right to treat me like shit, no right, and I don't care how fucking near death's door she is! Your Christ isn't my Christ, Frankie, you've been sold a bill of goods."

Frank had closed his eyes in defensive prayer against the Satan that had taken over Eugene's brain. What kind of life had poor Eugene fallen into? To blaspheme and cuss and argue outside his dying mother's door! He opened his eyes, strengthened, and said, "Boy, Eugene, you sure got yourself mixed up and turned around," and he pushed Eugene's arms that had him caged to the wall. "And keep your dirty hands off of me!"

Eugene held his hands up again, in surrender, and stepped back to the opposite wall, "Oh, that's right, I forgot, you might catch the queer disease, right?"

"I never said that!"

"Oh bullshit man! Why don't you speak your mind, *your* mind, for once! At least the old woman in there spews it out! You know damn well you've passed judgment on me, just like she did! Why don't you admit that you don't want me touching your family because I'm queer! You're just like Daddy! ..."

Frank broke in, "That's fine with me!"

"You're just like him ... full of the Church's excuses and hypocrisy, man. You tell me about being beholden to that woman in there, who beat the shit out of us, physically and mentally, for years! You're still taking it, Frankie, and offering it up, right?"

"I pray for your soul, Eugene."

"What happened to my little brother? Where'd he go? Did she kill him? How dare you pray for me! Who the hell are you?"

"I never lost my faith, thank God for that," Frank said, thinking a beer would be his first stop as soon as he left the hospital. "I never quit."

"I did," Eugene said, and abruptly reentered Clara's room and pulled the curtain back on his mother's bed, startling the girl who was finishing up wiping his mother's ass.

"Just a sec . . ." she started to say.

Clara's head turned to see Eugene. Their eyes met. Hers closed as they were shut by the rise of her cheeks at the drop of her mouth, as she screamed, "Eugene! Get away from me!! Oh, I can't breathe! I can't breathe! I ca . . ."

Frank grabbed him from behind, but Eugene shrugged him off. Eugene took the oxygen tube and shoved it roughly in his coughing mother's open mouth. His finger grazed her shaking lower lip, and it flopped rubbery. That was their last touch. She died five years later.

Before driving to the airport in Kentucky, Eugene went into Poachers Restaurant, which was adjacent to the Harrison Motor Lodge. Frank had told him that Bobby Schneider was the manager there. Eugene asked the waitress to call him from the kitchen. He walked across the dining room, slump-shouldered, balding, and heavy. Eugene stood to shake his hand, and they were the same height. Bobby had always been two inches taller. He seemed old and resigned to it, as if he was eighty instead of forty-five. They had coffee at a table that overlooked the interstate.

"Things sure change, don't they?" Bobby said, looking out the window. "When we was kids, who would've thought that it would be so built up way out here. This was country . . . You know, your old house was torn down years ago, and where Bess's . . ." He stopped, not wanting to bring up the fire. He grinned big, like a salesman, and said, "I don't think about it much. I'm always looking to the future. They say by the year 2000, there'll be suburbs to the Indiana border, and business here will double."

Eugene felt like an open book, looking beyond the excess of the man, to the kid, to the same inflections, and he saw the same halo for a second, around the shiny skull. He felt like he had stepped, out of the blue, into the tender territory of his innocence. They were all living their lives, biding their time, and he took a deep breath and let the reality settle around him like a blanket. He was no judge. He was no better or worse. The halo around Bobby's head was not of his doing.

"Your brother, Frank, told me . . . You know, Frank and I are both building new homes out in Oak Haven . . . and we got to talking, and he told me that you were a big-time poem writer, and had made quite a name for yourself. Is there money in that stuff? Anyways, I told him I wasn't a bit surprised that you made something of yourself, not a bit." He showed Eugene a picture of his three children, proudly explaining that they were all doing good, "though Candy is one of them Bushwacker nuts, but heck, I guess it's like the Beatles."

As he walked Eugene to his car, he asked him how he liked the ride, because he was considering getting one. "My Ford's been causing me grief."

They shook hands, and Eugene wished him "double business by 2000," and Bobby wished Eugene "a big improvement for your mother."

1997, New York City

"Lucinda," Eugene called from the shadows of the soundstage, "Ar!"

He had been sent to a stool in the dark, out of the way of the production. He was drinking. He was observing the formal adoption of his baby, *Barbara Wars Mark*. It was a wordwork he had signed away for money, and it was being made into a telepiece in Television Center on the West Side of Manhattan. He was permitted visitation rights, but his presence, loud and argumentative, was forcing one more confrontation between Lucinda, the director, and himself, the natural mother.

"The core of the piece is the *R* sound!" he argued, hearing the thin nasal sound of the actor playing Mark full of "R-lessness."

"Stop tape," the woman said, exasperated. She put her hand to her forehead, forming an awning against the lights, trying to see into the dark sidelines of the studio. "Goessler? Goessler? Are you back? I thought you were being interviewed?"

"Aha!" Eugene sang, "so I was right! You set that up to get me out from under your skirt!"

Lucinda's journalist friend had taken Eugene to an office. He had asked him questions for a piece he was "sure to sell to either *Rolling Stone Magazine II* or *Them*."

"Is it true that Spalding Gray opened doors for verbal films to be accepted into the mainstream?" he asked Goessler, who was drinking straight burning vodka from a cup.

"Yes," Eugene said, giving the question some thought, trying to be logical, looking back at the progress. "The films made money—but . . ." He opened the drawers of the desk he was sitting on, seeing pens, clips, and a hard rye stale pastrami

305

sandwich half eaten. He slid the drawer closed. "It melted some earwax . . . sucked out the blockage. The block, space, comma, age. Gray and Gullo both . . . and back to Jackson," and then he stopped with a thought. Lucinda was about to shoot "The Ball Jar" piece where Barbara cracks, and that was what this interview was really about, "getting rid of Goessler." He downed the vodka and moved to the door, "Look, I've got to get back to the soundstage. Just put down that before the word was the syllable, the grunt."

"But Mr. Goessler," the journalist continued, "what about ten years ago?"

Eugene opened the door and turned with a sly smile, having escaped, and said, "Lucinda put you up to this didn't she?"

Eugene was shushed at the studio entrance and told to take a stool, quietly.

"Aha! So I was right!" Eugene sang. "You were trying to get rid of me!"

There were sighs from the crew and actors at the disruption. Eugene sensed that everyone was taking the piece far too seriously, and he felt he was the only one accountable. They should have fun, and simply listen "to the mother." Out of his self-imposed solitary confinement up in his house in Massachusetts, he found himself in New York again, amidst the amusements and claptrap, the that and that and babble baggage, but he was getting paid $800,000. He would be able to retreat to Brazil or Florida or his stone house in the Berkshires, affording a freedom for himself, and all from the sale of one piece for video production. It was worth it. Obviously, he thought, wishing he had another drink, no one saw the humor in the situation but him, or for that matter, the "baby/mother" allegory.

"I know," he called over to Lucinda from the dark, "I know what makes baby gurgle and what makes baby bawl!"

"Goessler!" Lucinda ranted, frustrated that she had to have the author on the set ('his asshole agent has it written in the contract'). "Goessler, please trust me!"

"The Ball Jar" section of *Barbara Wars Mark* involved Barbara, the archaeologist, throwing her collection of jarred specimens of tar at her lover, Mark, the anarchist, who, in her aggravated state she felt had become her archrival for the heart and affection of their daughter, Arlene. Mark was to plead as he is pelted with the breaking shards and tar, "Sorry, Barb! Sorry!"

From the shadows, Eugene said toward Lucinda, "Tell him it is S-'are'-ree, not S-ah-ree, that's all."

The actor playing Mark addressed Lucinda, "Tell him to fuck off." The actor was dripping in fake black goo, naked and fed-up.

"Break! Take ten!" Lucinda yelled.

Eugene crossed into the light, still a striking figure at his age, though decidedly scruffy. He grinned sheepishly, counting on his eyes to appease the sour demeanor of the director.

"Goessler," she said, as everyone left, "you are a bastard. Don't you have anything better to do?"

"You need me," he said, sitting down on the blue block where Mark was to stand. "This is my baby, Lucinda. Ar, ar, ar. How many times do I have to tell you? And she throws the jars only after Mark calls them 'garbage of dinosaurs.' "

Lucinda finished counting to ten, took a breath, and said as calmly as she could, spacing her words very much like a Goessler wordplay unconsciously, "Do you think I don't know that? Do you think I am deaf? Do you think you are the director?"

Eugene shook his head like Clara's naughty boy, and said, "No. But, I am the mommy."

This was not funny to Lucinda, and she did not find men-being-boys cute. She had worked for years, through trivia shows and rock videos, and had only recently achieved marketable-money-maker stature with her *Bushwackers Live* docu-film. She slapped her palm with a coffee-stir and said, "You are a prick, Goessler," and added in a deep solemn voice, slowly, "You sold the baby. Now it is mine. Get it?"

"Nope," Eugene continued shaking his tangled mess of hair, seeing that his shoe was embedded in the drying fake-tar goo, "nope, I guess I don't."

"Okay," Lucinda said, sounding like a therapist, treading softly. "You wrote it. You sold it. You were paid for it. If I had my way, you would not be here, but you are, as an advisor, not as a 'mommy.' You wrote it. Yes. Now, I film it."

"It will always be mine," Eugene said, resenting her condescension, resenting her obliviousness to his cute act. He laughed strong like a wise adult.

She was losing her patience, "You never did own it, Goessler.

A parent doesn't own a child, if you want me to look at it your way."

Eugene got what she said, through the vodka and all, but . . . "No, no, it's not the same thing," he argued, now with himself too, "the piece is more mine than yours, that's all I'm saying."

Lucinda flicked the coffee-stir at him, and threw her arms out and down to her sides in surrender, "All right then! You fucking tell me which cameras to use and how many frames of lead I'll need, and you tell me how to get the fucking yellow!"

He stood up from the block and picked up the stir, then sat back down, using it to scrape the tar from his shoe. "Yellow?"

"Yellow!" she screamed, her voice echoing across the wide stage. "Yellow, Goessler! You pleaded for yellow the other day. Remember? You cried for yellow. The corncob barnyard scene. You demanded yellow. I delivered. Now," she faced him close, "I'll give up if you tell me how I got yellow."

He laughed.

"I'm serious, tell me, Goessler, because, dammit, that yellow is as vital to the piece, you said so yourself, as any *R* sound!"

He thought of all his theater work, the gels and filters, but he knew that was too simple. It was all digital coloring now, through the computer, and he said, "That's not the point."

"It is, Goessler, and you know it. I'm asking you to lay off. Go out. Get some air. Trust me. I chose to do this. I think it's great."

"You do?"

"Yes. Now give me a chance to take it somewhere else. You'll always have the paper."

Eugene stood the coffee-stir in the tar, planting it like a flagpole on the moon, and said, "One small step for Goessler, letting the baby go." He looked up to Lucinda and said, "I have a son, you know. He's a teenager out in California. Make this so that he might get it."

"I heard about that," Lucinda said, hoping that this time he would really get out of the studio. "I'll do my best, Goessler."

Eugene stood and shook her hand and walked out of the light, leaving a footprint of tar across the floor. "I'm going to get plastered!" he called back to the director, hearing her whistle blow, passing the returning crew who all acknowledged him with a slight nod or uneven smile. He wanted a drink before he started taking any of it too seriously. He rarely drank at home in Massachusetts, where he'd moved in 1992, but there was something about the blab and gaggle of the New York scene that egged him on to drink and smoke and have opinions like Lola and Joe and the rest.

The air hit him like a surprise party. Amber October late afternoon light and river breezes blew, brewing a punch, stirring him, seeing all the guests! The bar would be too much dark, he thought, and he opted for the open cafe on the Hudson River Esplanade, all part of Television Center. He ordered a vodka tonic at a table abutting the railing. The complex was a hug of media hustle and bustle. Not many people seemed to notice the river. They all seemed preoccupied, he thought, all unionized and expensive, definitely mainstream. He was an outsider. He was there to protect his work, to see to it that it translated clearly to film. He would compromise. Lucinda had her points, but he was suspicious of the "media savvy" that his agent had bandied about when he was selling Eugene on the idea.

"Cooper and Gullo have already signed," his agent had said, "so we are talking class and high-brow clout. We are talking breaking new ground."

"Money," Eugene said, drinking, watching a film crew file past the cafe. He had had complete control doing his Off-Off work, but rarely was there any money. The bodies he saw mercifully distracted him from the sodden regrets of what had already been signed away and legally adopted.

He eyed the young men. Octavio had said, "One gift of birthdays is that the older we get, the more younger there are of sizable age." Forty was young to Eugene and twenty was a boy. "Flowers," Octavio called them, and sometimes he would sigh, "such a garden!" when the two men were together eyeing the public. Eugene drank and watched and took deep long breaths, relinquishing his parental discretion to Lucinda. He'd found that when his spine was straight and his lungs inflated and deflated like waves, he would reach a dreamy consciousness where the dance of life became obvious. He could easily imagine, from a high-storied viewpoint, the jitter and jive, the glide and collide, of all the bodies, moving through corridors of the city, thinking they knew where they were going, as if they had a choice. They were pinballs, banging, reacting, and moving on. He and Lucinda had just clashed, bouncing off each other, he thought, smiling, deciding, he would think no more of *Barbara Wars Mark*. He would enjoy the river and the strobe of people passing between him and the Hudson's sun. Some bodies took his breath away.

One young man with long dark hair and black clothes looked three times back to Eugene at his table, and then said something to his friends and left them, returning toward the cafe railing. He was a bit hesitant, slowing as he neared Eugene. Eugene looked directly at him as the young man blocked the light. He exhaled.

"Excuse me," the young man asked, owning a dark rich voice.

Eugene thought, "Oh no, another actor."

"Are you Eugene Goessler?"

The young man must have been no more than twenty, he thought, nodding.

"I thought so. I thought I recognized you, but then I thought, 'Nah, not in Television Center, home of *Dancinggirls Express* and *Hoopla*,' not here. Don't you live in the woods upstate somewhere?"

Eugene laughed.

The young man became a little self-conscious at Eugene's laughter, and put his hands in his pockets. "You know, I think of you in the seedy side, downtown or you know, not television . . ."

"Mainstream," Eugene suggested.

"Yeah. I'm sorry. For all I know you are just sitting here having a drink, right? I assumed . . ."

"You assumed right," Eugene said, taken with the gleam of the young man's dark looks. "I'm a panelist on *The Brandname Game*," he lied.

The young man frowned, "I thought that was shot in Astoria? Hey, you're pulling my leg, right? Though, it's not such a . . ."

"I'll pull your leg," Eugene leered, kidding, and not kidding, well, kidding considering the kid. The light of the sun bouncing from the river to the black shine of hair made it seem blue. Not kidding, he would pull his leg. The young man's teeth seemed so straight white and new. All of him seemed new, like a stretched-out boy, still catching up to manhood, "No, I am kidding about the show, not about your leg, though," Eugene said. "What's your name?" he asked, sort of rising from his patio chair, and extending his hand across the railing toward the young man's pocketed right hand.

"Andrew Atwood," he said, pulling out his new hand from the tight black pocket and grasping Eugene's. "It's an honor to meet you, Mr. Goessler," then smirked. "Well, it is. I love your work."

"I too am honored," Eugene said, reseating himself, "I am honored at your recognition. What the hell, you are truly stunning. Quite the looker. Obvious assets. As you widen your smile, and redden. Your ponytail is very long."

Andrew beamed.

"Want a drink?" Eugene asked, offering the empty chair opposite his at the little table.

"Sure," the young man said, enthused, and swung himself, consciously agile, having been acknowleged for his physical beauty, over the rail and into the chair in one fell swoop.

Eugene enjoyed the move. This Andrew blatantly displaying himself. He drank the air of the soap the young man must have used, the fresh man's skin, he thought. He'd learned over the years to feast in the glorious flesh, that eyes can touch, and sometimes that's enough, because the taste could be foul, but the joy could be found, in "the architecture of even idiots."

"You are graceful," Eugene said, raising his hand for the waitress. "Are you old enough for alcohol?"

Andrew foolishly exclaimed, as if it should be obvious, "I'm twenty-three!"

The way he said "twenty-three" was somehow too toothy and forward, and Eugene thought, "Just be here, beautiful, but don't talk, or you'll betray yourself." Then he wondered if he wasn't somehow disappointed in his age, wanting him to be even younger. It didn't matter. "I imagine," Eugene smiled, "you'll have what I'm having." And then looking toward the river he said, "Look at that. Copper."

Andrew nodded at the order suggestion, as if he knew to keep quiet, but he was bubbly with his good fortune of meeting Goessler, sitting across from him, and he burst fast, "I'm so glad I stopped. I thought it was you. I've seen you perform before, I was at the opening of The Museum of Suburban Art. You were so good! And I thought, 'What do I say?' 'What if you aren't you?' and all that, and then I thought, 'Well, why not?' It's not like you would be a snob, and if it wasn't you, then who cares!"

Eugene looked away, trying to spot the waitress, and said, "I'm drunk."

"You are?"

Eugene turned toward the river and said, "It's still copper, see?"

Andrew Atwood looked. As he did, Eugene looked at him looking at the river.

He had bushy black pubic sideburns.

"Copper," Andrew said.

Eugene lapped at the air, like a thirsty dog, panting, noting how much like his father, Melvin, that was. "If the waitress would get over here, I wouldn't be tempted to drink the old Hudson," and again he raised his hand in her direction. This time she was caught.

The drinks arrived. Andrew asked the poet about other poets he knew he knew. They ordered another round and another. The sun was low and Eugene said, "Let's talk about the blood in your cock."

Andrew giggled, belched, and giggled louder.

"Tell me about your body," Eugene said, holding a civil tongue, though thick.

"Huh?"

"Are you hung like a horse?"

"Uhhhh . . ."

"With that tail," he said pointing to his head, and then toward Andrew's lap, "and that tail?"

The young man felt he was being ridiculed in some way.

"Do you think wonders who you are?"

Andrew settled back, recognizing the line from one of Goessler's works. "I know that one."

"Come on, boy," Eugene let himself sound like a drunk Melvin hick, drawling out his words, "if yer gonna talk, stop askin me about me and tell me about you. I already know about me. Shoot. Tell me, boy, now tell me. Do you pose yourself and comb the hair around yer cock jest so?"

"I don't get it." Andrew sipped, seeming hurt, as if nothing was genuine.

Eugene stopped his Melvin and the dares he was daring himself to say from his verbatim sacristonium. The psuedo-gaslights came on around the cafe. He stared across to Andrew, his face lined but truly lovely when he let himself show it that way. He shook off the Melvin, saying, "Bah! I'm sorry, young man, but seriously, tell me about your body."

"I don't get it," Andrew wriggled. "What do you want? You want me to tell you how big my cock is?"

Eugene realized there was about a half hour left before the sun would be set. He looked out over the river to New Jersey, as if he had not heard Andrew, then he turned quickly, breaking into a laugh. "There! So that's what I thought you would think I wanted to know. Well sure! Go on. Tell me how big you think your cock is!"

Andrew shrank away from the table, considering getting up and leaving. He had his pride, he thought, dramatically, but not yet undone.

"Forget it, boy," Eugene sighed, not wanting to rape the squirmer. "I apologize to you. I thought you might let me wander over your handsome body. To me, it is verbally and visually exciting."

Andrew said he was sorry. He said he had too much to drink. The sun was directly in his eyes at the level of New Jersey, and he was embarrassed to be overheard in the crowding cafe area.

Eugene reached over and touched the man's sideburns.

"I guess I should leave," Andrew said.

Eugene touched Andrew's pink pout of lips. He withdrew and pushed his chair across the bricks into the chair of the woman at the next table who'd been getting a shocking-to-have-such-talk-in-an-expensive-place-like-this earful. Eugene stood up, a bit dizzy, and raised his drink as if to toast Andrew, and announced loudly, "Hudson River! Hudson River! Andrew Blacktail! In you! The river! Let me know you! Heeeyyy!"

Andrew was embarrassed, but took courage from being with Goessler, who was somebody, and could get away with being loud in the classy place, and although he wasn't sure of anything at that point, he broke through, aided by drink and the power of Goessler's voice, to also stand, raising his glass, no longer caring about making noise, and sang out with Eugene, "Hudson River! Hudson River!"

The woman at the next table pickled her face bitterly and said to her companion, who was rolling his eyes, "Well, I never."

Eugene jumped the railing and Andrew followed. The waitress called for them to stop. Eugene placed a fifty on the marble tabletop. The woman, having told the waitress also that she'd "never," felt protected by the waitress's presence and the railing between her and the loud dirty man, caught Eugene's drunken attention, and said scornfully to him, "Shame on you!"

Eugene firmly grasped the railing and leaned down to look into her milky eyes that were caked with eyeliner and powdered bags. She stared back, determined to prove that her dignity overrode any uncouth drunk. Although she was aware for a second that she swallowed, audibly gulping, a sure sign of fear, and that the crease of her bent knees was damp, she remained staring. Eugene's green eyes cracked into the lines of laughs and he said, "Madam, I can't accept your shame no matter how generous the offer, but I will accept your apology. See that young man?" he whispered in her ear regarding Andrew. "That's Elvis's sideburns! And see beyond him? That's the fucking Hudson River."

Andrew pulled Eugene by his arm, feeling he was no longer just an admirer, but a protective friend. He saw the woman's companion rising to defend her.

"Come on!" he directed the drunken poet away from the cafe. "The Hudson River!" He sang, getting Eugene to join him. He thought that he had surely disappointed the famous author by not answering the body questions right, but then, he felt so drunk and suddenly free that he wasn't sure of anything but the river, the setting sun, and the poet holding on to him making *R* sounds.

Straight-black-haired, ponytailed, Andrew Atwood, with his Elvis sideburns and twenty-three-year-old lithe and artist-starved-thin black-clothed, black-sneakered body, walked on the esplanade at Television Center along the Hudson River feeling lucky. He calculated the opportunities of knowing Goessler. He sensed the power of the man might rub off. He could get to know the inner ticks of the poet he so respected. This was a fortunate break. He wisely knew how young he was, and how reclusive the man was, but he was made confident by his love for Goessler's work. Andrew considered himself a second-generation experimentalist word-painter. He was a production assistant on the *Giggles Laugh Show* that was produced at Television Center only till he could afford not to be. He hoped that soon one of his poem-plays would get produced and acknowledged, and he would be able to stop "whoring in pulp." As he acted as if he were listening to Goessler ramble on about the Hudson River and television production, he was thinking of how he might be able to enlist Goessler's help. He would wait till Goessler asked him about his work. He wouldn't push. For now, Goessler was so drunk he was using him as a walking stick. If he brought up his art now, the man would never remember what he said anyway.

"Are you listening? Ahhhh, you aren't, mi chevalebondiose," Eugene laughed. "You are off in your own mincemeat, eh?"

Eugene stared into Andrew's eyes. What dark lives had they dilated in? This boy was no youth. He may be calculating, Eugene thought, but that is of no importance. The connection, that was what mattered. This Andrew Atwood mattered more than ten *Barbara Wars Mark*'s.

"I was thinking of who you are," Andrew said, unable to lie to the green eyes that told him all that matters is honesty, "I'm sorry. I was thinking of how you could help me. Of when I should tell you about my poem-plays. I'm sorry. I really don't care. I want to just be with you."

"Television on the river!" Eugene announced drunkenly, kissed by Andrew's honesty, choosing to let the splendor of the fading light overrule a cranky meander around motives, "Television on the river! The virus on the vein, ah, my wash wash wash, ah my pregnancy!"

"Pregnancy!" Andrew sang out, letting his ears hear the word, trying to see what Goessler was seeing, letting the word roll out and override his need to file it somewhere.

"Without time, there is no first or last," Eugene laughed. "You are my tulip, Andrew. I am hearing the wheels. You shall see in this life." He held the young man's shoulder for stability, "The prig!"

"The nancy!" Andrew sang, feeling the heat from the poet's hand.

A woman pushing a baby carriage passed them by, the wheels squeaking over the irregular cobblestones that were once three streets in Brooklyn, one of which was the street Eugene had run down with Tex Houston two years before Andrew Atwood was born. A drop of Eugene's blood was under the stone his right foot stood on. They watched the carriage roll by. Eugene thought of his son, Jason. He thought of how nice it would be to be pushed around in a comfortable bed with a big bottle of vodka to suck through a rubber dickhead nipple. Then he felt like a prisoner of the carriage, too reliant on the pusher, just as Joe Bukovsky said he felt he was a prisoner of his limousine, then he saw the young neck near his hand, and the dark fuzz of transitional hair that grew into the straight black shine of Andrew's ponytail, and he remembered his own ponytail and when Scott had cut it off and where he buried it, near the river in Sonoma, and how Katherine had correctly interpreted their barbering as intimately sexual, and he tugged at Andrew's tail, and the young man turned to face Eugene, closely, eye to eye, and Eugene was warmed by the acceptance of his tug that he read in Andrew's face and the gentle give-back of his head, and he asked Andrew if he could cut it off.

"Why?"

"Because the sun has set," Eugene said.

Andrew smiled. It was a daring idea. A passing idea. He focused his eyes on Goessler's lips. They were full, thick, elongated buds that he wanted to bounce on. He pecked a fast buss, letting himself fall further into the new evening's oddness. The buds stretched and blossomed with that peck into a grin that sent rays of creases from the poet's eyes.

Eugene added another reason to cut the ponytail, "And because you must be edited."

Back at Eugene's suite in Hotelevisione, Andrew and Eugene urinated together with their eyes closed, listening to the dueling squirts, trusting their aim from the sound of the splash, choosing not to see each other's hoses in such utilitarian display just yet. Andrew followed Goessler, turning to stand in front of one of the two sinks along the tiled vanity. Each of them washed their hands and looked into the same wall of mirror. The white tiles glowed pink from the four heat lamps in the ceiling. Eugene studied Andrew's reflection and his own reaction to the reflection, and Andrew, still keeping to their rule of mimicry that had started in their ride up the elevator, did the same. Andrew admitted to feeling apprehensive about going to Goessler's room, and Eugene admitted that he felt just as apprehensive, so Eugene suggested that Andrew do "everything I do, and that way, we'll both feel equally comfortable or uncomfortable."

"Now," Eugene said into the mirror to Andrew, "tell me about your body."

Andrew said, self-consciously, "Now, tell me about your body."

Eugene had to own up to his own inquiry, which struck him as perfectly appropriate, there in front of the big reflection. He smiled at Andrew and wondered if Andrew was smiling back because he was copying or genuinely relaxing, whichever, the young man was Adonis and Cochise. Eugene said, "I am growing hair," he rubbed his week-old reddish-blond and graying beard, "I am a farm." He realized that just as in tic-tac-toe, whoever started had the upper hand, and until he could get Andrew to speak anew, he would be mimicked for the entire evening.

Andrew ran his thin hand across his smooth chin and said, "I am growing hair, I am a farm."

"My eyes are bloodshot."

"My eyes are bloodshot."

Eugene unbuttoned his shirt, saying, "I move my fingers and they undo and redo and do over and over."

Andrew was wearing a black tee shirt, and a black jacket, so he let the jacket fall to his feet saying, "I move my fingers and they undo and redo and do over and over without buttons."

Eugene let his shirt fall, and said, "Aha," seeing the break-down of the rule.

Andrew's lips parted, watching Eugene's eyes, then said almost inaudibly, "Aha," as his eyes moved to the man's chest. It was a muscular chest, tan from the sun and toned from splitting wood. The hair on the chest was light.

Eugene touched his own belly as he watched Andrew pull the black tee shirt over his head, seeing first the white skin and thin dark line of hair that rose with the shirt, up the white skin to the shoulders. Eugene said, "Belly up," and Andrew said, "Belly up without sun."

The young man looked away from his own torso to Eugene's and said, with modest apology, out of sequence, "I'm bony."

Eugene 'said, "You are Andrew."

"Bony Andrew," Andrew said releasing his comparative assessment.

Eugene said, "Tender framework."

Andrew said, "You look great for . . ." and stopped.

Eugene said, "For a forty-seven-year-old man full of vodka."

Andrew blushed, "I meant . . ."

Eugene said, "I meant for a forty-seven-year-old Eugene I am perfect."

Andrew recovered, "Yeah, I get it."

Eugene directed, "Look at you. Beautiful black-and-white life."

Andrew hesitated and swallowed and said, "Black-and-white life."

Eugene stepped back from the sinks so he could see lower and then grabbed at his own crotch through his khakis, holding his lips from breaking into a full blown grin, looking slyly to Andrew's reflection, and then said, "Eggs and sausage."

Andrew wanted to say, "I have the Paolo Certiano book with your balls in it," but he grabbed at his own crotch, feeling as if his hand had never been so bold, and his tongue thickened in a warm glue as he repeated, "Eggs and sausage."

Eugene was aroused. Andrew's innocence of his own reflection was the dare, the dagger, and the drive. "This is becoming," he said, undoing the belt Octavio had given him to hold him tight. He undid his button, lowered the zipper, saying, "This is becoming what we want, Andrew White-bone Tulip."

Eugene's khakis dropped to the tile floor. He wore pink cotton boxer shorts. His cockhead peeked when he bent to step out of his shoes and pants. Andrew removed his black sneakers by using each foot to push down the soft leather heels, then he unzipped his black jeans and tugged them down, as they were too tight to fall on their own. He was wearing faded black briefs. Brief briefs that reminded Eugene of ones he wore years before when he dressed as a poser.

"Inside the open tulip, in the shadow of the ivory petals, following the thin veins," Eugene said staring at the young man, "there is the secretion absorbing the light, a velvet. A velvet tulip, Andrew. Now the wind moves you. You touch yourself," he said, touching his own. Andrew did, the white hand moved over the dark brief, but he was watching Eugene, till the older man said, "Watch yourself touching yourself and see me peripherally as I'm seeing you."

"I have a scar," Andrew said, showing a four-inch pink line that ran up the inner side of his right thigh to his covered keystone. He self-consciously showed it, confessing.

Eugene touched the glass where the scar reflected and said, Mmmmmmmmmmm, that is where I will kiss first."

Andrew touched Eugene's hand with his hand. There was a remarkable difference in the two. Eugene's was big and ruddy, the knuckles red, and Andrew's was pale and blue-veined and smooth, with coal black hairs that introduced new masculinity. Their hands entwined and the two men turned from the mirror and faced each other. There was one more skin to shed. Eugene reached over and cupped the young man's crotch. Andrew said, confessing what to him was an original sin, "I'm not that big." His sense of proportion was distorted by his lack of sexual confidence, and had he been a giant, he would not have believed he was big down there. He disregarded the convolutions the poets hand caused, and reached over to Eugene's crotch.

Eugene melted at the feel of the youth's privacy, holding that vulnerability and source of flesh in flesh. Andrew's sin was venial, his cock was mortal. Eugene repeated, "I'm not that big."

Andrew compared, already knowing from the photos he'd seen, and he said, as if there was no question about it, "You are bigger."

"You are bigger," Eugene mimicked.

"Don't be ridiculous," Andrew insisted, "you are bigger."

"You are bigger," Eugene whispered, tugging Andrew by the young man's cock, through the black briefs, toward him, prepared to never say anything else till Andrew admonished his weights and measures and said something other than, "You are bigger."

Andrew kissed Eugene's lips, at first toying with the electric shock of touching those open nerves, those lips that talked and talked and talked. His hands, both of them fondling at the poet's pulsing ricardo, scratched at the door, wanting in, aching to touch the skin itself. He said to Eugene, "You ARE bigger."

And Eugene repeated, like an eraser on a pencil, "You ARE bigger."

Andrew laughed, seeing the gate was closed till he said the right password. He kissed Eugene's lips again and said, "Mmmmm-mmmmmmm, I think I know what to say. You asked me before at the cafe. You said, 'Tell me about your body.' I know I am good-looking. I use that, sure. But it's not like when you were my age, when everyone just went around doing anything. I pose, yeah, and now, on trial I feel so unprepared. What do you expect?" he closed his eyes, feeling Eugene's hand on him. His eyelashes as black and Octavian as the brushes that swept the poet off his feet years before. Andrew opened his eyes, showing a wetness from the sound of the gate being unlocked. "I . . . I am as big as big is for me."

In bed, Eugene kissed and licked the scar that Andrew received when the glove compartment door sliced into his thigh in the automobile accident on the FDR Drive that killed his uncle back in 1990. The young man held Eugene's head as the poet's tongue stoked up feelings along what Andrew had considered the dead red run of scar tissue. He started to cry with fear. At the first heave from the smooth white stomach, Eugene cried too, seeing the close-up truth of the thigh, the taut and tensing muscle, the black hairs of sexual fields, the instinct of licking wounds, and all of it so near Andrew's straining gender, bobbing to lure the poet from the beaten track that for years had been numb.

Andrew's thigh spasmed at certain points, and he went from tears to laughter, saying it tickled. Eugene was relentlessly lost down there, knowing, like a dog digging at a burial spot, that there was a history there to be revealed etched in the cells. Andrew tried to pull Eugene by the hair, laughing, "Enough! I give! Please!" But Eugene dug in, nipping with his teeth, and pushing with his Brazilian-educated fingers, the area around the scar, up and under Andrew's testicles. The young man lifted and fell back repeatedly onto the pillow, losing his strength and will to fight the recognition of that red line on his body, and finally in a last gasp to stop the probe, he swung with all his might at Eugene's head. The poet's teeth snapped down on the scar tissue and Andrew let out a piercing scream, along with a stream of fear and pain and hurt from the accident, as if it was happening there, in bed, in the hotel. He wailed like an innocent baby shocked at its first sense of sorrow. He wailed at death seeing his uncle's head split open through the windshield. He wailed at the sight of his leg and the thought that his cock had been severed. Eugene was an animal lapping away as if it had to remove the sac from the newborn pup. The young man felt the warm smooth tongue. It was wet and soft and not at all threatening anymore.

He felt a peace settling over him, and a grief and feeling of loss seemed to silently be sailing off the map before him.

Andrew pulled himself up from the pillow, growling, and devoured Eugene's hair, completing a circle of energy that traveled between the two men.

Eugene slowly lifted himself from the scar and looked at Andrew with a wide reddened swollen-lipped proud-to-be-a-human-animal grin, and Andrew looked likewise. Eugene panted, "Teeth marks on your scar," and Andrew said, "God, what did you do? Are you a magician? I was . . ." and Eugene covered the young man's lips with his own and howled in his mouth before Andrew tried to put anything into words.

Andrew studied the lines in Eugene's face as the man slept that night. Eugene had forgotten his promised appearance at The Museum of Suburban Art. In the left eyebrow, Andrew found a small scar that cut through the blond/red hairs, and at the poet's jawline, on his unshaven neck, there was a reddish scar, from a burn, it seemed. Andrew traced over these things, and kissed them as if they were the sweetest things.

Eugene slept in his bed next to Andrew. He was dreaming of red and blue triangles hanging dangerously close to naked bodies, the triangles beginning to sway, like pendulums, lowering, getting threateningly closer and closer. The pulsing tones from the telephone pulled him out, just in time.

"Yeah?" Eugene answered, pressing. Andrew was a pale-faced Indian at his side, framed in the white sheets. Eugene wondered if he had asked for a wake-up ring somewhere during the intoxicated night.

"Goessler!" Joe Bukovsky's voice sang out, wide awake. "Goessler! Come out and smell the coffee!"

Eugene had not spoken to Joe in months. There was a damper on their friendship, ever since Eugene had sold Joe's sculptures to buy the house in Massachusetts in 1992. They were still friends, but the footing was not as comfortable as it had once been, as there was always betrayal undertowing them.

"Joe?" Eugene said, sleep-dry. "Joe, I was going to get in touch."

"Sure you were, Goessler, sure you were. Lola told me you were in town. The PTA Show? Ring a bell for you?"

Eugene remembered that he was supposed to have gone to the

opening. "The PTA Show" was a collection of "Kansas Propaganda" that Lola had organized for display in the rec room of The Museum of Suburban Art. The opening had slipped through his fingers as he was manhandling Andrew Atwood's thigh scar. "Oh, yeah," he said, "yeah, I completely forgot, kaput." He smiled, and petted Andrew's head of straight black hair. "Was Lola pissed? Was everybody uppity there?"

"Nah, nah, she was on. The scene was the scene, you know, the out-do-you, but the Kansas stuff was exciting. You got to check it out."

Eugene yawned.

"Lola said you're doing a telepiece."

"*Barbara Wars Mark.*"

Joe chuckled wickedly, "You're too much, man. You sell out right and left."

Eugene tugged at Andrew's hair, ignoring Joe's dig. His silence was enough response.

"Don't get me wrong, Goessler, we do what we can to get by, right? I'm not talking about my pieces, that's water under the bridge, I don't want to start all that again."

Andrew's dark sleepy eyes opened. Eugene put his finger to his lips, signaling for him to remain silent.

Joe's voice continued in the room, "We do what we do, and value what we value, man. Hey? Goessler? I can hear your thoughts, man. Say something. You're saying, 'Go fuck yourself,' right?"

Andrew slid his arm over Eugene's chest.

Eugene said, "Not exactly, but you catch my drift."

"Hey! Goessler! Lighten up!"

Eugene felt Andrew's hand running down, and he relaxed back into the pillows, and said, "Joe? Can I call you later?"

Joe laughed, relieved to hear Eugene's voice unfettered, and then suspected he was not alone in bed. Everything fell into place. "Hey, I see how it is. Double sheath it, man. I'll be at my studio till four. You have the number. Hey, Goessler? You're too much." He disconnected.

Eugene cut three inches off Andrew's black ponytail before he said good-bye to him, giving him his private number in Massachusetts. Andrew had to get to work. Eugene called Joe's studio, but the line was busy, and there was no pickup on the interrupt.

An hour later, Lola called, her voice shaking, and she said that Joe had been shot by a Bushwacker freak. It was well publicized that Joe had refused the state's commission to do the memorial sculpture of the martyred rock group, because he was "not into exaggerating flukes of show business." The killer took Joe's remarks to heart, and coerced his way past the desk, and found his way to Joe's studio, and shot him point-blank, screaming, "The Bushwackers Live Forever, Fluke!" "It's all on the telephone-tape," Lola explained, choking up, "it recorded the whole thing. Zak is with Diane."

Eugene picked up the clump of Andrew's hair. Lola said she was coming up to the hotel to be with him, and disconnected. Eugene's tears fell onto the hair. He thought how if he had not put Joe off, or if he had gone to the PTA Show, they would have had plans for the day, and if he had not met Andrew, if he had not been out in that cafe, if he had not argued with the director . . . The tears fell at the futile ifs, knowing the resignation of deaths and the familiar feeling of being left behind.

When Lola arrived at the hotel room, she found Eugene writing furiously, in wide longhand strokes, in one of his large notebooks. He'd filled one, before she'd arrived, and it would become his famous prose-poem *Edge of Tulips*, which he dedicated to Joe Bukovsky.

1999, Brazil

Eugene was visiting Brazil till the new century, staying at Octavio's uncle's house in the northern jungle. On the night Clara Goessler died on the vinyl couch in the great room of Frank and Stephanie's new house in Oak Haven, Eugene was with Octavio, Maria Gustavo Breton, and others, all wearing white, and dancing in a circle, an Umbanda circle, chanting and singing and praising the powers of the trees. Eugene closed his eyes and saw his mother's face. It was a strong image, and he could not shake it. He broke the circle. Octavio looked at him, but Eugene motioned him to stay with the dance.

Eugene closed his eyes and walked toward the sound of lapping water. It was a river leading into the Amazon. He saw his mother, almost looking at him, and he trusted the image, trusted the sense of the trees to not be in his way, as he trusted the jungle and walked, following the sound of water. Fear and doubt, "What are you doing? Are you crazy?" dissipated in a white light and there was no such thing as "crazy" and there was no such thing as "harm," and his bare feet felt the cool moss of the riverbank. His mother was looking at him, open-eyed. He was a baby, and she was changing him, wiping his ass, and patting it with powder. With his eyes remaining closed, he squatted down, feeling the overwhelming power of this vein of river, and an overwhelming love of the earth and the people of the earth and of all people, his mother, Clara. He opened his eyes, crying with love, and said her name, "Clara Ethel Hackett Goessler," and he heard either himself or the smooth tributary say, "Clah-rah, meet your maker."

Eugene was full of love and the life love fed. He thanked Clara

324

for doing "the best you could." What had made her hold on for so long? She had been sick for five years. What had made her be? He cried in her arms as he felt her surround him with acceptance and love, and she said, "Honey, you were too late for my good side."

At midnight, when they were all back at Octavio's uncle's house, Eugene called Frank.

"You must've been reading my mind, Eugene, shoot," Frank yelled into the phone. "Me and Deb, both was trying to get you up there in Massachusetts. She died in her sleep, right in front of the TV."

"What was on?" Eugene asked.

"Say what?"

"What was on the TV when mother died?"

"Oh, shoot, I don't know . . . hold on . . . hey, Stephie! . . . Eugene here wants to know what was playing on the TV when Mother passed on! . . . Please? I can't hear you! Well, shoot, I'm on long distance to South America! . . . I don't know, Eugene . . . oh, she says the last show Mother watched was *Dancinggirls Express*."

Frank told him that she was going to be cremated. Eugene said that he thought cremation was against church law. Frank said, "Oh, shoot, they changed that, what with space being too valuable, you know." He said that he and Debbie had decided to each take some of the ashes. "I didn't think you'd want any, but Deb said she thought you would."

"Yes, I do. Send them to me in Massachusetts. I'll be there after the holidays."

"Shoot, Eugene, you know it's a shame . . . she was sick, Mother, but you know the last thing she said to me, yesterday, was, 'I wanted to see the new century, and I don't think I'll get my wish,' and it was like she knew. Up till then, anytime you'd ask her how she was doin, she'd say, 'a little better,' even when she looked drawn and sunken in . . . shoot, I still can't get over your calling like this."

Eugene and Octavio spent the entire last day of the twentieth century hiking through the jungle. Toward nightfall, they found in a clearing an altar from an Umbanda gira, an Afro-Brazilian spiritualist ritual. The site was deserted, although Octavio warned Eugene that they "may have visitors on such a special night."

They lay together on a blanket, and Octavio said, "What I find odd in you, sweetie, is you are so of words and yet you do not learn the Portuguese. You have been here eight trips now and know little."

Eugene watched the light from the candle they had lit on the stones light the undersides of the leaves. He was quiet, listening to the overwhelming noises in the jungle, all of them mysterious and frightening, and yet humbling. He had been thinking, "Man is arrogant to think of conquering this, he is arrogant to think he knows it."

"Eugene? Can you not speak English?" Octavio squeezed his neck for an answer.

"I don't want to know Portuguese. Here. Here I can listen with new ears, like a baby. If I knew the words being said, I'd be thinking of what they might mean, rather than hearing them as the garble they are. When I am here in Brazil, I am free of that, like what I told you about all the words of religions-un-religions."

"And now tell me again, while I rub your back," Octavio's dark voice soothed.

"Once a single word is put to religion, it is not religion anymore. Religion is not the domain of words. That is exactly what it is not. Even the Christ ones, oh so trapped in the words, should only hear clear and new, 'The word was made FLESH.' "

Octavio purred, "I will make your flesh, Eugene, always wondering."

"Mmm-hmm," Eugene exhaled full and slow, giving in to Octavio's strength, "I love the music of your language, sweetie, and I hear so much in the jibber-jabber of it. I don't want to speak its vocabulary. To me, then, it would lose its meaning."

"Shhhhhhhhhhh," Octavio said.

When the twenty-first century began, they were kissing.

2004, Massachusetts

Eugene's house was nestled in a valley near a river within the shadow of the Berkshires, surrounded by trees younger than it, getting a dusting of white early winter. It had a Ye Olde Christmas card look to it as the snow fell, the kitchen chimney vented smoke, and the door was hung with a pine and ivy wreath he'd made. It was a strong house, built of hand-hewn timber and mortared stone in the nineteenth century, haunted with history, according to the locals. Eugene and Octavio had found it in 1992 on a trip up to where they had first met. Widow Turner's Bed and Breakfast was closed. She had been put in a rest home by her son they were told by the owner of the motel they stayed in off Route 8. The owner of the motel also told them that he had property for sale, with "a solid workable house" on it. He said it was "way the hell out" bordering on Mohawk State Park. As the motel owner bent Octavio's ear with stories of the families that had lived there, Eugene went behind the house and pissed on the foundation, making it his. When he returned to New York, he raised the money for the down payment by selling five of his six Bukovsky sculptures. Joe resented that. Joe resented Eugene moving out of New York. He resented Octavio, whom he called Rio Rita to everyone but Eugene. He felt that the Stella Gold Gallery should have been offered the sculptures first, since it was where he showed exclusively in the United States. "I don't buy Rio Rita's touchy touchy sincerity," Joe told Lola, knowing she would tell Eugene. "He's upper-class down there. He can afford to be embracing. What does his family pay their workers? A pound of coffee? And if he wanted Eugene to move up there and buy that place, he should have given him the goddamned down payment."

It was December twenty-third and Lola and Eugene sat at the kitchen table drinking coffee. She had arrived the night before, with news that they might have his son, Jason, joining them for their quiet holiday. Jason had spoken to Lola in New York. Eugene asked her to repeat what she had told him about Jason's call.

"I offered to drive him up. He said he might have to help Stella hang a show. He said not to tell you, in case he couldn't make it. And he said, 'I think I'd like to see Pop.' Those were his exact words, 'I think I'd like to see Pop.' "

"What's Stella doing in New York? And what's she hanging a show for now?" Eugene asked, pouring milk into his coffee.

"I don't know," Lola said. "Jason did say that she was supposed to give him some money." Her blue eyes were puffed from sleep.

Eugene sat his spoon down, "Now see, Lola! You keep remembering more and more things Jason said. If he's getting money from her, we can count him out to come up here."

Both Eugene and Lola were now in their fifties. They sat at the old thick pine table near the hot cookstove in the kitchen. Snow was sticking, then melting, at the windows. Lola was wrapped in a polka-dotted flannel robe, but Eugene was naked. He had come down earlier wrapped in a blanket, but as the room heated from the fire, he'd let the blanket drop onto the chair. He and Lola had nothing to hide from each other. Lola's head was "Bozoed," curled bright orange, and Eugene could tell which side she had slept on from the flatness.

"I shouldn't have mentioned it at all," Lola said. "You should see yourself, Goessler. Anytime Jason is mentioned, you change. You get anxious and short-tempered."

Eugene had been moving into the fifth-floor loft in Stella's building when she confronted him with the news that she was pregnant. He was overjoyed at the thought of being a father, and she assured him he was the father, but they both agreed that marriage was out of the picture. They would be friends and share the work of parenting, as Stella called it.

Then in the hospital, after having Jason, Stella cried to Joe and his wife, Diane, that she felt like a tramp and that she was thinking, "Maybe Eugene and I should get married. Make an honest woman out of me. He loves the baby, and we tolerate each other." Joe blurted out that Eugene's affair with her was all his idea, a way for her to get into Goessler's pants, and a way for Goessler to get a decent place to live. She flew to L.A. with Jason and within two months had met and married the film producer Sidney Harris.

"You're gay!" she screamed into the phone to Eugene in New York. "God only knows if you've given me and Jason AIDS! Just forget he exists, Eugene. You owe me that much. My son. Your loft. Fair deal."

Eugene assured her he was healthy, and at one point even conceded that he would marry her, not knowing she was already seeing Sidney out there. He was in love with the baby Jason and was begging for her to understand his side. "It was innocent! I never planned it out to steal from you, it was Joe's idea, but we had fun, Stella, you know that's true! Yes, I wanted a loft, but I'm paying you for it, it's not as if it was free for the fucks!"

"But I gave you such a deal!" she screamed. "And a ten-year lease, you asshole!"

Eugene had no idea how much joy he would feel holding the baby. He held Jason tight, up to his chin, pacing the room, as Stella held court with all of her notable friends from her hospital bed. Eugene's hand fit over Jason's entire head. At one point he sang a song he had written with Scott, and promised to always sing to his son. The second day of holding Jason, he felt fear rise up his spine, and, worried beyond sense that Jason was suffocating, he ran with the baby out into the hospital corridor. Stella announced to her friends, almost lovingly, that someone should go after him. "The cheese has slipped off Goessler's cracker again." The third day Eugene went to the hospital, he was told Stella and baby had checked out. Only after frantically calling Joe did Eugene hear of her change of heart. Joe assured Eugene that "she just needs time, and she'll be back."

Eugene flew to Los Angeles, demanding to see his son. Stella assured him that she would be back and they would share the child. He left, not quite trusting her, but without a doubt that he would always see his son, and then she called to warn him to stay away. After the wedding, Sidney offered Eugene $25,000 cash to sign the adoption papers. Eugene hung up on the smooth talker.

"All told, Lola, I was figuring last night after we put up the tree, as I was writing this stuff about Ohio and Clara, I counted up all the times I've seen Jason, and if you put it together, it would be a month. Thirty days."

"I thought I heard you up," she said, teasing her hair out between her fingers.

"Did he say anything about what he's doing? Is he living in New York?"

Lola shook her hair, saying no to more coffee, and no to Eugene's questions. "I told you. It was quick. Don't get your hopes up. You might be stuck here with just little old me."

Eugene sighed, "Well," wondering if his sigh sounded like a father's concern for his son, "what can you do? I imagine, from what you've told me, he'll stay down in the city for the money. Stella raised him to love money. The little bastard is twenty-two and still under her thumb. I left home when I was eighteen."

"You weren't rich," Lola said, offhandedly, rubbing her face with the palms of her hands, massaging. "I think it may be time to consider the big baby boomer question, 'Time for a facelift?' "

Eugene raised a skeptical eyebrow, "You wouldn't do it."

"Easy for you to say, Goessler," she tugged at her cheeks. "I have all these crows' feet. On you they're called 'distinguished' or 'full of character,' but on us boomer girls, it's called 'withered.' "

"You're just suffering from your holiday horniness," Eugene said. "Why not try that new face tightener?"

Lola stretched her skin back, "No, no, no, it's been proven to have horrible side effects. I read in *Century* that one woman's skin dried to the point that she had to have skin grafts from her thigh." She sighed, letting her face drop. "Maybe if Jason comes I'll have him. I've always wanted a Goessler."

"You once said that you'd even consider a Sicilian on a lonely holiday," Eugene reminded her.

"I'm not alone! I have you, Eugene. I guess it's this quiet country setting. I don't know."

"Maybe you should have a face-loosening," Eugene suggested. "That would be truer to your perverse nature."

Lola Hampton defined herself as a Behavioral Restructuralist Artist. Her first noted work, before her *Mother Earth* tone poem, was *Walking Mother May I Over Her Dead Body*. She did a series of *Mother* pieces, after her own mother died in Pennsylvania. She had gone to the funeral and photographed her dead mother in her coffin, made ten life-size prints of "the coffin with Mom," and then she and nine other women, all dressed alike, performed giant steps, umbrella steps, dance steps, and improvised steps across the flat images that were placed end to end and picked up and moved around the entire rim of Manhattan. "The media coverage was great," Lola had remarked, determined to make a name for herself. She was quoted in the *Voice* as saying, "It's my way of saying, 'Bye Mom!' and 'So there, Mom!'" She believed in breaking whatever behavior pattern seemed expected. "It all started when they changed the time," she once said. "I freaked! What? Oh, just move it up an hour, or back, and everyone followed. It blew me away! And then I heard that people drove on the opposite side of the road in England! I realized I loved anti-manners." Lola and her troupe of players would dress in business suits and carry attaché cases, but walk sideways down Wall Street at rush hour. She made her own driving rules, never stopping at red lights after midnight. "I believe in my eyesight and my will to live," she explained in her media-covered appearance in court. She owed over two thousand dollars in tickets. "I will not let a light dictate my life, your honor. If I see there's nobody coming, I step on it." She called herself a Vehicular Terrorist and Freedom Fighter.

Lola pressed all of her facial skin toward her nose and through puckered lips, said to Eugene, "I'm not a comedy act, Goessler. Face-loosening!"

"All the boomers are sagging," Eugene said, slapping his chest to show the loose skin despite his muscle. He stood and plopped his balls and cock onto the table and said, "Breakfast is served. Two eggs well done and one overcooked sausage."

Lola picked up the crusted knife they'd used to cut the fruitcake the night before, and said, "I prefer eggs bene-dick."

Eugene removed himself from the menu, and bowed, "Agnus dei, bene-dick-shun."

Lola studied the crusty knife and picked it clean, sighing, "Really, seriously, Goessler, at this point in my life, I feel this overwhelming urge to clean. I want everything to be spotless, including my face. I want to throw out everything I've saved because 'someday I may need it.' I want to sand the flowers off the teacups and dye all prints solid."

Eugene extended his arms to display the mess of kitchen and said, "Here you go. If you want to clean, your prayers are answered."

"I'm serious! Seriously talking, that's all!"

The phone rang. It was Zero, Lola's houseboy in New York, calling to give her her messages. He had been instructed to call her every day around noon if she was out of the city. He was her gal Friday or her very bruised second banana. He had been with her for ten years, devoted and loyal, although completely spaced out. When he wasn't doing something he'd been told to do, he sat peacefully on the floor of his room and listened and watched old Bushwackers' discs. The Bushwackers were the biggest rock band of the nineties. They had only recorded three albums. A terrorist group in Germany set bombs off under the stage where they were performing outside of Frankfurt, killing forty-seven people, including every Bushwacker and roadie. A billion viewers saw the bombing, as it was televised worldwide. Zero was one of them. He suffered from TRSS, Tele-Reality Shock Syndrome.

"Zero," Lola asked, "would you look over by the service door and see if I left the color wheel there?"

The night before, after Lola arrived, she'd insisted Eugene open one gift. It was an authentic antique, in its original box, aluminum Christmas tree and stand, but she had forgotten the color wheel that turned at its base, illuminating it. "Shit! I'm so fucking forgetful lately!"

They decided that if they were careful, they could illuminate the tree with strands of traditional lights that Eugene had set out for, what he had expected, a traditional Christmas tree.

"You know," Eugene said, "these were illegal because of the shocks people got when they tried to do what we are doing. Be careful, Lola."

Lola insisted on inserting the branches into the pole according to whim and chance, not size. The branches each had curlicue aluminum slivers that made them look like silver poodle tails or metal feather dusters. The shortest lengths went to the bottom, the longest were inserted near the top. Some had to be moved in order to balance it. It was so wrong that they laughed hysterically, especially Eugene, remembering his early Christmases. Lola was busier, designing the look.

"Some Mother Nature you've turned out to be, Lola Hampton!" Eugene cried.

Lola heeded Eugene's warnings and was careful not to touch the tree once it was plugged in. Eugene suspected the hum he heard was coming from the wild electric aura surrounding the thing. He was not happy with the added tension of possible electrocution for the holidays, though the tree was delightfully bizarre. He wanted to turn it off. Lola insisted they have eggnog and fruitcake first, and toast the beginning of their holiday. "To tradition!" they sang, clinking glasses.

Then Eugene pulled the plug and kissed Lola goodnight. He climbed the stairs to his study where he began to write the *Clara Poems*.

Lola sighed and disconnected from Zero. Eugene stood up and stretched. It was already two in the afternoon.

"I'm going up to do some work," he said to Lola. "You know your face is getting very red from your kneading. Why don't you make cookies or something?"

She held her arms away from herself, but her hands flapped like fins, "I can't help it, Goessler, they've got minds of their own!"

Eugene left the room, draping a blanket around himself, as the rest of the house would be freezing compared to the toasty warmth from the cookstove in the kitchen. There were two large rooms on the second floor of his house. One was his bedroom, the other was his office, which was set up with three desks, a computer, a word processor, a laser printer, and an audiovisual monitor to his publisher in New York. The walls were lined in bookshelves that were stacked without order. He read anything that dropped. He believed books had wills of their own. His *Clara Poems* were on his leather couch where he'd left them the night before, having read the printout before going to sleep. He would work on them in the evening, he decided, and sat down at his correspondence desk. He heard the axe falling below. Lola was splitting wood to build a fire in the parlor. It was a pleasure having her there.

He was staring out the window at the barren hills, not answering an inquiry from the Bukovsky Foundation, when he heard a car crackle up the icy gravel drive.

"Jason!" he said to himself. He stood, and then sat back down. Maybe it wasn't his son. He only heard a car. From his window, he only saw the Berkshires and the threatening skies above them. If it was Jason, he thought, then the holiday had started.

Eugene's love for the young man was unconditional, but the young man's love for him was tentative. He disapproved of his father's works and lifestyle and philosophy. Stella had a hand in keeping Jason away, but that was years ago, and Jason was twenty-two and had made no great effort to know his father. Eugene stood again, and crossed the hall to his bedroom. He looked out the bedroom window to see if it was Jason. It was. The young man could be seen through the windshield, sitting there, tapping his hands on the steering wheel and singing something. "My son," Eugene said, "my son." He decided that it was too late to be competing for the boy. He would not say "my son" ever again. Jason was his own man. He warned himself to steer clear of expectations. He pulled on his old overalls and pulled his mess of graying hair back to a tail and snapped a rubber band around it. He heard the front door, and looked out the window. Lola was waving and walking from the woodpile to the car. She opened the car door and got in, kissing Jason twice and saying something that made him laugh and pound the dashboard with his hand. Eugene smiled. He was delighted by Jason's smile. That was what being a father was, he thought, it was the contagiousness of emotions. He hunted for his shoes, looking under the piles of coats and clothes and papers, always coming back to the window to see Jason and Lola sitting there. She seemed to have cheered up from her earlier heat.

"He really is looking forward to you being here," she said over the music in the car. Jason nodded. His hair was dark brown, almost black like Stella's, and he had her ice-blue eyes, but he looked like Eugene. Lola was always taken by that, how incredible the likeness was, but with all the colors changed. Jason did not sound like Eugene. He had a definite West Coast lack-of-accent accent, with the rounded O sounds, and his lips mouthed the words, "Bar-bar-eeeeeee-uns." And then he said, "Mother hates me to see him, she thinks he'll screw me up. She yelled,

'You're a Jew! How can you go to Massachusetts?' and I told her to fiddle a T-bomb, you know, cause I do what I want now that I have to work, but I'm glad you're here, Lola. I feel like you're my stepmom."

Lola's falling face fell further, "Oh please, think of me as an easy lay or your daddy's concubine or a horny bitch, Jason, I'm nobody's mother."

Jason turned the music down, "I didn't mean it like that, you know, like you know, you are hemline, Lola."

She pulled at her face, "I think I'll fuck it and have a facelift."

Eugene appeared opening the front door. He waved and picked up a few split logs and went back inside.

"Pop," Jason said, turning the music louder. Eugene had told him years ago to call him Pop, since Jason was accustomed to Stella's husband being "Dad" and "Father." But the way he said "Pop" was almost sarcastic. Eugene opened the door again and this time came down from the porch and crossed the ice and gravel, wearing flopping thongs and denim coveralls with no coat or shirt, as if it were summer.

"Jesus, look at him," Jason sighed, "he looks like a hillbilly, doesn't he?"

"What?" Lola asked, over the music, and thinking she saw admiration in Jason's eyes, she said, "Yeah, he looks great for fifty-six, look at his arms."

Eugene slapped the hood of the Quest, and approached Jason's window. Jason sighed, and pushed the button to lower it, "Ho, ho, ho, Pop," he said, putting out his hand for a shake, "I hope your hands are clean."

"Ho, ho, ho to you too," Eugene smiled, holding Jason's hand tenderly with both of his, telling himself "No my's, he is not mine."

Jason pulled his hand back into the car, bothered by the power and tenderness of Eugene's touch. He hated that. He hated what that gentleness meant. He interpreted that as a homosexual trait. "I'll be in when the sixth disc pops," Jason explained. "I timed the sounds for the road, but I overestimated the traffic. I got here in under four hours, and I was only monitored twice. So what, a hundred cues."

"Great," Eugene said, pocketing both hands and feeling the

snow on his feet. "It's warm inside, so I'm going back in. Make yourself at home."

Lola leaned over to see Eugene. She asked if he wanted her to get out so he could get in. Eugene shook his head "No," and said he would be inside and walked back to the house. He looked a little lost to her.

Jason pushed the button so that the window rose. He took a tissue from the console and wiped the few drops of ice that had rolled onto the leather window lip. "Looks like Pop hasn't shaved in a while."

Lola studied the young man's face. Finally she reached over to lower the sound and said, "Look, I'll just say this, and you tell me to blanket or whatever, Jason, but how do you feel? You just acted like Eugene was a stranger. You must want to see him, or you wouldn't have come up. That was mean, really, the way you greeted him."

"Pop asks for it. Once in L.A., when I was little, he showed up at the house with a backpack, you know? Uninvited. He was hitching to Berkeley, even though he could afford to fly. He looked like a bum, and my friends saw him. Look how he looks!"

"What? The way he looks?" Lola laughed, because for one, she thought Eugene looked great, and she also thought Jason sounded exactly like Stella, "You owe me, everyone owes me."

Jason started telling her about the Barbareeuns, and how he might try to see their concert in Worcester on the twenty-sixth.

She interrupted him with a pat on the thigh, "Jason, Jason, I really don't care where their tour will take them. Let's go inside."

Jason wore a chamois tie, a navy blue leather suit, and green suede boots. He took his luggage from the trunk, and at the porch remembered he'd left his can of leather protectant under the seat, and ran back for it. Lola hurried to the porch and opened the door to the house. She shivered. Eugene was there waiting. He smiled, somehow hurting, she thought, although his face broadened and he kissed her, as if to say everything was fine, and they both heard Jason curse, slipping on the ice, yelling that he'd ruined the side of his boot. He ran up on the porch and in, showing them the can and telling them how it was the best stuff around for suede and leather.

"Nice luggage," Eugene said, as Jason proudly showed him the digital lock and clamps. "Bet it cost a pretty penny," he said, making his voice drawl like Melvin's voice.

"State of the art," Jason said, stopping all of his moves at the sight of the bizarre aluminum tree. "Wha?"

Lola proudly stood next to her creation, the deliberate mis-shapen choices of which branch where. She turned the lights on for Jason to see, with Eugene's warning, "Be careful of shocks." Not only was the tree lopsided, but lopbottomed, because of her perverse insistence on inserting the tarnished long branches in the upper holes, and the smallest in the lower holes. Jason laughed apprehensively, put off by one more weird distortion in his Pop's reality.

"You two are endangered," Jason said. "What's it supposed to be?"

"History!" Lola announced, gesturing with her arms as if she was a professional game-channel hostess displaying the big prize to shoot for. "This, Jason, is a genuine antique. Not that Eugene and I didn't alter it, but this was, for one brief shining moment, modern American yule."

"The existential essential Ex-mass," Eugene said, letting himself relax about the possible electrocution from the old lights on the metal. "Just keep in mind, Jason, it is volatile and we may all fry. They were banned way back before you were born."

"I know," he said, feeling like Eugene was always explaining and pushing information at him as if he was ignorant, "I've seen pictures, somewhere, of'm, you know, not so fucked, but yeah, aluminum, you know."

Lola told Jason that she liked his blue leather. Eugene stoked the fire in the stone fireplace that separated the parlor from the dining room. Both rooms had thick hewn beans and were dark-ened from years of soot and smoke and dirt.

"Where should I put my stuff?" Jason asked.

Lola looked at Eugene. She had jokingly but not so jokingly asked him earlier in the day to have Jason in her room. Eugene smiled surreptitiously at her, and then at Jason. Jason did not like feeling like they were doing boners on him. He somehow felt he was missing the point, and he'd only asked a simple question.

"You can have my room," Eugene said, and I'll sleep in my

study, or you can have the other bed in the guest room. Of course, that would mean you'd have Lola to deal with."

Jason laughed. Was he being dared to share a room with her, as if he couldn't take care of himself? There was no choice, he knew Eugene's room would be uncomfortable and wrecked. This was not his first visit to the Massachusetts house. Lola posed in her robe, faux-seduisant, daring. Jason carried his bags across the room toward the guest room. He laughed to himself at what fools they seemed, always so odd.

"Oh Santa Holy Santa!" Lola squealed. "I'm going to spend the holiday with a genuine cock!"

Jason was always shocked at how foul-mouthed Pop and Pop's so-called friends were. He was tempted to say something to Lola, like, "Hey, if you're trying to get to me, or shock me, or make me feel like a backliner, you can crow, it isn't going to work," but he didn't because any reaction he'd have would certainly be ridiculed. He thought for a second that he would really fuck Lola to show her that he was no kid and no one to blast.

Eugene came to the guest room door and opened it for his son. "Here, Jason, let me get that for you. She's just being 'Lola,' you know that don't you?"

"Sure," Jason said.

Lola sang from across the parlor room, "What the hell does that mean, I'm just being 'Lola'?"

Jason set his bags on the double futon, the straightened one, not the one twisted from use, and told Eugene that he wanted to try to save his suede boot by quickly setting to work on it with his protectant. "They were handmade," he said.

Eugene felt he was doting, so he left the room and went back to the parlor crossing to Lola, eyebrow raised, kissing her cheek, thankful for her presence, for her friendship, and for her shock.

She held his bare arm, "Oh, Goessler, I love you. Seeing Jason and seeing you with him makes me feel so warm."

"The fire helps," Eugene said, blocking that love. "It's always so awkward."

Lola read him, recognized his unsettled role, and squeezed his bicep, "Yeah, the fire helps, thanks for stoking it."

"I'm sorry," Eugene said.

Lola smiled, tugging at his overall straps, "You know, I love the way you look in these baggie things, the way the skin and

your hair gradually disappear, but obviously go on, the line and
the curve of your back." She ran her hand down his spine across
the crossed straps to the loose waist, "Down to where the naked,
you know, goes on so available."

Eugene finally let himself feel her touch, as she brought him
to his senses, out of the fog of Jason's arrival and the weight of
that unsettled relationship. He took a deep breath, and another,
slowly releasing a very sad feeling, an almost tired feeling, from
way back, of self-consciousness, wanting to please, wanting to
explain the unacceptable. The reality was, he sighed, that he
loved Jason, no matter how estranged they were. His back tin-
gled from Lola's finger skating designs on him. Jason was under
roof, he breathed, and Clara was in his word processor, and Lola
was under his skin, healing long-gone events with her hands.

Jason rubbed the scrape on his green suede boot with the
leather solution. It easily came clean. Lola's words repeated,
"You must want to see him or you wouldn't have come up."
Why did he fight the facts? Eugene was his real father. And it
wasn't as if he was a bum, although he dressed like one, he was
careless, Jason thought, he was selfish, as Stella showed time
and again, but Pop wasn't a nobody. He had books published
and awards and a couple of Jason's teachers at UCLA had re-
ferred to Eugene Goessler. He decided that, for what it was
worth, he wanted to make an effort to enjoy his visit, and try to
see what others saw in Pop. And then a cry from Jason's childhood surfaced and he heard in his head, "If only he wasn't queer.
If only Pop wasn't queer. I hate those tests!" Was that it? Was
that why he resented Eugene? Eugene was no more hemlined
than Lola, so maybe it was because of all the AIDS tests he was
forced to have as a baby and, at Stella's insistence, yearly till he
was seven. Maybe it was the real fear and thought that his Pop
might have been infected and infected him. He didn't hate gays.
He loved the old Bushwackers and in most of the biographies of
the ill-fated band, it was a matter of fact that the lead guitarist
was gay. And a lot of his mother's and stepfather's friends were
gay. It wasn't just that. Maybe it was the threat of the deadly
disease, and his mother's fear that as a boy he had to absorb. He
closed the leather-and-suede cleaner can tight and unclasped his
large suitcase, removing two wrapped boxes. He brought them
out into the parlor.

"Where should I put these presents?" he asked, seeing Lola rubbing Pop's back over by the fireplace.

"Oh!" Lola sang. "Under the tree of course!"

Eugene looked across the room to Jason. How handsome and tall he was, how young, especially his smile. Eugene let himself take the smile in, and tears swelled in his green eyes, seeing a fact of life, a stray seed grown.

Stella had so often pointed out to her son, "Goessler wanted to get a good deal on a loft, Jason, he was hung up on his own sexuality and thought by having an affair with me, he'd prove he was a real man, you don't owe him anything. How often does he ever send you a gift?" Jason had hesitated about getting Pop a Christmas gift, but it felt wonderful carrying the packages across the room, seeing the broad grin on Pop's face. He seemed like a strong mountain man, standing in his overalls there, against the stone fireplace, with a woman at his side.

Lola said, "I should put a little something around the base of the tree before we put the presents there. She pulled a sheepskin pelt off the back of one of the chairs that faced the hearth, and said, "There, the little lamb, the baby Jesus, in a remote way," and she examined each box. The one said, "To Pop from Jason," and was square and light, and the other read, "To Lola, luh, luh, luh, Lola, luv, Jason." She shook it. It was heavier and more of a rectangle.

Eugene said, "Be careful you don't touch the tree, Lola, you're too close."

Lola looked to Jason, "He's really hung up on electrocution."

Jason saw snow falling out the window. "It's snowing, look!" His Quest and Lola's car were both covered in a brush of white dust, "Hey, Pop? Is there room for my car in your garage? Snow'll eat away on the finish."

Eugene thought of old television series from his childhood and the sons asking the fathers for the keys to their cars. Jason likes cars, he told himself. "Here," he said, taking the keys from the mantel, "go on out and move the old pickup out, and you can pull yours in, and watch out for the old garage door, it's not electric."

Lola stood at the window, "Watch out, it's electric, watch out it's not electric, watch out, it's almost electric."

Jason went to his luggage for his all-rubber shoes.

Eugene said, "Well, he's used to everything being automatic. This is primitive."

Lola started singing "White Christmas."

Jason came out wearing brownish-swirl-colored rubber boots, "You like these?"

"Oh God," Lola stooped to touch them, "they're great. They look like marble or the inside of a jawbreaker! And they're all rubber! Where'd you ever find these, Jason?"

"Palm Springs," he said, "this all-rubber place you'd crave, out by my mom and dad's place ..." He realized that his real dad was Eugene. "You know," he laughed.

Eugene thought, "He loves cars and clothes, and he is not 'mine.' "

Jason went outside.

Lola looked out the window, and Eugene thought how the three of them briefly seemed like a family. He stood next to her watching the snow fall, watching Jason make footprints across the drive and out of sight. Lola said things seemed to be lightening up and that the snow seemed perfect. Eugene nodded. Lola said she loved weather. Eugene nodded.

"Pop! Hey, Pop!" they heard, and then saw Jason tramping back around the house.

Eugene went to the door, "What's wrong?"

Jason had snowflakes glistening on his eyebrows and dark hair. "I can't get it going. Must be some trick, right?"

"Let's see," Eugene said, going out with him.

Lola grabbed the other sheepskin from another chair and tossed it to Eugene, "Goessler! Wrap this around you, you'll freeze!"

Now Jason looked at Pop, in thongs and overalls and a sheepskin around his shoulders, walking alongside him to the garage. He was no longer a hillbilly, he thought, "Pop is a Neanderthal."

"I turned the key, you know," he explained to Eugene, "like they used to, and it jumped, but then I didn't know what to do, whatever I did, it didn't work. The thing just died."

"Hmmmm?" Eugene said, approaching the pickup and wishing he knew more about engines. Knowing about engines was what Jason wanted a father to know, to have the television dad solve another weightless suburban crisis. Jason stood outside the driver's seat, looking for Eugene to "fix it."

"Come on baby," Eugene pleaded with the truck, turning the

key, but getting nothing but a dying grind. "I know what," he said. "We'll push it out."

He set the gear in neutral and he and Jason grunted and pushed and Eugene felt like they had done something together. He ran to brake the rolling pickup before it hit the house. Jason, also enthused by their joint effort, shouted, "I'll get mine!"

Eugene stood in the garage, so he could direct the young man in. The other side was filled with old furniture, the printing press he'd never set up, and the eight boxes Lola had taken off a delivery truck in Manhattan destined for the popular "appropriation" artist, Sherrie Levine. Lola had never bothered to open them. She told Eugene, "I don't care what's in the boxes. That is the ultimate 'appropriation.' " Jason pulled in, and Eugene praised the shine of the car. He closed the door cautiously.

"You should get someone to fix those doors, and get rid of all that junk in there," Jason said as they hurried through the falling snow back to the house.

"Why?" Eugene said.

Jason stomped the snow from his rubber boots on the porch floor. Eugene stepped out of his thongs and shook his sheepskin pelt.

"Whataya mean, why?" Jason laughed, shaking his head. Wasn't it obvious?

They entered the house. Lola still stood at the window, holding her arms.

"Coffee," Eugene said, rubbing his hands together for warmth.

Jason followed him to the kitchen, seeing a snowflake melting into the man's scraggly ponytail, and he wanted to suggest that Pop get a good haircut and dress better and have the driveway paved and heated instead of the dirt and gravel that would be impossible to shovel clean if it snowed heavy and they would be trapped there, but he didn't, because he knew that his suggestions would be laughed at. He worried that he might miss the Barbareeuns concert because of the weather. "You like all this mess, Pop?"

Lola came to the kitchen. "What mess?"

"The garage," Eugene said, lighting the gas stove, as the cookstove was now cold. "Jason thinks I should fix the doors and clean it out, and I asked him why." Eugene looked at the young man, "I'm not arguing with you, Jason. I just wondered why you wanted me to do that, not why it should or shouldn't be done, just why you cared?"

"Oh, forget it," Jason said, "just forget it." He sat at the kitchen table and picked up a stack of Christmas cards that were on top of a pile of *Century* magazines. "Hey, Pop? Are these from this year? You should have them up somewhere." Lola sat down next to Jason. "Whoa!" he exclaimed, "this one's great from Amy Carter."

"Let me see," Lola said, pushing closer, smelling Jason's wet hair and cologne.

Eugene ground fresh coffee beans from Octavio's family's plantations in Brazil. He missed Octavio. He missed Ohio. He missed everything that wasn't in his kitchen. "Holidays," he sighed, "they're like scars."

"You got one from Diane Bukovsky?" Lola shouted. "That bitch never sent me one!"

Eugene let himself absorb the unfamiliar man, sitting there in his familiar spot. He would remember that, the closeness of Jason for these days. He felt that Jason's concern about the garage was the young man's way of telling him that he cared. Eugene poured the coffee. He smiled to himself at the truth of it. There was no reason for it to be clearer.

Later, Eugene spoke to Octavio on the phone, wishing him a big holiday on the beach. Then he spoke to his sister, Debbie, who was in Indianapolis, awaiting word on her daughter's labor. "I hope she can hold out to tomorrow, Eugene, so the baby will be born on Christmas. Lord, to think I'll be a grandmother!" And then he spoke to Rubinstein in New Mexico, and Belle in Paris.

Meanwhile, Jason and Lola were dancing in the parlor under the dark and dusty beams. He was showing her how to do The Clamp and she was telling him that it was just like The Alligator.

"Hey, Pop!" Jason pushed through the door, sweating. "Get out here and dance!" Jason was drunk.

Eugene came in, and after dancing with Lola and somewhat with Jason, they decided to open gifts. From Lola, Jason received a reworked silver print of herself, framed and signed, "To Jason Goessler and his genes, Love, Lola." Eugene gave him the *Collected Works of Bernard Rubinstein*, which had just been published in book and disc, and Eugene thought Jason might like it.

Rubinstein was very hemline with straight youth. He also gave him a mirror that he'd bought in the jungle outside of Octavio's uncle's place, from an old woman who pounded out the bits of tin that framed it, and then performed an Umbanda ceremony over the mirror, filling it with "good fortune." He gave a similar mirror to Lola, along with a box of toucan feathers he'd collected. Jason gave Lola a toy kangaroo. Lola gave Eugene a gold pin that was inscribed with the words, "Eugene, the metaphor, Lola." And Jason gave Eugene a cedar box with brass hinges, and in it was a note that said, "Pop, you can keep things in this, Jason."

Eugene noticed that Jason, who had been bothered that his father had simply stacked the holiday cards he'd received out in the kitchen, had arranged them across the mantel over the stone fireplace.

"Did you do this?" he asked the young man, who was dancing suggestively with Lola.

"Yeah," Jason grinned, drunkenly goofy, "it must be the decorator in my genes!"

Eugene started to tell him about his grandmother's obsession with Christmas cards, but Jason would not stand still; even after Lola ran to pee, he kept dancing and drinking, nodding to his father, but not hearing what the man was saying.

Christmas morning, Lola asked Jason if he was at all curious about Eugene's family.

"Hey, what's there to know?"

Lola kissed his sweet Goessler lips and said, "You'd be surprised."

Before he left the next day to catch the concert in Worcester, Jason sat with Eugene out in the sunroom. He asked Eugene what it was like to grow up poor.

Eugene thought about it, explaining that he didn't know anything else, and that he often thought that if Melvin and Clara had money, they wouldn't have been so ornery, and then he smiled, remembering things, and he said, "I had a river."

"No," Jason said, "I mean, what is it like? Not poet scat, Pop. Did you get welfare?"

"You learn to make do, and to count."

Jason threw up his hands in frustration, "Blast the pung, man, this is why I never got along with you! You never give me a straight answer, a straight anything. Man . . . why do you fuck with my head . . . even when I was a kid, Pop . . . it's not just me!"

Jason stood. Eugene stood, grabbing him, and pushed him back onto the teak seat. "You are who you are, Jason, and I am glad you made your way up here, but I want you to hear this, and then get out and on your way, if you want to know poverty, ask yourself."

2012, Panacea, Florida

Eugene Goessler's luggage, for his last winter in Bungalow #4 at the El Caribe Bungalows, consisted of mementos. A shell he'd found on the beach at San Felipe, Mexico. A shell he'd found with Andrew Atwood on their trip to Maine. A shell from the beach in Rio. A strange bag, he'd thought, as he'd packed it. Some of the things meant something, but he couldn't remember what, but he brought them anyway. A stone from somewhere. The rock that he and Scott split in half. The cedar box from Jason. His third of his mother's ashes. Andrew Atwood's ponytail. He spread everything out around his bungalow. The relics. One at a time, he was giving them back. "Rented," he said, smiling, thinking of Lola, "all the things we shop for, even on the beaches, something to capture." His shopping was completed.

That day, he let go of Jason's cedar box and returned to write his son this note: "Jason, One Christmas you brought me a gift. Remember? It was a cedar box. It is the only thing I've brought down here with me that will not sink." He sent it with his last stamp.

He threw the shell that he thought was the shell he and Scott had brought back to the cabin after their day at the beach near Bodega Bay. He saw Scott's surfer face, tan and lean, his body strong, never having seen the deterioration, the wasting away, only the vital man who had shown him a path, telling him he could put every cell back together. He was still doing that, he thought, putting every shell back, every rock. He said, "Scott."

Octavio had called again. Tonio had the hydro belt refitted, and they were leaving the Keys, heading up to Apalachee Bay. He told him he was ready.

346

He threw a piece of quartz given to him by one of his students in Boulder where he'd taught a few times. She was a poet. She gassed herself. A seagull swooped down at the flying quartz thinking it was something else. Eugene felt his shoulder ache from the way he threw. He heard his father criticize his throwing.

2006, Tallahassee, Florida

Cleaned up in a bronze-toned sharkskin suit, Eugene Goessler stood at the podium on the stage in Ruby Diamond Auditorium at Florida State University, where he had been awarded an honorary Ph.D. He had listened as three drama majors read from his books. Then the president of the university had asked Eugene to read "something new. Something recent, to give us a glimpse at the poetic inner process, to honor the university with a reading of your own words." Eugene was recovering from the misinterpretation he had just witnessed by the drama students. He felt apologetic for ever claiming any skill at literary communication, if that was what they were getting from his words. He welcomed the opportunity to perform and hopefully redeem some confidence in his ability to make sense. He read the "Clara Poems" from *Goessler/Goessler/Back/Forth*, which had been published in 2005. He stood back and bowed to the audience after the reading, and motioned with his hands for them to applaud louder and louder, letting the sound of their clapping embrace him warmly. He yelped like a dog, and a few students, having fun, yelped back.

Once, Eugene had insisted at a performance that the audience snap their fingers beatnik style, and on another occasion, at Berkeley, he had asked everyone to remain silent, and allow him to applaud himself. "Because I love myself so!" he'd sung over his own uncomfortable laughter at such a claim, "and more than your applause, I deserve my own!" And the audience laughed extra-hard when he gave himself a standing ovation, but he was serious. He was truly trying to break through his selfish humil-

348

ity and take credit for, if nothing else, the concentration he had had to develop, to have fun.

As the yelping and clapping in Rudy Diamond Auditorium subsided, he again approached the podium and spoke. "Now, to receive an honorary degree, is a fine kiss for me. But, the sweeter honor is in standing here before all of you young ones, so tan, seeing your necks long and your jaws opening, your eyes gawking up to me, hungry for something, like featherless baby birds in a big packed nest. I wish, I wish I had some big lively night crawler to drop squiggling to your lips," at which point there were more than a few lascivious laughs, "something more than words. Words. It is words that I am known for, at least it is words that have brought me here before you. I am not being honored for my ability to make a full stop at a stop sign. Words. Words are not sustenance, they are not. They are merely the menu." He paused, consciously and conspicuously taking slow deep breaths that could be heard audibly from the stage to the back of the auditorium. "Words are the menu, not the meal. The poem is not the words." He paused again, stepping back and breathing. A few chuckles rose from the quiet, reverent audience. Eugene smiled his big grin out to those laughs, and he lifted his arms up high, as if he was an official declaring a touchdown, and from the depths of his being, he gave out a wriggly squirm of a yell, "AyeeeeeeeeeeeeYoooooooooooooooooooooooooWoooooooooooo!" his voice ricocheting from the walls, reverberating through the ears, in one and out the other and in the next and so on, till it softened down to a fuzzy hum, and then he again approached the podium and spoke, slowly, precisely, separating his words into syllables. "Words are sounds. Lang-guage is when two or more voy-cess a-gree on a met-ah-for for a spuh-ciff-ick sound. Words are masks. You on-or me not for words, but for LOVE-ing my self. Riv-er wah-ter oh-ver rocks make words much bet-ter."

Eugene approached the edge of the stage, doing a fey twirl and feigned toe dance, then flexed his biceps. "All I can tell you people, students and teachers, jocks and bookworms, is, dig your physical body. That is the one thing we know dies. Words and the metaphors and beyond are unkillable. Don't miss out on the fun of this," he grabbed his crotch, "and this," he did the already outdated dance, The Clamp, "and this," at which point he took a deep breath, slowly stepping back from the edge, exhaling and shaking the hand of the president of the university. Eugene shouted back to the audience, "Dig your lives, you sweet souls!" And he took off to the side exit, where he had parked his rented luxury Scorpion.

"Mr. Goessler!" the head of the English department called out, pursuing him to the car, "Mr. Goessler! Please, the reception! Wait!" she demanded, blocking him from driving off. "You forgot your degree!"

Eugene honked and inched forward, then stopped and said to the woman, "Professor, I will run you down if you don't get out of my way." He revved the engine and she stepped out of the way, believing he just might mean what he said. The degree was later sent to his agent in New York.

Eugene drove south on Route 319 hoping to find a room overlooking the Gulf of Mexico. One of the reasons he'd agreed to accept the degree was to spend some January in warm weather. The sun was setting as he drove through the Apalachicola National Forest. Kudzu vines and Spanish moss hung from bare trees, and stumpy squat palms, uncut and scraggly, lined the highway. He hummed and wore his sunglasses till it was dark. Then, outside of a little town called Panacea, he saw the fizzly fading sputtering neon pink sign for El Caribe Bungalows. He stayed there till February, and returned the next year, and the next, each winter from then on. When he signed the register, he wrote, "Eugene Goessler, Ph.D.," and the woman at the desk, a teenage girl actually, although her breasts were nursing twins under a flimsy white shawl, so he thought of her as a woman, said to him, "Oh, what kind of dentist are you? Root or gum?"

2008, Brazil

Eugene had a twisted ankle. He was at the coffee plantation in Brazil. He had his leg up. Octavio came out onto the terrace with drinks and set them on the table. The housekeeper, Dorotea, was at the market with Lola Hampton, who'd insisted on preparing "American" for all the Brazilians who were coming out to the house for Octavio's celebration. His clinic had finally received official status, a breakthrough long overdue, considering his extensive recognition in the United States and Europe and Japan. His work incorporated touch therapy and spiritualism. "Finally," Octavio had said to Lola and Eugene on their arrival for the big party, "finally the government has acknowledged the power of ignorance. They admit our work cannot be challenged, yes, and it cannot be denied. We have now taken it to reality."

Eugene sipped the drink, a tangy concoction of banana, coffee, and liquor. He looked pathetically at Octavio and said, "Thanks, sweetie."

Octavio sat down next to him and said, "You like your injury, no, Eugene?"

"No," Eugene frowned, and then saw Octavio's game. "Oh, don't start. Yes. Yes, I chose to twist my ankle getting off the horse. I was thinking, for some reason, of when I was hit in the head by my mother, and then as I was dismounting, I thought of how long ago that was, and how old I am, and how my bones were . . . okay, so you're probably right, somewhere in my head, I wanted to limp about and feel sorry for myself, and, no, that wasn't it, Octavio. I remember, right before I fell, I thought that it was not so good to have government sanctioning for your clinic. Then I twisted my ankle."

Octavio laughed, "You speak fast to deny and admit in one breath. You share my party, sweetie, but not my country, and here, the government does not interfere, but they do need our work. I'm sorry you must limp because of it, but this is one way for me to serve you as you do when I am North."

"Could it be that I'm clumsy?" Eugene sighed.

"Of course!" Octavio laughed, and caught himself before he rattled Eugene's set-up with a shake, "You think clumsy, you are clumsy. You worry of me being middle-stream."

"I do not, I know you. I know Umbanda is sacred and 'Touch' is sacred and they are a far cry from government."

"A far cry, yes, sweetie. Look at it as a passport, that is all. Now people here, like in the other places, can say openly that they are spirits, no?"

"Boo!" Lola called out, coming from the kitchen doors onto the terrace. "How's the patient?"

Eugene moaned.

Octavio stood to pour Lola a drink. "How was the shopping?"

Lola removed her wide brimmed sunhat, revealing white-blonde dyed hair. "Let's just say, Octavio, this will be Lola Hampton's conceptual restructuring of American cuisine, and I hope you sign the official papers before anyone tastes what Dorotea and I are cooking up. They will definitely see the spiritual side, they'll be fucking breathing it."

Eugene moaned louder.

Lola kissed his dark tan forehead and said, "Don't worry, old man, for you, we're making french fries."

2009, Venice, Italy

Within the bark of tree, dog, and man

"Wearing a brown suit for you, standing across the way, there now, as always. Long gone. I use these words, these metaphors, and speak to you, and I'll call you, Eugene," Goessler heard the light say. He was in the hotel. He was in the bed in the hotel in Venice. Damp horsehair mattress, soaked in a century of sinking sweat, only beaten for dust and covered in bleach, warmed by the sun of Italy, sheets. His eyes were tight to the voice. It continued, "You run to me with your open arms, so thrilled to see me, thinking I'm still alive and with you, that it has all been a misunderstanding, that there is no plague, that we will all wash up on shore someday, and it will be understandable. You grab my brown-suited shoulders and shake me down, begging me to tell you what it's like, to put into words what it's like. TO PUT INTO WORDS! GOESSLER! Here: Gold light reflecting off the strands of a torn weave, frayed, but with still some color remaining, gold light absorbed. I surround you forever and zsha zsha zsha zsha zsha zsha zsha zsha zsha zsha WORDS?"

Filtered sight burned his eyelids, and he was forced to open them. He was ecstatic and terrified at losing himself, at losing his life, his world, no matter how painful or grave, he fought looking at the gold being shown him.

"Well, you asked, Goessler. You wanted to know what it was like. It is zsha zsha zsha ten thousand times and the word 'wasps' repeated over and over till you're stung by two. It is Venice only golden, always morning, always the bug on the step, the ladybug. Open! Open! Goessler! You asked. Now, look!"

Eugene was blinded. The light from the canal shone into his

room, over the walls and religious symbols. The cross was dimmed. The rosary draped around the cross dripped and melted like wax. He said, "Still, I want to stay. I want here. I want to smell with my Eugene nose and taste with my Eugene tongue and see with my Eugene eyes. I want the physical world with all of the language and rules and drives, and I want to live like this, in gold for a moment, then . . ."

"Why?" God asked him, directing his question to Goessler's stomach.

"I don't know why," Eugene cried to himself, "I only know that I love life and I love being me in it, and I'm afraid, like the rosary that was on the cross on this wall in this house from the sixteenth century, that if I look any longer I will melt, and I don't want to melt."

"Why?" God asked him, directing her question to Goessler's luggage.

Eugene struggled with words, wanting to say "zsha" ten thousand times as a reason, being true as an atom, and his tears rolled, adding to the canal, "I want to hold out. Hear the train on schedule. Put titles to things."

"Why?" gods asked him, directing their question to Goessler's world.

"Because when I hear a bird in the dark morning, and I hear a growl and a bark out there, and I smell fresh-cut willow that harbored a white fungus that killed it and it became a hollow hive for the Brazilian bees, and I need people who count things up or bury hatchets, it is all a joy to me and I love it. All of it, and oh . . . oh!" And Eugene wept for his love of life, with all of its sorrow and drama and sums. He was all of it. He was the bed and he was Venice and he was a baseball and the radio waves weaving the gauze round and round. He was the Lido and the follicle in the nose of the man dead near the open sewer in Florence, and he had never been to Florence, and was there then. He laughed, "All I know is nothing. All I know is the paper is delivered outside my door and I cannot read Italian, but I pick it up and open it and it tells me . . . all I know is nothing. I know that. That I don't know. I don't want to argue!"

"Well, you asked. You wanted to hold me. Apologize for living on. No apologies, Goessler. In lieu of flowers, say 'wasps' over and over till two sting you."

"I love so," Eugene said, hearing, seeing, tasting, touching, breathing the message that transcended words. Into words, the answer to what it was like, was Love.

The sky was green and blue and red and yellow. He thought, "What a fool I must be to hold on to this. What a fool I must be to have the book opened before me and to choose to look away, denying what is written in plain down-home phantasmagorical jibberwasps, wasps, wasps, wasps, wasps, wasps, wasps, wasps, zsha zsha. What a fool I must be to sleep and think that wake is reality. What a fool that with such melting, I still wonder if Octavio will make his flight and meet me in Rome next Tuesday. What a fool," he thought. "Oh, how I love being this fool. Oh, how I love the fool, weak-kneed at beauty and losing bowel control over truth."

He'd stained the ancient mattress. Since the mouth opened to speak to the brown-suited god, so did his colon loosen. The warm stink too, he thought, was life. He heard Clara complain about so much poop. He was a baby. "What a baby I am," he laughed, sounding mixed half scratch of old and half goo-gurgle new.

2010, Massachusetts

"I wonder," Eugene said to Lola on the sunporch of his Massachusetts home, as they had Brazilian morning coffee, "I wonder."

Lola was basking in the sunlight, her head back in the chair, her long legs stretched out and over to the windowsill. It was spring, and the Plexiglas panes were still in place, so the room heated up as if it were a summer morning. She was staying at Eugene's till May. She had been there alone, with Zero, all winter, while Eugene was in Panacea at his El Caribe bungalow winter home. Lola had had a facelift in 2006 and looked younger than forty, which was how she put it after Eugene had pointed out to her that younger than springtime could be interpreted as winter. She had to have the facelift, she claimed, because of the scarring she'd had from her bout with AIDS, which she'd gotten from Tobey "Too Tall" Thomas, or so she assumed. Eugene said she was just looking for excuses. All winter, there in her self-imposed isolation, she'd been taping her autobiography. "You know, Goessler," she said, her eyes closed, seeing the dark red of the sun through her lids, "I'm always surprised at how different our lives were, and yet we've been so close for so long."

"Different?" Eugene said. "Lola, you are becoming an analyst with this book. Spare. Spare. It is words that are different."

"Please, hear me out," she said, frustrated at the man's constant denial of the value of words, "let's pamper my little late-blooming literary career and assume that words, or metaphors, suit yourself, whatever, have meaning ... okay? Now, look at your childhood, and look at mine ... completely different, and yet here we are."

Eugene nodded and stirred his milky coffee with his finger.

"You had a tragic puberty," Lola said, shading her eyes with her hand and looking at him in a half-baked squint, "most teenagers back then were . . ."

Eugene touched her hand, "It was what it was . . ."

She slapped his hand, "I mean, compared to mine. I hated the fact that my parents filled in the pool! The most trouble I ever had that had anything to do with the real world were my few run-ins with the law."

"Wasps," Eugene said, "wasps, wasps, wasps . . ."

"I used to . . ."

Eugene heard "wasp" yodeling inside his mouth, although he heard her, on some level.

"Would you just let me talk, Goessler? I've been holed up here for months. As a matter of fact . . ." she said, pressing her wristdot to record her words, "as a matter of fact, I get lost back there, my criminal days of shoplifting at the shopping center. I hated to pay." She laughed at herself.

Eugene thought he heard the split tweet twirp of a cardinal.

"I know I was caught stealing a pink cashmere sweater, and I remember thinking in the manager's office, as they called my parents, 'oh please, do you really think they're going to believe your word against mine?' because, you see, I had told the manager that I was fed up with waiting in lines and would obviously pay for it, when they hired another cashier. It wasn't as if I even wanted the damn sweater. Hell, I didn't know why, but I sounded so convincing to myself, that I knew my parents would believe me . . . they got me credit cards to all the department stores in Philadelphia, thinking that would help me . . ."

"Shhhhhh!" Eugene shushed Lola and pointed up to one of the convex Plexiglas bubbles. He whispered, "There's a cardinal, right over your head."

The red bird shit a yellow runny ooze and flew off. The ooze curved a drizzle down the skylight. For ten years the cardinals had been dying off, and according to the Audubon Society, they would soon be extinct. Years before, cardinals had flocked to Eugene's house, and nested in the trees by the river.

"So much for shoplifting," Lola said, as Eugene spoke to the local chapter of NatureWatch on the phone. He described the color of the shit as egg yolk and gave the size of the bird and directions to his house.

"You're quite the conscientious citizen," Lola said, having heard the entire conversation since Eugene had not muted it. "They seemed very excited."

Eugene stared up at the drying cardinal shit. As it was heated by the sun, it seemed to be darkening in color, to a shade of green. Avocado-green. Lola studied the concern on his face. He was tan from his three months of sun on the Gulf of Mexico. He was lost to her, she thought. Each year, upon his return north, he seemed further and further removed from his old self. His green eyes watered at the sight of the bird shit. She could only imagine what he was thinking, because Eugene had ceased to, as he had taken to calling it, "garble, garble, garble," and had once been more explicit, saying, "most talk is a smoke screen. What is behind those words? What? Lola? What is behind the word? It has a rear door to it. I use that, as I've done for years with Octavio."

She had once asked him how he spent a typical day at El Caribe Bungalows, and he told her that he had yet to have a typical day. One day, and this was documented by a woman who lived there year-round and took photographs, Eugene spent all of low tide writing in the wet white sand with his finger, and then watched it wash out into the Gulf with high tide. He told Lola that it was his best work, his most true, and he said it was a revelation to him, to watch the words wash away, knowing all along that they would, and yet their actual demise was shocking. "I have such hope! Even knowing, I thought, maybe one word would withstand the pressure of the sea, and, the next day, I went out again, and wrote again, hoped again, and laughed again at my folly. What fun it was," he'd told her. "I used the beach as my notebook, and at times felt like I was wasting such wonderful material." That was the season he returned empty-handed to the north, without a word to publish.

"Cardinals are your favorites aren't they?" Lola asked him.

"Cardinals are my favorite cardinals," he sighed, and lowered his head to sip his coffee. "I'm afraid that I'm not being very responsive to you, Lola. You talk. Your voice is a song to me. Garble."

"Do you want more coffee?" she asked, checking the pot, seeing nothing left, and turning her head to look into the house to see if Zero was near at hand. "I'd like another fresh pot. Where is that Zero?"

Eugene rose from his chair, wearing no shirt, but loose draw-string pants. "I'll go put up another pot, Lola, leave him be."

"No! Sit, dammit. Just stay put and watch your bird shit dry, Goessler. I pay Zero to work for me, and I ask very little of him. This has been going on since we came up here. He thinks he's on vacation, I guess." Then she laughed. "I don't think he knows anything but vacation, actually. Zero! Damn." She stood up as Eugene sat down, and she whistled a high pitch in, through the open french doors, and then sighed, "He knows we drink at least two pots. Zero! You know, sometimes I think, especially after this past winter, that having Zero with me is a little like having one of those little pocket puzzles, and whenever I feel frustrated, or stifled, I play Hunt for Zero, and then when I find him, it's nothing, and I put the puzzle back in my pocket."

Zero appeared at the open doors. He was a very thin, pale man. Thirty years old, but seeming like a youth, a youth of no distinct gender. His head was shaved so that it resembled a gray egg. He sighed, and stood with one hand on his hip, the other extended with an eardot resting on the tip of his index finger, as if it were a contact lens. He seemed bothered by Lola's call. He wore a long white robe that had been Lola's. If it hadn't been gathered and draped at the waist, it would have dragged along the floor. "Yes?" he said, as if he was saying, "You rang?"

Their heads were eye to eye, because Lola was down a step on the sunporch. She mimicked the way he stood there, so put off, and she mimicked his tone of voice and said, "Yes?" Then she calmed down, and said, "Yes, dear. We would like another pot of coffee, if it's not too much to ask."

He slowly blinked and nodded, and reinserted his eardot, and turned to go toward the kitchen.

Lola sat back down and looked at Eugene, who was staring at the skylight. She sighed, wondering if she should even have any more coffee. Then she noticed her wristdot, and said, "Now what were we talking about?"

Eugene looked at her and smiled.

She smiled back, determined to keep him down to earth, "I remember, we were talking about shoplifting."

Eugene said, "Our garble."

2011, Massachusetts

Eugene packed his notebook, his Baden, and three Bosc pears into his old green knapsack, and set out for a hike into the hills above his house. It was late September, and the trees had turned early. He would be going to New York for what he knew would be his last performances and so, he walked with an open heart, collecting the autumn to a condensed day.

Orange and red leaves floated fast on the rocky little river as it cascaded past his climb. He used a walking stick that Octavio had carved for him during one of his times at the Massachusetts house. He stopped to watch a specific leaf that caught his eye as it fell and then disappeared into the crowd flowing down. It was brisk and clear, so that the blue sky seemed solid and the red hues of the trees vibrated against it. He smelled the wet mud kicked up by the river, and the smoke from his own chimney. He repeated to himself that he *had* doused the fire with sand, and what he was smelling was the fire smoldering out, and there was no need to worry, and if the place burned down, and if all of his papers went up in flames, if every disc melted, if the file cabinets became ovens, what he couldn't remember wouldn't be any loss at all. "Loss," he said, "loss of. Loss of what? Hearing? Light? Loss. Loss of breath?" And as he spoke, he deliberately forced air out to see it in the cold. "Loss of words?" And he watched his words visibly disappear into thin air. He saw a blackbird and thought of the cardinals that used to be seen in the woods, and he thought how like Bukovsky that was, to see one bird and regret the loss of another, instead of seeing the bird that was.

"Gain," he said. He sang the word loud and the blackbird flew

360

out of sight. "Gain weight. Gain the world. Lost sight of the bird." He adjusted the brim of his hat that he realized was blocking a crescent of overhead leaves and blue. He was wearing his leather jacket that he'd had since 1986. He thought of it as a gift from Scott because he could never have afforded to buy it at the time if he hadn't received money from Scott's estate. The jacket still fit, and he thought of how frugal he was and how he maintained his weight and health and shape if for no other reason than he did not have to buy bigger clothes. So many purchases he didn't have to make, he thought, time better spent sleeping or waking. He passed his property line and was in Mohawk State Park, which ran for miles up to the Vermont border. He remembered seeing Scott at the height of the trail in Sonoma for the first time, the sun behind him, and Eugene said, "So perfect was the light and the man in the light." He saw himself there in California and said, "I'm bronzing everything." He thought, Scott was so real in his mind, so real right there on the trail, he could feel the heat from his tan skin that always glistened with golden hairs.

He walked higher and higher, crossing the park bridge and returning to the dirt trail, and the one constant he'd known, the fleshy physical world, licked and leaped and combed him with its branches and earth and air. Sense was not to be made, like a wheel, he'd once written, sense was the maker.

The river was below him, a Chinese snake so skinned full of color, and he sat on a rock looking down and then up to the evergreen points that jagged the blue like sawteeth, threatening to cut. He remembered the hills of Kentucky from the Ohio side of the river, and how they really did roll and really were almost blue-grassed, and how, when he would lie on his side on the riverbank and stare across, it seemed that Kentucky was lying across from him, hipped and legged and sleepy, and he remembered the porch at the house on River Road and how, as the leaves fell from the trees that climbed the hill, the river was revealed, all the way to the bend in it. He had always wanted to cut down the weeds, and cut off branches from the trees, so that the river could be seen unobstructed from the porch, even in the summer. Clara refused to let him cut, because she insisted that the leaves kept the house cooler, and "at least for half the year, I don't have to feel ashamed of people seeing how we have to live. For all they know, there's nothing."

"For all I know," Eugene said from the rock, "there's something."

He walked on, to the rows of towering pines that Andrew Atwood called Needle Cathedral. Both Andrew and Octavio had come to this place with Eugene on their visits. He knelt down into the soft pine needle carpet, breathing in the scent activated by his knees' press. He remembered running the length of the pines with Octavio on one side, him on the other, their hiking sticks out, playing the trunks as if they were running their fingers along a fence.

"I love this earth," Eugene said, rising to his feet.

He looked down and noticed a white card stuck to his knee. It was a business card. It read, "For all your hunting needs see Jack Diamond Bait and Ammunition, Readsboro, Vermont."

"Jack Diamond," he said out loud, and his heart skipped.

2012, Massachusetts

Eugene had insisted that Lola come to his house. She said she would if Eugene would speak, "and not gibberish."

"I'll speak," he assured her.

In the sunroom, this is what he said. "I'm going to Panacea soon, and I won't be coming back. I am leaving my estate to Andrew."

On the trail, up from the house, along the river, this is what Lola said. "Your words are music, Eugene."

He kissed her as they made their way back to the house, and said, "What is unknown cannot be feared."

Before Lola left to return to New York, Eugene said, "I'm a gambler, and I'm putting all my cards on the table, and I'm saying, 'Okay, show me your hand, Life, show me your hand, Death.' I dare all of it, Lola." And he laughed, his green eyes watering with love for the woman. "I dare all of it to be anything but glorious light and dark and, our word for it, LOVE."

Her link with him would be through Octavio, but to the world of Eugene Goessler, he would be considered drowned, body never recovered from Apalachee Bay, no links left.

"Burn your bridges," Lola said. "Always, I love you," and she drove away.

Eugene cried, enjoying the last drama of Eugene Goessler, letting all the times appear before him. He was beside himself, weeping.

2012, Panacea, Florida

Eugene sat on the beach watching the sun set before him, as the moon rose full behind him. Spread out on the sand was his leather jacket, and on it, he had placed the ace of diamonds given to him by Jesus Lo Dichodicho, the king of diamonds from his mirror, the queen of diamonds from Andy Warhol's service, and the Jack Diamond business card from the Needle Cathedral. The joker, which he'd found behind the other mirror, was placed to the side. He held Andrew Atwood's black ponytail like a brush, dusting the surfaces of the cards. The joker was not true. What he wanted was the ten, and he felt a doubt rising in him that he should wait, till a ten came to him. He could tell Octavio and he would understand. He swept the joker with the hair and said, "Turn. Change."

"That's not it, cowboy," Charity Ball said, walking toward him. "Don't you see? You sought that card, the others came to you. Trust yourself, honey. Trust all of this, and let go of your doubt."

The white-haired poet was struck by Charity's exquisite beauty. Her hair matched the sky in brilliance. He said, "I let go," and handed her the joker.

She laughed a deep male laugh and put the card behind her ear. "If I had underwear on, cowboy, you know where I'd put it." She lifted her gown and revealed a blinding light. She spoke: "It's all happening, honey, and it is funny. They land on the moon. Take pictures of the earth. One blue-green ball. It's the truth. We are one. The conscious is seeded. They can have all the border wars they want and fight in the name of their gods, but it's over, cowboy, the spring has sprung. When the conscious mind accepted the possibility of blowing itself up, it also conceived the power to transcend. The veil is saturated, the bridge is built. Hell, we blew up a long time ago, and you guessed right, cowboy, we all survived. You hear the air raid sirens? You smell the gas? You see the tubes keeping you breathing? And you give in. One way or another, you give in. Beyond words, beyond pain, but, honey, it ain't beyond much."

"It's beyond me," Eugene said.

Charity laughed, "Yes! Yes! That's the first step, baby. Knowing that you don't know. Trusting that. Do you have any idea how many waves are rolling with the ones we surf on?"

"No," he said, "and I leave the numbers to the Mayans."

"Cowboy! That's it! It is all calculated, but so what? You're the poet, not the calendar. You're the metaphor, not the print," she said, lowering her gown, revealing the night sky. "And honey, you can walk on water."

1965, Ohio

Eugene walked out into the frozen river and looked back to the black ruins of Bess's. He stared out and relived the fire, and his sister's screams and Michael's cries, and the funeral, and the stupid words of sorrow. Something had not been said, he thought, something about dying and living, and it had not been bridged. June was as real as the ice he stood on. Seeing her dead, in the half-open coffin, a blond wig and plaster face making her look like a statue, confirmed that it was not a dream or a nightmare, or was it? What was a dream? It was as real as the ice he stood on, in the middle of the frozen Ohio River. He could hear June singing, "Sugar Shack," and he could see her standing up to his mother in the kitchen, and he decided, out there in the river, that the words that were missing were just that, words, and for some things, it must be that there are no words. There had been a time in his life when there were no words, as a baby in Kentucky. Tears started to fall as he allowed himself to remember, and he fell to his knees on the ice, and let himself scream gibberish and see flames and colors and feel the blood in his veins, and then he heard his father calling him from the river's edge.

"Eugene! Eugene! Get back here! Come back over here! You don't know how thick it is out there, boy! Get yourself over here this instant!"

He saw his father and stood up. Melvin's arms were outstretched to him, to lure him off the ice.

"Come on! It was forty yesterday!"

Eugene walked cautiously, sobbing, as if he was a toddler taking his first steps. The closer he came, the clearer he saw his

366

father, and then, it was not his father, through his tears, it was outstretched skin and blood, held together with something beyond words, a bead next to his own bead on an endless necklace.

"Now, now, boy, come on," Melvin said. "You're too old to be crying."

Eugene could not hold back his tears, no matter how hard he tried. His father's words could not scold him into closing up. He had a mind of his own.

"Now, Eugene, we'll go home and get warm. We got to look ahead. Your sister's in heaven with Jesus and her Michael. Lord, that's all your mother would need, is to have you go through the ice and drown."

He grabbed Eugene's arm and pulled him onto the riverbank.

2012, Panacea, Florida

Eugene put his cards in the plastic pouch along with the shard of mirror and Andrew's hair, and he shook the sand off the jacket, kissed it, and said, "My father had a jacket just like this."

Charity said, "You always did dress like such a man, cowboy."

Eugene heard a boat, then nothing, then saw a flash of light. It was Octavio signaling for him to swim out. Eugene said, "Would you like it?" offering the coat to Charity, but she was gone.

"Over here!" she sang out from the water's edge.

Eugene stood, wearing only the strip of June's towel around his waist. He tied the pouch around his neck and walked toward her. The light from the boat flashed again.

"Oh, I love your new look, cowboy! Aborigine!"

Eugene looked back to the jacket on the sand and took a deep breath.

"And, aborigine," Charity said calmly, as if there was no hurry, no time at all, "dig this. Take a taboo and crack it. Turn a trick into truth. That's what I did on my cross. That's what you're doing, honey, traveling so light."

He kissed her and thanked her for being there. She laughed and said it was nothing. He dove into the cold water.

"Place your bets!" Charity called out after him.

Octavio helped him on board. Tonio was at the controls of the hydro. In the moonlight, Eugene removed the shard of mirror from his pouch. It was a piece of mirror he had found in the ruins of Bess's. It was the mirror that June had used to set her hair that night. He looked at himself and smiled, wrapped in the blanket Octavio had put around him. He studied himself. He loved his lips. He loved his eyes. He said to Octavio, "Come here, sweetie, and kiss the man known as Eugene Goessler one last time."

Octavio said, in a strange deep low voice, "What is a name, my fidalgo? I've decided to change my voice."

They kissed.

Eugene took Andrew's ponytail and threw it overboard and yelled, "Take care of Lola, Andrew!" Then he yelled, "Joe Bukovsky!" because that hair had always reminded him of Joe's last call to him at Hotelvisione.

He kissed the mirror and threw it out into the white wake of the boat, into the Gulf of Mexico, and he sang out loud and clear, "EUGENE GOESSLER!"

A note left on his desk back in Bungalow #4 read: "I have gone to drown my self."

2013, Brazil

"Claudia Cardinale. Claudia Cardinale. Claudia Cardinale. Claudia Cardinale. Claudia Cardinale. Claw-dee-aw-car-dee-now-lee . . ." the man said all day, till Joe Bukovsky appeared on the other side of the river, as a sabia, squawking. Joe cawled over to the old man, "Charity is having a party! Just a little get-together! Do you want to come, Goessler? The Bushwackers are playing."

The man laughed hysterically and flapped his arms like wings and squawked in mimicry.

Joe flew to a branch overhanging the river, and cawled, "Here's the ticket." He flew above the laughing man, and from his beak he spit a crystal that shattered on a rock at the man's feet into ten diamonds.

1950, Kentucky

Pregnant Clara Goessler sat on a bench by the Ohio River in Covington, Kentucky. She smoked a Lucky Strike cigarette. It was a warm May day. She was due in eleven weeks.

"Go on out and get some fresh air, then," Melvin had said to her after she complained that the smell of his stale beer and the noise from the baseball game on the radio and the closeness of the dark apartment on State Street was all "gettin' under my skin like hives."

She took deep breaths of the air breezing off the river in between deep inhales of smoke, and she said to three-and-a-half-year-old June, "Ain't that wind delicious."

June looked up from the riverbank where she was running a stick through the shining gold water. She wondered how long eleven weeks was, because that's what her mother had said on the walk from the apartment. "Eleven weeks and you'll have a real live baby doll to play with, girl." She jumped for joy and squealed a high note, so happy just knowing.

"Now you are the dizziest little girl," Clara laughed. "What made you jump like that? I thought you saw something."

June turned back to the water and looked at the bridge crossing the river to Cincinnati. Her ponytail blew on her neck and it tickled her and she laughed.

"And you watch yourself so close here, little miss giddy," Clara inhaled, "and be careful of all that wet mud."

What was to be Eugene was round and bone and swirls of red and no light, light and liquid pink banjo cells. What was to be was rubbery and pliant and wrapped in a hum of rippling water and drips of nutrients from bacon and eggs and nicotine from

371

Clara's Lucky Strike. When she coughed, there was a wave. Her voice was a lark and then a bark and her la-la-la hum trying to remember the song she'd heard on the radio was celestially glorious. The sun warmed her skin and what was to be Eugene.

"Now see, there!" Clara yelled, ever watchful of June. "Look at the mud on your one shoe!" And June looked up to her mother, and the wet stick dripped river water on the other shoe, "June! Look at what you're doing!"

Clara felt the baby sliding, moving, ever so, around. What was to be Eugene was spirals of cells and shocks of blood pumped from Clara's heart. There were no words, no consciousness. There was no time. No separation of self. What was to be Eugene was a metaphor. A puddle. A drop in the bucket. The metaphor was to be a baby, but to be, was a time, and there was no time, and there was no space, no wall, no separate conscious-ness. What was to be Eugene was not limited to "he" a baby, a body, a fetus. "He" was his mother. "He" was the sun. "He" was his sister's stick skimming the river. "He" was God and God was all things and then some. "He" was the smoke from the Lucky Strike. He, God, was the river. God was the ball being hit over the wall at Crosley Field right then. God was not separate from Eugene, or Joan, or Lou, the three names Clara and Melvin were considering.

"Little Lou or Joanie sure is kickin up a storm," Clara said to June as she laid her palm on her stomach and clouds covered the sun and the sky darkened, threatening a shower.

"Where'd the sun go?" June asked.

"Scared away by a thunderstorm," Clara said. "If it gets any darker we'll head on home."

In July, the evolutionary membrane that sequestered man from all else and made him think he was separate and had his own thoughts, that allowed him the illusion of ownership, began to assemble itself within what was to be Eugene. It started as a trickle, but it was a separation, between God and Eugene. As it became a creek, Eugene began to stretch and feel confined and Clara said, "It's time, Melvin, I just know it." And on August first, Eugene was born. The creek had become a river and he screamed air. All that within the sweet pink body moving on its own was named Eugene Louis Goessler. The clouds were clouds and he was looking at them, when his eyesight developed, and the leaves were falling and he saw their flight, and he was delighted by the sight, but he was not very much the leaves, or the cigarette smoke, as the river became wider and deeper and the bridge between God and Eugene was drawn. The World Series on the radio in the living room was not him, although he did feel the waves of it. And then he was not his hair as he cried and cried as his sister, June, tugged at it with her dollbrush. He himself learned his parts. He cried at the rough wipe of his behind by his mother who was "fed up" when he shit for a fourth time in one day. He felt anger and danger from the hands he depended on and he absorbed all of it, because he was all of it, but he no longer crossed the bridge easily. A veil was forming. A veil that hid the bridge in more and more metaphor, but he absorbed what he could, Melvin, Clara, June, the radio, the air pressure, and the river. In his sleep, the veil was lifted and the drawbridge was lowered and there were dreams of colors and swirls and pinks and music. There was the sound of breath and the trust of breath and a hum in the walls and a trust of the hum and all of the sounds were blue, and it was the same blue as the sky and the bunny on his shirt, and when he came to, awake, he learned more of the limits and the sensational metaphors, and the veil and the drawn bridge that made him a boy in a crib in Kentucky and not the wood in the crib from the tree in North Carolina were in place.

, *Brazil*

In the jungle mangrove on the bank of the Bardo River the man who was once Eugene Goessler sat naked on a tattered striped piece of towel, humming, humming as if he was the wind. The trees overhead were filled with sabias, toucans, and papagaios singing. There was a low rumble in the distance, as if the earth was quaking.

Octavio approached the man from behind, touching his shoulders, and said, "Those machine sounds are bulldozers, sweetie. They're building a road. They're ten kilometers from you. I've come to take you away. We'll find you another river, my fidalgo."

The white-haired man turned to Octavio and stood facing him. His green eyes watered with love. His mouth opened into a full smile. He took Octavio's hand and held it open, and from his fist he dropped ten crystal diamonds onto the Brazilian healer's palm. He inhaled deeply and turned to the river. Two black wasps descended from the trees and stung the shoulders of the man who once was Eugene. He exhaled and walked out across the river, the word made flesh, the flesh made love, the love made sense. The rest was untranslatable.